PRAISE FOR *WHAT'S NOT SAID*

"Taylor's dialogue is snappy aɪ   ften
amusing marriage drama."

₂ws

"In this dramatic tale of love, lust, and lies, author Valerie Taylor
crafts an entertaining and gripping story...a shocking novel full of
secrets, twists, and turns, but it also has elements of pure humor and
deep love. If I had to pick one word to describe *What's Not Said*, it
would be the word 'captivating.'"

—Readers' Favorite

"*What's Not Said* is highly recommended for women who look for not
just stories of marital relationships, but the unexpected revelations
that revolve around life purpose and the immortality of love."

—Midwest Book Reviews

"*What's Not Said* is oh-so-clever at illustrating the unintended
consequences of secrets. Valerie Taylor's characters face a tangle of
events and emotions that keep the reader turning pages!"

—Joan Cohen, author of Land of Last Chances

"Wonderfully entertaining! You'll find yourself rooting for the main
character from the beginning as she finds herself divided by mixed
loyalties and her own desires. Taylor has written a sharp-witted and
fun story, so grab a seat, buckle in and enjoy!"

—Marianne Lile, author of Stepmother: A Memoir

What's Not True

What's Not True

A Novel

Valerie Taylor

SHE WRITES PRESS

Published 2021
Printed in the United States of America
Print ISBN: 978-1-64742-157-1
E-ISBN: 978-1-64742-158-8
Library of Congress Control Number: 2021905129

For information, address:
She Writes Press
1569 Solano Ave #546
Berkeley, CA 94707

She Writes Press is a division of SparkPoint Studio, LLC.

*This sequel to **What's Not Said** is dedicated to*
Ayse, Lyn, and Vicki . . .
for making this book, and my dreams, come true.

A List of Chapters

In honor of Kassie

Facts do not cease to exist because they are ignored.

—Aldous Huxley

Truths and roses have thorns about them.

—Henry David Thoreau

There are two ways to be fooled. One is to believe what isn't true; the other is to refuse to believe what is true.

—Soren Kierkegaard

Truth is like the sun. You can shut it out for a time, but it ain't goin' away.

—Elvis Presley

1

Say Cheese

We should've stayed in Venice. For once, Kassie kept her thoughts to herself and planted both feet on the bottom of the private water taxi Chris had arranged to take them to Marco Polo Airport. Quite the balancing act for a woman with a reputation for opening her mouth and inserting her foot without much forethought.

The challenge of booking a hotel room should've been the first clue that going to Paris in July was a bad idea. The second should have been how difficult it was to get there in the first place. Kassie suggested they take a Thello night train, but trains from Venice to Paris at any hour that Saturday were filled to overcapacity. When she checked flights, she stumbled on two seats on a late morning flight that would land them midafternoon. Perfect timing. The goal was to get to the hotel by dark. They had fireworks on their minds.

"*Sei fortunato. La domando ha guidato l'offerta,*" the fellow at the airline ticket counter said.

Kassie's eyes begged Chris to translate.

"We're fortunate. Demand drove supply." Chris fed her the

words, as usual. "They've added flights." When he smiled at her, she melted as she did in their early years.

After landing at Charles de Gaulle Airport, they grabbed their carry-ons and found the Uber driver Chris had scheduled. That was the easy part. The ride into the center of the city was ten times as tedious as normal as the driver meandered through the narrow cobblestoned alleyways, avoiding as much as possible the gridlocked thoroughfares and army of traffic cops, who battled to instill calm among chaos.

"What a cluster," Kassie said under her breath, not wanting to annoy the Frenchman, be branded an ugly American, or have Chris accidentally hear what she'd said and interpret it for what she really meant.

If he had, she'd blame the sea of raucous Parisians and wine-fueled tourists that swarmed the boulevards and sidewalks or the rank smell of diesel fuel and car exhaust as the final proof that Paris wasn't always the best idea.

"*Vous êtes courageux,*" the driver said. "*Coupe du monde demain!*"

"World Cup tomorrow!" Kassie and Chris shouted in unison. That explained it. Had they been so into each other the night before they'd forgotten what else was happening in the world? Seemed so.

In any normal year, Paris in July was mayhem but manageable, with the Tour de France and Bastille Day celebrations. Add France playing in the World Cup finals? *Mon Dieu.*

Chris wrapped his arm around Kassie's shoulder. "I don't know, I think being fortunate and brave in one day is a good thing." He leaned in and kissed her cheek. "A sign, wouldn't you say?"

"Perhaps you were fortunate to have found me alone last night," Kassie said with a slight shove of her shoulder into his chest.

"And you're the brave one to take another chance on me," Chris whispered in her ear.

Kassie turned and gazed out the car window. The squabble that ensued between her heart and her mind prevented her from noticing the quaint and bustling neighborhood bars, cafés, bookstores, and wine shops they passed. Preoccupied, she wondered whether their time in Paris would launch Kassie and Chris 2.0, or would it be a summer pilot that would be cancelled once they returned to Boston and their attempt at reconciliation became a reality shitshow.

Paris was easy. Three thousand four hundred and thirty-five miles away from home, they were free to take up where they'd left off a year ago with no ramifications. Lovers, albeit with a past. A past they'd swept aside the night before in her hotel room in Venice. But second chance? Not so sure. Not so fast.

Chris had caught her off guard. She'd had no time to assess the situation, to make a list of the pros and cons of going round two with him. He didn't even ask. She didn't say no. Would she have if he had?

Once the driver pulled up to Hotel de Fais de Beaux Rêves, Chris jumped out and ran to open the car door for her. She interlaced her fingers with his, as she had in bed last night, and stepped out of her comfort zone and into unforeseen territory. Before her trip to Venice, she'd taken the year to demonstrate her total commitment to the company, to her boss, and to the board. No more distractions, she'd promised herself. Achieving the gold ring at the top of the corporate ladder had replaced the possibility of a lifetime with Chris.

And then he showed up uninvited. In St. Mark's Square of all places. Pandemonium exploded inside of her. Maybe if she hadn't been sitting in the same café where she'd met him six years before, she would've had the strength to rebuff him. Flashbacks blurred her ability to think logically. His piercing blue eyes fixed on hers dismantled any strength she had to tell him *this*, whatever *this* was, would not be a good idea. She feared if she blinked, he'd be gone. And truth was, she didn't want it to be a dream and had touched his hand, almost pinching him.

Kassie thought she'd buried the memories. Damn it. Where was

Bad Kassie when she needed her alter ego to stand firm—or sit firm, as it were—and reject the game Chris and her best friend, Annie, conspired to play?

"Let it be," he'd said. So she gave in, letting the magic of Venice reawaken her desire and longing for him.

Last night under the covers, Chris had suggested moving their reunion from Venice to Paris. A fresh start, he proclaimed. Kassie agreed, though sensing she was losing control. Fast. Of herself and the situation. She'd surrendered to Chris, to Annie—co-conspirators at the top of their game—when her plan was to be on top of hers.

That's how she found herself in Paris.

As Chris grabbed their roller bags and slapped the driver on the back, Kassie stood like a statue gawking at the faded green splintered doorway and sorrowful facade of the hotel.

"Doesn't look like they've painted since the Revolution." Kassie bit her lip.

"Beggars can't be choosers." Chris nudged her toward the entryway.

"Less than twenty-fours?"

"What's less than—"

"Spouting proverbs already?"

"That's your gig, Kassie, not mine. Just saying, we're lucky again. Lucky we've snagged a place to stay at all. If it doesn't work, we'll try somewhere else."

Kassie had called her assistant, Vicki, late Friday night and didn't have to beg her for help finding a place to stay in Paris. Always the resourceful one, Vicki phoned her counterpart in the local office of Calibri Marketing Group. Didn't matter it was in the middle of the night; global partners ignored time zones. Vicki's contact found a room for them at a centrally located Saint-Germain hotel.

Vicki peppered Kassie with questions about the change in her vacation plans.

"You're with Chris? How'd that happen?"

"A setup. Between him and Annie. What are friends for?"

"You okay with that?"

"What? Their grand plan, or being here with Chris?"

"Either. Both."

"They gave me no choice. It is what it is."

"A new beginning maybe? And Paris, the City of Love, Kassie. Ooh la la!"

"We'll see. Nothing's changed. I'm just taking one day at a time."

"Is Chris?"

"*Ciao,*" Kassie said.

"It'll be *au revoir* in France. Don't be confused. Think before you speak. Remember where you are."

Kassie signed off knowing exactly where she was. And who she was. Neither time nor country would change the past. Twenty-four hours ago, a future with Chris appeared inconceivable. Now, that impossibility faded like the doorway of the Sweet Dreams Hotel.

"This is a first, you know?" Kassie said, turning toward Chris.

"For what?"

"We've never checked into a hotel together as a couple before," Kassie whispered as her eyes widened, yet blind to the vaulted ceiling and rich antique interior of the lobby.

"*Passports, si'l vous plaît.*"

The clerk opened their passports and announced *Kassandra O'Callaghan, Christopher Gaines* aloud.

Kassie swiped her damp forehead and tapped her fingers on the mahogany reception desk. *Oh, God.* They weren't married. Would that be a problem?

"We're in France. Relax," Chris mumbled, standing to her left and giving her a reassuring squeeze around her waist.

I'm having an affair with my husband's son, and he's telling me to relax. Kassie hoped the clerk wasn't a mind reader.

She reached for the gondola necklace Chris had a jeweler craft for her more than a year ago, pressing her lips together as she remembered she'd left it home, swapping it for her Moissanite solitaire pendant when the gondola came to symbolize a wish she'd assumed would never come true.

I'm having an affair with my husband's son. Kassie continued praying the clerk didn't have Superman powers and couldn't see the invisible crown of thorns she'd worn for more than a year bearing those words. A mere scarlet letter would've fallen far short of describing what she had done. And what letter would it be? *A* for adulteress? *C* for cougar? *S* for stepmother?

Oh, no. The clerk looked at her and then at her passport. Had she said the words out loud?

"Is something wrong?" The saliva in Kassie's mouth vanished like the onset of a tsunami. She tried to lick her lips. Nothing. She rummaged in her purse for ChapStick.

"No, no, Madame. Or is it Mademoiselle?"

"Madame," Chris interjected, saving Kassie from having to answer.

When Kassie's eyes hit the floor, she noticed the exquisite Persian rug she'd been standing on, shifting from one foot to the other.

"We have a message for you, Madame. An envelope." The clerk disappeared.

"What's wrong?" Chris said.

"You have to ask? What if he knows?" She gulped.

"Knows what?"

"Who you are. Who we are. I don't even know if I'm a mademoiselle or a madame."

"Standing here, you're a madame. Upstairs, you're my mademoiselle." He winked.

The clerk handed Kassie a light green envelope. She stared at it and stuffed it in her purse.

"Aren't you going to open it?" Chris accepted the room key from the clerk and led Kassie to the stairs.

"Later. Probably a snarky welcome note from Vicki. She's the only one who knows I'm here."

"Or Annie."

"How's that?"

"I emailed her. She wanted to know about Venice. If the flamingo had landed."

"Really? You two have become rather chummy."

"I needed someone to talk to. You don't have a problem with that, do you?"

"I'll think about it. But a flamingo? Am I a code word now?"

"It's her idea. She feared someone had kidnapped Bad Kassie. Have you been keeping your head in the sand lately?"

"Don't believe everything you hear. Bad Kassie is on hiatus. Keeping her head down, but not out. She'll be back when the time is right."

They gasped for breath and laughed as they reached the fifth floor, neither willing to admit how they'd struggled to get there.

"Wow. If this is the last room they had available, I'd like to see the others," Chris said.

Kassie flipped on the antique chandelier, tossed her purse on the floral slipcovered Queen Anne chair, and twirled. "It's beautiful."

She flung open a door to a modern full-size bathroom. "Look! A shower and a tub. Imagine that!"

"But is there a toilet?"

"Ah, yes! And toilet paper too!"

Chris ran his hand across the light blue French provincial drop-leaf desk in the far corner of the room.

"Don't get any ideas. No work while we're here, you hear?" Kassie walked up behind Chris and wrapped her arms around him.

"You're right. This week is about you and me. No distractions from me, I promise." Chris turned and kissed her forehead.

"We have a great view. Look." Kassie pulled away, opened the French doors, and walked onto a small deck with a round wrought iron table and two chairs. The aroma of freshly baked bread wrestled with the box of pink, purple, and white geraniums on the railing of the deck. The bread won.

"I'm starved."

"Me too, Mademoiselle."

An hour later, Kassie was sure she'd died and gone to heaven. The boulangerie across the street, not Chris, was the source of her desire. Confident she was onto something before they were otherwise occupied, they followed her nose and discovered croissants of every variety imaginable. Baguettes to die for. And melt-in-your-mouth chocolate bread, reminding her of the bread she and Annie pigged out on every day when they'd vacationed in Saint-Martin.

A few doors down, the distinctive smell of fresh cheese was too delicious to ignore. A quick stop at the fromagerie and then the wine shop was all they needed for the perfect late lunch on the intimate porch off their hotel room.

Chris found a corkscrew in the desk and poured the chardonnay in wine glasses also provided by the hotel.

"To us," he said. "May today be the first day of the rest of our lives. Together."

"To us."

Kassie sliced the brie and fed Chris, followed by a kiss.

"Reminds me of Meg Ryan in *French Kiss.*"

"Hope not. We have plans for the night." Chris laughed.

"Hold that thought." Kassie went inside to find her purse. "Time for a selfie." She returned with her iPhone and the envelope the clerk had given her.

She sat on Chris's lap, took a picture and a sip of her wine. "It's not Italian, but it'll do." She giggled and settled in her chair.

Kassie delicately unsealed the envelope, planning to add it to her cherished souvenir box at home. Her eyes widened and her cheeks flushed as she read it to herself.

"What's French for *oh, crap*?" She covered her mouth.

She handed the letter to Chris. He read it aloud.

Kassie, Sorry to intrude on your vacation, but your timing couldn't be better. I need you to swing by the Paris office. Since you're in town, Mimi wants to bounce an idea off you. She's expecting you Tuesday at 10. I know I can count on you. Merci et bonne chance, Tom.

"Maybe we should've stayed in Venice," Chris said.

2

Mommy Dearest

The crowds in Boston that July weren't as insane as they were in Paris. But the sports mania was, and the craziness would last more than one day or one month. On that Friday the thirteenth, the Red Sox entered the weekend with a ten-day winning streak. They were in position for a winning season if they could hold off the Yankees, who everyone knew sucked.

With Patriots training camp opening in two weeks, proverbial paranoid purveyors of any and all things related to Boston sports were already down in the mouth coming to grips with Julian Edelman's four-game suspension and the continual undercurrent of a Brady-Belichik-Kraft feud lingering from a disappointing end to last season. Nevertheless, the mid-80s, low-humidity weather kept the mood of Beantown sports fans pumped.

Karen could care less about the Boston sports world. She had her own competition to contend with. Nor did she care she'd be late for work that morning. She was the boss's girlfriend, and he was the reason she was running behind her usual morning schedule.

"Get in here, doll face," Mike shouted from the bedroom as she stepped out of the shower and the glass door clanged shut. She knew what that meant. Wasn't last night enough?

With her frosted blonde hair dripping down her shoulders and onto the carpet, Karen stood next to the waterbed, wrapped in one of the yellow waffle towels she'd bought with his Nordstrom card, refusing to use any of the plush white towels his soon-to-be ex-wife had left in the hall linen closet. She wanted nothing associated with Kassie O'Callaghan to touch her skin, except for Michael Ricci, of course.

"Shouldn't you be getting ready?"

"I am ready." Mike raised his eyebrows and drew back the new six-hundred-thread-count blue Egyptian cotton sheets, also from Nordstrom, displaying just how ready he was.

"We'll be late." She dropped her cover and stroked her fingers over the two-inch scar below her naval, reminding him not for the first time what she did for love.

It was nearly ten fifteen when Karen pulled into her son's reserved space in the Ricci and Son parking lot in her shiny new silver Lexus hybrid sedan. She'd sold her two-year-old Ford F-150 the year before she relocated to Boston from Elephant Butte, New Mexico, leaving part of her past behind before donating another part of herself to Mike.

"New son. New city. New wheels." Karen had rationalized the expense to Chris when she had him drive her to the dealer to pick up the car.

"But a Lexus? A little over the top for a receptionist's salary, don't you think, Karen?"

"Karen? When will you start calling me Mom or Mother? Either would work," she said, attempting to divert his attention away from the topic of money.

"What about Mrs. Ricci? Would that satisfy you?" Chris said.

"You're kidding, right? Even after I marry your father, you still won't—"

"For over forty years Sarah's been my mother. She still is."

"And what about Kassie? You call her stepmother?"

"I don't call her anything. Haven't called her in months."

"I'd say that's a good thing."

"Enjoy your car." He'd left rubber and Karen with her hands on her hips in front of the car dealer.

With conversations like that swirling in her mind, Karen was relieved Chris was in San Francisco on vacation. Not only could she take his parking spot, but she'd also have the opportunity to host Sarah and Charlie Gaines for the weekend without having to listen to Sarah and Chris reminisce about his childhood.

"Remember how I'd leave work early three times a week to take you to swimming lessons?" Sarah would say.

"Not sure it helped straighten out my back," Chris would laugh.

"Or how every six months I'd have to buy you a new pair of Nikes to keep up with your growth spurts?"

"They were way too expensive for kids' shoes," Chris would recall.

"You should've seen him, Karen. He shot up like a rocket."

During Sarah and Charlie's previous visits from Chicago, she'd clench her fists as Sarah rubbed her nose in the close mother-son connection she wished she had with Chris.

Yes, I should've seen him. I should've never given him away, bitch.

That weekend would be the first time Chris's biological parents would host his adoptive parents at Mike's house. On their other trips, Mr. and Mrs. Gaines stayed in one of the fancy hotels on Boston's waterfront, giving them convenient access to Chris, who still lived in Charlestown in the furnished apartment he'd rented when he moved there from San Francisco the year before.

Karen looked forward to her role as hostess. It would be good practice for her to be the lady of the Ricci household, soon to be her household once she and Mike were married, and he removed Kassie from the deed. Every chance she got, Karen suggested he sell the house and buy something for the two of them. Maybe one of the fancy townhomes popping up in the suburbs with lavish swimming pools, club houses with entertainment centers, and libraries of all things. They had maintenance crews that handled everything. She had no interest in tending to the garden and all the flower beds Kassie had planted and nurtured over the years.

Karen had raised the issue with Mike as recently as the night before. "This house is paid off, right? Why don't you sell and invest in a love nest for us?"

"Not so easy. Kassie owns half. I'd either have to buy her out or sell and give her half. I have no interest in taking on another mortgage at my age. I hope to retire someday, ya know."

Karen wouldn't be discouraged. She had no intention of giving up. Baby steps. First the towels, then the house. By the time Karen was finished, any memory of Kassie would be erased from the brain of her husband and her son. Anything she could do to eliminate Kassie from their lives was priority one.

Without his knowing it, at least Chris was doing his part. Thank goodness he'd ended that ridiculous affair he'd had with her. What the heck was he thinking? She was old enough to be his mother. Well, not quite. Sister maybe. When she ranted about Kassie the night before, Mike reminded her Kassie was only ten years older than Chris.

"I thought you liked her?" Mike said. "If she hadn't reached out to you on my behalf last year, you wouldn't be here in Boston with me today."

"But I'd still have my kidney." For effect, she touched her scar through her jeans, reminding him she was his lifesaver.

"And I'm eternally grateful to you for that. As I would think you would be to Kassie for reuniting you with your son. You should be thankful he was attracted to an older woman. If he were with someone younger, you could be a grandmother. Try that thought on for size."

"Well, there's still that possibility now that he's free of *her.*"

With that thought, Karen's stomach growled. She needed coffee bad. Mike's sexual appetite left her zero time for breakfast before she left the house. Now at the office, she could hear laughter and the microwave timer pinging in the kitchen, where some staff members were getting their second or third refill of the morning. When she walked in, you'd swear crickets made more noise.

"Good morning, everybody. Sorry I was late. Something came up with Mike." Karen grinned as she forced her eyes to twinkle.

No one laughed as all but Bill scattered to their desks.

Bill broke the silence. "Some calls came in, Karen. I left messages on your desk."

"Anything critical?"

"Chris's father called."

"What? Mike?" Karen squinted, confused.

"No, Charlie Gaines called. He asked for you."

"Mr. Mahoney, when will you accept that Mike is Chris's father? Ricci and Son. Get it?"

"My bad. Chris is a lucky guy. Two fathers and three mothers."

"Three? Just me and Sarah."

"Don't forget Kassie. Stepmother, right?"

"She's yesterday's news. Technically, Bill, she's nothing to him."

"Time will tell."

"What's that supposed to mean?" Karen popped the K-cup into the coffeemaker. She waited for an answer that failed to come. Bill walked out, yet his quip lingered as he left her all alone in the kitchen.

"Damn it." Karen burned her tongue, rather than holding it. She had no regrets. In a few months, she'd be Mrs. Ricci, the majority owner's wife. Bill would not be able to deny that. He'd be farther down on the ownership succession totem pole than he was since Chris became a partner last year.

Tough luck, old boy.

Karen grabbed her iPhone and the pink messages off her desk and closeted herself in the conference room to call Charlie. The other messages would have to wait.

"Hey, KC."

"Don't call me that, Charlie. You know how much I hate it. It sounds too much like Kassie."

"I know. That's why I do it. I love to tease you. Reminds me of old times."

"You'll need to keep those memories under wraps this weekend, okay? Promise me that."

"You got it. Where were you when I called earlier?"

"Taking care of business. Not that it's any of yours. You still arriving at five?"

"Yes. Sarah can't wait to see you . . . and Mike. She's disappointed Chris won't be there."

"I bet she is. Maybe next time." Karen hoped her pissed-off attitude hadn't traveled through the airwaves. "Boston Coach will meet your flight. Look for a man with a sign."

"A man? That's pretty sexist even for you."

"Whatever. Just get here."

It was after eleven when Karen finally started her work day. The switchboard buzzed as soon as she sat at her desk.

"Good morning, Ricci and Son. This is Karen Copperman speaking." *Soon to be Karen Ricci.* She inspected her nails, making a mental note to leave the office early to get a mani/pedi, then forwarded the call.

She pulled the *National Enquirer* out of her bag. Pretending to read, she felt hands on her shoulders. Only one person at the office would do that.

"You were great this morning," Mike whispered in her ear.

"Watch it. No PDA in the workplace, boss. I might have to report you to the authorities." Karen licked her lips, ensuring the game played on.

"Hate to ask you this."

"What, here? Upstairs? I'll get someone to watch the phones." It wouldn't be the first time they'd had sex in his office.

"You wish. But that's not it. I need you to run to the house. Amelia's locked out."

"Amelia? Who's Amelia?"

"Teresa's daughter. Teresa's not feeling well, so Amelia's going to clean. She thought she had a key, but then remembered she gave it back to me a while ago."

"Can't she come here?" The last thing Karen wanted to do was get involved with the hired help.

"That'd be rude. Listen, take the rest of the day off. Get ready for Charlie and Sarah. Go have a massage, get your hair cut. Whatever floats your boat." Mike took out his wallet and handed Karen both his AMEX and a Visa card. "Knock yourself out."

"You think I need a haircut?" She pulled a small compact mirror out of her desk drawer and ran her fingers through her hair. "Really?"

Though happy to get the hell out, Karen lollygagged as she departed from the office. She dropped her coffee cup in the kitchen sink, made a trip to the ladies' room, and swung by Bill's office to tell him Mike gave her the afternoon off to get ready for dinner that night. She'd catch Bill and Nancy at the house later.

"See you all Monday," Karen announced as she strolled out the door. No one returned the sentiment.

She took her time driving to Mike's house, stopping at every yellow light, and going at least ten miles slower than the speed limit.

Indeed, a car was parked in the driveway when she arrived, but no one was in it, and no one loitered on the front steps. *Where the hell is she?* Maybe Amelia had a key after all.

"Hello?" Karen called out when she entered the house. No answer. She walked around the first floor, a bit spooked. Standing in the family room, she recognized a squeaking sound coming from outside.

"Oh, there you are," Amelia said as she got up from the back porch swing. "You must be Karen."

"You're Teresa's daughter?" Karen hoped Amelia didn't notice the surprise in her voice.

"I am. You took so long to get here, I thought maybe Mike changed his mind."

"About what?"

"Oh, nothing. Let's go inside." Amelia followed Karen, who tucked a lock of her hair behind her ear.

Karen stepped aside as Amelia headed for the kitchen.

"Would you join me for a cup of coffee? No time for lunch today," Amelia said.

Stunned, Karen passed on the offer as she observed Amelia move around the kitchen as if it was her own.

"You don't live here, do you, Karen? Mike said you don't. Not until after the divorce."

"No. Not full time yet." Karen was at a loss for words. Her brain cells exploded as she tried to figure out how this woman, who looked like Sophia Loren in her prime, was a cleaning lady. Since when were skinny jeans and a red V-neck tee shirt appropriate for scrubbing floors and toilets?

"So, you probably don't know if there's anything that needs particular attention?"

"No, the usual, I guess. I assumed you'd know what to do."

"When Kassie lived here, she'd leave a list. She loved lists."

"Is that so?"

"Grocery lists. Exercise lists. Instructions for taking care of her cat."

"Cat? I forgot about the cat."

"Yes. Topher. What a lovey he was. I miss him, even though he made it harder to clean."

"Don't worry, there'll never be another cat in this house," Karen murmured.

"What? Oh, never mind. I know how Mike likes things."

Karen disappeared to the master bedroom to get out of Amelia's way, but mostly to think. How did this woman know so much about Mike? He'd never mentioned Amelia, but Amelia sure as hell knew about her.

"Excuse me, Karen?"

Karen turned toward the doorway, where Amelia stood holding what appeared to be DVD cases.

"Do you mind if I come in and put these away? I don't mean to disturb you."

"No. Come on in. What have you got there?"

"Oh, just his porn," Amelia winked at her and headed for Mike's walk-in closet.

"Where did you find those, and how do you know—?"

"Tucked in the side of his Pleasure Chair. He used to keep them there. Apparently it's true—old habits do die hard."

"I guess." Karen realized there was much about Mike she had yet to learn, if she was so inclined.

"You know, when I walked in here and saw you sitting on the edge of the bed, I could've sworn you were Kassie. Mike was right. There is a strong resemblance. Of course, she's thinner than you."

Amelia went back to doing whatever high-and-mighty, hot cleaning ladies do.

Karen did what she had to. She picked up her phone and called her salon. "Hi, it's Karen Copperman. Can you take me now? What? The works."

3

Splitting the Difference

Mike looked forward to spending the weekend entertaining the Gaineses. In a way, they'd have their own University of Chicago mini reunion. The four of them had partied hardy there, and it would be easy to pick up where they'd left off. Combined with good food and a steady stream of liquor, there was sure to be lots of laughs and do-you-remember-whens.

But there'd be no sex. At least not in his bedroom. He made sure he'd given Karen a more-than-satisfying poke that morning, hoping it would hold her until next week after the Gaineses were gone. He had no desire to broadcast his huffing, puffing, and middle-aged orgasm to Charlie and Sarah, who'd be sleeping within earshot in the spare bedroom.

Speaking of Karen. More than likely she was at the mall, shopping till her bags weighed more than she did. He'd given her the opportunity and means to enjoy herself. No reason why he shouldn't enjoy himself as well.

Mike packed up his briefcase, wished his employees a good

weekend, and whistled a happy tune on his drive home. Leaving early on a Friday afternoon was not a habit of his. If the team stuck it out until the bitter end of the week, then Mike would as well. Yet, if there were a better excuse for skipping out early than Amelia, he couldn't think of one. And with Karen off with his credit cards, she'd be occupied and contented as a dog getting a tummy rub for hours.

Sure enough, Amelia was still doing her handiwork when he arrived home.

"Amelia, where are you?"

She greeted him in the kitchen with an ear-to-ear smile that stirred him below the belt.

"Glad it's you, not Karen again."

Mike walked to her, pulled her close enough to let her know how happy he was to see her, and kissed her slow and hard. The pressure of her breasts against him and the smell of her perfume reminded him of the last time they were together.

"How far have you gotten?" he whispered, stroking her long dark hair.

"Almost done. Why?"

"Come with me, sweetheart." Mike took Amelia's hand and led her to the family room and the Pleasure Chair. History was about to repeat itself.

"What about Karen?" She unzipped and slid his pants down and slung them on the couch.

"She won't be back for a while." His breathing intensified. "I gave her my credit cards." He chuckled as he returned Amelia's favor.

"I mean, if you're going to marry her, should we be doing this?"

"That never stopped you when I was married to Kassie."

"Actually, you still are."

"Oh, right. Then this shouldn't be a problem for you, or me."

And it wasn't.

Amelia left the house at about four after straightening up the family room for the second time that day and after Mike wrote her a check for three times the normal cleaning charge.

"Hope this isn't for services rendered." She waved the check and tucked it within her cleavage. "I'm not that kind of girl."

"I know you're not. I'm just feeling generous today. And I missed you. Think of it as an anniversary gift."

Amelia kissed his cheek and held his hand. "Here's Karen's key. She asked me to lock up when I was done. Let her know I took care of everything." Folding his fingers over the key, she winked and was on her way.

Mike climbed the stairs two at a time. He felt better that day than he had since the transplant. As he showered, he realized he'd had sex three times in twenty-four hours. If his kidneys weren't going to kill him, his sex life certainly would. *What a way to go.*

Mike checked his watch. He had some time to kill before Karen got home and Charlie and Sarah arrived. They'd be lucky to get to the house by six if their plane was on time and Logan wasn't insane. And then there was Friday night rush hour to battle.

He patrolled the house, ensuring no evidence of his latest escapade with Amelia lingered. Kassie never had a clue. Now was not the time to slip up with Karen.

Everything appeared in order, if order meant the way Kassie had liked it. Relatively little had changed since she'd moved out. Oh, there were minuscule changes, like the yellow towels Karen bought that reminded him of urine and the new blue sheets too. Nonetheless, the house decor was vintage Kassie. Each room appeared as if it had frozen in time, museum-like. Not a piece of furniture had been rearranged or removed. Bookcases throughout the house still shared their shelves with his favorite biographies and Kassie's historical fiction and best-selling novels. Every nook and cranny in every room, including the bathrooms, contained reading material of one form or another. Mike was good with that, even if it irked Karen, who rarely picked up anything to read other than the latest supermarket tabloid. Maybe that would change after they were married and his habits rubbed off on her.

Mike wandered into the room that had been Kassie's office. He still thought of it as hers. Hard not to. Like Kassie, it was neat as a furniture showroom. Though uncluttered, framed pictures of various sizes of family and vacations were aligned like soldiers taking a stand along the credenza and sofa table. A lone eight-by-ten picture of Topher stood watchful guard on her desk. Was it his imagination or could he smell vanilla, her favorite bath gel? He soaked it in and rubbed a twinge in his chest. He parted the drapes, which Amelia must have closed, and pulled the door shut.

Next stop, the dining room and the wine rack. Out of habit, he grabbed two bottles of pinot grigio. He removed Christmas gift tags that read "To Kassie, Love, Mike," and put the bottles on ice. There was plenty more where those had come from.

Mike picked up the checkbook he'd left on the kitchen counter and headed to his home office. He returned it to a small box and locked it in the bottom drawer of his desk. He sank into his big leather chair and flipped through the past week's mail. Amelia had sorted the envelopes and magazines mostly by size, putting *Playboy* on top. A sticky note with a smiley emoji stared at him. He left it there.

Without opening them, he set aside the gas and electric bills, water bill, trash collection bill, a Visa bill, MasterCard bill, AMEX bill, and Nordstrom bill. "You really should get e-bills," Kassie's voice echoed.

He opened a letter from his lawyer. It simply confirmed completion of the work they'd done in conjunction with his accountant over the last month to finalize the divorce settlement and review his will.

The divorce agreement with Kassie was pretty much locked down. With the court date set for September, they'd determined his will was in good standing until such time he might want to make any changes, perhaps after the divorce.

As things stood, if something happened to him, Kassie would inherit a sizable amount of his wealth. It would have to stay that way. At least for now. That was okay with Mike. Though their marriage failed, he owed her a lot. Just because you can't live with someone doesn't mean you don't care for them. Maybe he'd even leave her something in the revised will after the divorce, as a reminder he was a nice guy after all.

At first, they both thought the divorce process would be complicated. There was a lot at stake. His business, the size of their combined and individual wealth, her inheritance from her mother, and the new tax laws. In one joint meeting they'd laughed when his lawyer said, "At least there's no alimony or child support to fight over." Mike figured Kassie went along with the joke only to be polite.

And they didn't have a prenuptial agreement. When Mike and Kassie married thirty years ago, prenups weren't popular. Even if they were, they came into the marriage with little in the way of individual assets. All of their wealth came from working hard, building Ricci and Associates—now Ricci and Son—investing, and inheritance.

Before negotiations got serious, his advisors warned him the business could be a bone of contention with Kassie. When he'd made Chris a partner, Mike gave him a small ten percent share, leaving ninety percent divided evenly between him and Kassie. If he were going to buy her out, the business would need to be valued and a cash payment made to her.

Rather than get into a pissing match with the attorneys, one morning Mike invited Kassie to breakfast at Panera Bread. On his way he stopped at the florist and still arrived a few minutes early to snag a quiet booth away from incoming traffic. He placed a single yellow rose on the table and had her favorite English breakfast tea and a blueberry scone, warmed, on a plate with a knife and fork ready and waiting. Four brown paper napkins aligned the white kidney-shaped plate. The tea was double-cupped and sleeved just the way he knew she preferred.

"Hope this is okay?"

"Great. Thanks. What's this all about?" She rubbed the tips of her fingers as she always did, anticipating the cup would be too hot to handle, then lifted it and nodded. "Perfect."

Mike talked about how the business was thriving and how Chris brought new energy to the office even though Bill was a little ill at ease with him.

"Competition can be healthy," Kassie said without mentioning Chris's name.

Mike complimented her, reflecting on how critical she'd been in making the firm a success over the years. He'd always admired her for maintaining her marketing career separate from his.

"Thanks. I thought if we'd worked together, we'd have divorced much sooner than now."

Mike let that slide. Instead he moved on.

"I'm wondering," Mike said, "how to handle the value of the business? Your forty-five percent could be a significant chunk of change for me to come up with or finance along with everything else."

"I've been wondering about that too. My attorney keeps telling me to get all that I'm entitled to. It's been such a long haul. I have no desire to screw you, Mike. You must believe that."

"I do." Mike resisted reaching across the table to touch her hand.

"Where have I heard those words before?" They both laughed and shook their heads.

"We're both creative, Kassie. Surely, we could come up with an alternative that works for both of us *and* our attorneys. Don't you think?"

Kassie abruptly excused herself and got up. Mike could see her put her phone to her ear as she walked past the registers.

Mike wasn't sure who she was talking to or where this was headed, but he appreciated how cooperative she'd sounded so far. Bad Kassie was nowhere in sight.

"Listen, Mike," she said, sliding back into the bench seat. "Like I said, I have no appetite to make any of this any more difficult on you than it already is. You've had a helluva year. I get that. Looks like you're doing okay?"

"Yes, I am. Thanks. Go on."

"Here's an idea. Obviously, if I received a huge lump sum from the business, I'd get screwed tax-wise. Why don't we amortize my share over a period of years?"

"Spread it out, you mean, over time? How many years?"

"I have no clue. Why don't we have those that do have a clue value the business and then give us several different scenarios?"

"Good idea. See, that's why I married you," Mike said.

"It's important they know what our goal is."

"Which is?"

"Minimization. The burden on you, and the tax impact on me. It could be a win-win, I think."

"And then there's our retirement accounts?" Mike rubbed his hands together.

"Isn't that out of our hands? As I understand it, soon after the divorce we'll need to retain a separate consultant to value and distribute those accounts. From the statements I saw last year, the size of those accounts is pretty equal. There are laws and formulas. It is what it is."

They'd finished their meetup by talking about Topher and how Kassie was thinking about going to Venice with Annie in July.

"I need to get going." Kassie moved to leave.

"This is for you," Mike said, sliding the rose toward her. "Still friends, right?"

"Ouch." A thorn pricked Kassie's finger as she picked it up.

"You okay?" Mike asked.

"Yes," Kassie said, sucking the slight cut. "You doing okay?"

He leaned down to kiss her cheek. "Yup. And Karen's fine."

She stepped back, her neck and head rising like ET. "Really? I don't recall asking."

Mike shook his head and touched her arm, reminding himself that Bad Kassie was never more than a heartbeat away.

The doorbell and a knocking woke Mike. It was 6:23 according to the digital clock on his desk. He gathered up the mail and shoved it in a drawer and shuffled to the front door.

"Hey there, you two. Come on in."

Charlie crossed the threshold past Mike as if he owned the place, leaving Sarah and their bags on the front porch.

"Let me help you with that," Mike said, picking up the largest gray roller bag and guiding Sarah into the entryway.

After hellos and how are yous were exchanged, Mike rolled the biggest bag in front of Charlie and directed the Gaineses to their upstairs bedroom in case they wanted to get settled and freshen up. *Where the hell is Karen?*

"Where's the lady of the house?" Charlie said.

"Charlie, you know Karen and Mike aren't married yet. Technically, Kassie's still the lady of this house, am I right, Mike?" Sarah piped in.

"Yes, she is. Legally. For a few more months anyway," Mike murmured as he showed them their room and the adjoining bath, hoping to change the subject.

"Once you and Karen are married, I'm sure you'll change all that and make a proper woman of her. You'll make her part owner of Ricci and Son too, right? How about that? You could change the name again to Ricci and Family." Charlie laughed.

Neither Mike nor Sarah shared his joke.

The doorbell rang again.

"Excuse me." Mike left his houseguests to unpack. He pulled back the white lace curtains covering the narrow window next to the front door. He didn't recognize the redheaded woman whose back faced him and hoped she wasn't trying to sell him something he neither needed nor wanted.

"What took you so long? Charlie and Sarah should be here soon." Karen spun around and sped past him.

"Uh, they're here already. Where have you been? What's with the red hair?"

"You like it?" Karen primped in front of the small blue-framed antique mirror in the hallway.

"Why'd you ring the doorbell?"

"I had to give Amelia my key. Speaking of, how well do you know that broad?" Karen closed in on Mike.

"Later, Karen, okay?"

"Oh my God, thought I heard your voice. Look at you!" Charlie descended the stairs two at a time and spun Karen around. "Hey, Sarah, doesn't Karen look fabulous?" Charlie said, never taking his eyes off her.

Leaving Karen and Charlie behind, Mike touched Sarah's arm and led her to the family room. "How about a drink?"

4

Let the Games Begin

Charlie grabbed Karen's ass, curled a strand of red hair around his index finger, and whispered in her ear. "How about a kiss?"

"Not here, not now." Karen giggled, cupped Charlie's crotch, then pushed him away. "So, you are glad to see me."

"I am. What's with the new 'do?"

"Thought I'd shake things up a bit. I'm tired of being compared to Kassie. I'm finally getting Mike on my own terms. I want all that he is all to myself." Karen nudged Charlie toward the family room. "I'll be there in a second. Behave."

"Look who's talking."

Karen retrieved from the refrigerator a cheese plate she'd arranged earlier that morning and threw two different types of crackers around the periphery. She grabbed a cheese knife and opened a drawer, looking for cocktail napkins. Staring back at her were three unopened packages of purple napkins with K and M embossed in silver. Biting

29

her lower lip, she considered using them—after all she was the K of the household now—but then thought twice, tossing them in the recycling bin. She opted for plain yellow napkins that would have to do until they were officially K and M.

"Aren't you the brave one?" Sarah said, helping herself to a slice of brie from the plate Karen offered to her.

"Regarding?"

"Your hair. I've thought about going red, but I hear it's not easy going back if you don't like it."

"I like it," Charlie chimed in. "Don't you, Mike?"

"Karen looked fine just the way she was."

"Oh, honey, that was the old me. Wait till I introduce you to the new me. Later." Karen winked at Mike, then smiled at Charlie.

"It's after seven. Bill and Nancy should be here soon. You guys hungry? Thought we'd order in," Mike said.

The three couples gathered around the dining room table, taking their assigned seats. Boy-girl, boy-girl. Mike at the head, Nancy to his left, then Charlie. Karen at the other end, Bill to her left, then Sarah. If you didn't know any better, you'd think this was a reenactment of *The Big Chill*, without the funeral. Wait a minute? Was that Marvin Gaye playing in the background?

Though it may seem otherwise, Karen wanted dinner to be a success, or more precisely, needed it to be. By hook or by crook, she had to build a relationship with Bill, Mike's best friend and now her coworker, and to chink away at any connection his wife, Nancy, had with Kassie.

When Charlie called and said he and Sarah had to be in Boston for client meetings, Karen jumped at the chance to host them. If she could reestablish the friendship she and Sarah had when they were in college, Karen believed Chris would come around and accept her as his mother sooner rather than later.

Karen concocted the seating arrangement without consulting Mike. She figured they'd agree it was a great way to stimulate conversation. They were all adults, right? But she had an ulterior motive, and it worked. Right on cue, Charlie curled his ankle around hers. She didn't pull away, relishing the tingling sensation running from her toes all the way up her leg to her nether region.

Dinner fare was anything but your typical takeout meal. She'd seen a menu from Tryst in Arlington in the same drawer she'd found the monogrammed napkins, and though it smacked of Kassie, it would save her from having to research caterers. *Boring!* As she was still new to the area, Tryst would have to do. Karen ordered prime rib tips and scallops, mashed and sweet potatoes, green beans and broccoli, and an enormous garden salad with three different salad dressings. She wanted something for everyone.

"This is fabulous, Karen," Nancy said as Mike filled her wine glass with pinot grigio. "Thank you for remembering I don't eat red meat."

"Wish I could say I cooked it all myself, but I'm a working girl, you know."

"You left early today. You had all the time in the world to prepare this meal," Bill said.

"Not necessarily. Didn't you notice her hair?" Sarah jumped in.

Is she really trying to defend me for once? Karen's eyes widened in hope and with doubt.

"A haircut and dye job doesn't take all afternoon, does it?" Bill said.

"You don't like it?" Karen tilted her head, running her fingers through the back of her hair.

"Down, you two. Let's leave the sparring at the office." Mike picked up his butter knife and tapped his water glass. "I'd like to make a toast. To old friends and older friends." He lifted his wine glass first to Bill and Nancy and then Charlie and Sarah. "May we all live long and healthy lives in peace and harmony."

Hear, hears all around.

"Speaking of harmony, what is it with you and Bill?" Charlie asked Karen. "Sounds like foreplay to me."

Karen punched Charlie in the arm and shot him a don't-go-there look as the others waited for her to answer.

"Actually, Charlie, we're all good here," Bill spoke up. "Just a little growing pains at the office. With Chris settling in as partner and Karen in the front office, so to speak, I think some people are unsure of what's going to happen when the music stops."

"Well, my dear friend, that's one thing you don't have to worry about. You'll always be taken care of. I'll make sure of that," Mike said.

Karen tapped her fingers on the table, contemplating Mike's comment. *Not on my watch.*

Done with dinner, Karen stood up and threw her napkin on the table. "How about dessert?"

"We went to the North End. Cannolis for everyone!" Nancy announced.

"I've got something better than cannolis. Of course, we can eat them later. Actually, we'll want to eat them later." Mike pulled away from the table and ran upstairs, laughing. "Get some pillows and flip on the fireplace. Let the fun begin."

Karen wasn't surprised when Mike returned with pot. After all, there was college. She figured he had it somewhere in the house, though he'd never shared it with her.

"Well, it's about time," Karen said. "Thought you'd given it up or run out."

"It's been a while. Last time was with Kassie, if my memory serves me right." Mike smiled. "Oh, what a night that was." He held the joint to his lips and tweaked it like Groucho Marx. "But that was the beginning of the end. So there you go." Mike lowered himself to the floor next to Karen and squeezed her shoulder.

"You're with Karen now," Sarah piped in. "You've got a new kidney, a soon-to-be new wife, and your son, um, our son. Time to rejoice." She inhaled.

"Speaking of . . . too bad Chris isn't here. He'd enjoy this scene, don't you think?" Charlie imbibed and then passed to Karen sitting next to him. No ankles locked in full view of the others.

"Just look at the four of you," Bill said. "Who would've ever guessed when you all were in college that you'd share parenting forty years later? And be civil about it?"

"I was very lucky to have had Sarah as my sorority sister when I needed her most." Karen put her right hand over her heart, hoping she sounded more noble than she felt. "No way my parents would've let me keep the baby."

"And great timing. Since Sarah and I were about to get married, we could adopt Chris. The best thing that ever happened to us. Except getting married, that is." They all giggled.

"So where is Chris?" Nancy inquired after coughing and waving smoke away from her face.

"San Francisco," Sarah said. "You know he lived there for quite a while. He has friends there, and I think he may be with his girlfriend."

"Girlfriend? What girlfriend?" Karen and Mike said together.

"Oh, didn't he tell you? He's been seeing a gal named Lexi. Who do you think he went to Greece with in March? Wonder why he didn't tell you guys? He told me," Sarah said, scrunching her nose with a smile.

"At least she's closer in age to him than Kassie. Probably more in common. Especially in the sack," Charlie said.

Karen glared at him and took in a pained look on Mike's face.

"Oh, sorry, old man. Just saying."

"Don't call him that. We're all around the same age, except you and Sarah are even a couple of years older. Remember?" Karen said, not defending Mike, just not wanting to be linked to the idea of getting old.

"Sex is sex, and good sex can be great sex, no matter what your age. If the urge is mutual." Bill grabbed his crotch and winked at his wife.

"Maybe we should get going," Nancy said with a knowing grin.

Mike piped in and suggested they stay in the other spare bedroom. He wouldn't want them driving under the influence. They all agreed driving would be a bad idea.

"Three couples. Three bedrooms. Hmmm. Why don't we do what we did in college?" Charlie suggested. "We guys put our car keys in a bowl and let each gal pull out a key. Whoever is the owner of the key . . ."

Sarah interrupted Charlie. "I know you thought that was a hoot back then, but times—"

"Coffee and cannolis anyone?" Nancy said, apparently trying to save the night.

"Aw, shucks."

5

C Stands For . . .

Bedtime. Wishes of *sweet dreams, nighty-night, don't let the bed bugs bite* echoed as the three cooked couples wobbled their way up the stairs. Charlie and Sarah peeled off into the bedroom they'd settled in earlier that evening, as Karen, being the host-ess-with-the-mostest, ushered Bill and Nancy into theirs.

"Have you ever stayed the night before?" Karen asked as she pulled the drapes shut.

"Nada. Nope. No siree," Nancy said, cozying up to Bill.

"Strange, after knowing Mike for how many years?"

"There's a first time for everything. Better late than never," Bill said, massaging Nancy's back.

"Whatever. Make yourself at home. The towels are fresh, and I think you'll find whatever you need in the bathroom vanity." Though she'd never checked—she had no reason to until now—Karen assumed the spare bathrooms were fully stocked by the previous woman of the house.

"Thanks, Kassie. I mean Karen." Nancy guffawed, putting her hand over her mouth. "Sorry."

Karen bit her lip. Nancy wasn't the enemy.

As Karen closed the door, she lingered and heard Bill say, "Not the best way to win friends and influence people, eh, my dear?"

"Not my job. But this is." Nancy giggled.

Karen rolled her eyes and shook her head as she closed the master bedroom door behind her. Mike had made quick work of getting ready for bed. Things were looking up until he opened his mouth.

"What do you think Charlie meant?"

"By what?"

"Aw, shucks."

"Nothing really. Just a saying. And he's stoned." Karen threw her hands in the air.

"What if you pulled his key? Would you—"

"Only a game, Mike. He knew no one would go along with it. Only a game." She and Charlie played the game once before without Mike's key in the mix. A night etched in her mind forever.

Karen took her memories and retreated to the bathroom to freshen up. Catching a glimpse of herself in the mirror, her red hair startled her. It would take some getting used to. But it was all for a good cause. She brushed and tossed it, giving the woman in the mirror a knowing wink.

She slipped on a black satin baby doll nightie with a plunging lace neckline and spaghetti straps, tucking the matching panties in a drawer in the bathroom. No need to make things difficult for Mike tonight. She was mellow and horny. A winning combination. She hoped Mike was as hot to trot as she. With Charlie just down the hall, it would be easy to play out her recurring fantasy, and Mike would never be the wiser.

The bedroom was as dark as a dungeon.

"What the hell? Mike, turn on a light before I stub my toe," Karen hissed. Silence.

Karen felt her way around the bed, tapping one palm at a time until she reached her side and climbed in. As she rolled toward Mike, she touched his back. Actually, she touched the back of his T-shirt. Her fingers slid down his body until she inserted them into the elastic of his boxers. She rolled her eyes and pinched her lips. His measured breathing indicated his back and his attire were more than a wall between them. She'd seen this movie before. It was his way of saying *not tonight* without having to utter the words.

Her eyes adjusted to the darkness, helped by her cellphone's blue light. It was nearly midnight. She exhaled and coughed. Maybe that would wake Mike up. She waited. Coughed again. No reaction.

She resorted to happier thoughts. At first, the memory of Charlie wrapped around her ankle earlier that evening stilled her mind, then stirred a longing. She faced away from Mike and squeezed her hand between her thighs. *What a waste.* She could have had either of two men in the house that night, and she had neither.

There was only one solution. Karen got out of bed and went into the bathroom and took care of business, without even a groan. It wasn't the first time, for sure. After her husband Barry died, she reintroduced herself to self-pleasuring without guilt. Once she'd reunited with Mike, though, she figured that was behind her.

After, she sat on a small round vanity chair in the dressing room, careful not to make noise swiveling or rolling on it. There were guests in the house to consider.

Guests. Karen wondered what they were doing. Hard to imagine Bill and Nancy having sex—though Mike had told her about their rocky marriage and how they reignited their relationship after Bill had a rip-roaring affair a few years back. And then there was Charlie and Sarah.

In more than one conversation over the last year, Charlie said he and Sarah had no sex life at all anymore. Could she believe him? Was the way he came on to her that night a deep-felt emotion for her, a memory of a mini-affair in college, or just a sex-starved middle-aged man?

Karen found the satin panties she'd tucked in the drawer and stepped into them. She grabbed a mid-calf black silk robe and her cellphone and tiptoed downstairs. In her travels, she noticed no lights shining under the doorway from Bill and Nancy's room. Whatever they'd started when she closed their door was either finished or still in progress, but quietly. A smidgen of light and voices came from the other room. At first, she hoped she hadn't wakened Charlie and Sarah, but then dismissed that wacky idea with Mike's familiar snoring filling the hallway. Any complaints by the guests of a sleepless night would be directed toward the homeowner.

God, she was hungry. With the kitchen at the opposite end of the house from the sleeping quarters, Karen was able to shift the bowls of leftovers in the refrigerator without fear of disturbing anyone. Paydirt. She found the cannolis. As she grabbed a knife out of the drawer—eating an entire pastry in the middle of the night was out of the question—her cellphone lit up. A text.

That u downstairs?

Yup.

Company?

Why not? Hungry?

Starved.

By the time Charlie arrived in the kitchen in his light blue pajama bottoms and dark blue Chicago Cubs T-shirt, Karen had clicked on the Keurig.

"Couldn't sleep?"

"Sarah had other ideas." Charlie grinned.

"Really? Thought you'd said—"

"Talk. She wanted to talk. She wasn't happy about my key suggestion."

"Neither was Mike. Did you really think anyone would go along with that?"

"What about you? You had no problem with it way back when."

"So, does the *C* on your shirt stand for the Cubs or for Charlie?" Karen teased and tried to change the subject.

Charlie approached her and pushed her against the counter. She fed him the other half of her pastry. As he chewed, he said, "Cannolis," and tried to kiss her. They busted out laughing.

"Shhhh," Karen whispered. "Don't want to wake the house."

"Maybe it stands for clitoris." Charlie untied her robe and slid his fingers into her panties. He kissed her deeply. "You're wet. That was quick. Like the good old days. Yum."

And it was quick.

Karen traced the huge *C* on Charlie's chest. "Perhaps it stands for Chris. The one thing everyone in this house tonight, except for Nancy, has in common."

"And Bill too?"

"Oh, there's a Bill connection. You know that. He's competing with Chris, and eventually me, for stakes in the company."

"What do you think Mike meant when he said Bill would be taken care of?"

"Not sure. But once we're married, I'll have full view of Mike's plans for divvying up the company, when and if the time comes." Karen pushed him away ever so slightly.

"Maybe the *C* stands for *collusion* or *conspiracy*. Popular words these days, don't you think?" Charlie gave Karen a peck on the cheek, a swift pat on the ass, and headed back upstairs.

Karen gazed out the kitchen window, reflecting on the risk she took hosting Charlie and Sarah that weekend. She'd have to keep Charlie under control. Keep her eye on the prize. She gave Charlie a five-minute head start, then went upstairs to the master bedroom, a.k.a., the promised land.

6

Getting to Know ... Him

Vacationing in Venice was not Kassie's idea. Returning to the city where she'd met Chris six years earlier was the last item on her bucket list, if it was there at all. Apparently it was a major component of Annie's grand scheme.

"Write a book," Annie, her BFF, had nagged her. "It'll help get Mike and his vasectomy, Chris and his lineage, and your mother and her misguided love out of your system once and for all. You have an unbelievable story to tell. Movies are made with far less intrigue. You'd be rich. Be on *The View* and *Ellen*."

"More like *Dr. Phil*. 'What were you thinking?' he'd yell at me for sure. I'd be so embarrassed. More than I am already."

"If you won't write to cleanse your soul, Kassie, you must return to Venice, the scene of your original sin. It may be the only way to close the circle and get on with your life."

She thought she'd moved on. After the shit had hit the Mike/Karen/Chris fan, Kassie plowed her energy into her work, much to the delight of Tom and her team. She was grateful they'd remained loyal to her when she needed it most, giving her time and space to handle her affairs—the romantic one with Chris and her financial and legal affairs with Mike. She'd committed herself to returning to the Kassie they, and she, once knew—putting in long hours, challenging the design and copywriting teams to break boundaries, signing new clients, beating the competition, and being the leading revenue producer in the firm. She was back.

Or was she?

"Are you just filling time with activities you could do with your eyes closed? Classic denial syndrome," her therapist diagnosed.

"But I slept with my husband's—"

"You also saved Mike's life."

"Did I? Karen would claim first prize in that regard."

"Enough self-pity. Change the tape that's on an endless loop in that head of yours. Find a new love. Something other than a man to make you happy," her therapist challenged.

So she tried. She thought about her past volunteer work: reading to second graders, cleaning cages at an animal shelter, raising money for AIDS, participating in telethons at the local public television station. Those were fulfilling, happy times. And none included either Mike or Chris.

Convinced, Kassie declared she needed a new cause. She didn't have to look far. She discussed an idea with her therapist.

"I could help you with that. I'm on the board of the Boston Adoption Center. We're always looking for volunteers. You could be a big sister to one of the children. How does that sound?"

Her therapist was right. Working with children who'd been discarded by or taken from their parents filled one hole that had ached for thirty years. Payback or pay-it-forward, she didn't know which, but she was willing to do whatever she could.

But that wasn't enough to put the past behind her to satisfy Annie. Venice. It just had to be Venice. Annie was sure of it.

Kassie wasn't but gave in anyway. Who could turn down a trip to Venice? So, as she waited to meet Annie at the same café on St. Mark's Square where she'd first met Chris, her doubts that a trip to Venice had the power to heal the emptiness she felt without him brewed inside her. How many nights had she fallen asleep imagining the arms wrapped around her were his, not her own? Her eyes watered as the dance bands dueled and couples coupled. She yearned for his gentle touch, his Hollywood smile, the subtle ways his outward confidence balanced her internal anxieties. Without him, her entire being shrieked, "Tilt! Check engine light." She definitely was out of alignment.

Kassie sipped her twenty-euro Cosmopolitan at a table she chose specifically to be near the one she had sat at long ago when Chris descended into her life from out of nowhere. He became a five-year gift from God, getting her through her mother's illness and the final downward spiral of her marriage. And then in a nanosecond his love was zapped away as unexpectedly as it had appeared.

Before last night—before Annie's bait and switch—she couldn't have imagined how she'd replace him in her life. Maybe now she wouldn't have to. Could Paris change all that? If they could make it work in Venice and Paris, could they make it in Boston? In Europe they were out as a legitimate couple for the first time since their affair began. Would they endure when they returned to Boston? Or would they uncouple, be like 7 Up, the uncola?

Kassie left Chris on the terrace with the letter from her boss. She'd better get her shit together. Lifting her red roller bag, she slung it onto the queen-size bed with a thud so forceful the bed's metal legs shifted and scraped. She pressed both hands on the mattress.

Hope it's strong enough to take a week's worth of pounding. God bless the guests in the room below. Maybe we should send them a bottle of wine now before we need to apologize.

They'd left Venice in such a rush that morning she'd thrown everything into her bag in a heap. It didn't matter then. There were no big plans. The letter from her boss changed all that.

She removed her Clarks sandals and dropped them on the floor. So much for minding the noise. The plastic bag with dirty clothes found its way to the narrow closet that had just four hangers, probably left there by previous guests. She found the black skirt she'd worn the night before rolled up in a ball. Even unfurled and shaken, there was no way it would work for her meeting Tuesday. She hung it up anyway. She mumbled something about not having anything to wear, not sensing Chris standing behind her.

"We're just going to cruise the Seine tonight. You're fine the way you are. Not sure you'll even need a jacket. It's pretty warm."

"What?" Kassie whipped around. "You didn't tell me—"

"Ever hear of surprises? I gather it's one of the best ways to see the fireworks. Isn't that why we came here? To see the fireworks?"

Is that why we're here? Fireworks? She'd thought it was to light a fire under their love. Not from where they left off, but from a new starting place. Was she foolish to think his insistence on coming to Paris would mean anything other than that? Maybe she'd read him wrong.

Still, Kassie wondered if she'd ever get used to Chris's surprises. Showing up in Venice, now the cruise. Throughout most of their affair, gifts or surprises were mostly off-limits. They'd be too difficult to cover up with Mike. That changed when he gave her the gondola necklace, which she hoped he hadn't noticed she wasn't wearing.

"Come with me. We need to talk." Kassie took Chris by the hand and with a slight shove directed him to sit in the Queen Anne chair.

He stumbled into the chair, and his eyes twinkled. She didn't need to be clairvoyant to know what was on his mind. She had other ideas. Unless they were prone in bed, this was the only way she could look him eye-to-eye. She leaned on both arms of the chair, her nose leading the way.

"Listen. I'm okay with the fireworks. But this, all this, is Annie's fault, and yours too." She tapped him on his chest. Probably instinctively, he grabbed her wrist.

She pulled away, ranting and pacing and shaking her finger at him. No way was she supposed to be in Paris with him or to be meeting with the managing director of the Paris office. None of this was in her plans. It wasn't what she had worked so hard for over the past year.

"You don't know what I've gone through." Kassie raised her voice, flailing her hands in the air. "While you were off becoming a partner in Mike's firm, moving from San Francisco, making nice with your new mother, probably dating, for all I know . . . ."

"Sounds like you're losing your superpowers, KO. Three out of four ain't bad." Chris got up from the chair, poured himself another glass of wine, and sat back down. He was right; she wasn't done.

"Whatever." Kassie ranted on and gave him a pass for the moment. "I haven't moved on quite the way you have. While you built a new life, I unbundled my thirty-year marriage and resurrected a career some people assumed I had put on the back burner. You know I've been pitching Tom about making me a partner after twenty years' sweat and blood. No one's built that business like I have. But no such luck with that." Stopping, she took a deep breath. "And I'm still living at Annie's with Topher."

"Speaking of, how is my namesake?"

Kassie shook her head and warned him not to change the subject. What did he mean three out of four? And why didn't he jump to deny her dating accusation?

"I feel like I've been marching in place since we—"

"Broke up?" Chris said, pulling her onto his lap. "Me too."

Chris nibbled at her neck and held her close as if she was a toddler needing to be calmed. She kissed him softly first and then with purpose. French-like, of course.

"You didn't answer my question," Kassie said.

"Was there a question in all your railing?"

"Have you been dating? Is there someone else?"

"What do you think? Venice was no coincidence. Paris is no one-week stand."

Chris had left the door to the terrace open. Five flights up, the sound of revelers gearing up for a night of Bastille Day celebration confirmed they weren't in Boston, or Venice, and interrupted Kassie's inquisition and Chris's chance at defense.

"Let's move along. Your cruise boat awaits, my lady."

They walked to the boat dock swinging hand in hand as if they were in high school. That scenario would've been impossible given the ten-year difference in their ages. Shrugging off that thought, Kassie's busy mind wrestled with three competing problems—readying herself for a meeting she was ill-prepared for, not having Paris-appropriate clothes either for the meeting or for a week with the sexiest man alive, or finding out who and when Chris had been dating in her absence.

Once they checked in for their cruise, they were escorted to a VIP section of the dining room near a window.

"*Monsieur et Mademoiselle.*"

Kassie rolled her eyes; Chris grinned from one ear to the other.

"See, you don't look like a madame," Chris whispered.

A cozy table for two, decked out with a white tablecloth and fine bone china, awaited them. Two empty champagne glasses called their name.

"Kir royale?" the waiter suggested, removing the long-stemmed glasses.

"*Oui.*"

"Actually, make mine a Cosmopolitan. I'm on a mission to taste-test cosmos every place we go this week."

Kassie picked up her empty water glass, tilting it back and forth. "Wow. How'd you arrange this?"

"You're not the only one with connections in Paris." Chris took Kassie's hand and squeezed it as they reviewed the special gourmet menu for Bastille Day.

The boat disembarked precisely at 20:30 hours, a.k.a. 8:30 p.m., and Kassie and Chris lifted their cocktail glasses to the finer things in life. A violin and piano played dinner music courteously in the background.

Kassie laughed. "No jazz here tonight, I gather. Where's Ryan Gosling when we need him?"

"If you'd like to go to a jazz club, I'm sure I could find one."

"No, silly. Just remembering a scene from *La La Land*."

"Really? I thought you'd be thinking about our first boat ride. The gondola in Venice."

Out of habit, Kassie reached for the necklace. There was nothing she could do to make it appear out of nowhere. It sat in a purple box in her bedroom at Annie's house.

"I think about that ride and our time in Venice every day of my life."

"Is that right? You're not wearing your necklace. There was a time you said you'd never take it off."

"That was before."

"Before what?"

"You left me."

"Left you? You left me, as I recall."

The waiter appeared and took their order. She'd have the fish; he'd have the lamb chops. And she'd switch to champagne, *s'il vous plaît. Keep it coming. Sounds like I'm going to need it.*

The mood at the table shifted from happy and expectant to

cranky and rejected. A momentary break in their conversation allowed Kassie the opportunity to decide whether or not she'd go down the road they'd traveled before Paris. At some point they'd have to address why they'd broken up and how they'd been living their lives over the last year. Was this the best time?

"Pain," Kassie started, gazing out the window. "Wearing the necklace made me sad. It represented not only the past but also the future I thought we'd have but didn't." She returned her eyes to his. "I believed over time thinking of you and what might have been would shred every fabric of my heart and soul and kill me. I'm sorry."

"Me too."

For what?

Interrupted by the clanging of dinner plates and Chris complimenting the waiter in perfect French, Kassie put the need to follow up on ice. They enjoyed the meal with minimal fanfare. There was enough razzle-dazzle distracting them.

The Seine was beautiful, though not as quiet and serene as it normally would be. As they cruised through the heart of Paris, the lights of the city reflected off the river in perfect vertical lines, as if they were counting the days that were left on their trip. The other boats crossed the lights, creating glowing hashtags on the river.

"Good thing we're here and not up there," Chris said, motioning to the crowd gathered on Pont Neuf bridge. "I'd like to take you there later in the week."

As they drew closer to the Eiffel Tower, the soothing violin and piano melodies that played on board faded and were replaced by classical music from a concert along the shore. More relaxed, Kassie swayed in her chair. Chris moved alongside her and draped his arm around her shoulder. He rested his hand on her upper thigh. The moment was surprisingly more intimate than she figured it could be with other diners around. Maybe they were having their own special moment as well. After all, it was Paris. She turned to kiss him.

"I love you, Kassie. I always have, and always will. No matter what happens."

Kassie just about jumped into the Seine. Fireworks burst into the dark Parisian sky.

Oohs and aahs echoed throughout the boat. For about thirty minutes, they were willing captives in a multicolored, multidimensional world, marveling at a dazzling display that could rival Boston's, or even New York City's, Fourth of July celebration. A world that, though spectacular, was fleeting.

Kassie wondered whether the reunion with Chris was as well.

All that was left of the fireworks was light gray smoke drifting eerily down the night sky. So what next? There seemed to be more people swarming the streets on the walk back to their hotel than there were on the way to the boat. Kassie clutched Chris's hand more out of fear of being separated than of affection. What would she do if she'd lost him? Did she remember the name and address of the hotel? Lord only knew she wouldn't be able to pronounce it. She should've taken a matchbook or napkin or business card, or something.

Back in their room again, out of breath from trudging up the stairs, Kassie dumped her purse on the carpet and sat cross-legged in a huff.

"I don't have any business cards," she said, throwing her wallet, tissue, sunglasses, pen and mini travel notebook, passport, and pink Post-it notes back in her bag.

"So?"

"You ever hear of business etiquette? We're in a foreign country, for crying out loud. I'll be meeting with the head of the company.

And I have no cards. She'll think of me as unprofessional, classless, which of course, I am not. Mercy buckets."

Chris laughed at her. "Don't you think she'll give you some slack? After all, you're on vacation and didn't even expect to be in Paris, let alone meet with her." Chris stripped off his clothes faster than a Chippendale at a local dive bar.

Kassie gawked at him. "Excuse me? Just like that. Drop every thing and go at it? What a difference a year makes. What have you done with my young lover?" She looked to the ceiling.

"Your stud needs a shower, if you don't mind." Chris moved toward the bathroom, reaching down and squeezing her shoulder as he passed. "You've met Mimi before, right?"

"Once a few years ago. At a joint planning conference. She seemed nice. Doubt she'll even remember me."

"How's that possible? You are unforgettable. You'll see."

Kassie undressed, assessing what she should toss in the dirty clothes bag and whether or not her slacks and shirt were salvageable. She grimaced, giving up on everything she'd worn that day. Rifling through her suitcase as she had earlier in the evening, she realized not only did she have nothing professional to wear on Tuesday, but she had nothing sexy for Chris. Even her lingerie was white and middle-aged, like her.

A short deep blue silk robe would have to do double duty—cover her when needed and seduce Chris when the mood suited her. She had to do something to make their first night in Paris unforgettable. There must be music. She scanned the music on her iPhone, confident she hadn't deleted their favorites. Managing the content on her devices was not one of her virtues.

She searched her purse for a small travel-size vial of perfume. It had to be there somewhere. Once on a trip, a spray bottle she'd stored in her cosmetics bag had exploded and damaged her clothes, forcing her to shop in a strange, unfamiliar city. She learned from her mistake, about the perfume anyway. Breathing a sigh of relief, Kassie found the vial sealed in a plastic snack-size bag, tucked safely in a zippered pouch.

Rolling the scent along her neck and under her breast, Kassie was comforted that she still wore Chris's favorite vanilla scent. The necklace might sit in a box across the ocean, but she held in her hand one key to turning Chris on.

Her eyes caught the passport in her purse. How long ago was that conference when she'd met Mimi anyway? Five years ago according to the Paris stamp in her passport.

Ah yes. Mimi was pregnant then. How could she forget? Kassie couldn't take her eyes off of her during the meeting. Mimi was showing. Probably six months pregnant. Could she feel the baby moving? It wasn't fair. That joy would never happen to her. Mike had made sure of that at a time she could've conceived. Now the years outlived a dream, a wish she kept tucked in her heart. She wondered if she'd ever stop envying pregnant women.

Chris's gold Rolex sparkled on a small round marble table near the Queen Anne chair. Picking it up to check the time, she saw his passport. Probably a good idea to keep them together. As she put hers there, she realized she'd never looked at his before. She opened it. Christopher Charles Gaines. How is it she never knew his middle name? What else didn't she know about him?

She flipped the pages of country stamps and stopped. Two pages before Venice had inked impressions she didn't recognize. She looked closely. Entry and exit stamps for Athens, Greece. Last March. What was he doing in Athens? How come he hadn't mentioned it to her?

"Whatcha doing?" Chris appeared with a towel wrapped around his waist.

"Waiting for you." She slid his passport under hers and picked up her phone, clicking on Barry White. She took his hand and led him to the chair. This time she had no intention of lecturing him. "Can't

Get Enough of Your Love, Babe" pulsed through the room. Kassie moved with the music, her hands exploring her own body, her tongue exploring his.

Chris carried her to the bed, peeled off her robe, and as Barry sang "You're the First, the Last, My Everything," images she had of the Acropolis vanished.

7

Taking Care of Business

Before opening his eyes that Saturday morning, Mike rubbed his chest. His T-shirt was damp and so were the sheets, again. He made a mental note to tell his doctor about this at his next appointment, whenever that was; he couldn't remember. Where was Kassie when he needed her?

He opened one eye and quickly shut it. He lifted both eyelids and gasped. He didn't recognize the woman sleeping next to him. Maybe he'd died and gone to heaven or was dreaming. Visions of Goldilocks and Snow White swept through his mind. But that didn't compute. The black spaghetti-strapped woman next to him had sleek red hair and was breathing.

He sighed. He'd forgotten. Karen. Once a blonde. Now a redhead. Whatever for? Who was she trying to impress? Surely not him. From where he sat, or lay, she'd already gotten what she wanted. After it was determined they were a match and the surgeries scheduled, he agreed to marry her after his divorce from Kassie, but never officially proposed.

On more than one occasion, he tried to convince her they could live happily ever after without a marriage license. She'd have none of it, arguing their kidneys matching was proof they belonged together. With her parents and first husband deceased, no one stood in their way. Marriage would fulfill their college dreams, and it would be good for Chris to have his parents married.

"He's in his forties, a grown man for Chrissakes! He's had loving parents all his life. And now that he knows who his real mother and father are, the circle's been closed. For him that should be enough. For me it is. It should be for you too."

But apparently it wasn't enough for Karen. Mike recalled how she shrugged off his counterargument.

"I can take care of you for the rest of your life," Karen said, as she massaged an area below her belly button where she wore the surgical scar like a badge of entitlement.

He figured she had a point. He was alive because of her. Because of her kidney. Granting her wish was the least he could do. And to be perfectly honest, living out the rest of his life alone was not the future Mike saw for himself.

But Karen wasn't Kassie, and he couldn't expect Karen to replace her. Despite their relationship going completely south over the last six years or so, he'd grown comfortable with Kassie. And dependent on her. She was like a Duracell battery, or maybe it was a Timex watch. Whatever. She kept the marriage ticking through thick or thin, allowing him to do his own thing, whenever and whatever that was.

Whether it was when he started the business or branched out and expanded it, Kassie supported him and didn't interfere. Smart, savvy, and spunky, Kassie became successful in her own right, right in front of his eyes. An intelligent, independent, ambitious woman. He figured many men would've swapped places with him in an instant.

Mike wasn't surprised Chris was attracted to her. Looking back, he could kick himself for being the worse part of for-better-or-for-worse.

For lying about Karen and about having a son. Oh, and the vasectomy. He'd never forget her reaction to that revelation. The straw that broke the marriage, or any possibility for reconciliation, for good.

His kidney disease and the divorce forced him to admit he'd been a shit all their years together. He took all that Kassie had done for him for granted and never gave her the credit and attention she deserved. If he had been a better man, perhaps he would've happily joined her on that trip to Italy six years ago, and there would've been no Chris in the picture. Of course, that would've meant he would've had to chart a different path to finding a donor. Too late now. Mike rationalized he made his past a prologue for whatever was to come.

Over the last year, what-ifs crept easily into Mike's thoughts, perhaps driven by the prospect of his demise or the finality of the end of his marriage. To say he had doubts about the path he'd chosen would be a gross understatement. He'd found it impossible to get Kassie off his mind and had sunk into an impractical habit of comparing the wife he was losing with the one he'd be gaining.

Take selflessness: Kassie one point, Karen almost zero. Their reactions to his chronic kidney disease were a perfect example. Though she was ready to leave him for Chris, Kassie put that on the back burner and hung in there with him, making sure he got to his doctors' appointments, ate the right foods, took his meds. And then she made the ultimate sacrifice: When she discovered the Mike-Karen-Chris connection, she gave up her relationship with Chris forever, introduced Mike to his son, who could've been a donor but wasn't, and then arranged for him and Karen to reunite. After all that, their divorce was inevitable. Yet, if it weren't for Kassie, he could've been dead and buried instead of lying next to a redhead. Kassie didn't have to put his needs ahead of her happiness. But she did. He'd be indebted to her forever.

On the other hand, Karen donated her kidney, but not without a price, a quid pro quo, baked into her original offer to do so.

Ostensibly, her gift was out of her timeless love for him. But Mike questioned her motive. Was it payback for the years he supported her after Barry died? Or was it her jealousy of Kassie? Donating her kidney gave her bragging rights over Kassie. A clear case of one-up-manship. He couldn't explain why, but a gnawing feeling haunted him. Maybe Kassie's sixth sense was contagious.

Next, take sex: Karen one point, Kassie half a point. Hard to honestly compare the two, since his sex life with Kassie petered out, gradually and literally, after his vasectomy. With Karen, though, once they were given the all-clear signal from the doctors after the transplant, they'd picked up where they'd left off in college. Except this time there was no chance of a pregnancy. *Thank God.*

Enough daydreaming. Time to get up and get the show on the road.

As he stood at the toilet smiling, happy that peeing was no longer a struggle, he realized he'd never understood women. You'd think he would have after being married to Kassie for decades. But no. Still a mystery.

Take Charlie's suggestion the night before of throwing the guys' keys in a bag. Charlie said it was a game they'd played in college. Mike didn't recall it, though he was certain he would've been open to it if he'd been invited to play. What surprised him was that Nancy and Sarah vocalized their objection, but Karen didn't do so at the time. She poo-pooed it only when he'd raised the prospect of it with her afterward. Would she have gone along with it?

What if she pulled Bill's key? Mike laughed as he retrieved clean underwear from his armoire, careful not to wake Karen. Could a roll in the hay thaw the icy waters between the two of them? Mike snorted. *Fat chance.*

What if it was Charlie's key? How weird would that have been for her? Bedding down with the man who was her son's adoptive father? Of course, they would have Chris to talk about post-coital. *Wonder if Charlie needs Viagra to get it up at his age?* Mike filed that as something he could probe Charlie about delicately if he had the chance over the weekend. Man-to-man. *Real-dad-to-fake-dad.*

Mike wasn't surprised the house was as quiet as a couch full of napping felines. Karen and the others more than likely were sleeping off their high. On any other Saturday morning at six thirty, Mike would still be between the covers asleep or at least contemplating getting laid. But something woke him. Was his mind working overtime thinking about the letter he'd decided to write last night? Or was it the damp shirt that interrupted his sleep? Didn't matter. He was glad to be up before the other roosters and hens started gathering in the kitchen.

The kitchen looked a bit disturbed itself and smelled like hazelnut. The Keurig light was on, and a variety of coffee and tea K-cups were lined up ready to be brewed. Two coffee mugs mingled—half a cup of coffee lingered in one, the other appeared untouched. A white bakery box sat on the counter next to the sink, its lid beckoning a look-see. As he did, he stepped on something that crunched. He bent over and picked up what looked like a remnant from a cannoli shell and tossed it in the trash. He brushed white sugar off the counter and into the sink.

Someone had the munchies. Despite the crumbs on the floor, Mike was pleased his guests—his friends—made themselves at home in the middle of the night. Would they admit their midnight raid or even remember it?

Mike took advantage of the Keurig being ready and the convenient empty mug. He carried his coffee down the hall, passing Kassie's office. The door was still closed. His palm touched it as he walked by.

Settling into his leather chair, Mike powered up his computer and opened a new Word document. In less than five minutes, he fulfilled the promise he made to Bill the night before. He saved the letter in two places on his hard drive—his personal file and his Ricci and Son file. He printed six copies, slid them into a blue folder, and then took it out to his car, tossing it onto the passenger seat.

Still early, he refreshed his coffee and cozied up in his Pleasure Chair in the family room. He lifted the footrest and shook his head, deciding he should let in some fresh air. He got up and opened the sliding doors as quietly as possible, hoping not to wake anyone, and then made his way to the laundry room. A healthy spray of Febreeze should help eliminate the skunk smell from last night's party—a trick he'd learned from Amelia.

None too soon. Above him Mike could hear footfalls and running water.

"You're up early," Bill said, running his hand through his hair.

"Hey, man, look at you. Let me get you some clothes."

"How about a shirt for Nancy too?"

As Mike and Bill made their way upstairs, Charlie and Sarah waited at the top.

"Good morning! Sleep well?" Mike greeted them a little out of breath.

"Like a baby! Sarah had to feed me every two hours!"

"Did not." Sarah punched Charlie in the shoulder.

"So it was you who had the munchies?"

"Don't know what you're talking about." Charlie shrugged.

"You guys make yourself at home. We'll be down in a jiffy."

Mike could hear laughter from the kitchen as he and Karen came downstairs.

"Sounds like they're getting along," Mike said as they walked down the hallway.

"Glad someone is."

Mike grabbed Karen's arm and pulled her toward him. "Hey,

kiddo, sorry I fell asleep last night. I'll make it up to you later, if you behave," Mike whispered and kissed her on the nose.

"There you two are. Thought you were going back to bed," Charlie teased. Mike noticed his wink at Karen. Probably everyone did.

"Actually, I'm going to leave you guys for an hour. I have a couple of errands to run. Have some coffee. Make some bacon and eggs," Mike suggested.

"I'd have a cannoli, but they're gone," Nancy said. "Weren't you the first one up, Mike?"

"I was, but I didn't."

"Okay, fess up, you guys. Who's the culprit?" Nancy continued her research.

"I confess. I couldn't sleep with all you guys snoring. You sounded like an out-of-step marching band. I was starving," Karen said. Mike sensed coyness in her remark.

As he grabbed his keys, Mike recalled Charlie's game, the two cups, and the crumbs on the floor but decided to let it slide. For now.

Mike pulled into the bank parking lot as the manager unlatched the front door.

"Mr. Ricci. You're bright and early today. Can I help you?"

Yes, she could, and she did. She notarized and had witnessed his signature on six copies of the letter he'd written earlier that morning, shook his hand, patted his back, and let him into the vault.

"Good for you, Mr. Ricci, keeping your ducks in order. I've always said if you fail to plan, you plan to fail."

The voice of Kassie's mother and her annoying habit of quoting long-dead poets echoed in his mind. *Was the whole world populated with epigrammatists?*

Pushing those thoughts aside, Mike focused on the task at hand. While his health may have failed over time, he'd be damned if the future of his business would. Taking care of the people who'd made him a success should help make up for his sins and ensure the longevity of Ricci and Son.

After placing one of the letters in his safety deposit box, Mike drove to the post office and overnighted one letter to his lawyer and one to his accountant, including a Post-it note letting each know that the other received a copy. He checked his phone for Annie's address. He tried to remember if that was the week Kassie was in Italy with Annie, but it didn't matter; the package would be waiting for her when she returned. He shoved two envelopes in the cardboard container: one envelope addressed to Chris, the other to Kassie with a note to hand deliver the envelope to Chris. Perhaps this would break the stalemate between them and give them a reason to get back together. It was the least he could do.

One more stop and one more envelope to deliver.

Bill and Nancy were climbing into their Hyundai SUV as Mike pulled into his driveway.

"Leaving so soon? I have donuts. I know they're not quite cannolis, but sugar . . ."

"Sweet. But no thanks, Mike. We need to get going. Saturday, the boys and all," Nancy said.

As Bill approached Mike to shake his hand, Mike slapped an envelope in Bill's palm.

"What's this?"

"See you Tuesday. Remember I'm taking Monday off. One last day—"

"Before they leave?" Bill laughed. "Have fun, if you can."

Mike waved, backpedaling toward the house. Bill threw his hands in the air and mouthed the words, "What the . . . ?" confirming Mike had accomplished his goal that Bill would see the message he'd written in red on the envelope.

Open in the event of Michael Ricci's death.

8

Duck, Duck, Goose

Dutifully, the five "friends" Mike left behind in the kitchen as he ran some errands busied themselves with breakfast. While Karen and Nancy set the table, Bill and Charlie fired up the griddle. Where was Sarah?

Clever girl to escape having to do anything like work. The pungent smell of bacon redirected Karen's negative thoughts about Sarah to her stomach, which gurgled on its own.

"Was that you?" Charlie teased as Karen brushed his arm as she passed him to get the silverware out of the drawer.

"The bacon. Guess I'm hungrier than I thought."

"It's the nitrates working their magic." Sarah moseyed into the kitchen out of nowhere from the direction of Kassie's office.

"She should know, a nutritionist by training and all," Charlie boasted a little too proudly for Karen's taste.

"So, I suppose you don't eat bacon?" Karen taunted Sarah.

"Oh, I do. Sometimes. I'll probably pass this morning. It can make my hands swell."

Sarah held up her hands, spreading her fingers. Her obscene diamond engagement ring competed in size and stature with the emerald-cut emerald on her right hand.

Fuck that. Karen massaged her ringless hands as if she was rubbing in lotion and plucked an extra piece of bacon off the platter to accompany her two eggs over easy. She had her man—men, actually—right where she wanted them. They could care less if her hands swelled, as long as they were serviceable.

"Speaking of hands, where were yours when we were pulling this spread together?" Charlie half scolded, half kidded Sarah.

"In the back office. I guess it's Kassie's?"

"Wish Mike would get rid of everything in that room." Karen tore a piece of toast in two and proceeded to mop up the yolk of her eggs.

"You think he's keeping it as a monument to her?" Charlie added his two cents. If he was trying to make Karen feel better, it wasn't working.

"What were you doing in there? Isn't that off-limits? I thought the door was closed." Nancy spoke up, sounding accusatory.

"Just looking around." Sarah either ignored Nancy's tone or was oblivious to it, as Karen figured she was with most things. "There's adorable pictures of her cat in there. Topher's his name. Isn't that funny?"

"Funny teehee, or funny strange?" Karen's curiosity kindled.

"Neither," Bill chimed in. "Story goes, she adopted him from a shelter in Newburyport after she'd met Chris. His previous owners had named him Moguls. Guess they were skiers. Kind of hard to pronounce unless you have marbles in your mouth." Bill tried to be funny, puffing out his cheeks and mumbling, and then exhaling. "So Kassie renamed him in honor of your son, Sarah."

"My son," Karen said, her nostrils bulging as she inhaled, her fork and knife upright in her fists positioned squarely on the table.

"Our son." Charlie announced, appearing to placate both Sarah and Karen and attempting to take the wind out of a brewing argument, or cat fight.

Karen clanged her utensils across her plate, gripped the side of her chair, and crossed her ankles, doing everything possible to prevent an outburst she might be sorry for later.

With their mouths full, the five "friends" finished breakfast without a murmur, barely grunting even when asking to pass the butter.

"It's time we head out," Bill said, finally breaking through the silence. "Nancy, let's go."

"Nice having you both. See you at the office, Bill." Karen fake smiled, trying to clear the air as she ushered Nancy and Bill out the door. *Good riddance.* She chalked it up to another brick in the wall when it came to her relationship with Bill.

"That went well," Charlie laughed.

"Don't be such a fool. You didn't help. I have to work with him." Karen gestured for Charlie and Sarah to sit back down at the table.

"You really don't," Sarah said. "I understand you needed a job when you first moved here, but you've been here awhile. I'm sure you could find a job somewhere else."

"And once you and Mike are married, you shouldn't have to work," Charlie prodded.

"I like being there, with Mike and Chris. We have so many years to catch up on. And anyway, working there isn't the problem."

"What is?" Sarah needled.

"I know you don't want to hear this, Sarah, but it's you." Karen looked her straight in the eye. "And Charlie." She bowed her head toward the placemat.

"What?" Sarah leaned forward in her chair. "You've got to be kidding."

"I'm not. People still consider you two Chris's parents." Karen pointed at Sarah and Charlie in turn. "Not me and Mike." She pounded her chest.

"What people?" Sarah pressed.

"Obviously, Bill and Nancy. Chris. Probably Kassie too."

"I wouldn't worry about Bill and Nancy. They seem like nice folks. They'll come around. Just give them time." Charlie patted the back of Karen's hand.

"What about Kassie? Seems she considers Mike his father." Sarah wouldn't let it go. "I bet every day she chastises herself for shagging her husband's son." Sarah tilted her head and wrapped her arms around herself. "Sends shivers up my spine when I try to put myself in her shoes. Poor woman."

Charlie reached over and rubbed Sarah's back. "Don't feel sorry for Kassie. Sounds like she's moved on. Mike told me he thinks she's in Europe on vacation—"

"On the prowl for another sucker." Karen attempted a joke no one got.

"I beg your pardon. Are you calling my son a sucker?" Sarah's face flushed, her eyes tearing.

"I rest my case. You see, you guys are the problem. If you can't stop referring to him as your son, how can anyone else start referring to him as mine?" Karen started clearing the table.

"Really, Karen? You gonna go there?" Sarah picked up her dishes and followed Karen to the sink. "As I recall, by your choice, we've been Chris's parents all his life. We're all he's known. He's an adult now, not a child. You can't expect him to rewrite his life just because you want him to."

Biting her lip, Karen decided not to fight this fight. She had bigger fish to fry. She grabbed Sarah's dishes and dropped them in the sink. The silverware clanged against the plates. She looked out the window over the sink as Mike pulled in the driveway. With reinforcements arriving, she turned toward Sarah with renewed confidence.

Karen leaned back on the edge of the counter over the sink as Sarah invaded her space, continuing on her high horse. She raised her eyebrows and covered her nose as Sarah's tea breath was already souring.

"Maybe you should've thought all this through, Karen, before you cooked up your little scheme. You haven't changed."

"All's fair in love . . ."

Meow.

Karen rocked from one foot to another, loading the dishwasher as Mike came into the kitchen carrying a box of donuts. Moments earlier, from her vantage point peering out the window, she saw Mike and Bill shake hands as Mike handed him what looked like a white envelope. *Why did Bill throw his hands in the air?*

"Kitchen's closed already?" Mike slid the donut box onto the small counter next to the stove. "Guess I'm too late."

"Yup. Looks like the party's over. For the time being anyway," Karen said with her hands on her hips.

"Shouldn't you be getting ready? What time is our duck boat tour? Should be a beautiful day to end up in the Charles. *Quack. Quack.*" Mike laughed and tweaked her nose.

"Aren't you in a good mood?" Karen slammed the dish towel on the counter. "I've got to get dressed."

As Karen turned toward the hallway to go up the stairs, Sarah and Charlie arrived in the kitchen, looking as though they were ready to go.

"Oh, it'll only take me a few minutes to change. More coffee? Mike brought donuts." Karen pointed to the box on the counter at the far end of the kitchen.

"No coffee, thanks." The polite Sarah seemed to have returned.

"We're going for a walk." Charlie gave Mike's shoulder a squeeze as he passed him.

"Don't be gone too long. We'll need to leave in an hour."

"No problem. We'll be back shortly." Charlie flashed a thumbs-up as he and Sarah walked out the front door. "Could you leave the door unlocked?"

Karen shrugged and went up to the bedroom. Enough of Sarah for a while. She had more important things to think about. Like, what would she wear? She'd been gradually moving her clothes and essentials from her apartment to Mike's house in anticipation of settling in once and for all when the divorce was final. She couldn't wait. The uncertainty of whether she had the right clothes for every occasion was driving her batty. Though having the right clothes wasn't the only thing she had to change at the house.

She stepped into her capri jeans and held a red scoop neck short-sleeved shirt in front of her. She groaned. *No can do.* It clashed big time with her new hair color. For sure Sarah would tell her she should've thought about that too.

She swapped her black bra for a nude one and slipped on a white V-neck T-shirt. "Hmmm. Better." Inserting the half-carat diamond studs she'd bought with the thousand-dollar monthly stipend Mike had sent her after Barry's death, she laughed, recalling how Mike had asked her if they were real. "Hell, no. I can't afford diamonds on my income," she'd said without bothering to cross her fingers. Dressed, Karen admired herself in the mirror, ran her hands through her hair, and gave herself a wink of approval.

Thank goodness Mike wasn't there to witness her earlier exchange with Sarah. Whose side would he have taken? She needed to keep him in check, on her side, focused on making her Mrs. Michael Ricci.

The weekend thus far was kind of a bust. Dinner and their smoke fest weren't too bad, and certainly the midnight snack was intriguing, but this morning was a disaster. Why had she agreed to host these guys? Except for Charlie, she couldn't give a hootie-toot about any of them. But the weekend was still young. She had until Monday to make nice with Sarah and make it with Charlie. Finally, again.

"Are you ready?" Mike said as he huffed and puffed into the bedroom.

"Almost. Where'd you go earlier?"

"The bank. The post office." He leaned against the bathroom door.

"Why?"

"Business stuff."

"Couldn't it have waited till Monday? You left me alone to entertain the whole lot of them." Karen tried to insert a positive lilt in her voice, careful not to give Mike any inkling coffee wasn't the only thing that brewed while he was out.

"I've decided I'm not going into the office Monday. Taking the day off. To be with you." Mike snuggled behind her.

As she put the final touches on her makeup, she could feel his body pressing against hers, but her focus was on how she needed a full makeover to go with her new hair color. She'd have to figure a way to get to Nordstrom that day or the next. Before Monday.

"We should do something special."

"When?"

"Aren't you listening? Monday. Our guests will be leaving and—"

"I can't. I have to work." She wasn't ready to surrender an entire day to Mike when she'd already committed an extra-long lunch hour to Charlie.

Mike cupped her breast. "No, you don't. I'm the boss, remember."

Clang. Clang. Click. She cocked her head. "Must be Sarah and Charlie back from their walk."

Mike thinks he's the boss? We'll see about that. Suddenly, the idea of having sex with Mike while Charlie was downstairs made

her horny as hell. She wanted more of what she'd started during the
night, even if it wasn't with the partner she'd been dreaming about.
Karen turned her body toward Mike and unbuckled his belt.

"Can't it wait till tonight? We'll be late."

Karen slipped off her capris, rubbed her scar, and guided Mike's
hand into her black lace panties. When he'd taken care of her desire,
she knelt and tugged his pants to the floor.

"You know what we can do Monday?"

"Besides this. Can't think of a thing." Mike moaned.

"Let's purge Kassie's office."

"Don't even go there, missy." Mike pushed Karen away and
yanked up his jockey shorts and his slacks.

"Why the hell not? I could turn that room into something for
me."

"Like what? You don't have any hobbies that I'm aware of."

"Not yet, but I could if I had a place to call my own. I used to
knit."

"You need a whole room for needles and yarn?"

"As a start. Please, Mike, I don't ask for much, do I?" He didn't
notice her rub her right earlobe.

"That's true. But it's still Kassie's house. She doesn't have to move
her things out until after the divorce is final. In fact, if you're not
careful, she could ask you to remove your belongings or claim half
ownership of them."

"You're kidding. She'd never do that."

"You're right, *Kassie* never would." Mike walked out of the dressing area into the bedroom.

Karen got Mike's message loud and clear and swallowed the
"fuck you" she wanted to say to him. She vowed to bide her time.
Soon Kassie's office, the house, part of the business, and Mike would
all be hers. And Chris would come around in time too.

When she closed the vanity drawer with more oomph than necessary, Mike returned and wrapped his arms around her.

"I'll talk with her when she gets back from Italy if it'll make you happy."

Look who's the boss now? Karen gave him a quick peck on the cheek and a pat on his chest. "I'll let you know if I'm free Monday. Let's get going, our guests are waiting. *Quack. Quack.*"

Karen led Mike down the stairs. She would've skipped down them if she could. They found Charlie and Sarah standing in the family room with their luggage.

"What's this?" Mike lifted his palms in the air and glared at Karen as if she knew what was happening.

"Charlie called a cab. We're going to a hotel."

9

Memory Lane

Without a word, Charlie picked up his suitcase and headed for the front door. Mum as well, Sarah was close behind, rolling her bag across the carpet and into the tiled foyer as Mike stepped in and took it off her hands.

"What the hell? What's going on? Did something happen while I was out?" Mike moved aside and ushered Sarah ahead of him through the front door.

"Karen can fill you in," Sarah said as she thanked him for managing her luggage.

"What hotel are you going to?" Mike hustled to keep up with Sarah, who made fast tracks to the black sedan idling in the driveway. "Wherever it is, you don't need Uber to take you. I'll drive you."

Charlie finished loading their bags in the trunk. "Thanks, man, but we're all set here." He shook Mike's hand.

"Wait. Wait. What about our plans? The duck boats? The concert tonight?"

"I think we'll pass." Charlie slammed the trunk closed.

"But you'll come to the game tomorrow? We can pick you up. I'll call and let you know—"

Charlie looked to Sarah. She shook her head from side to side and let out an audible sigh.

"Sorry, bro. It was fun while it lasted." Charlie signaled Sarah to get in the back seat, while he climbed in the front.

"Wait right here. Don't leave yet," Mike said, pressing his hand downward toward the pavement.

Mike heard Karen come up behind him before he turned and passed her on his way into the house. "Stop, you guys. Really, no reason to leave," Karen said to no one in particular.

Charlie turned his back on Sarah and walked over to Karen. He said something in a voice only the two of them could hear. She tapped him on the arm, slipped her hands in her pockets, and kicked a small rock out of the driveway onto the lawn.

"What's this?" Charlie asked as Mike handed him two Red Sox hats, one navy and one pink.

"Planned to give these to you tomorrow. Before the game. Take them anyway. You can fight over who gets the pink one." Mike tried to make a joke, though he wasn't in a laughing mood.

Karen waved as the car backed out of the driveway and slipped her arm through Mike's as they headed up the slope to the house.

Mike unhooked Karen's arm as they entered the foyer and closed the front door. She jumped and glanced back at Mike as the bells on the doorknob clanged louder than usual.

"Did Charlie tell you where they're going?"

"Nope." Karen headed for the kitchen.

"Well then, darlin', why don't *you* tell me why they're going wherever they're going? What did you mean, no reason to leave?" Mike stayed close on her heels.

"I think it's Sarah. She said something about having a headache.

Bacon will do that, ya know. She probably didn't want to be a drag on the weekend."

"Ridiculous. But you're right. She could've skipped this afternoon, taken a nap, and then joined us this evening. You women—"

"How about those donuts?"

The rest of their Saturday went as originally planned, but with just the two of them. Mike called Bill to see if he and Nancy would like to use the Gaineses' duck boat and concert tickets. Bill reminded him they already had plans with their sons.

"What gives with Charlie and Sarah?" Bill said.

"Beats me. Karen said Sarah may have gotten a headache after eating the bacon."

"Really? If she had a headache, it came on from the time Nancy and I walked out of your house till the time you walked in. Sarah never mentioned a headache. And she didn't eat any bacon. You can take that to the bank."

Mike checked to see whether Karen was nearby before he said, "If not the bacon, what? You were here. What do you think happened?"

"Could've been my fault."

"How so?"

"I mentioned Chris. Conversation seemed to go downhill in a flash after that."

"Poor guy. He's not even here, and he's causing trouble."

"Sorry, pal, if I said something to mess up your weekend."

"You didn't."

If Chris was the topic of conversation that caused a falling-out, Mike was certain Karen was involved in some way, shape, or form. Bill may have fueled it, but Karen lit the match. He decided to let it pass for now. Let it all die down. He'd check with Charlie before they headed back to Chicago. Smooth things over if need be. Life was too short to allow something out of his control ruin his weekend. He'd just let things ride the tide and enjoy the day, such as it was, with Karen.

Which he did. Especially the duck boat tour. Without Charlie and Sarah, he and Karen each had their own row in the boat, allowing him to spread out and relax. He might even learn something new about Boston.

Later that day, he breathed a sigh of relief when Karen suggested they head over to the concert early. It was her first time at the Hatch Shell, so she wanted to get a good seat, or blanket space, as it were. Going early had its advantages. Parking wasn't the usual chore, and their slow walk to the esplanade on that hot, muggy July night was less taxing on his body, though his light blue shirt with the little green alligator on the pocket did little to hide the sweat circle forming under his arms. Luckily, he had a handkerchief to wipe off his brow.

The humidity seemed to have the same effect on the folks sitting so close to them it was impossible to distinguish one's body perfume from another's. Everyone was equally soaked in sweat, so no one noticed his embarrassment.

"Once the sun goes down, it'll be better," Mike heard more than one concertgoer forecast. He hoped so, feeling moisture gathering around his waist. Wearing khakis clearly wasn't a good idea, but his wearing-shorts-in-public years were far behind him.

That said, Karen wasn't bothered by the heat. Her sleeveless white knit knee-length dress looked as crisp as when they'd left the house.

"Your hair," Mike said. "The sun bouncing off it. Amazing, like the rocks of Sedona." He squeezed her waist and pulled her closer to him despite the heat. Was he mistaken, or did his compliment catch her off guard? She reached for his hand and put his finger in her mouth, his middle finger. *Nice. Down boy.*

"I thought there'd be more young people here."

"It's an oldies concert!" Mike shouted in her ear as the band's tune-up reverberated through the speakers. He kissed her cheek after he gave her a hand so they both could stand. So much for the blanket. "Baby boomers!" he bellowed, swayed, and cupped his ears.

After an hour of standing and singing to Aerosmith, Rush, and The Doors, Mike felt the urge to pee.

"You okay if I go search for a porta potty? Or do you want to come with. . . "

"I think I'm good till we get home. I hate those things."

"At least I don't have to sit." Mike said he'd be right back.

He would've been too, except for the line of guys who all had the same urge when there was a break in the music. He passed the time in line by estimating there were about twenty fellows ahead of him, and given the pace it was moving, he could be shifting from one leg to the other for at least ten minutes.

"Hey, Mike!" someone yelled as he felt a tug on his arm.

"Hi, Annie! What are you doing here?"

"Duh. Best concert of the season. Where else would I be?"

"In Italy with Kassie. You back already?"

"Uh, Mike, this is my friend Jack. Jack, this is Mike, Kassie's husband."

"Hi, Mike. Thought Kassie was—" Jack reached out his hand to Mike.

"Okay. Gotta run."

Well, that was weird. She didn't answer my question. Crap. Should've told her to look out for the package I sent to her house. Or maybe Kassie's back. Oh, well. My turn to hold my nose.

His zipper was down before he'd flipped the sign to occupied.

Hoping not to step on anyone's foot, Mike shouldered his way through the crowd toward the area where Karen was holding court. Along the way, he scanned the jumping crowd on the off chance he could pick Annie out of the throng. He gave up when the rowdy bunch started singing "Sweet Caroline," though it was worth a shot. Truth be known, as the band played the Eagles and Foreigner, Mike's eyes continued to wander as far as he could see. Even if he hadn't run into Annie, he knew he would've been thinking about Kassie. Mike sighed deeply when the band played "Don't Stop Believing" as their final number.

"Did you enjoy it?" Mike interrupted Karen's humming when they finally made their way through the departing crowd to the parking lot and the quiet confines of his car.

"I did. Lots. So many of the songs reminded me of Barry. Those were good times."

He raised his eyebrows as he pulled out of the garage. She rarely mentioned her late husband. Not the response he'd expect, especially after the nice day they'd had. He caught himself short from a tit-for-tat and saying many of the songs reminded him of Kassie. No need to hurt her. Fact was, he and Karen's music history was limited. They were only together for a short time in college, whereas he and Kassie had more than thirty years together. Made sense his and Karen's memories—music or otherwise—would be grounded in their first marriages. He'd have to do something to change that.

It didn't take long. On the way home from the concert as they drove past the Citgo sign, Mike brought up the idea of blowing off the Red Sox game the next day and instead taking a drive out to Provincetown. They could walk the dunes, another first for Karen.

"Great idea. I second that. You know how much I love baseball."

"We'll need to get up early if we want to buck the traffic on Route 6."

"Works for me."

"I feel guilty about not using the tickets. They're great seats. Behind home plate. You sure you don't want to go? You just might change your mind and like baseball."

"I think I'd like the Cape better. Isn't that where you found all the shells in that lamp?"

"You noticed the lamp. Yes, along the beaches out there." Mike felt a memorable twinge in his chest and gazed straight ahead as he drove the rest of the way home, deep in thought.

As he walked in the house, Mike called Bill. This time Bill accepted the offer of the baseball tickets for his whole family. Since he and Karen were heading out early in the morning, Mike offered to leave the tickets under the mat by the front door.

"What do I owe ya?"

"Oh, I don't know. Maybe you could think about treating Karen with a little TLC. She's not so bad when you get to know her."

"For you, Mike, anything."

With his legs tired from standing at the concert, Mike filled a glass with ice water from the refrigerator spigot and pulled up a chair at the kitchen table.

"Karen." Mike threw his voice loud enough to find its way into the family room, where he assumed she'd curled up on the couch and was at that very moment clicking through the TV searching for something to watch.

"Hey, lady, would you do me a favor?" he asked once she walked in the room. "Could you go into my office and get the Red Sox tickets? They're right there on top of my desk. And an envelope in the right-hand top drawer. Please."

"How come?"

"Bill's gonna take his family to the game tomorrow. I just told him I'd leave the tickets under the mat."

While Karen was off doing what she was told, Mike rummaged through the clutter in the small built-in desk in the kitchen. He found a notepad he kind of liked, one of Kassie's custom-printed Post-it notes notepads, and stacked the other five on the desktop.

"What are you going to do with those?"

"Give them to Kassie. They're hers. She loves them." He scribbled a note to Bill about having a good time and a beer on him, which he stuck on top of the tickets, then shoved everything in the white envelope. "We'll have to get you some of these," he said, adding the last pad to the pile.

"You look tired, Mike. Why don't you head upstairs? I'll close up down here."

"Good idea. I'm beat. Maybe too big a day for this old body. I'll just put—"

"Let me. . . ."

About twenty minutes later, Mike was drifting off to sleep when he heard the bells on the front door clang once and then again. *The tickets.*

He lifted one eye as Karen passed the bed, heading toward the bathroom.

"You put the tickets under the mat?" he mumbled just above a whisper.

"All taken care of."

10

Putting Off the Put-Off

Mike stepped out of the shower, stretched to the ceiling, and wrapped the jumbo towel around his middle. He felt as bright as the first light streaming through the sheer curtains in the dressing room.

"Rise and shine, honey child. It's a beautiful Sunday morning." Mike stood in the bedroom doorway, hands on his hips.

"You've got to be kidding." Karen pulled Mike's pillow over her face and rolled away.

"Nope. We've got miles to go before we sleep. Told you we'd be up at the crack of dawn if we want to beat the traffic to Provincetown. Route 6 can be a parking lot."

"It's just across the ocean, isn't it? How many miles could it possibly be?"

"It's Cape Cod Bay, not the Atlantic. It's about one hundred and fifty miles, give or take. You can nap in the car if you want, but I rather you didn't."

"Why not?"

"Driving to P-town is an experience you should have at least once."

"You make it sound as if it'll be my one and only."

"You never know. If you don't take in the whole thing, you might not want to do it again. After a year, it's time you spread your wings beyond Boston and Cambridge. Anyway, with your red hair, you'll fit right in out there."

"What's that supposed to mean?"

Mike packed a couple of tote bags with a change of clothes, water, bug spray, and his trail runner shoes to switch into when they got to the dunes. For the ride out there, he preferred his dark brown leather slip-on driving shoes that looked more like comfy moccasins, but they were too precious to get filled up with sand and dysfunctional for hiking to boot.

"You'll need two pairs of shoes. One for the car, one for the dunes."

"Really, Mike? You know I don't have all my things here yet. Not sure I have anything that'd work for the dunes. How about flip-flops?"

"No can do. Check the tall gray cabinet in the garage. Kassie probably hasn't thought to empty that yet. I bet you'll find something in there that would work. You're both the same size, I'd guess." He chuckled to himself at the thought of how similar the two women in his life really were, except of course now one of them had red hair. Would Kassie go red once she saw Karen? Probably not. Kassie wasn't a fan of change, and she'd already had plenty of that to deal with over the last year.

Leaving Karen to get ready on her own, Mike fired up the Keurig and made them each a tumbler of coffee for the road. The door to the garage rattled, confirming Karen had taken his advice. He gave her a few minutes to explore Kassie's shoe selection without any interference from him.

"How's it going?" Mike opened the back of the SUV.

"I think I found something that'll work." Karen lifted a pair of blue, green, and taupe Nikes out of a box and waved them above her head.

"Are they new?"

"Look to be."

"You can't take those. They probably cost a hundred fifty bucks."

"Why not? If the shoe fits. I'll consider it a wedding gift. She obviously doesn't miss them. She can well afford a new pair."

"What's in the bag?" A large black plastic trash bag sat open on the floor next to Karen.

"Oh, this?" Karen laced the orange ties, tried to kick it, and grunted as she shoved it in the corner next to the cabinet. "Did her a favor and packed up her boots and things. I'll let her know they're here. She can pick them up when she gets her office stuff."

"Whatever. You ready?"

"I need to pee first," Karen said.

"Make it fast. Time's a wasting. Grab my phone while you're in there. It's on the kitchen counter."

Sitting in the car waiting for Karen, Mike stared at the cabinet and the black trash bag. Is this what his marriage to Kassie amounted to? He stepped out of the car and opened the cabinet. *She emptied the whole fucking thing.*

He turned as the clunk-clunk of Karen's black roller bag announced her arrival in the garage. Along with the designer purse she'd slung across her body, the glittery, strappy sandals that showed off her French pedicure from Friday, and her sunglasses propped on her head, Karen looked more as if she was heading for a stroll down Rodeo Drive than a hike in the sand.

"I'm gonna make us coffee." She turned on her heel, heading back once again for the house.

"Coffee's in the car. Already got it." Mike tapped the hood of the car.

"Of course you do." Karen patted his chest as he held the car door for her.

Karen tilted her head against the window, closed her eyes, and drifted off to la-la land before they reached the highway. So much for her taking in the sights of the Cape. With her hair and dark sunglasses, she reminded Mike of a movie star. Maybe Jane Fonda. Or maybe he was beginning to like her new look, or just getting used to it the same way he was growing accustomed to having her next to him in the passenger's seat.

Mike's eyes wandered away from the road, looking around the front for his iPhone. He figured he could take advantage of the quiet time to listen to a jazz appreciation course he'd downloaded. *Aw, shit. It must be in her bag.* Conceding his planning skills weren't as honed as Kassie's, he turned on his favorite jazz station, keeping the volume low. It was the least he could do. If Karen could sleep on this stunning day, she must need it.

Traffic getting onto Route 6 wasn't as heavy as Mike predicted. *Of course.* Saturday was more the changeover day when weekly renters arrived and departed. The madness would occur later that day when weekenders extended their mini-vacations as long as humanly possible and then flooded the roads in a dash to get home for work on Monday. Why hadn't he thought of that before he suggested this adventure? Kassie would've known better. He could've avoided the hassle altogether had they gone to the ballgame. Too late. The tickets would be in Bill's hands by now.

About two-thirds of the way to Provincetown, Karen shifted enough in her seat for Mike to tap her arm and ask if she was hungry.

"Starved. Are we there yet?"

Mike laughed. "You sound like a kid."

"That may be. If you don't get me some food quick, I may get carsick. Damn it. This coffee's cold."

He pulled off the highway in Dennis, not needing any further motivation. The last time he thought about possibly puking in a car was the Good Friday Kassie had rushed him to Boston Clinic and his life turned upside down.

The line at the diner was out the door and wound around the side of the red building with white shutters. Full breakfast on Sunday mornings on the Cape was almost as popular as three-scoop ice cream cones in the evenings. The best thing, though, was Mike had been there before.

"The line moves fast. You'll see."

"Really? Wait here," Karen said. She brushed ahead of families of men, women, children, babies, and elderly with their walkers and pushed her way into the restaurant.

Oh, no. What's she up to now?

The people in front of him turned and glared. He lifted his shoulders and raised his eyes to the cloudless blue sky, except no one could see his embarrassment behind his sunglasses. Glares continued, accompanied by murmurs: "Who does she think she is?" and "Maybe she's a movie star. Did you get a close look?"

"There you are."

Karen grabbed Mike's hand and dragged him to the front door.

"What the hell?"

"Just shut up and come with me."

Once inside, Mike and Karen were hustled to a table for two in what appeared to be a private room near the kitchen in the rear of the building. Probably belonged to the owners or a staff break room. As soon as Karen ordered two No. 2 Specials and hot coffee from a waiter who was not more than sixteen years old, she left Mike at the table, scratching his head.

Karen returned as their meal arrived.

"Okay, Einstein, spill it. How'd you manage this?" Mike said.

"It's the hair, big guy." She tossed it. "I told the gal taking names I landed late from LA and had to get to Provincetown by ten for a film I was shooting. If I didn't eat soon, I'd faint, and then what would Martin Scorsese do?"

"She bought that crap?"

"Yup. So keep your mouth shut except to chew."

Mike stared at his eggs and poked at the bacon, his appetite nowhere to be found.

"Oh, and I gave the first two families in line twenty dollars each. Good idea, eh?"

"You didn't." Mike lowered his coffee cup.

"Sure. I made their day. They'll have a story to tell. They'll rack their brains all day trying to figure out who the pushy, yet sexy, red-head was."

Karen was right when she said she was starved. She finished her meal; stole his bacon, though he didn't plan on eating it; and helped herself to his whole grain toast. Mike suffered in silence through his eggs and cantaloupe, knowing it could be five hours until his next meal.

Though her fraud may have made the day exciting for some of the restaurant's patrons, she was wrong about one thing. She hadn't made his day. Perhaps he could give her some slack about filling the trash bag with Kassie's shoes since they'd had that conversation about clearing out Kassie's office. But her public display of entitlement was a side of her he hadn't seen, or noticed, before. He'd have to talk with her about it, but the diner was neither the place nor time to cause a scene. He couldn't risk the sprawling headline he imagined across the front page of the *Mid-Cape Herald*: "Man Dresses Down Actress, Wears Egg on Face." He had Ricci and Son to protect.

There would be the dunes.

11

Climb Every Mountain

Karen couldn't pinpoint her newfound energy. Was it the protein breakfast, the way she made her way to the front of the line at the diner, or the chummy text from Charlie she'd seen when she slipped off to the bathroom at the restaurant? Probably all of the above, except Charlie's text was the cherry on top.

Whatever the reason, Karen's eyes were wide open during the remaining forty-mile drive to Provincetown. Yet for the life of her, she didn't know why Mike characterized it as a not-to-be-missed experience. *Looks like the usual tourist trap to me.*

"Was it always like this?" Karen turned her attention to Mike.

"What do you mean?"

"Mini-golf. Ice cream. Junky craft stores. Lobster shacks. Bumper-to-bumper traffic?"

"Always?"

"Yeah, like forever, since you began coming here?" Karen deliberately excluded Kassie in her question, as in "since you and Kassie began coming here." It was bad enough she'd be walking in her shoes most of the rest of the day.

"Seems like more traffic now. But it could be an illusion. The roads are filled with SUVs and vans, all jockeying for space once taken up by sedans and station wagons. So it's hard to tell."

"Then why . . ."

"You'll see."

And that was the extent of Karen and Mike's conversation for the rest of the trip. Oh, she tried to keep the chitchat flowing, but all she got back in return was either a nod, a grunt, or a "You'll see."

After ten miles of his apparent disinterest in her or in what she was saying, she gave up and simply stared out the window, wondering what she was doing there in the first place when they were supposed to be spending the day with Sarah . . . and Charlie. If only Sarah was still the kind sorority sister who'd come to Karen's rescue when she'd gotten pregnant in college, rather than the rich bitch she'd morphed into, she'd be rubbing knees with Charlie at Fenway instead of riding shotgun next to Mike, going who knows where.

"Here we are."

"Where? Where's the parking lot?"

"There isn't any. Lucky we're here early enough to get a space along the road."

Unlike Mike, who seemed to jump with glee getting out of the car, as if he were seven years old again, Karen took her time, in no rush to explore the unknown.

By the time she joined him on the side of the car away from the road, he'd slipped off his khakis and slipped on a pair of asphalt-gray cargo shorts that were frayed along the pockets.

"Nice knees." She patted his backside.

"Let's get going. Don't be a slowpoke. Change your shoes." He already had his sneakers on, bending down to lace them up. She offered her hand to help him stand.

She unzipped her roller bag, retrieving her—or rather Kassie's—shoes. A thought whipped through her mind. *What if she'd accidentally left them behind? Would Mike have called off this wild adventure?* Too late now to test that theory.

"Come on, before it gets too hot." Mike slapped on a blue Red Sox hat, handing a white one to her. "You'll need this. And put this on." He flipped a tube of sunscreen at her. It burped when she tried to squeeze some on her arms.

"Great. It's empty." Karen threw it back at him.

Of course, he'd come prepared. Rifling through the totes he'd packed, he put a new tube on the hood of the car and proceeded to load two black day bags with the water bottles, bug spray, and paper towels.

"My phone. Grab my phone, Karen, so we can take pictures."

Karen claimed one of the day bags and tossed her phone into it. "Can we lock my purse in the back?"

She didn't notice him mouth the words, "Anything else, my lady?" as he locked her purse in the secret compartment in the rear of the car.

"Welcome to Cape Cod National Seashore," Mike read the sign aloud, as if Karen couldn't read.

"Out here, sweets, the area's also known as the Province Lands." He was suddenly in a babbling mood. That is until they reached the first sand hill. He stood with his hands on his hips, reminding her of a Jack Nicholson movie where he was told he couldn't have sex until he climbed a flight of stairs. Eventually, Jack conquered the challenge. She assumed Mike would as well.

He warned her the trek up the hill was a doozy, but she thought he was just pulling her leg.

She was wrong. Though her calves screamed, "You've got to be frigging kidding me," Karen led the way up the giant incline, dragging Mike behind her. At the crest of the hill, they stood bent over, arms linked, breathing heavier than they ever did after sex. But, to be honest, a roll in the hay was the last thing on Karen's mind.

"Is this what it's like the rest of the way? 'Cause if it is, maybe we should turn around now."

"Don't give up, Karen. This was the worst. Can't say it's all downhill from here, but no pain, no gain."

"Glad to hear it. I think."

Karen retrieved her water bottle and took a swig.

"Pace yourself."

Indeed, the pacing began. As Mike took the lead along unmarked trails and the hollows of the dunes, Karen followed in his footsteps and those of previous hikers who were most definitely more experienced than she. The sandy grit seeping into her shoes reminded her she'd need a pedicure even though she'd gotten one just two days before.

Every few minutes, they'd stop, allowing Mike to tutor her on the flora and fauna of the dunes, as well as its history. She welcomed each break and, to her surprise, grew to enjoy the time in the sun and with Mike.

"I'm not in Elephant Butte anymore." Karen waved her arm across the breathtaking vista.

"No, you're not. Would you like to stay here tonight?" Mike pointed to one of the weathered shacks they were nearing.

"You're kidding."

"I am. But writers and artists do live here between April and November. There's about twenty dune shacks with no electricity, running water, or toilets."

"Better them than me."

Mike continued, "Imagine living here a century ago. You

could've helped mariners navigate their ships through the Cape's shifting sands."

"Really? That long ago?"

"Yup. There were a lot of shipwrecks."

"Did they find them all?"

"Probably not. Did you know the Mayflower . . . you are familiar with the Mayflower, aren't you?"

She gave him a don't-be-an-asshole punch in the shoulder. "What about it?"

"Provincetown Harbor, which was called Cape Cod Harbor back then, was their first stop in November 1620."

"I thought they settled in Plymouth."

"Eventually. Their original destination was the mouth of the Hudson River, but storms and tides blew them off course. If you're interested in the story, there's a fabulous book by Nathaniel Philbrick aptly named *Mayflower*."

"Maybe I'll read it sometime."

"Check out the bookshelves in Kassie's office. It's probably there. You took her shoes. She probably wouldn't mind if you borrow a book."

Karen turned her attention to the sprawling beach they were approaching and smiled. *I've got the men in her life too.*

Closing her eyes, she took three deep breaths through her nose, pulling into her lungs a mix of salty sea air and sweet wildflowers. The late morning sun bore down on her SPF 30 skin. Trickles of sweat formed beneath her hat and streamed near the outer corner of her right eye.

"What the hell?" She dropped to the sand.

"What happened?" Mike turned and rushed to her.

"My eye's burning. I forgot I had sunscreen on my hand."

Mike knelt beside her, whipped out a paper towel, poured water on it, and dabbed around her eye.

"Better, sparky?" He removed her hat, kissed her forehead, and lifted her chin to kiss her lips.

"Um. While you're down here, you know, you never officially asked me to marry you."

12

Magic Moments

Mike hoisted Karen to her feet, rubbed his chest, and led her down a sandy path to the uninhabited beach. "Did you see that? Look. I think I see some seals bouncing around out there. Let's take some pictures."

Hoping his diversion wasn't too obvious, he reckoned Karen had a point. He'd never officially proposed to her.

When neither Kassie nor Chris were a donor match, Karen shocked him when she offered to be tested. Once the test results confirmed she was a match, chaos ensued. Before he knew it, they shared more than a hospital room. While recovering, they joked that even if they weren't legally married, their kidneys were physically joined for his eternity.

"Don't you think a-kidney-for-a-kidney is the ultimate sacrifice deserving a ring around my finger?" Karen had posed that question to the doctors, nurses, candy stripers, phlebotomists—anyone who had ears. He guessed she kept asking because no one answered.

And it didn't stop once they were released from the hospital. Talk of marriage seeped into their daily intercourse, in and out of the bedroom. Mike's gratitude toward Karen left him no choice. He'd gone along for the ride, but without the ultimate commitment—a proposal and a ring.

Now, as the *i*'s were dotted and *t*'s crossed on his divorce settlement with Kassie, his mortality, not marital status, occupied his mind more often than he figured mindfulness experts would agree was healthy. Coming to grips with his almost, but not quite, near-death experience and the demise of his super-long marriage competed for his precious few remaining brain cells. When he added the prospect of getting married again at his age to the equation, he began to have doubts. Who wouldn't?

"Later, maybe?" Karen interrupted his quiet self-flagellation.

"Why wait? Hand me my phone."

Karen dug into her backpack. "I meant, are you ever going to ask me to marry you, silly."

"Oh, right. Sure. When you least expect it, my dear." He rubbed her back as they approached the water lapping onto the shore.

Mike picked up a pebble and skipped it across the water. Karen stood back fiddling with the phone, rotating it in different directions, holding it close to her body, probably in search of shade.

"Looks like there's no cell service out here."

"No, but we can take pictures." Mike reached for the phone. "Where's mine?"

"Guess I left it in the car, in my purse."

Pissed, but unwilling to be a prick about it, he coaxed Karen to stroll along the coastline with him, stopping to take panoramas of the barren beach, videos of a colony of seagulls cawing and dive-bombing for fish, and selfies of the two of them with the bluest of blue seas and whitest of sails in the background.

Karen stretched out on the sand, offering Mike a come-hither look. He lowered himself above her, push-up style. Her fingers found their way up the leg of his cargo shorts.

"Later . . ." He leaned down, kissed her breast, and sat beside her. "Tell me, what was that all about this morning?" He picked up a shell and tossed it toward the water.

"When?"

"At the diner. I've never seen you that pushy before."

"You mean, when I got us a table so we didn't have to wait in line for an hour?"

"A bit rude, don't you think?"

"We wouldn't be here right now if I hadn't done that." She sat up and brushed sand off the back of her arms, some of which landed in his lap. "And, if you recall, I politely thanked people for letting us get to the head of the line."

"Did you think it may have embarrassed me?"

"It never embarrassed Barry."

"So this was a repeat performance. Something you're skilled at."

"Oh, come on. It was fun."

"Ya think?"

"Growing up, my mother encouraged me to break a rule every day—do something out of the ordinary, unexpected."

"Except when it came to marrying an Italian Catholic." He chuckled as he tossed another shell, and his annoyance, toward the sea.

"You got me there." She laughed so loud she scared the seagulls.

They looked away from each other, lost in their own private worlds. He wondered if she were thinking, as he was, about what their lives would have been like had they broken the rule, defied her parents, and gotten married when she was pregnant with Chris.

"What other extraordinary things did you do when you were married to Barry?"

"You really want me to show you?" She took his hand and placed it low on her lap.

That wasn't what he meant, but the stirring in his shorts confirmed an intense desire to unzip her shorts in front of God and the seagulls. Instead he rubbed her inner thigh. "Now that's an infraction that would cost us more than what you paid those families at the diner this morning."

"You're no fun." She pushed him away.

"Really?" He flipped over a smooth, weathered pink rock he'd been massaging as they'd sat there, and rolled to one knee as best he could.

"Sweetheart, to me you're my beacon of light. The flame was lost for a while, but it's burning brightly now. I never want it extinguished again. Will you marry me?"

He lifted Karen to her knees and pulled her so close to him he could smell a mixture of vanilla and sea spray.

"I don't think it's appropriate for me to give you a diamond until after my divorce. But here, take this rock instead."

"What the . . ." She shoved him, knocking him on his ass. "You bastard. Is this your idea of a joke? You're making fun of me?" She marched away in a sandy huff.

"No, Karen. I'm serious." He caught up with her, grabbed her arm, and spun her around. "I'm doing something unexpected. Isn't that what you want?"

"How can I believe you?"

He wiped a tear that followed the same path her sweat had moments before.

"Look. Here." He twisted off his wedding band and cupped it in his hand as if he was going to hurl it into the ocean.

"Don't," she gasped.

He held the ring close to her face. "As long as I live, I'll never wear this ring again." He tucked it into a pocket of his shorts and zipped it. "That's the best I can do." He put his hands in his pockets and bowed his head.

"YES," she wrote in the wet sand as a lonesome wave crashed on the beach and ebbed toward the sea, whisking away her promise.

If they were teenagers again, they'd have collapsed right there on the beach and screwed their brains out—damning the rules. Instead they giggled, held hands, and hotfooted their way back to his SUV as fast as their sexagenarian calves could maneuver the broiling afternoon sand and seemingly unending rolling hills.

Once at the car, sharing not a word, only a knowing glance, they kicked off their crunchy shoes, banged them against the tires, and brushed off their feet. Mike placed the sunshades against the windshield and side windows and, with the rear window shade already lowered, created a den of iniquity.

Karen climbed into the back seat and wrestled off her shorts and shirt that were soaked with anticipation. He was glad she'd left her bra and panties for him to remove. Which he did, as she tugged off his shorts.

All was said and done in ninety-five seconds. They might as well have been nineteen again.

They straightened themselves up, changing into the clean clothes they'd brought with them. As Mike pulled out of their parking space, a large gray SUV flew by bearing a sign, *Sam's Dune Tours.*

"Tours? You mean we could've taken a tour?"

"Um. Sure. But then you wouldn't have that special pink rock. You still have it?"

Mike caught Karen searching each pocket. "Tell me you didn't lose . . ."

She unbuckled her seat belt and reached into the back seat. "Thank goodness. Here it is."

She held the rock up to the sunlight shining through her window. "Do you think a necklace can be made with this?"

"I know just the place."

Mike wanted to show Karen there was more to Provincetown than sand, sun, dunes, and sex. Well, at least the first three. There could never be too much sex in P-town, where *fuck*—whatever its part of speech—was not an unspeakable four-letter word. Good thing. Given their recent escapade and afterglow, they'd fit in nicely among the uninhibited denizens of Commercial Street.

Mike opened the car door for Karen and escorted her to the crowded sidewalk filled with vacationers, day-trippers, and the cadre of folks who called this celebrated LGBTQ community home.

"I bet you've never seen anything like this in New Mexico?"

He could tell she was baffled as to where to set her sights first: on the bare-chested, tattooed man passing her, wearing a neon-orange G-string and chaps; on the extremely tall woman across the street with long straight white hair, parading confidently in an extremely short fire-engine-red negligee and five-inch yellow patent leather platform shoes; or on the two bearded men strolling down the middle of the street, arms snaked together, wearing pink and green matching tutus with sparkling tiaras on their bald heads?

Rescuing Karen from culture shock, Mike clutched her hand and dragged her, dropped jaw and all, into Guy's and Dolly's Galleria of Jewels. The wood-carved sign over the door read, "Handmade jewelry for handy-guys and handy-dolls. You know who you are."

Truth be known, after half a day on the sun-drenched dunes and their steamy after party, the blast of icy air conditioning on Mike's sun-tinged skin provided much welcome relief.

"A restroom. Please, Mike." Karen tugged at him while rubbing the goosebumps on her arms.

"No problem. Hey, Guy, how are ya?" Mike shook Guy's hand. "Before we look around, could we impose?" Mike tilted his head toward the rear of the room. "Gotta go."

There was only one bathroom, so Mike moseyed around the showroom admiring the handcrafted silver, bronze, and white-gold jewelry while Karen did her thing. It'd been a couple of years since he'd been in the shop. Not much had changed, except for Guy, who'd replaced the robin's-egg-blue streaks in his chin-length chestnut hair with alternate strands of lime green and Barbie pink.

Mike introduced Karen as his lifesaver and blamed his surgery for the reason he hadn't been in the store for a while. He chose not to complicate their reunion by getting into the pending divorce or anything at all about Chris.

"Looking for something special today?"

"We found something special. I'm hoping you could make it into a necklace for Karen." Mike gave her a friendly tap on her back.

Guy oohed and aahed over the unusual smooth pale pink rock and speculated as to how it got its lovely, unique color. "Perhaps from the blood of a whale or from a slain pirate. Wouldn't that be a luscious story, especially a gay pirate?"

Karen didn't hide her grimace at Guy's conjectures, but she assured the two of them that she loved the rock as long as the blood wasn't hers.

Mike and Karen turned from the glass case as a fellow dressed identical to Guy in white linen pants, scuba blue Birkenstocks, and a black collared polo shirt approached from the rear of the store. The man with "Dolly" embroidered in rainbow colors on his shirt greeted them with "Did I hear there's a gay pirate here to rob us blind? Arrr!"

"Hey, man, how are ya?" Mike slapped Dolly on his back. "It's been way too long. A pirate perhaps, but not gay, I'm afraid."

"Don't ever give up the ship, mate. It's never too late, Mikey, to come out into the sunlight. It took Guy here decades." Dolly bearhugged Guy. The three men laughed. Karen stared at the basket weave seagrass rug, shifting from one foot to another.

It took her less time to choose a medium-weight eighteen-inch

Argentinean silver snake chain and a simple circular setting to house the pink rock than it did for her to order breakfast that morning.

As Mike and Guy settled the bill, Dolly slid around the counter and stood next to Karen, who had her eyes fixed on diamond rings displayed on black velvet. "You've got excellent taste."

"How's that?"

"In jewelry, men . . ." Dolly winked toward Mike. "And hair." Dolly flipped Karen's hair in one swift expert motion. "Love the color. Would you email me the formula? I'm ready for a change. Amethyst is so last year, don't you think?"

Mike interrupted the chitchat. "Hey, Karen, should Guy ship the necklace, or would you like to come back in two weeks?"

"Oh, let's come back." Karen perked up, still hovering near the display of diamond rings. "He proposed to me today," she stage-whispered to Dolly.

"Congratulations, old man." Guy seemed to catch on to Mike's tiny head shake cluing him not to go down that path much further. "Come see me when you're ready to seal the deal, and I'll fix you and this lovely lassie right up."

After fist pumps and air kisses all around, Mike shooed Karen out the door as the chimes announced their exit.

"Did he call me Kassie?"

"He didn't. You hungry?"

"Starving. But I think he said Kassie."

"You've got sand in your ears. The word was *lassie*, Miss Sassy. You ready to take in one more P-town tradition?"

A mere three-minute stroll up the street from Guy's and Dolly's sanctuary on Commercial Street, Larry's Lobster Landing had a line out the door and around the corner to rival all lines. In their quest to find the end, Mike and Karen passed a potpourri of patrons who seemed to care less how long their wait would be. There were the obvious residents sprinkled among a slew of families whose kids sat on the curb feasting on ice cream cones and, for whatever reason, thought it would be super fun to put cotton candy in each other's hair.

Karen offered the woman in front of them a pack of hand-wipes from her purse and asked how long the wait was.

"That was nice," Mike whispered in Karen's ear. "Look what we missed. At least forty-year-old children are better behaved."

"Ninety-minute wait. What do we do now? Should we go someplace else?"

Mike got out his wallet and handed Karen three twenties. "Here, mama. Go work your magic."

13

Hello Dolly

Never once had Mike called her that. "Mama." Finally, someone had recognized her for what she was. Thank God for small favors.

Karen thanked herself for an even bigger one. Feeling emboldened, she'd created her own path around and through the quirky queue. "Excuse me. Pardon me." *Get outta my damn way.* Despite the where-does-she-think-she's-going murmurs, she arrived unscathed inside the restaurant's front door, where an attendant in a black miniskirt and lobster-red T-shirt keyed names into an iPad.

In reverse this time, she gave a barely believable song-and-dance about being on a short leash to catch a flight back to LA—"You know, Hollywood's my home"—But she really, really must eat at this esteemed and fabled establishment that Matt Damon had insisted she and her bodyguard give a whirl. She crossed her fingers hoping no one, like the owner or a bartender who'd worked there for twenty years, would pipe up and call her bluff. It didn't occur to her anyone would doubt her preeminence.

With total gratitude—"I'll be sure to give Matt your regards"—she slipped the red-shirted lady and the woman first in line each a twenty and stuffed the third in her pocket.

Karen leaned out the door and gave Mike a wave, a thumbs-up. "Remember, you're my bodyguard, so act like one." She backhanded his chest.

This time they weren't relegated to a back room. Instead they were seated at a square table large enough for four but set up for two, overlooking Provincetown Harbor, a.k.a. Cape Cod Harbor from days of yore. *See, I listen.*

"Why is it that restaurants that claim to be traditions are all the same? Crowded, noisy, with un-fucking-believable menus."

"Watch your language, lady. Children . . ."

"You're kidding. You think anyone can hear me?"

"I can. As your bodyguard, *cough cough,* I'm protecting you. And me. Don't want to be tossed after spending sixty bucks just to get in here. You did pay for this table, right?"

"Yup. Look at this. There must be thirty ways to cook lobster. Broiled, steamed, grilled. With or without stuffing. Spicy lobster pasta. Bland lobster pasta."

Karen caught Mike's head tilt.

"Joke. It's a joke, Mike. But wait, there really is more. Block Island lobster salad. Where the hell is Block Island? And lobster stew. Fra diabolo. Pickled. Soup. Rolls. Tails. With shrimp, steak, scallops. Whatever happened to just plain boiled lobster with butter?"

"First of all, you sound like Forrest Gump discovering shrimp."

"Or Paul Simon. Do you think there are really fifty ways to leave a lover?"

"I don't know. Never thought about it."

The waiter took their order. Two boiled lobsters with butter, baked potato, broccoli. A bottle of wine and two bibs.

"Now, about Block Island," Mike lectured. She sipped her wine.

"It's a quaint resort island off Rhode Island, though you can't drive there like Rhode Island or Long Island."

Karen freaked, afraid Mike was about to launch into the history of Block Island and recommend she read a book Kassie most assuredly had tucked neatly into her super-organized library at the house.

Which reminded her. "Why did that guy call me Kassie?"

"You mean Guy. Not *that guy*."

"Whatever. Why did he—"

"He really didn't. He referred to you as *lassie*. Though he may have been thinking about Kassie."

Oh great. Here we go. She squeezed the handle of the lobster cracker, which was really a nutcracker. Lobster cracker, nutcracker. Provincetown Harbor, Cape Cod Harbor. Rhode Island that's not really an island. *Give me a break.*

"Guy worked for me years ago, about five years after I opened the business. First as an intern from Emerson, then full time. Graphic design."

She fought with a small clear cellophane bag of oyster crackers, the kind often served with soup—*why didn't I order chowder?*—finally using her teeth as scissors. Half of the half-smashed salty round devils spilled down her bib and onto the red paper placemat. As she brushed the crumbs to the floor, Mike handed her another pack he'd opened for her.

"You do take good care of me."

"What are bodyguards for?"

"Protecting me from your past with Kassie, perhaps?"

"Shouldn't it be the other way around? You were the other woman, not her."

"Except that she fucked our son."

"Not after she found out who he was."

Unwilling to relive the year before, but curious about the Kassie-Guy connection, Karen recalibrated.

"So, how long did Guy work for you?"

"About six years. He lived with his family mostly, saving most of his paycheck. The rest is history."

Karen turned both hands toward the ceiling and shook her head. "Where does Kassie come into this story?"

"She was my wife. She knew the staff well. And she's a successful marketer in her own right."

"Yeah, so."

"Guy took his savings and investments—apparently he had a knack for stocks and bonds—and moved here to Provincetown. He fell in love with Donald, who also had a sizable nest egg, and they opened the jewelry store."

"Donald? Who the hell is Donald?"

"Dolly. Donald is Dolly. That's where Kassie comes in."

Mike stared, glassy-eyed, past Karen's shoulder as he told her the rest of the story. Seems Guy asked Kassie to help name and brand the new business. She toyed with the name Guys and Dolls, as Guy sketched potential logos. One night at dinner at Guy and Donald's apartment over several bottles of wine, Kassie played with making the name possessive. It wasn't a far stretch for them to move from Guys and Dolls to Guy's and Dolly's.

"That still doesn't explain—"

"Sure it does. Simple. That night, Donald decided to officially change his name, and the rest, as I said, is history. They've made a name, or names, for themselves here. So to them, Kassie is a god-*dess*."

To you too, it seems. The long, narrow, sharp stainless-steel lobster fork Karen used to etch deep Ks on the placemat slipped out of her hand and became airborne, whirling tine over handle and landing on a table behind her in a bowl of New England clam chowder.

"You okay?" Mike asked the fellow seated behind Karen.

Ignoring Mike, she reached in her pocket and handed the guy with milk and potatoes in his lap the twenty she'd thought would be hers to spend. The waiter brought her another lobster fork, and they enjoyed their meal without any further drama.

There was still a line outside Larry's when they walked out, though not as long. Up-tempo music, live and recorded, competed with the laughter of boys and girls sitting on the sidewalk with chocolate ice cream dripping down their faces.

"What's next on the agenda?" Karen asked only to be polite. She was ready to bail and head home and thrilled Mike had the same idea.

As they neared the car, Mike handed her the keys. "Mind driving? I'm bushed."

"I'm not sure I can find the way back. I slept—"

Not taking no for an answer, Mike set up the GPS on the dashboard. "Just follow the yellow brick road."

"Before you nod off, answer me one thing, Mike. You're the least liberal person I know. How is it you enjoyed yourself so much today?"

"Easy. First, I'm more liberal than you think. And Provincetown is Happy-town. What's not to enjoy?"

They'd barely passed pale lilac, mustard-yellow, and pilgrim-blue cape and colonial homes and entered the town of Truro before Mike had reclined his seat, drifting off to oblivion. His jaw dropped an inch, and he sucked air through his mouth, snorting it out his nose. Small price to pay for peace without quiet.

Confident Mike would sleep until she pulled into his driveway, she scanned the radio, bypassing news stations and talk radio. Mike had filled her brain with enough reality for one day. She was in the mood to have oldies keep her company. Stumbling upon a voice announcing, "an hour of eighties love songs," Karen's shoulders softened, allowing her to relive what she'd achieved over the last twelve or so hours.

For one, Mike had formally asked her to marry him. *About time.* And she discovered a way to keep chipping away at Kassie's fan club.

Without a doubt, she'd return to Provincetown to pick out a ring that would make Guy and Dolly crown her the true god-*dess*.

Despite sitting in traffic getting off the Cape, Sunday had been a good day. Monday was only hours away and Charlie only miles.

Karen and Charlie's relationship spanned four decades. A spotty, inconsistent four decades to be sure, but four decades nonetheless.

Consider the beginning—now fondly referred to as the Key Hookup. Then the barren middle—where the adoption agreement forced them to keep their mouths shut about who had adopted Karen and Mike's baby. And then the here and now.

They'd arrived at the here and now just over a year ago, when Karen invited Sarah and Charlie to her hotel room in Chicago to meet Kassie O'Callaghan, a.k.a. Kassandra Ricci, who was searching for Mike's son in hopes his DNA would match Mike's, and he'd be willing to give him one of his kidneys.

In an unlikely scenario, Karen became the conduit to the father-son reunion, which in turn revealed—and promptly destroyed, much to Karen's delight—a tawdry cougar-type affair between Mike's long-lost son, a.k.a. Christopher Gaines, and Kassie. When tests determined Chris was an unsuitable kidney donor match, Karen saw an opportunity to play the hero. Gain some atta-girls, some notoriety. Could she be a match? The selfless offer alone would curry favor with Mike for a lifetime. She'd owe him nothing further in return for his kindness and generosity after Barry had died. Her debts would be paid once and for all.

Anyway, what were the chances she'd be a match? Fifty-fifty? Either she was or she wasn't. She liked the odds until they were no longer in her favor.

But once the news was out, and family and friends were thrilled and relieved Mike would be saved, there was no way she could renege on her offer. And she relished the love and attention she was getting and the prospect of a new life away from Elephant Butte.

So she rented a small apartment in the same building as her newfound son and became quickly consumed in all things Michael Ricci—saving his life, living his lifestyle, and hanging around the office. He promised her if she chose to stay in Boston, he'd give her a job at Ricci and Son. Cool. A family business. *Just what I always wanted.*

Not.

Security for a lifetime. That's what she wanted. To Karen, security was spelled *Michael Ricci.* Her parents had stolen him from her when they forced the adoption after she got pregnant. Now the only thing standing in her way was Kassie.

And that's where Charlie, the near family lawyer, came in. As luck would have it, before Karen signed her kidney away, Charlie called offering his legal services pro bono. He'd review any paperwork the medical authorities put in front of her just to be sure her interests, not just Mike's, were served.

Wonderful idea. Karen had no professional connections in the Boston area, so she accepted Charlie's offer. Then she bounced a burning question off him. If Mike died during the transplant, who would get his assets? She feared a scenario where she'd be kidney-less and penniless all in one day. Shivers ran down her shoulders, through the backs of her legs, and to her toes just thinking about that horror.

That was a chance she'd have to take, Charlie advised, but he assured her that was highly unlikely. And he was right. They both survived the transplant, and life went on.

A week after the surgery, Charlie called Karen while she was at her apartment recovering.

"See, I told you," he'd said.

"Okay, okay. But what happens now? To his assets if something happens to Mike . . . God forbid."

"You're getting married, right? After the divorce—"

"He hasn't formally committed, but he will."

Charlie explained that Mike held all the cards—in his will, in his estate, in the business succession plan. More than likely, Kassie would get a chunk, Chris a slice. After all, Mike had made Chris a junior partner, and as his wife, Kassie would get the lion's share of his retirement assets. It was the law.

"If I were you, if you love him, I'd marry the guy soon," Charlie advised.

"What happens then?"

"Some assets would shift easily to you as his wife, while others, like the business and the house, he'd have to purposefully change. Which I'd imagine he would. When the time comes, I'll guide you through all the legal mumbo jumbo."

"Free of charge?"

"No charge."

"What's in it for you, Charlie?"

"Christopher. I'll want to make sure he's taken care of. And you, of course."

"You'd do that for me?"

"There's a lot I'd like to do for you, and to you. . . ."

And so, Karen took Charlie up on that offer too, admitting to herself she cared about Mike but wasn't in love with him. Before that weekend, she and Charlie hooked up the only way they knew how, by phone. Tomorrow would be another day. Where had she heard that before?

14

Ticketless in Boston

The bump woke him. The inch difference between the street and his driveway was ingrained in Mike's psyche. He'd driven over it a million times. Though he didn't have to look, his sleepy eyes confirmed he was right. They were home. Not their home, his home. At long last. He felt beaten to a pulp—his legs ached, his arms tingled hot. Clearly, his nap back from the Cape failed to conquer the punishment the dunes and the sun imposed.

"Honey, wake up." With one hand, Karen nudged a particularly angry spot on his left arm as she pressed the garage door opener with the other.

"I'm awake." The palm of his right hand touched the spot. He hoped Kassie had left behind a tube of aloe vera.

"See, Ka . . . Karen, you made it." He stopped short of calling her Kassie. He'd done that more than once before, always thankful she hadn't noticed. "Don't know what you were worried about, babe. And in record time too." By the digital clock on the dash, he figured she'd shaved fifteen minutes off the trip. "You in some kind of rush?"

Mike wasn't. He sat for a few moments, wiggling his toes, rolling his shoulders, needing to loosen the cobwebs before stepping out of the car. Karen was more than a step ahead of him, already lifting the rear door of the SUV.

"Can't believe we brought so much shit for a day trip."

"Leave it. We'll unpack in the morning."

Sitting sideways in the passenger seat and gazing down at his dangling feet, Mike heard the *thump thump* of Karen's roller bag before he felt her hand on his knee.

"Didn't you hear me? We'll do it in the morning."

"I think I'll go to the apartment."

"What? Now? What about tomorrow? I'm off. We're off. Thought we'd do something. Together."

"Haven't been there in a while. I should check on things."

"Can't you do it Tuesday?"

"I could. But I need clean clothes."

"Last time I checked, I have a washer and a dryer. Imagine that."

"My mail. Need to pick up my mail. Pay bills. I'll be back tomorrow night. We could go out for dinner."

"I give up. Go if you want. Where's my phone?"

And just like that, Karen handed him his phone, loaded her suitcase in her trunk, and kissed his cheek. He heard a metal-on-asphalt screech and a clunk as her muffler bumped the street pavement pulling out of the driveway.

Now nearly awake, Mike headed toward the house and turned on his phone as he lowered the garage door.

In the months since his transplant, there were few days he'd entered the house alone to utter silence. Often Karen was either with him or waiting for him, and then of course, there was Amelia last Friday. Before all that, even if Kassie was traveling, Topher would be there to greet him. Now that he was gone too, living with Kassie at Annie's, Mike had to admit he missed the orange-and-white ball of meowing fur. At least he was company.

Mike grabbed a bottle of water from the refrigerator and sat at the kitchen table. *Maybe we should get a cat.* Nah. Karen would never go for that. She'd say one pussy in this house was enough. Probably right.

Karen had become more of a handful in her later years than he'd remembered. She'd developed a mind of her own. Not the malleable coed he charmed during their college years together. She let him into her pants on their first date in the back of his roommate's Chevy. If recollection served him right, their first time was fast and furious. *Just like today.* He chuckled, noticing two messages waiting on his phone.

First message. "Hey, Mike. Bill here. Where did you say you left the tickets?"

Second message. "It's me again. We looked under the mat in the back too. Nothing. No problem. We're gonna head over to Fenway anyway. Hit up a scalper. Catch you later."

"What the hell? Must be a mistake." Mike shuffled to the front door as he decided to see for himself. As the bells hanging from the front door handle jingled, he recalled hearing them as he drifted off to sleep the night before. The tickets had to be there. *I heard Karen put them there.* She even said she had, hadn't she? Maybe the envelope had stuck to the underside of the mat.

Bending over to lift the mat, he felt pressure in his chest. He lifted the left corner of the mat and peeled it off the concrete slab. Nothing but a dark moist impression. *What the hell?* He turned the mat over on its underside. Nothing there either. He left the mat to the side to dry.

Stolen? Had somebody, maybe neighborhood teens, seen Karen put the tickets there and swiped them after they'd left that morning?

Inconceivable. To believe that would require too many assumptions, including that his neighbors of more than twenty years were thieves. There must be some other explanation.

She probably forgot to do what he'd asked. Maybe he was already asleep and dreamed the front bells banging against the door because he was expecting to hear them. The brain often plays mind games. If that's the case, the envelope with the tickets would still be somewhere in the house in plain view.

He shuffled through the first floor, his eyes scanning every tabletop, every desktop, the two toilet tank tops. You never know. She could've placed them there if she'd stopped to pee.

No luck. Intent on checking out the entire house before calling Bill, Mike reached the last step of the staircase leading to the second-floor landing, gripped the railing, and stopped to catch his breath. He walked through his bedroom, the two bathrooms, and then wandered through the two spare bedrooms.

He needed a rest. He sat on the chaise lounge in the larger of the two spare rooms. This room. That bed. The last time he'd made love to his wife was right there under those covers. He remembered, he'd always remember, even if Kassie chose not to. After that night, he was hopeful they could work something out, not move forward with the divorce. But oh no, his hope faded fast. Patricia O'Callaghan screwed up everything with her letter. Damn her mother for outing him, haunting him as much in her death as she did when alive.

Mike rubbed his hands back and forth along the arms of the chair, as if it were a bottle with a genie inside that would instantly make the tickets materialize. Or was it Kassie he wished would magically appear? If she were there, she'd make things all better. If she were there, they would've gone to the ballgame, and none of this would've happened.

He closed his eyes, reflecting some more. Truth was, he was the one responsible for the demise of his marriage. For the secrets, the lies, the vasectomy. The straw, or cut as it were, that broke Kassie's back. She had every right to leave him. He'd made his bed; now he'd have to sleep in it. Alone . . . for that night anyway.

Ticketless, Mike made his way back down to the kitchen, to his bottle of water and phone. He scrolled through his contacts, pressing Bill's number.

"Hey, man, wassup?" Bill answered after two rings.

"Not sure. We just got back and heard your message. My phone was off all day."

"Oh. That explains why—"

"Yes. Sorry about that. Wished I'd gotten your message earlier when I was with Kassie."

"You mean Karen."

"Right. Did I say Kassie? Shit, second time I've done that tonight."

"Maybe it's a sign."

Mike chose to ignore Bill's remark, but not the missing tickets. "Hey, bro, I've no clue what happened to the tickets. Karen—right? Karen—got me an envelope. I put the tickets in it with a note. Handed the envelope back to her and went to bed. She said she'd put them under the mat. Like I asked."

"Sounds like you'll need to ask Karen. She's not there?"

"No. She's sleeping in Charlestown tonight."

"Well, I'm sure you'll figure this out the next time you talk to her. We're all good here. Don't lose any sleep."

"Not to worry, I've got miles to go before that happens."

15

Queen for a Day

"It's open today from nine to six."

"What is?" Kassie asked as she rummaged through what clothing lingered in her suitcase and hadn't found its way to the tiny, hardly functional closet.

"The Louvre, of course." Chris stroked his chin.

"Impossible."

"No. It says it right here on their website. Monday nine to six. Closed Tuesday. That's an odd day to be closed, don't you think? But today is Monday, so . . ." Chris pushed his iPad between Kassie and the clothes she'd scattered on the bed.

"I see that." She pushed his arm away. "Impossible. Impossible. I have to meet with Mimi tomorrow. I have absolutely nothing to wear. This could be my big chance to show Tom I can haul in a really, really big deal."

"Is that what you think this is all about? A big deal? An international client? Maybe you're just a courier, a messenger. Or a spy? A ruse. Tom sets you up under a pretext, and then you're compelled to report back to the mother ship what Paris is really up to."

"I don't think so, Hercule." Kassie picked up the note she'd received from Tom and read it aloud for what was probably the tenth time.

"'Kassie, Sorry to intrude' . . . yeah, right, he's already succeeded with that. Thank you very much." She waved the letter in the air. "Blah, blah, blah." She paced the room, rubbing the back of her neck. "'Since you're in town, Mimi wants to bounce an idea off you.'" She stopped in front of Chris, who lay across the bed, lifting one garment at a time out of her suitcase.

"Stop that." She grabbed her red bra out of his hands and slung it across the room. "Next thing you know you'll be sniffing my clothes."

"What's wrong with that?"

"Just stop it. This is serious. My whole career may ride on what happens tomorrow."

"You're being a bit melodramatic."

"Am I? Mimi has an idea. An idea doesn't sound like she's giving me a package to bring back home, does it? And then he says, 'I know I can count on you.' What a crock of shit. Finally, after years of my loyalty, dedication, and being pissed on, he says he can count on me."

"Whatever it is, Tom knows you won't screw it up."

"But I have nothing to wear. And it's all your fault." Kassie covered her face with her hands and dropped to the floor.

Kassie recovered when Chris offered to postpone their excursion to the Louvre until Wednesday and suggested a better idea: shopping. A shopping spree would take her mind off the why of the meeting and concern herself with the how. It should be easy to find something to buy in Paris that was business appropriate, and while she was blowing up her credit cards, he could window shop, because according to Chris, isn't that what men mostly do? God forbid they shop for themselves and try something on.

"Do you think the internet exists so men don't have to shop in public?" Kassie asked.

"Look it up. There must be stats comparing online versus brick-and-mortar buying behavior by sex."

"Doesn't matter. I do both."

"That's obvious. Shoes. Maybe I'll look for shoes. Or a belt. Anything leather," Chris said as they scurried like starving mice to the boulangerie across the street for their morning coffee and pastry. Two days in a row they'd started their day this way. On the third day it would officially become a habit, according to people who professed to know these things. Whatever would they do when they were back in the States?

"How do French women stay so thin?" Kassie whispered as she spread butter and raspberry jam on her croissant. "At this rate, even if I had a suit with me, I probably wouldn't fit into it."

"Not to worry. We'll work it off later." Chris stroked her hair.

Kassie sighed and leaned into his warm, sturdy body.

"This is good." Kassie didn't mean the croissant. At first, in Venice, she was unsure of the viability of taking up with Chris again. In reality, it took less than seventy-two hours to suppress her anxiety. It was déjà vu. The butterflies she'd felt years ago on the Rialto bridge in Venice sprung loose once again. Flooding her heart. Filling her lungs with the love she once had for him but was forced to surrender when she discovered he was Mike's son.

Over the last year, she'd convinced herself her number-one priority was her career; not Chris, who obviously was persona non grata; not Mike, who was soon to be her ex; and certainly not her mother, who actually was dead. No one was stopping her. No one in her way. Her time had come.

"Go for it, girl," her assistant Vicki had encouraged her as they fist bumped after a week of long nights at the office.

Sitting there now with Chris, in Paris, seemingly away from the

stresses of business and divorce, she wondered whether she could
have both—her career and Chris—and succeed at both. Would she
be happy having one without the other?

"What's that you're humming?" Chris interrupted Kassie's
meanderings.

"Oh, you probably wouldn't know it."

"Try me."

"My mother used to sing it to me. 'Love and Marriage.' Frank
Sinatra, if I recall."

Kassie sang the lyrics softly, hoping only Chris would hear it.
Then she explained, "You can't separate love and marriage. You can
never have one without the other. They're like Laurel and Hardy."

Chris gave her an oh-come-on look.

"Or Belichick and Brady," she said, confident he'd get the more
contemporary reference.

"Marriage? Is that what's on your mind?"

"Uh, no, not really." Without thinking, she rubbed her wedding
ring. "Not marriage in the literal sense. More like love and career.
Can a relationship based on true love and a career based on ambition
survive?"

"Are you talking about us?"

"I want my career, Chris."

"And I love you. So I think we're like Sinatra's other song. Two coins
in a fountain." Chris snuck his hand under her arm and tickled her.

Kassie dissolved into laughter. "It's three coins, you idiot!"

An hour later, they walked into La Maison de Paris, stopping dead in
their tracks in front of a two-story fountain whose cascading water
appeared to change colors. Chris reached over and lifted Kassie's chin
that'd dropped to her chest, kissed her, and slipped three coins into
her hand.

"Did you know, this was the first department store in the whole wide world? Opened 1862," Chris said.

"You mean 1962," Kassie corrected.

"No, Madame, your husband is partially right. We opened in 1862, ten years after Le Bon Marché, making us the second in the world." Kassie and Chris turned toward the voice.

"Oh, we're not married." Kassie waved her finger between her and Chris, caring less about the age of the store. She wasn't there for a history lesson.

"Dazzling," Chris mouthed, gazing upward. Kassie hoped he was admiring the five-story atrium with its gleaming chrome railings and glass partitions, not the long-limbed lady with straight pewter-colored hair who'd greeted them.

"How can we help you *aujourd'hui*?"

"I came here with no clothes."

The femme fatale's eyes widened. *Dollar signs. She sees dollar signs.* Kassie tried to convey her thoughts to Chris.

"Not no clothes. Just not the right outfits for tonight and tomorrow," Chris piped in.

"Plural?" Kassie said.

"Don't argue. Take my word for it."

"Well, Mademoiselle, I'm Gabriella. I'm happy to be your personal shopper. Be *trés* sure La Maison de Paris can fulfill your every desire. Won't you come with me? *Comment vous appelez-vous?*"

"Kassie." Proud she knew that much French, she touched her hand to her chest and then his arm. "Chris."

"Um. If you ladies don't mind? I'm going to leave you two. Do a little shopping of my own." Chris gave Kassie the "call me" hand signal and said, "When you're done. Take your time."

Kassie gasped, "What the?" as Chris hustled out the sparkling glass doors, leaving her in a fantasy world to fend for herself. "Not sure where he's going?"

Gabriella ushered Kassie toward a bank of elevators. The doors opened and dinged as if they sensed their arrival. "Ready, Mademoiselle?"

"It's really Madame, for now. It's a long story. How much time do you have?"

Feeling like a queen, or even a princess, was not on Kassie's travel itinerary, no matter where she traveled in Europe—whether vacationing with Annie in Venice as originally planned, or touring in Paris with Chris, or shopping with Gabriella, to be precise. All she needed was something businesslike to wear to a business meeting. Not a lot of hoop dee doo required.

But Gabriella had other objectives.

Rather than look through racks of petites and haul mostly separates into a claustrophobic dressing room, Kassie was directed toward a mirrored room three times larger than the walk-in closet she had in the Ricci house back in Boston. A woman named Louisa asked for the clothes she was wearing, which just an hour before were crunched in her suitcase, and handed them to an even younger woman named Zoe, who hung them on hangers covered in pink silk.

Louisa held her hand and led her to a circular platform, where Kassie was immediately embarrassed upon hearing Louisa announce her measurements to Zoe.

"Maybe you don't have anything to fit me," Kassie said, prepared to grab her garments and run like hell.

"*Absurdité,*" Gabriella chimed in, frowning at Kassie's stretched-out lingerie as she assisted her into a pink silk knee-length robe. "And new undergarments too, *oui?*"

"*Oui, oui.* Kind of sad, but there's a reason. . . ." Kassie looked down, embarrassed.

Gabriella handed Kassie a flute of champagne, winked, and gave a nod to her assistants to leave them alone.

"Sit, *s'il vous plaît,* Mademoiselle."

"Madame," Kassie corrected, half wondering if she should just give up on that.

"You have *un histoire?*"

"History? Me and Chris? Yes, you could call it that."

"Handsome, *oui. Certainement.* I mean, you have a story about why you are here today? What event can I help you with?"

Embarrassed again. Kassie decided it best to focus on buying clothes, not on Chris, who was off doing who knows what. *KISS. Keep it simple, sweety.*

And thus began Kassie's spiel about her predicament. Starting with the trip to Venice—how her best friend had pulled a fast one on her, which in the States would be called a bait and switch; how the same music played when Chris showed up again in St. Mark's Square, serendipitous and freaky; how they thought Paris would be a good change of pace, but they'd forgotten about the World Cup—they had to be out of their minds; and how when her boss learned she was in Paris, he had the nerve to schedule an impromptu meeting with Mimi, the head of the Paris office, on Tuesday without asking if she had anything to wear. She didn't. The nerve of him. That's why she was there.

Kassie polished off her second glass of champagne with "Oh, did I tell you I'm having an affair with my husband's son?"

"It's *Paris,* Madame. *C'est la vie.* And Monsieur Chris is *chaud, non?*"

"Hot? You noticed, like half the women in the world," Kassie mumbled as she tried on the thirteenth dress. She hoped it was the lucky one.

"*Belle. Belle.* This is it, *tu ne crois pas?*"

"Yes, I think it's beautiful." Kassie slid her hands down the sleeveless midnight-blue tulip-shaped dress.

"*Vos yeux*. The cowl neckline attracts your eyes."

"Not right for the meeting." Kassie shook her head and chewed her pinky. "Something a little less sexy. Something that makes a strong statement."

"*Rouge?*" said a soft voice.

"*Non, Zoe, pas rouge,*" Gabriella said.

"*Noir?*"

"*Oui.* Perhaps black." Kassie wiggled out of the blue dress. "Depending—"

Zoe uttered something foreign into her headset and disappeared.

Kassie gazed at Gabriella as she whisked the blue and black dresses out of the dressing room. Clearly this wasn't Gabriella's first rodeo. She'd sized up Kassie in more ways than one and together with her accomplices found the perfect dress for the meeting with Mimi. Though a bit *cher* for her budget, Kassie decided to check with Chris before purchasing either or both of the dresses. As she waited for Chris to return, Kassie wandered around the store, humming the piped-in music, spritzing the latest designer perfumes. For the thrill of it, she felt the luscious fabrics of the latest French fashion trends draping skinny, yet shapely, mannequins. *I'd be broke if I lived here.*

In her wanderings, she practiced how'd she'd rationalize the expense. The black dress spoke power and confidence. The simple three-quarter-length-sleeve boat-neck sheath fit her like a glove, and Zoe's suggestion of a wide silver belt was pure stylistic genius. It accented her smallish waist and suggested Kassie had a flair for fashion. She thought if she could find the right shoes, the ensemble would impress Mimi. And the dress could be worn for many occasions, even a funeral, without the belt. But the blue dress cost twice as much as the black dress. It would be perfect for a night of frolicking in Paris and for special occasions back home. So the cost of it could be spread across multiple events, making the shopping spree a reasonable return on investment.

Okay, that all made logical sense. But to whom? They were her dresses; there was no need for her to justify anything to Chris.

Kassie felt his presence before she saw or heard him. He'd found her at the handbag counter and wrapped his arm around her waist.

"What is it with women and pocketbooks?" Chris said.

"You sound like my mother. Purses, not pocketbooks."

"Are you ready to go?"

"I haven't checked out yet."

"I took care of it. Where next?"

"You're shittin' me!" Kassie said under her breath but loud enough for Chris to hear.

"I bumped into Gabriella—nice name, by the way—on my way in. She said you'd selected two dresses like I suggested."

"Did she show them to you?"

"Nope. I just gave her my AMEX card. So we're good to go. Unless you have more shopping to do."

"I need shoes and a purse, not a pocketbook. But it's too expensive here," Kassie said as they pushed through the doors to the street. "Where are my dresses?"

"On their way to the hotel."

"You think of everything, don't you?" Kassie stuck her hands in her pockets and smirked. *Not sure I can get used to this.*

16

Lunch with Tiffany

As they pushed their way out the revolving door of La Maison de Paris, a tall blonde Uber driver greeted Kassie and Chris. *WTF? Is every woman in Paris a ten?* The driver looked to Chris and asked, "*Quelle destination maintenant?*"

"*Ou est le meilleur* shopping?" Once again Chris demonstrated he was comfortable asking for directions whatever side of the Atlantic he was on.

"Rue du Commerce, Monsieur. Anything you possibly could want to buy you'll find there." The driver caught Chris's eye in the rearview mirror and winked. "American?"

"*Oui.* Yes," Kassie responded, smacking that interaction in the bud.

"Me too."

"Where?" Kassie jumped in before Chris could.

"Chicago."

Oh, Christ. Here we go. Kassie slumped in the seat, giving up. She might as well have been left behind on the sidewalk.

The next five minutes sounded like an episode of "This is your life, Mademoiselle Uber driver." Though ten years younger than Chris, the driver had lots of friends who attended the University of Illinois, just as he did. *What a coincidence.* She had a degree in art history from the Art Institute of Chicago, which of course he had frequented when he lived there. *Of course he did.* She'd applied for a position at the Louvre and picked up this driving gig in the meantime. He applauded her for that, saying he'd do the same thing if he was in her shoes.

At least he didn't say in her pants. Kassie gazed out the window at the Paris hubbub, as the multilingual chatterboxes carried on their tête-à-tête.

Kassie's ears perked when she heard the words *Chicago Cubs.* Finally, baseball. Her turf.

"You don't look like the typical Cubbie fan," Blondie said, admitting the White Sox were her team.

"Red Sox will win the series this year." Kassie tried to join the confab, not really understanding the genesis of her prognostication.

"That's because my first allegiance is to the Giants," Chris said.

Did he just ignore me?

The driver's sister lived in San Francisco. *Oh, no, here we go again.* Blah, blah, blah. Apparently, she'd visited a couple of times but couldn't live there.

"*Tremblements de terre!*" Miss Coquette rocked her hand from side to side.

"I get it. Earthquakes. Rumblings, like my stomach." Kassie put her hand on her waist. Her intestines were talking to her. At least something was.

"Hungry?" Chris finally took notice.

Just in time, Kassie grabbed Chris's attention and his hand and let her nose steer them toward the aroma of chicken frying and grease oozing from sizzling burgers. Sure enough, Le Petit Café was two doors down from where the Uber siren dropped them. One more minute in that car and Kassie wouldn't have been responsible if Bad Kassie had eaten her alive.

Standing outside the café, Chris stared at the sign that posted the hours. "Look." He pointed to 14h30 and checked his watch. Always the help, Chris stopped her from counting on her fingers. "They close at two thirty. It's only one, we're good."

"Let's eat inside." Still holding his hand, Kassie led the way past those who chose the sidewalk tables. "I have to pee," she mouthed to Chris.

Billed as a small restaurant, Le Petit Café was anything but. And fancy too. Crystal water glasses, off-white plates, white linen napkins, and what looked like, but couldn't possibly be, gold-plated forks and knives decorating the white tablecloths. Dull yellow and white tile laid pattern-less, most likely by a Parisian who'd had one cognac too many, broke up the monotony in the room. But it was the vintage French magazine posters that hung haphazardly around the restaurant and the mirrors that stretched from the ground floor to the ceiling of the second tier that made Kassie say, "Wow." This was not your typical hamburger joint—be it French or American.

"We're lucky we got a table. Seems World Cup mania continues."

"Maybe it's just uber popular." She peered over the top of the menu, expecting him to get the joke.

His eyes twinkled back.

"Look at this menu, Chris. Is it the smells in here or reading the menu in French that's making my mouth water? Asking for *pommes de terre frites* sounds so much better than saying, 'I'll have fries with that.'"

This time he laughed.

Once Chris ordered for the both of them in French, *mais bien sûr*—fish and chips for Kassie, salmon for him—she excused herself for the ladies' room, which, wouldn't you know, was up a long mahogany staircase. Halfway up, she turned to look at Chris. He was in deep conversation with a dark-haired lady wearing a white blouse, black miniskirt, and white apron. She looked more like a French maid than a server. Ever the chick magnet. Kassie brushed the green-eyed monster off her shoulder when the lady handed him what looked to be a menu. *Hope that's not the wine list. He should know I want a cosmo.*

For a busy restaurant at a busy time of the day, their meals arrived quickly. So did the cosmo Chris ordered for her. She offered him her fries. No way would she or could she eat all of them.

"I have two new dresses to fit into."

"Tell me about them."

"One's blue. One's black. The blue one's fancy. The black one's practical. I can wear it to the meeting tomorrow. Or a funeral."

"That's a happy thought. You're not thinking the meeting with Mimi is one and the same?"

"Of course not. Just making a joke. I bought enough black clothes to wear to my mother's funeral two years ago. In fact, they're taking up way too much space in my closet at Annie's."

"Maybe you should think about moving them to my place in Charlestown, like you were supposed to before—"

"We'll see." She cut him off, not wanting him to take her down memory lane. She did that too often on her own.

A suave-looking waiter, not the French maid she'd seen chatting him up earlier, tried to fill their water glasses. But his hand trembled and water splattered on Chris's side of the table. No big surprise. She figured it was Chris who caught his fancy, not her.

"We're good." Kassie flipped him off politely, not colloquially, with a wave of her hand.

"You two on your honeymoon?"

"No, we're not married." Kassie smirked and slid her left hand under the table.

"Not married." Chris echoed as the waiter turned to leave and tripped over himself, almost falling into the table behind them.

"You should've told him I was your stepmother. He would've dumped the whole pitcher on us!" Kassie covered her mouth, stifling a laugh.

"I trust in time you'll get past that."

"Past what?"

"Referring to yourself as my stepmother. Once you and Mike are divorced, are you going to call yourself my ex-stepmother?" Chris polished off his glass of wine and poured another. "Isn't it time to let it go?"

Stunned, Kassie placed her knife and fork across her plate, leaving half her fish and most of the potatoes untouched. Over the last year, she hadn't given much thought to being connected to Chris in any way after the divorce. Why would she? Until four days ago, her relationship with him was over. *Fini.* Did his showing up in Venice jumpstart it for good? Or just for the next few days?

"We're not married. We're not living together. You're my husband's son. If I'm not your stepmother, what am I? What are we, Chris? Two former lovers having a fling in Paris?"

"Don't make this difficult, Kassie. It doesn't have to be. We're two mature adults, granted with some baggage."

"Ya think?"

"I think it's time for us to put the past behind us, don't you? Let's throw all the craziness that was out of our control into the Seine. Let's keep the good memories that brought us together in the first place and move forward. Together. What do you say?"

Kassie finished her drink and turned away from his gaze.

"I love you, Kassie. We can make us work."

Oh, God. She smeared black mascara on Le Petit Café's linen napkin.

"It's almost two thirty. They'll be closing soon. Before we finish shopping, I have to . . ." She pointed toward the ceiling.

She climbed the staircase again. Through her tears, she noticed Chris had his hands in his pockets. She hoped her non-response hadn't made him regret finding her in Venice, either this time or the first. She loved him. If she was ever to believe in magic, a future with Chris might be her last shot.

When she got back to the table, champagne flutes had replaced their drink glasses. Chris stood behind her chair, which he pulled out for her as he touched the small of her back and kissed her cheek. A small light blue box with a white bow prevented her from taking her seat.

Her mouth felt like sandpaper. She tried to swallow. Nothing doing. Her eyes blinked, fighting another flow of tears, and her left eye twitched.

"What's this?"

17

Crossing That Bridge

Kassie and Chris spent the rest of Monday afternoon holding hands, playing tourists and shoppers along La Rue du Commerce.

It didn't take long for Kassie to agree with Mademoiselle Uber-Know-It-All. La Rue du Commerce was the best hidden shopping street in all of Paris. Just around the corner from the Eiffel Tower and across the street from some famous gardens Kassie didn't know the name of, La Rue du Commerce was its own feast for the eyes and the wallet. Its tree-lined street held court to high fashion boutiques, as well as to stores displaying everyday bargains bursting with every shade of red, green, and blue. Inventors of the Pantone color wheel would be proud.

She came to a screeching halt in front of a baby store. Its windows were adorned in girly pink and baby-boy blue, with just one bright yellow onesie thrown in for accent. Her feet became cemented in place. Her eyes watered on instinct. Her breathing showed signs of hyperventilation. *Get ahold of yourself.* Too late. A cheery pair of pregnant ladies strolled out of the store, each carrying two white store-branded shopping bags so filled to the brim, Kassie envisioned a little bump on the shoulder of one would be all it would take to knock them both over to the curb like bowling pins. *Down girl.*

Chris looped his arm around her waist, pulled her in tight, and led her away to safer environs. A leather store. It was pay dirt for them both. Chris tried on a half dozen jackets, settling on a classic black bomber jacket, its leather softer than butter, if that was even possible. All she could think of when he posed in front of a three-way mirror with his hand in his pocket of his gray jeans and winked at her was *Eat your heart out, Karen. He may be your son, but I sleep with him.*

She hadn't thought much about Karen since Chris surprised her in Venice. She wondered if Karen was as happy that day with Mike as she was with Chris and why images of both Karen and her mother flashed through her mind at that moment. *Mother, what are you trying to tell me?*

Kassie shook off the eerie feeling, rubbed the goosebumps on her arms, and focused on leather. Like Chris, Kassie succeeded too. So many shoes and purses to choose from. It would make any American girl giddy. Cleverly, Chris grabbed an empty chair along the front window, giving her time and space to behave like a kid in a candy store.

She touched and sniffed the earthy, sweet smell of more than a dozen handbags, returning more than once to one that caught her eye—a red crocodile designer label knock-off that would complement both new dresses. At first, she'd put it aside because it had two handles, not a cross-body strap. But when she returned to explore it probably for the fourth time, a wise saleswoman stepped in to rescue her, pulling out a strap that was hidden in an inside pocket, hooking it up, and draping it across Kassie. Sold.

Finding two pairs of shoes, one black leather and one red to match her new favorite bag that would work with either of her two new dresses, occurred with far less drama. So too, the process of checking out. This time, Kassie paid for her own purchases and Chris for his jacket, shipping costs and all.

"Where to now? A drink celebrating our shopping extravaganza?" Chris said.

"How about coffee? The day is young. I don't want alcohol to slow us down." With that, Chris spied a Starbucks. Yes, Starbucks, in Paris, where his prepaid rewards card worked with only one tap.

When Kassie returned from her obligatory trip to the ladies' room, Chris was sliding his phone into his pocket. "How do we get back to the hotel from here?" she asked.

"No problem. Let's go."

Of course, as if right on cue, a car pulled up and Uber Blondie jumped out and popped the trunk. "I see you had much success. Fueling our economy. *Merci beaucoup.*"

Kassie hesitated, shook her head, climbed in the back, and gave in. During the ride to the hotel, Bad Kassie took a back seat as well.

"I'll be right in, babe." Chris asked Kassie to wait for him in the lobby of the Hotel de Fais de Beaux Rêves, which she did but with reservations, trusting him, not Blondie. Parting a long sheer curtain, she saw an exchange going down. Something was up between Chris and Tanya. Oh yes, she had a name. On that last ride, Kassie asked. Not just to be included in the conversation. It's important, you know, to name your adversaries. To put a name with a face. An unforgettably gorgeous face who was at that moment getting a slight shoulder rub from her man.

"What was that all about?" Kassie tried not to sound as jealous as the bile inside her chest cavity suggested.

"You'll see. We've got to get a move on. Can you be dressed in an hour?"

"Where are we going now? I might have nothing to wear."

"*Mais oui*, you do." Shooing Kassie toward the stairway, Chris stopped by the front desk, giving the bellman a thumbs-up as he joined her. "Remember Cinderella, your dresses? They wait for you upstairs."

Kassie showered first. Though a fully equipped bathroom, the tub could only accommodate one at a time, to her dismay. Right alongside Red Sox and Patriots games, having sex with Chris in the shower ranked high on her list of favorite pastimes. She'd have to wait until they were back at his place in Charlestown for that wicked indulgence. A little grin sparkled her eyes as she realized she was warming to the idea that whatever this was with Chris had the potential to last beyond Paris.

While Chris took his turn in the tub, Kassie put on the lace lingerie she'd bought—or rather, he'd bought—earlier that day. She unclasped the Moissanite solitaire necklace she'd worn for the last year post-gondola and draped it on the bedspread.

"Here, let me do that." Chris emerged from what could rightly be called a steam room. He removed the solitaire from the chain and slid on the diamond-accented Eiffel Tower pendant from the light blue Tiffany box. Standing behind her in front of the full-length mirror, he draped the necklace across her chest and clasped it.

"Now that's better. The other was lovely, but not as meaningful as this or the gondola. Agreed?"

She turned toward him, gave him a suggestive smooch, and tugged at the towel around his waist.

"Later." He held the towel in place, protecting his jewels.

Pouting, she mindfully agreed, although the throbbing between her legs had other ideas.

"Have it your way. Could you get me the blue dress, *s'il vous plaît?*"

In front of the mirror again, after Chris snipped off the tags, Kassie slid into the midnight-blue tulip-shaped dress. He approached her from behind, his hands massaging her, starting from near her breast and moving down along her hips.

"Perhaps I was wrong."

Kassie didn't need to ask what he meant by that. The answer was peeking out of his boxer shorts.

"Too late. I'm almost ready to go." She twirled around.

"As always, you're right. And gorgeous. Give me a minute." He disappeared in the bathroom for five, returning with a Cheshire cat grin.

"You're insufferable!" She gave him a sweet punch in the shoulder.

"What? I brushed my teeth."

"Liar. Not fair."

"I'll make it up to you later." He gave her a sweet kiss on the cheek.

They giggled all the way down the stairs, out the lobby, and into Miss Tanya's car, whose black leather back seat was covered in red and white rose petals.

"Isn't it rather early for dinner? I thought Europeans were late eaters." Kassie held Chris's hand as he led them toward the base of the Eiffel Tower.

"Two seatings. Remember your meeting tomorrow with Mimi? I booked the early one."

"Good thinking."

She touched her new pendant.

Just hours before, after lunch at Le Petit Café, she'd held her breath as she opened the Tiffany box, and then she exhaled in utter relief. She prayed her fear the gift contained a ring wasn't written all over her face, though her leg twitch could've easily ratted her out. Chris wouldn't be that presumptuous, would he? They'd only been reunited since Friday. Under the lunch table so he wouldn't notice, she'd counted off four, four days, on the fingers of her left hand. Was four days too soon? *Crazy girl. You fell in love with him the first time in two. Four days is a lifetime.* The voice inside her head tried unsuccessfully to calm her nerves. *And I'm still married to his father, no less.*

Somehow Kassie recovered, putting two and two together—the gondola memorialized their first time in Venice and the Eiffel Tower signified Paris. Her response was genuine: "It's perfect, Chris. I love it . . . and you. I thought—" She was saved from opening her mouth and inserting her foot by the waiter with their bill. And that was that.

Now, rubbing the new pendant as she often did the gondola, she wished she'd brought the gondola with her so she could see how they looked dangling together on the chain. Like sex in the shower, that would have to wait until they got back to the States.

Chris picked up their tickets, and they rode the lift to 58 Tour Eiffel, located on the first floor of the monument, which wasn't ground level as one would imagine when something is said to be on the first floor.

"I read," Chris explained after they were seated, "the height of the restaurant is fifty-seven meters from the ground. But to accommodate the open kitchen range over there, they added another meter, making it fifty-eight."

"So, does that mean if I wear a hat that's four inches tall, I can say I'm five foot six? Or more to the point, can I say these three-inch heels make me five foot five?" She leaned down and rubbed the top of her right foot.

"You okay? Would you like a cosmo before wine?"

"But of course. My mission continues."

Once Chris ordered their drinks and dinner, Kassie reached for his hand, weaving her fingers through his. "This is spectacular, Chris. How did you ever get reservations?"

"Connections. Remember?"

"By any chance is her name Tanya?"

He pursed his lips and shook his head no. "The hotel concierge and I have become *bons amis*."

Kassie gazed out the window at the humanity two hundred feet below, if her math served her right. Even for a Monday evening, the Eiffel Tower was a magnet for tourists. From their table for two next to the massive windows, she could see hordes of what looked like mini-Lego characters, with their phones and cameras flashing, fingers pointing skyward. She wished she were wealthy enough to rent out the entire restaurant and invite those who were not as fortunate as she to savor Paris in all its panoramic and gastronomical splendor.

"Paris is quickly becoming my second favorite vacation spot."

"Let me guess. Seattle? No. Hmm. San Fran—?" Chris's phone chimed before Kassie could answer.

"You know what? I'm going to shut this invader down for the rest of the week." He held up his phone, turned it off, and slid it into his pants pocket.

"And who was invading?"

"Just a friend. West Coast. It can wait until we get home. Now, where were *we*?"

They were exploring their roots, their genesis, their raison d'être. Starting with Venice, six years ago. It would always be Venice. Yet, over a span of five years they'd taken their love affair primarily bicoastal, and so they reminisced—she about their spontaneous meeting at the Space Needle in Seattle, he about a lascivious weekend at a B&B in Napa, both about a roll in the sand on a beach on the Cape, their literal undercover meetups in and around Boston and the apartment in Charlestown that was supposed to be theirs, but ended up as his . . . alone.

Ultimately, their romantic walks down memory lane arrived at the doorstep of Annie's condo just about a year ago to the day. There was no way of ignoring the elephant that would forever occupy a seat at their table, even if both the seat and the elephant were invisible: Mike. Mike and Karen's forty-year secret had brought father and son together, splitting Kassie and Chris apart.

Regrets? In retrospect, hell yeah. They'd allowed Karen and Mike's buried past and Mike's illness—all of which they had no control over—to separate them for a goddamn year.

"We sound like victims," Kassie said.

"Aren't we, though?"

"Perhaps. Past tense." Kassie poked at her profiterole, knowing full well how uncomfortably full she'd be if she indulged and scoffed down the entire dessert as she really, really wanted to do. Instead, showing unusual restraint, she wiped off the fork with tines shaped like the Eiffel Tower, opened her brand-new red handbag, and plopped it in.

Rather than feeling melancholy about their past, reliving the journey that rekindled their love made Kassie calm, bullish on the future, and playful. "I've got you back in my life, and the prospect of something mysteriously exciting at work." Kassie raised her champagne flute; they toasted, and she slugged back the inch or so that was left. If there were a fireplace nearby, Kassie . . . or Bad Kassie . . . would've given hers a heave-ho.

When she returned from the ladies' room—again—Chris asked if she'd like to take a ride to the top of the Tower.

"Maybe another day. I should get ready for tomorrow. We have five more days—"

"One last stop before we head back, okay?"

Surprised, and a bit relieved, there was no Tanya waiting to whisk them away, Kassie hooked her arm through Chris's as he navigated the evening crowd to a taxi stand.

"Pont Neuf," she heard him attempting to whisper to the driver.

"Are we going to jump off the bridge? A new twist on Romeo and Juliet? The Riccis versus the Gaineses. Whatever will your mamas and papas say when we show up in Boston together again? I'm nobody's favorite, except for perhaps Mike."

"What? Are you worried? I'm not. We might jump, but not off the bridge."

The sun had set as they left the Tower, and the moon was on the rise. The hot, sticky July day had lingered into the evening, giving tourists and Parisians alike a reason to stroll Pont Neuf, as if anyone ever needed a reason to do so.

Never the shy one, Chris stopped midway across the span and pressed Kassie against the stone wall. She allowed her arms to wrap around his neck, and he kissed her deeply, with a passion befitting the moment. Her left ankle collapsed outward a bit. *How did I ever let a year go by without you?* He held her in this embrace, kissing her forehead, and then turned her so she could see Paris from his vantage point. He enclosed her body with his arms, and they swayed to their own music.

"What are you humming?" Chris asked.

"'Something's Coming' from *West Side Story*."

"That's weird. We're in Paris?" Chris spun her around facing him but didn't let her go.

"Not so weird. Being here with you and my meeting tomorrow. It's all grand, don't you think?" Kassie looked deeply into his eyes, feeling their souls unite. *My life doesn't get any better than this.*

"You're right. With you, it is all grand and absolutely perfect. Over the last twelve months, I hardly lived. I hardly breathed. Without you I am nothing."

Chris dropped to one knee and a red box magically appeared in his right hand. "Marry me, Kassandra O'Callaghan."

She leaned down and massaged the top of her right foot. "Fuck. Pomegranates."

18

Come Again?

"**I**s that a yes?" Chris steadied Kassie, preventing her from falling to the pavement. *Could 'pomegranates' be an unfamiliar French way to say, 'Absolutely, I'll marry you, love of my life'?*

"Not a yes, or a no. It's . . . get me back to the hotel. I'm starting to itch like hell. Can we talk about this later?" Kassie returned the box to Chris's hand. "I'm so sorry."

Chris was sorry too. Until that moment, he'd pretty much rate the day five stars. Kassie's reaction when she opened the Tiffany box at lunch and found an Eiffel Tower pendant, not a ring, was priceless. By deliberately asking the salesperson to put the delicate diamond-studded Tower in a ring box, his ruse worked. He'd knocked Kassie off her game. Her need to control the situation, every situation, was foiled.

He thought he'd gotten her good, right where he wanted her. Especially because he knew the rest of the day would be a humdinger. Boy, would she be surprised.

Except he was the one surprised when his phone rang at dinner.

He hadn't talked to Lexi in a month, not since they'd mutually agreed to end their long-distance relationship, giving him an open runway to conspire with Annie about Venice. Time would come when he'd tell Kassie about Lexi, but not that night of all nights.

Things went downhill after that call. He looked the other way when Kassie pilfered a fork at dinner. Had she become a klepto-maniac over the last year? Or was this an innate urge of hers he'd ignored over their years together because he was blinded by his love. And what was with *pomegranates*? So much for believing he was the master of the moment, or that he really knew this woman he just asked to marry him. What a cluster.

Chris grabbed Kassie by the arm, guided her through a bottle-neck of folks out for their evening stroll, ensuring she didn't bump into man, woman, or heaven forbid, baby carriages—though he stubbed his toe on an unforeseen part of the sidewalk that was an inch higher than the rest. A metaphor for the day.

Making matters worse, there were no taxis in sight, and Tanya had told him when she'd dropped them off at the Tower that she was off the grid for the rest of the night.

"Can you make it back to the hotel if we walk? Or do I need to call . . ."

Kassie kicked off her shoes, pointing toward the direction of the hotel. "Let's hoof it."

And so they walked. Every two hundred paces or so, Kassie stopped to rub pebbles off the bottoms of her feet.

Waiting to cross an intersection with chattering pedestrians and honking traffic, she leaned up and yelled through tears Chris could see streaming down her face, "You'll have to work your magic with the concierge. I need some antihistamines and a cream too."

As he swung the hotel door open, Chris tapped his palm to his forehead as if he should've had a V8 juice. "You're allergic to pome-granates? Is that what this is all about?"

"Ya think?"

"But you didn't have—"

"My bad. One of the cosmos, I bet. Probably at lunch. I felt something weird at dinner, before I drank that one. Damn it."

Chris told her he'd meet her upstairs. A night-duty concierge, not the one he'd made nice with since they'd arrived on Saturday, just had to make Chris a hero and help him turn the evening around. Chris touched his pocket. The ring was still there. *Thank God.*

The concierge disappeared into the back room and reemerged with salvation—a six-pack of Avil tablets, betamethasone lotion, and two bottles of water. Grateful they were in Europe, where medications could be obtained in a heartbeat, Chris placed ten euro on the desk, said *"merci"* to the concierge probably six times, and continued giving thanks as he bounded the stairs two at a time.

"Here, take one of these." He handed Kassie, who was stretched out on the bed still dressed, the package and water, which he unscrewed for her.

"What is pheniramine?"

"It's the French answer to antihistamines. More effective than ours, I bet."

"And this isn't cream. It's gel."

Chris grabbed the tube and massaged the translucent goo onto the top of Kassie's feet, which looked raw and bubbly.

"Better?"

"Better." Kassie inhaled and exhaled loudly. She grabbed his hand and pulled him onto the bed next to her.

"I'm sorry, Chris. You didn't expect all this. I've ruined . . ."

"All is not ruined, unless you want it to be." Leaning toward her and brushing the hair off her face, he gave her a kiss that was both sweet and intimate. He reached into his pocket and placed the box on her lap.

"Not as romantic as Pont Neuf—" Chris held her hands as her eyes gave him permission.

"Tell me again. . . ."

He'd memorized the speech he'd given earlier, but considering the location and events of the last hour, he knew he had to make some adjustments.

So he began, "When I'm with you, nothing in the world is ruined. The whole world is unspoiled. The air I breathe is filled with your essence." He paused, hoping his setup words were sinking in. "Over the last twelve months, I hardly lived. I hardly breathed. Without you, I am nothing. You are my oxygen."

He paused and lowered his head, his tongue circling his upper teeth. He feared Kassie would find a reason to change the subject, flee the moment, or need to pee for the eightieth time that day.

"Is that it?"

19

What's Fair Is Fair

On days like that Sunday, Karen longed not just for Charlie but for Elephant Butte. Like the Cape, it had sandy beaches and boats and fishing. Year-round, for that matter. As the largest state park in New Mexico, tourists were the lifeblood of the two thousand or so folks who were proud to say they were from Elephant Butte. Jokes be damned.

What it didn't have was the never-ending traffic and congestion in and around Boston that made getting from one place to another, whatever time of day, a friggin' nightmare. *You'd think it'd take ten minutes to drive from Newton to Charlestown on a Sunday evening.* Karen slammed her hands on the dashboard as she rolled to a stop behind a line of red taillights that looked a mile long.

Bored and anxious, never a good combination when driving, Karen picked up her cellphone she'd tossed on the passenger seat and turned it on. Creeping along at less than ten miles per hour enabled her to see she had two recent calls and two voicemails. No text messages. Though she would've liked a flirty message from Charlie, she was relieved he finally honored her plea not to take the chance Mike would see it.

Wouldn't you know, just as she was about to listen to the voicemails she was sure were from Charlie, traffic rolled. She plopped the phone in the open storage compartment below the dashboard. *My hot Charlie will have to wait.*

And there was another thing she hated about Boston. If you didn't live in a house with a driveway or attached garage, like Mike, parking was an event unto itself. And not a pleasant event. Oh, her apartment complex had a secure garage, inconveniently located the length of a football field away from the front door of the building.

"Think of it as exercise," Chris had said. "If you walk back and forth a couple of times a day, you won't have to go to the gym." *Like that was going to happen.*

Karen decided to keep the place longer than originally planned. The one-bedroom second-floor flat provided an oasis away from Mike if and when she felt a noose tightening, and a perch from which to spy on Chris. Though he said he wasn't seeing Kassie, Karen wasn't so sure, especially since he hadn't told her about Lexi.

On that Sunday evening the apartment was a staging area in anticipation of Monday, when it would transform into a love nest. For once she was glad Chris was away so there was no chance he'd bump into Charlie.

She dragged her roller bag over the bumpy slate pavement, keyed in the front door code, and backed in through the glass entryway. When she entered her apartment, a sour smell whiffed up her nose. She hadn't been there in a week. She fiddled with the thermostat until the air conditioning clicked on. The place was in need of a significant airing out. Thank goodness she hadn't waited until Monday to take care of it.

She opened the refrigerator, hoping there was something refreshing to drink. Just water. As she leaned on the counter and peered through the opening to the dining/living room area, the pungent odor cloud still lingered. *Good Godfrey.* It was her, not the apartment.

Time to shower. *Get the dirt and sweat and all things Mike and Cape Cod off me. But before I do that . . .* Karen looked around for her phone. Not in the pocket of her suitcase. Not in her purse.

She stood in the middle of the living room, hands on her hips, reconstructing in her mind where she had it last. *Crap.* She grabbed her keys and the water and hoofed her way down the carpeted hallway, only to have to wait for the elevator. The stairway beckoned her, but she flipped it off. Pushing through the glass exit doors, she held them open for a young couple she recognized as tenants and marched her way to the garage, mumbling all the way, "I'm hot and sweaty and I stink. Charlie's messages better be good."

By the time she retrieved her phone and headed back, pearls of salty sweat dripped from her hairline into her eyes. She poured what was left in the bottle of water over her head, which didn't help clear her vision. Rubbing her eyes with the back of her hand allowed her to see she'd received three, not two, recent calls. One from Bill, Charlie, and Mike, in that order. The two voicemails weren't both from Charlie, but from Charlie and Bill.

She had a hunch why Bill had called, so she clicked on Charlie's message first as she waited for the elevator, wet head and all. She scrunched her eyebrows, as if that would help her hear Charlie, whose voice was barely a whisper. "Loverly Lady, how are you this spectacular Sunday morning? Such a drag not spending the day with you. Sarah quickly arranged a brunch for us with some of her museum blowhards. At least it'll pass the hours until—"

As she stepped off the elevator onto her floor, she pulled the phone away from her ear as Charlie came through loud and clear, "Sounds like a plan, Harry, see you tomorrow." *Ah, Sarah must've walked in on him.* Made her laugh. "Yes, you will see me tomorrow."

Entering the apartment for the second time, she latched the dead

bolt and headed for the bedroom. She stripped off her capris and prepared to listen to Bill's whining. As she laid the phone on her bed,
she noticed the call had come in while they were way out on the Cape
without cell power. *Yes!* Just as she hoped. She took a deep breath.
This was going to be good.

"Hey, Karen. Couldn't reach Mike, so I'm trying you. We're at
the house. We looked under the mat by the front door and the one
in the back. No tickets. We'll wait ten minutes. If you get this, please
call back. Thanks."

Poor Bill and Nancy. No free tickets. *He better get used to no free
lunch once I'm Mrs. Ricci.*

Before jumping in the shower, she listened to Charlie's message
three times and deleted Bill's.

Toweling off, it occurred to her that Mike hadn't left a message.
She checked. Indeed, he'd called while the phone was in the car. *Too
bad.* She guessed he and Bill had probably connected. No way she'd
call him now and get into a pissing match. She'd wait and cross that
bridge tomorrow night. Charlie had to come first.

Which he did, the next day. Twice, in fact. She did too, just not as
quickly as Charlie. His mature, experienced hands made sure he finished what she'd invited him there to do.

He didn't need the little blue pill he'd placed in the palm of her
hand when she greeted him at her door.

"What's this for?"

"Just in case. It's kept Sarah happy . . . and me a kept man . . . for
years." Charlie swatted her ass as he entered the apartment.

Karen put the pill on a napkin in the kitchen and the white wine
he'd brought in the refrigerator. Now with the dirty deeds, plural,
behind them, she uncorked the wine and tossed the pill in the trash.
We won't be needing that *today.*

She curled up on one end of the dark blue couch, Charlie stretched out at the other end with his feet resting on the coffee table. They clinked their wine glasses.

"Nice place. Similar to Chris's upstairs."

"He's got a better view of the Harbor." Karen walked to the big picture window. "It's okay. Serves its purpose until I totally move in with Mike."

"And . . . how is that going?"

"Oh, Charlie. I have so much to tell you. You'll be so proud of me." She returned to the couch, curling up alongside him, caressing his neck and shoulder with her fingers.

"It's official. He asked me to marry him. On the dunes yesterday. And I'm gonna get a big fat diamond."

With that as a backdrop, Karen monopolized the conversation, recounting the highlights of the trip to the Cape the day before, leaving out the episode in the back seat of Mike's SUV.

"They thought I was a movie star. Imagine that?"

"The hair. It's the hair." He ran his fingers through her red hair. "I like it. Makes you look even younger than you do already. Takes me back to our first—"

"My God. That was decades ago. We did it twice, remember? But not at the same time, like today, you horny toad. Maybe if you got out more, you wouldn't need . . ." She rubbed his thigh.

"Nah. I'm pretty contented with Sarah. Don't want to rock the boat too much, blow a good thing."

"Then why are you here?"

"Same reason you are. Just grateful Sarah's museum gig gave us the reason to be here in town. I was getting tired of fantasizing about you and our time way back when."

"We did have fun in school, even if it was only twice."

"Twice." Charlie gazed at the ceiling. "Yeah, I'll never forget the first time. You were the lucky gal who grabbed my key out of the bucket at that frat party."

"The other time. In the back of your car. You cheated on Sarah then, and you're cheating on her now."

"That makes us even . . . again. You're cheating on Michael now, just as you did then. Only difference is you had his son, who I raised."

Karen backed away from Charlie, not wanting to reenact the scene from breakfast on Saturday. "And I'll always be grateful to you . . . and to Sarah." She fiddled with her fingernails.

"Not sure she knows that, Karen. You treat her like shit."

She poured herself another glass of wine, ignoring Charlie's empty glass and his honest assessment of her treatment of his wife.

"If you truly feel that way, why are you here?"

"I'm a lawyer. You need a lawyer—that is, if you really are going to marry Mike."

Karen said she was going to marry Mike if it was the last thing she'd ever do. It was time for payback. She'd given herself to Mike, twice. First, she gave him a son, and then a kidney.

"You actually gave *me* his son."

"But *he's* got Chris now. Ricci and *Son,* remember?"

"True."

"And what did I get? You've seen his house and the life he made with Kassie. And his business is thriving. And it's wrapped up in him and Kassie, with a little something for Chris and that asshole, Bill, probably." Her tears were forming.

Charlie put his arms around her, reminding her that once she married Mike, he'd help make sure all the legal paperwork was drawn up on the business and the house and his investments. He'd be sure she got her fair share of all of Mike's worldly goods.

Karen raised her fist and pounded his chest. "Fair share? I want more than a fair share."

20

Eyes Opened Wide

Mike didn't spend Sunday evening fretting over the baseball tickets, nor did he leave a message when he called Karen to find out what the hell happened to them.

As he changed for bed, thoughts about the whole weekend bombarded his mind. Charlie's key game suggestion still gnawed at him forty-eight hours later. Why would a grown man propose such juvenile behavior? Maybe times had changed more than he realized over the three decades he and Kassie were married. "If only we'd had a wider group of friends," he said to the bedroom's four walls as he tossed his clothes toward the hamper. He shook his head at the futility of that thought. Why waste time on if-onlys and what-ifs? There was no way to go back, to get her to come home. As he leaned to pick up the striped boxer shorts that had fallen short of the basket, he grabbed the edge of what had been Kassie's bureau to prevent himself from falling.

Once he'd regained his bearings, he sat on the side of the waterbed, frankly not caring if it broke and flooded the house. Getting in and out of it was becoming increasingly problematic. Outwardly, he blamed it on the surgery; internally, he knew better. Karen was probably right. Time to get a new bed for the two of them. But there were so many types to choose from these days. Where would they start?

He'd ask her about that, and the tickets, when he saw her next.

After he brushed his teeth, he turned on the tube. He flipped through the politicos, NCIS of who knows which city, and the Yankees game. Forget that. Not in this house, unless they were playing the Red Sox. He settled on some visually appealing show about living in Alaska. That was a place he and Kassie never visited, or ever talked much about visiting, even after his sister had vacationed there and jabbered on about it forever. She'd brought him back a large raven totem he'd displayed on his credenza at the office, in which he squirreled away keys to the lockbox that had precipitated the collapse of his marriage.

He thought about the day before. How he took care of business, literally, ensuring Bill got a piece of the company's pie. For the time being, until sometime in the future when he actually married Karen, all his worldly possessions would be dispersed among Kassie, Chris, and Bill. Well, mostly among those three. He'd left a directive for Kassie to provide a small stipend for a couple of other folks, confident she'd follow his wishes, if it ever came to that.

Lying in his bed in the dark, barely watching the television, Mike grimaced at the lights bouncing off the ceiling, picturing what might have been. That weekend had not at all gone according to plan. The house was not supposed to be quiet that Sunday night. He had his own headache just thinking about the real reason Sarah and Charlie bolted after breakfast on Saturday. Reaching for his phone, he considered giving Charlie a call to make sure everything was okay between them and that his and Sarah's plans for Monday were all taken care of. Did they need a ride anywhere? It was later than he thought. He decided to wait and call Charlie tomorrow, maybe around midday when Sarah would be at the museum doing whatever philanthropists do. He tapped a reminder note on his phone.

And that was that. Monday morning Mike woke up to an invasion of sunshine streaming across his bedspread. He turned on the television to MSNBC, expecting Morning Joe. What? 9:17. When had he ever slept that late before?

He commenced a routine one of the nurses at Boston Clinic last year had recommended. Wiggle toes. Rotate ankles. Place feet flat on bed, knees up. Cross one leg over the other and press on that knee. Repeat on the other side. Then get up. He swung his left leg over the bed and began to lift his body, and some tweak or twinge made him think better of it. Slinking back under the warm covers, he buried his head in his feather pillow, vowing not to part with it when they replaced the bed. When he pulled Kassie's old pillow over his face to block out the morning, the deep lingering smell of her perfume helped further postpone his decision to get up.

After drifting off again, Mike finally decided it was time to greet the day around ten thirty, and he shuffled into a much-needed shower. He stood, letting the warm, not steamy, water flow from his head and down his back, balanced by his palms against the tiles. Why didn't he wash off the sand and stench last night? *I'm slipping.*

Slipping a bit, perhaps, but not completely. In an unusual move, he made the bed, or let's say he pulled up the covers and fluffed the pillows, sniffing Kassie's perfume one last time. Then he went downstairs; retrieved *The Boston Globe* off the front stoop, straightening out the mat he'd flipped over on its side to dry the night before; and settled down at the kitchen table with a cup of coffee. He'd have his morning joe one way or the other.

Something fluttered by the bay window. A bluebird perched on the outdoor thermometer, poking its head to-and-fro. Listening for friends to come by and pay a visit perhaps, or fly off with to a shady pond where they could be protected from the July sun and quench their thirst at the same time.

Midmorning and the mercury registered eighty-two degrees already. The day portended to be a scorcher. "Hotter than a griddle," his mother—*God rest her soul*—would always say on days like this. "Better get your ass out there and enjoy it while the gettin's good," she'd say, literally pushing him out the screen door. Figuring he ought to follow her advice at least once in his life, Mike took his coffee and paper and headed to the back porch, pausing to adjust the air conditioner's thermostat.

That lasted a little more than a quarter hour. He got through the op-ed page, but when he flipped to the comics and a pearl of sweat the size of a penny from his forehead landed smack dab in the middle of Dilbert, Mike folded the paper and went inside. He tossed it on the floor next to his Pleasure Chair, patted his face with a wad of tissue, and moseyed around the first floor until he stood at the doorway of his office. *Now, what did I come in here for? Maybe I'm slipping after all.*

Mike turned around, thinking he'd go back where he started and retrace his steps, and whatever he was planning to do in his office would come back to him. "Isn't that what they say you should do?" He threw back his hands but didn't move. A cold sweat took over where the hot sweat left off. Maybe he should sit down.

The closest chair was behind his desk. He wiped his forehead, around his neck, and under his chin. Lucky for Mike, he took Kassie's lead and stored bottles of water in his office closet. Even luckier, two unopened ones stood like soldiers on his desk within arm's reach. He unscrewed one and guzzled all but an inch of it, leaving some to pour on a napkin that he used like a cold washcloth. He folded the napkin in thirds, applied it to his forehead, and leaned back in his chair, letting his arms flail toward the floor.

Ten minutes later, feeling revived, Mike removed the half ban-
dana he'd concocted with the napkin. "The bills." That's why he'd
come to his office in the first place. He shuffled through a stack of
envelopes on his desk, unfolded his checkbook, and paid the Visa
bill, the electric bill, and the bill to the waste management, a.k.a. gar-
bage, company. Maybe it was time to set up electronic bill pay, just as
Kassie had nagged him to do on more than one occasion.

Almost done with that monthly task, Mike slid his chair over to
the portable shredder. Ugh. Something was stuck. He groaned, and
using the arms of the chair like a cane, he got up to unjam it.

"Holy shit." Red Sox tickets.

21

Where There's a Will

Mike's body may have been slipping, but his mind was as sharp as a tack, if you ignored the most recent incident when he forgot why he needed to go into his home office. Even at his advanced age, he could put two and two together as easily as a four-year-old.

He spun his chair around to check the Seth Thomas antique mantel clock he'd acquired years back when he first launched the business. He always liked that clock, but he had to move it to the house after Kassie's mother had redecorated his office with a more modern, contemporary flair.

By sheer coincidence, as his eyes met the clock's face, it chimed twelve. Bingo. FedEx would've delivered his three packages by now.

"Hello, Wendy. It's Mike Ricci here. Fine. Thanks. You?"

Mike's left knee quivered.

"Did you get a FedEx from me this morning? Saturday, I sent it."

How do you steady a knee that has a mind of its own?

"Good. Is Stephen in today? Can I . . ."

Not only because he was heading out to meet his lawyer but also because he'd soaked through the shirt he was wearing, Mike trudged upstairs and swapped his gray T-shirt for a blue button-down oxford, going full business casual, except for the socks. Too hot. And who'd be looking at his feet anyway?

He cranked up the air conditioning in his car for the fifteen-minute ride to Stephen's office in Arlington, wondering how long it would take to cool it down on his return trip home after it baked in the sun for an hour or so. He'd cross that bridge.

Normally, he'd turn the radio to a jazz station, or even the local news once he settled in his car to occupy his mind and pass the drive time away. That day, more than enough noise occupied his brain waves. No additional distraction required.

Suffice it to say, it was Karen who flashed across his mind's eye. At a stop sign, he shook his head as if to get the cobwebs out, but in reality he struggled with the color of her hair. Most of his life he'd known her as a blonde, and now all, or most, of his visions of her were red.

Putting that quandary aside for the moment, Mike switched the movie reel in his mind to the events of the weekend that provoked him to make changes to his will in the first place and why he was in such a rush to see Stephen that afternoon.

Clearly the first triggering event was dinner Friday night when he realized he hadn't taken care of Bill quite at the level he should, given his longtime loyalty to the company and to him and to Kassie. That Karen and Bill would need to improve their working relationship going forward was an understatement. "Just give it time. What will be will be," Mike said, stuck behind a bus and pounding the steering wheel, though he hadn't a clue who he was more exasperated with at that moment, the bus driver or Karen.

Wanting to take care of Bill had nothing to do with Karen, really. But certain words kept popping up that did. *"Aw shucks"*—Charlie's key-in-the-bag game. *"Headache"*—Sarah's excuse? No, that was Karen's excuse for Sarah cutting their weekend together short when it had just gotten started. *"All taken care of"*—Mike was sure Karen told him she'd put the tickets under the mat. Now he was dead certain she'd lied.

Something was rotten in Newton. He knew it right down to his achy bones. He didn't need Kassie's finely tuned intuition to tell him to beware. There just had to be some intrigue between Charlie and Sarah and Karen beyond the familial issue of Chris. They'd had forty years to come to grips with Chris's adoption. Of course, they'd had only one year to get used to the new state of affairs. But damn it, of all the parties involved, the two folks who should've been pissed beyond belief were Chris and Kassie. It was their relationship, their future, that went to hell in a hand basket.

For all Mike knew, the friction among Karen-Sarah-Charlie could be traced all the way back to college. Did Charlie's key game suggestion rekindle a smoldering fire among them? *Who the hell knows?* And since Charlie and Sarah were heading back to Chicago that night, there was no need to dwell on it or solve it now. Yet, if he got the chance, he still planned on reaching out to Charlie to clear the air. Mano a mano. *We'll see how the afternoon goes.*

Mike didn't need to be behind a car with a Red Sox bumper sticker to remind him Karen's lying about the baseball tickets was the match in the powder barrel—the driving force behind his need to see Stephen to make sure his affairs were in order.

From his vantage point, two problems existed. Karen's lying, the first and most obvious. A clear affront against him and an insult to the dignity of their relationship. But secondly, why in God's name did Karen want to screw up a day at Fenway Park for Bill and his family? No one in their right mind living in the Boston area would ever purposely shred game tickets to pieces and prevent someone from going to a Red Sox game. It was mean and cruel. *A sin, yeah, that's what it was. A sin.* Plain and simple.

All kidding aside, what was in it for her? Hell if he knew. Only she would be able to answer that, and Mike was willing to give her a chance to explain herself even if whatever her reasons were didn't save her.

Of course, there were other red flags too, inconsistencies over the weekend that gave him the heebie-jeebies. Kassie would call them clues. Maybe she was right. Whatever moniker you applied, the chill traveling up his back and goosebumps on his arms gave him pause.

Why did Karen bring up Barry after the concert, after spending a nice day with him? Why was she so pushy and embarrassing at breakfast? Why did she leave his phone in the car when they hiked the dunes? Why did she pressure him to officially propose when it was a given they'd get married at some point after the divorce? *Yeah, what was that all about?* Did he really get down on one knee?

For that matter, why did she sleep at her apartment in Charlestown after he'd just proposed? What woman does that? Isn't there an unwritten rule that all women follow? When your man proposes, you go fuck his brains out as soon as humanly possible. Didn't she know the quickie in the back seat of his car was just an appetizer? She had to have known there'd be more lovin' in the oven once they returned from the Cape.

So I was tired and slept all the way home. I'd have done her even if I wasn't up to it. Wouldn't have been the first time I turned on my charm, and my skills.

But Karen didn't stick around to find out. She didn't follow the rules. Didn't even come in to pee after a long drive. What woman doesn't do that, for goodness sake? She hotfooted her way to Charlestown. Didn't even call or text him when she got there.

Mike pulled into a visitor's parking spot alongside Stephen's office and reached for his phone that occupied the seat next to him. He palmed it to eye level. *This explains it.* She knew Bill would try to call him about the tickets. No phone was no accident. She manipulated him. Big time. All weekend. Did she take him for a fool? Was it the first time, or the last?

As he sat in Stephen's waiting room flipping through one of the dozen or so law journals staggered on the coffee table, Mike thought about all the hoops he'd jumped through during the last year—the surgery, Chris joining the firm, the divorce. He'd learned the importance of staying on top of the legal aspects of his life, even if he hadn't done the same on the medical side.

The uneasy feeling he had about Karen when he went to bed after talking with Bill the night before became a reality shitshow when he saw the tickets half-shredded that morning. Piecing together the rest of the pie on his way to Stephen's reinforced in his mind he had some serious decisions to make about his future. Taking care of the business was a good first step. He'd deal with Karen later.

"So a codicil will take care of it?" Mike sat across from Stephen, his lawyer of thirty years.

"Yes, Michael. Since you were heading in, I had my paralegal draw it up. It should be ready for your signature and witnessing shortly. Now tell me, what's this all about?"

Since Mike wasn't making substantial changes to his will, mostly adjusting the business ownership percentages to leave something to Bill, he focused on that as the reason he sat there sockless. He felt no need to bore Stephen about his issues with Karen and decisions he knew he'd have to make. Those were personal, not legal. At this juncture, Karen was only marginally in his will, with a directive to Kassie to continue the stipend he'd started after Barry had died, should anything happen to him. Until he sorted things out with her, his will, including the business side of his estate, would remain the way it was being updated that day.

After the paperwork was signed and notarized, Mike and Stephen sat for a spell. Stephen peppered him with questions about the health of the business, his relationship with Karen, his own body and soul. If it were any other lawyer than Stephen, Mike would accuse them of probing for too much information. But this was Stephen, a longtime friend and confidant.

"You've gone through a lot this past year, Mike," Stephen said, tweaking his mustache. "How you really doing?"

The business was booming. Chris was a youthful shot in the arm it needed to rise to another level. They were now competing with firms who had embraced social media a step ahead of them.

"Funny thing, though. Working with Chris every day, I think of him as a partner, not my son. Not sure why. Folks like Bill see a resemblance. I just don't get it."

"Any residual resentment about his affair with Kassie?" Stephen asked.

"Resentment or regret? Guess it depends on who you talk to. Seems they both have moved on. He's got another long-distance romance, I hear. Imagine that. You'd think he'd look for someone in his own backyard. And I hear Kassie's in Europe, I think Italy again. Wonder if she's wishing for lightning to strike in a bottle a second time."

"Well, it did for you and Karen, right?"

"Right. We'll see."

"Looks like we're done here," Stephen said in a dismissive, yet familiar, way—a way Mike customarily used himself when he needed, or wanted, to move on to bigger and better things. "I'll let you know when we get the court date for the divorce." Stephen patted Mike on the shoulder, his hand squeezing it ever so comfortingly.

"Thanks," Mike said aloud, and *I needed that* to himself.

22

Men and Directions

Mike stood outside his car in Stephen's parking lot, letting the air conditioner work its magic—the bridge he predicted he'd need to cross came to pass. Unpredictable was the bile taste invading his throat and an unexpected queasiness he usually felt after overindulging. He got in the car, rifled through the console, and popped an Altoid. That should do it. *That's weird.* It didn't.

Of course, it wasn't what he ate but that he hadn't eaten all day that was his problem. It was already after two. No real breakfast or lunch. Not quite living according to doctor's orders. He pulled into a diner and solved that issue.

A cheeseburger and fries later, Mike decided to take a bite off Eve's apple and tempt fate. Or if not tempt it, at least see if he could redirect it from the downward spiral path it seemed to be taking.

Mike needed to see Karen. He had to find out what the hell was going on with her. Though he felt he was her puppet and she was pulling the strings, he believed she must have a reason for behaving so out of character. She gave him her kidney. Gave him life. He owed her the chance to explain things before he told her he couldn't marry her under the circumstances.

In his mind, he practiced the words, rather than being spontaneous as he was once too often with Kassie. The word *vasectomy* popped in his head not out of nowhere. If only he hadn't blurted it out. If he'd kept his mouth shut, he was certain they would've worked things out as they had multiple times before. He let out a big sigh. Of course, that was before he knew she had Chris on the side. Oh well, that was ancient history. Back to current events.

He checked Karen's whereabouts on his Find My Friends app. She was in Charlestown. Not at the office. Not in transit to his house, or off shopping with his credit cards—her favorite pastime. He keyed her address into the car's GPS. He'd figure out what to say to her on his way.

Without a doubt, Karen would be surprised to see him. He'd only been to her apartment once before when he helped her move in. Never a real reason for him to go there, before now. Best he be honest with her, perhaps break her heart, on her turf. Or was he just being a coward, not wanting her in his territory? What would he do if she melted down, cried in his family room? How would he get her to leave? Could he simply say to her, "Looks like we're done here," the way Stephen had, and show her the door?

Maybe it wouldn't be as difficult as he feared. She'd immediately sense something was wrong just by his showing up unannounced. The look on his face could be more than enough signal she was in dire straits. If she had a conscience at all, she knew what she had done with the tickets was deplorable. And that by now he and Bill would've talked, compared notes.

A tiny voice in his head repeated over and over, *Give her a chance to explain. I owe her that much.* He could show another side of him— be magnanimous, big-hearted, forgiving even. Like him, she'd had a helluva year, one in which she got as well as she gave. Reuniting with

her son, sacrificing her health all to save him, uprooting herself, starting a new job in a strange city. All traumatic life events categorized by
insurance and health experts as major stressors. He chuckled. Boston
might as well be a foreign country when compared to Elephant Butte.

Another side of his brain, he didn't know if it was the left or the
right, whispered, *Cut her some slack.* Wait until he saw her face-to-
face and heard what she had to say. Remain calm, cool, and collected.
Adopt a mantra. That's it. *Vasectomy.* Repeating the word *vasectomy*
would slow him down, remind him to not shoot off his mouth, to
think before he passed judgment. Now was not the time to adopt
his wife's not-so-endearing knee-jerk reactions and lack of filter.
Creating his own version of Bad Kassie at this stage in his life would
not serve him well, though he was certain Kassie, bad or otherwise,
wouldn't be silenced when she got a load of this story.

What do ya know? It was shaping up to be his lucky day after
all. A mammoth Chevrolet Suburban pulled out of a parking spot
on the street adjacent to Karen's apartment building. He wheeled in
his SUV, which looked like a Dinky car in comparison, shut off the
engine, and decided to gather his thoughts, rest a moment, but not
long enough for the heat of the sun to replace the cool air in the car.

Mike drew in as deep a breath as he could muster. *It's now or
never. Just go for it.* As he stepped out of the car and turned to press
the automatic key lock, he saw Karen emerge from the building. At
least he thought it was her. Though the woman's back was to him, the
red hair was unmistakable.

"It can't be," he murmured. The woman, walking less than half a
football field away from him, clung to the arm of some tall dude wearing a blue Red Sox hat. His initial instinct to call out to her vanished
as he watched the couple, their arms swinging to-and-fro, amble to
an idling black car on the street on the opposite side of her building
from where he spied them. Mike covered his squinting eyes, focusing
on the incident unfolding before him. His bare feet felt glued to his

shoes, though he had no desire to move even if he could. A little bird told him to let the scene play out no matter what the outcome.

Seconds later, before the man slid into the back seat of the car, he released the woman's arm, patted her on the ass, and pulled her in good and tight for a shamelessly hearty kiss in broad daylight in front of God and everybody, including Mike. He swallowed hard as the woman turned to leave her lover. He saw Karen clearly now. And the man too, who shouted, "Hey, KC," as he tipped his cap to her. Well, well, who'd a thunk it? Charlie Gaines, a paramour, in all his pompous glory, got into the car and sped away.

Mike got into his car too, and cranked up the A/C. No GPS needed on this trip. He knew his way home.

23

Mother, Please

Confident that her body clock and need to scratch would wake her, Kassie didn't set the alarm on either her phone or the small digital clock on the table next to the bed. In fact, an urge to pee coupled with a sliver of sunlight peeking through the curtains provided key indicators she should get up and set Tuesday in motion.

6:12 a.m. She tiptoed to the bathroom, held the door handle steady, and closed the door with only a slight click. Sitting on the john, she calculated her meeting with Mimi was in less than four hours. If she allowed thirty minutes to get there by car, she'd need to leave the hotel at nine thirty.

That leaves me three hours to get my shit together.

The face she saw in the bathroom mirror didn't give her any confidence that getting ready would be an easy task. Between the alcohol and allergy, her skin drooped and the dark circles under her eyes appeared as big as dinner plates. On the bright side, she remembered kissing Chris on Pont Neuf after dinner and walking barefoot back to the hotel. A vision of him sitting next to her on the bed passed like wildfire through her mind. Maybe she was dreaming. She placed her hands on her thighs, fingers spread. Two rings. Her wedding band on her left hand, a new brilliant ring on her right.

Her feet twitched. She checked them out. Still bubbly, but not as red and raw as when they'd returned from dinner and Chris applied the cold soothing gel.

But then, her left shoulder spoke to her. She turned toward the mirror. "You've got to be kidding me," she whispered, not wanting to disturb Chris. He deserved to sleep even if she couldn't. He had as bad a night as she, and it was all her fault. She planted her two hands on the sink and bowed her chin to her chest. *Why this on all days?* How could she bring her *A* game to the meeting when her body was on strike? At this point her only saving grace was the new black dress with its three-quarter sleeves, enough to cover most of the crud creeping over her body.

How stupid she was to let her guard down. A few years back after breaking out in hives after she drank cranberry juice containing pomegranates, her mother warned her to check the ingredients in recipes she didn't create and control. She'd totally forgotten how popular pomegranate cosmos had become. Being with Chris disarmed her, made her careless. What was she thinking? Obviously she wasn't. Enough of that recklessness.

Kassie grabbed her blue silk robe, the tube of goo, and headed for the balcony. The French doors resisted her push, the heat of July expanding the wood. She welcomed the coolness of the dawn on the back of her thighs as she lowered herself ever so quietly onto a wrought iron chair, hoping the scraping of its feet on the deck wouldn't wake Chris or their neighbors.

As she rubbed a thin layer of medicine onto her shoulder and slid into the robe, keeping it as loose as possible, her stomach gurgled. Good thing she didn't live in Paris full time. She'd be as big as a house. The smell of buttery croissants wafting up from the boulangerie across the street tantalized her brain. Her mouth watered. Even if her body was scarred, her senses were working in overdrive. *Don't give in. Wait for Chris. Be patient.* Yeah, like that's going to work.

She knew what would—or hoped would—work. *Focus. Breathe.* Kassie positioned her feet side by side on the deck, bowed her head, closed her eyes, laid her arms on her thighs with the palms of her hands open to the deck roof above her, and breathed. *Focus.* She willed the inner conversations competing for her brain cells to relax. *Chill.*

The thumb on her right hand reached across her palm and rubbed a foreign object. Her left-hand thumb mirrored the right. *Don't look. Breathe.* She envisioned a small red box. Cartier. Not Tiffany, but what the hell. He'd said, "Kassandra O'Callaghan, marry me."

Marry me thoughts morphed into *Mimi.* How could she prepare to meet her boss's peer without a defined agenda? *I'll just cook one up of my own. I'm good at that.* She envisioned her list of clients on her whiteboard. Who's the biggest? Most profitable? Most impressive? What could she say about the success of the Boston office that would cause Mimi's jaw to drop? What personal achievements could she weave into their conversation without being too much of a braggart? *Stop overthinking. You'll do fine. Just breathe.*

A morning breeze passed. Her knees jiggled. *Not now, mother.* Despite imagining external forces out of her control, Kassie sensed her body settling, praying if she found peace in the moment, the bad pomegranate juju would subside.

Starting at the top of her head, she tapped into her energy field, steering all her spiritual and emotional positivity throughout her limbs, commanding all the negative forces that allowed the pomegranate seeds to invade her blood system to escape through her fingers and toes.

A warm wind blew her robe open. She tied it tighter, trying with all her might to reject the distraction. What time was it getting to be?

Her phone. His phone. A call he didn't take at dinner. The passport stamp. Athens. Her thumb rubbed the foreign object again. *Inhale.*

She'd given him space last night to do something that was unthinkable five days ago. She could've shut it down, turned him down, but didn't. Because she loved him. *Exhale.*

Kassie opened her eyes. Chris sat in the wrought iron chair across from her. Tea and pastries were spread out on a white linen napkin on the table.

"You were off somewhere. Somewhere wonderful, I hope."

"Trying to get my act together. Trying is the operative word. It's spreading." She pushed the robe off her shoulder.

She couldn't miss Chris's lying reaction. Eyebrows up, eyebrows down. "It's not that bad. Take another pill before you head out."

"I'd better eat before I do that." Kassie sipped her tea and reached for a raspberry scone.

"I see you're still wearing it. The ring." He pointed at her hand and disarmed her with his Crest toothpaste smile.

She splayed her fingers and raised her right hand to the sky. "Incredible, Chris. I've never seen anything like it."

"That's the idea. I wanted something unique for an unusual woman. To represent our unorthodox relationship."

"I think you succeeded on all counts, including your alliteration. Even at this hour." She turned her hand toward him as though she were showing it to him for the first time. "Didn't notice until this morning. It looks like a curved nail with diamonds at its head and tip." She held both hands out, comparing the traditional rings from Mike she'd worn for thirty years to Chris's *un*conventional offering.

"Symbolic, wouldn't you say?" Chris puffed out his chest, rooster-like.

"Are we fixing something that's broken?" Kassie scrunched her eyes and pursed her lips.

"Or nailing down our love once and for all?"

"You understand, right? Like I told you last night, it's not an official engagement ring until after the divorce."

"But you will marry me. . . ."

"I will." Kassie walked two steps to Chris and lowered herself onto his lap. "Let's just say we're engaged to be engaged."

"Let's just say we do what we ought to have done last night."

Making love to Chris was not on Kassie's agenda that morning. With her skin screaming like the aftermath of a bikini wax and her mind racing as if she was on the final lap of the Indianapolis 500, she wondered if it was possible for her body to relax enough to enjoy a roll in the hay with Chris.

Silly girl. Have sex with Christopher Gaines? The man with the Midas touch. With a tongue more talented than a giraffe's. And fingers able to find the G-spot . . . *oh* . . . in a flicker. Chris made making love a delicious appetizer ahead of her audience with Mimi. Kassie didn't know the French word for orgasm, but she knew she'd had it when it happened.

Spent, Kassie relished being wrapped in Chris's muscular, warm arms that morning, any morning. The tips of his capable fingers danced along her back. Their panting subsided, their breath syncing to a natural rhythm. Give it time, and they'd both be sound asleep.

Oh shit. Kassie raised one eyelid, squinting. 8:07. She slapped his chest and bounded out of bed. "Look what you've done."

"What? I thought that was damn good."

"Not that, you goof. It's after eight. I need to get my show on the road."

As one might expect, Kassie had a get-ready-for-work routine down to a science. Forty-five minutes without fail. But that was at home, assuming she'd laid out her outfit, lingerie, shoes, and jewelry the night before. God forbid a wardrobe malfunction. Except she wasn't home, and other than knowing where her dress was hanging, the rest of her accoutrements were scattered about the hotel room and in her luggage. She calculated she'd need seventy-five minutes to make herself presentable, which would land her close to her nine thirty goal. Hopefully taxis were easy to flag at that hour, otherwise she'd be sunk.

Feeling pretty perky after the tea, scone, and sex—especially the sex—Kassie kicked herself into high gear. She was able to shower in ten minutes, not her usual twenty, due mostly to her inability to shave her legs with the spreading rash. Luckily, Gabriella recommended light tan pantyhose, which would serve to cover the rash and discourage her from scratching.

After Chris glided the black sheath over her head, she secured the new wide silver belt around her waist. With her hands on her hips, she swiveled from side to side, checking out how she looked in the mirror. The Cartier ring sparkled as bright as the belt. She touched it for good luck.

Hurry up. 9:23. Almost witching hour. She dumped the contents of her new purse on the bed. "Ha, I forgot about this," she said, holding the Eiffel Tower fork in front of her nose. "See, I have more than your ring to remind me of last night."

"You stole that."

"Duh. Like every other tourista. It's baked into the price. I bet hundreds of forks a day walk out the door." She turned it on its tines and walked it across the bedspread. "Some families probably end up with a place setting for four . . . or eight . . . if they should be so lucky." Kassie continued despite Chris shaking his head. "Believe me, it's true." She laughed.

"Okay, Doris Payne. Just don't—"

"Who's that?"

"I'll tell you later. You better get going."

Kassie finished reassembling the contents of her purse. "Oh, crap. I have two purple pens, but no business cards, no notebook, just this small travel piece of shit. Won't do any good—"

"Here. Take mine."

Kassie swiped the black leather journal out of Chris's hand and gave him a quick smooch.

"Wish me luck."

"You won't need it."

"What I need is a cab."

"Not to worry. Tanya's outside waiting for you."

Why am I not surprised?

Still breaking in her shoes, Kassie headed down the stairs one step at a time. The leather tops rubbed against her chafed skin, reminding her she needed to be on her toes in more ways than one.

"Have you been waiting long?" Kassie asked Tanya, who stood near the rear of the car, holding the passenger door open for her, and hoped her tone came across as bright as the Tuesday morning sun.

In the few minutes since she'd left Chris in his boxer shorts, she'd decided accepting Tanya's presence in her life that day, and most likely throughout the remainder of their Paris vacation, was better than bitching about it. Perhaps the antihistamine she'd taken an hour ago had knocked out Bad Kassie for a while. One could only hope. That morning Kassie needed to be great, not just good, Kassie—new business genius, colleague extraordinaire, *mistress of the universe*. Well, she had that one covered.

Kassie climbed in the car and settled in, her new bag on her left. She placed Chris's leather journal on her lap. Bowing her head and taking a deep cleansing breath, she noticed three bumps had just popped up on her right ring finger. *Shit.* Maybe she should call off the meeting, postpone it until later in the week. Too many distractions. Her body was inflamed, and her mind was on the man she'd left in the hotel.

Too late. Tanya had already pulled away from the curb, and Mimi was expecting her in less than half an hour. It would be rude for her to cancel, and almost impossible to explain. Oh, can't make it today. *My skin is on fire, and anyway, I'd rather stay in bed with my fiancé.*

"I see you said yes." Tanya interrupted Kassie's half-hearted attempt at changing the course of the day.

"Excuse me?"

"You're wearing the ring."

Kassie looked down and then up at Tanya, whom she could see looking at her in the rearview mirror.

"Yes, I did. How—"

"Bravo! You are engaged."

"Engaged to be engaged." Kassie held up her wedding band. "Still married. Not quite divorced yet."

"You know what they say?"

"No, what do they say?"

"You should marry the second guy you love."

"Never heard that. Given Chris was a child when I married his . . ." Kassie caught herself from sharing too much personal information. She changed the subject. "Ever heard of Doris Payne?"

"Sure. She's a legend here in France, and in America, I'd imagine."

"A legend for what?"

"She's a jewel thief. A convicted one, at that. Probably in her eighties by now if she's still alive. Rumor has it she stole a ten-carat diamond ring from a jewelry store in Monte Carlo back in the seventies. It was worth a half million dollars."

"Why a rumor?"

"Police never found the ring."

"Wow." Kassie stared out the window as they stopped at an intersection. "Speaking of rings. How'd you know about this one?" She lifted her right hand and wiggled her finger.

"Chris told me that when you were shopping at La Maison de

Paris, he went to Tiffany's to get the pendant and then to Cartier to pick up the ring."

"You mean, to pick it *out*."

"No. Quite clearly, he said *up*. It was ready for him."

Really. Suddenly the trip to Paris sounded less spontaneous than she originally thought. Chris was more presumptuous than she gave him credit for, or maybe he just knew her better than she knew herself. Whatever. He knew she loved him and this time she wouldn't let him go.

"How long before we're there?" Kassie had no desire to question Tanya any longer about her cozy conversations with Chris.

"About ten minutes."

Kassie opened the journal, flipping through it to find blank pages she could utilize. One page stopped her cold. A mind map.

Circled in blue in the center of the page was the word *LEXI*. Probably a name. A female name. Branching away from the center on the left was a series of *L* words in green: *lovely, lusty, leggy, lips, longing.* On the opposite side were *C* words in purple: *curly, curvy, chesty, crave.* Along the right side of the page, stacked one letter on top of the other, was *GREECE.*

Kassie's breathing accelerated. She adjusted her glasses, unsure if her eyes were focused correctly. They were. And there was more. Reading left to right were three words in black: *conflicted-confused-tangled.*

Her fingers walked to the bottom of the page. Her name, *KASSIE,* was written in calligraphy inside a red heart. She didn't know he knew calligraphy. Go figure. Arrows leading away from the heart contained the words *affirm, commit, adore, engage, swoop.*

She clutched the armrest. Now was not the time to spiral out of control. *Who the hell is Lexi and why is she juxtaposed with me on a page in Chris's journal?* Just two of the questions the lovely Mr. Gaines would have to answer.

"We're here. Kassie? Kassie, we're here."

Getting out of the car, Kassie gave Tanya her hand, afraid if she didn't, she would've collapsed to the pavement. She looked up at the nine-story ultra-modern glass building; her eyes widened not only in awe but to prevent tears from falling.

Tanya handed Kassie her card. "Call me when you're ready. I'll stay in the area."

"*Merci,* Tanya." Kassie hugged her, hanging on for dear life.

Kassie checked in with the guard in the lobby, who directed her to Calibri Marketing Group on the eighth floor. The elevator ride gave her enough time to transform herself from whatever she was—wife, stepmom, fiancée, *fool*—to the consummate marketing executive.

"*Bonjour,* Madame O'Callaghan."

Here we go again. "Call me Kassie, *s'il vous plaît.*"

"Mimi is running a few minutes late. Please have a seat. Can I get you anything?"

"No. Thank you."

Kassie made her way to one of the four black leather square-shaped chairs in the lobby's waiting area. The chair was bigger than she, so she had a choice to make—either sit uncomfortably on the edge or squiggle her butt to the rear of the seat. Moving one side of her cheek, then the other, she squiggled. Once positioned profession-ally with her two feet barely touching the floor, she couldn't help but notice how her black dress blended in with the chair. Amused, she imagined anyone looking at her from a distance might only see her silver belt and think she was a tuxedo slung across the chair. Shifting her body to the left, she wedged her red purse between her butt and the arm of the chair. *That should help. I don't want to fade into the woodwork.*

When she'd conquered the chair, she eyeballed the rest of the seating area. Modern artwork with splashes of every shade of every primary color interrupted the monochromatic black and white furniture and stark white walls. And with the panorama of Paris in full view out of the nearly floor-to-ceiling windows, Kassie knew she wasn't in Kansas anymore—in spite of the red shoes she wore. This was Paris.

Forgetting how difficult it was to settle herself into the chair, Kassie pulled herself up and walked over to the receptionist.

"Pardon me. Can I give you this card now? Would you be kind enough to call my driver when I'm ready to leave?"

"*Mais bien sûr.*"

"May I ask your name?"

"Madame Bisset. You can call me Patricia."

But of course.

"Patricia?" she mouthed as she returned to the seating area and reacquainted herself with the chair. *Well, Mother, you finally made it to Paris. I'd tell you to stop following me.* "But I need you now."

"Can I get you something, Kassie?" Patricia, the receptionist, asked.

"No, just talking to my . . . my . . . self."

24

Tea for Two Times Two

Not knowing how long Mimi would keep her waiting, Kassie contemplated what to do in the meantime. She could turn on her phone, read messages and news. But that would be rude. She kept it off and tucked it in her purse. She could stare at the page in Chris's journal where he compared someone named Lexi to her. But that would boil her blood and frustrate her when he wasn't there to confront. She chose, instead, to ignore what was out of her control, at least for the time being, and do what she did best.

Kassie pulled out a purple pen from her purse, opened Chris's journal to a blank page, and started a list, actually a two-column ledger—*Mimi* on the left, *MeMe* on the right. She chuckled, two puffs of air escaping her nostrils. She glanced at Patricia, who was busy doing whatever. If she'd heard Kassie's mini snort, she didn't let on.

Under the Mimi column, she doodled areas of inquiry Mimi might possibly explore. Why in Paris? How long? Alone? Kassie's right-hand thumb rubbed the ring. She wondered how easy this new habit would be to break once she moved it to the rightful left hand?

Ten minutes passed. No sign of Mimi. She continued her list-making, still focused on the Mimi side. Boston and Tom? New clients? Strength of the business? *Nothing I can't handle.*

Kassie shifted her attention to the other side of her ledger. What would she ask Mimi? Family? Daughter—four or five now? Kassie frowned at the thought of discussing how successful Mimi was at balancing family and career when she'd never had the chance to give it a go herself. Nevertheless, she'd bite her lip and swallow her pride and go down that route if need be.

A vision of her Uncle Dan flickered through her mind. What was it he always said? *Remember the end game.* She scribbled nonsensical circle and square shapes at the bottom of the page. Killing time, willing her thoughts to stay centered. Time check. 10:20, according to the multicolored ball clock on the wall behind Patricia.

She'd already waited twenty minutes for Mimi, a managing director, which was five minutes longer than she'd have given her college professors. She couldn't leave as she would've then. She decided to suck it up and wait. Back to her list. "Where was I?"

The end game. How could she remember it when she didn't know what the end game was? Tom hadn't given her much of a clue. Mimi had an idea to bounce off her. He could've given her more information than that.

How's business? Kassie wrote in the MeMe column. She drew a small arrow and then wrote the word *Idea*, followed by four question marks. Across the bottom of the page she wrote END GAME and underscored it twice.

Nearly thirty minutes passed. Still no sign of Mimi. Maybe if she went to the ladies' room. It's like buttering a wedge of bread at a restaurant. As soon as you do, your main meal arrives.

Kassie stood.

Patricia stood. "Mimi will see you now."

The Paris arm of the Calibri Marketing Group had half the staff of the home office in Boston. Comparatively—actually, to be honest, there was no comparison—the Paris office shimmered and shined in a way the Boston office never could or would. Tom was too image conscious, always concerned clients would accuse them of charging exorbitant fees if they worked in the lap of luxury. Apparently, French clients preferred to align themselves with firms as good as or better than themselves.

Taking it all in, Kassie followed Patricia down a long hallway, past a conference room large enough for twelve seated. The transparent glass walls had the faintest smoky tint and three-inch Eiffel Towers conspicuously etched in the glass, most likely to prevent head-on collisions.

"*Pause-café*," Patricia said as they passed a small room where three people laughed as one of the fellows shared something on his device.

"Coffee break?"

"*Oui.*" Patricia led the way up a spiral staircase, stopping at a doorway at the top. She stepped aside and pointed a French-manicured index finger to a chair in front of a white desk large enough to land a small airplane, or perhaps a drone, where Mimi sat with her eyes down, obscured by a seventeen-inch Apple laptop screen.

"*Bonjour*, Kassie. Give me a couple of moments, *s'il vous plaît*. Finishing an email."

Haven't I given you more than thirty moments already? Bad Kassie's voice echoed inside her head.

Nodding her permission to take her time, Kassie lowered herself into a leather high-back swivel chair that resembled marshmallows in its look and feel—much better than the lobby chairs—and tried to suppress her alter ego by scanning the office. No matter how hard she tried, she couldn't take her eyes off Mimi in her ladybug red V-neck top with sleeves that flowed to her elbows. Her face looked older than Kassie remembered. But then, she probably looked older too, to Mimi.

Cut yourself some slack, girl, you've been through a lot the last five years. She touched the tip of each finger as Bad Kassie silently counted them off—her mother's death, Mike's illness, the divorce. Oh, and the on-again, off-again, on-again Chris affair. *How many is that?* Too many to count and no time to dwell on the past. *Time to choose a different fork in the road.*

A different fork? The Eiffel Tower fork. Swiping it must've been a sign. A good one. She reached for the spot just below her neck. Not there. Her teeth gnawed a section of the inside of her mouth. *Damn it.* In a rush to get ready, she'd left the new necklace on the desk before she'd showered. Another sign? A not so good one. *KO, focus.* This time it was her mother's voice she heard.

All right already, she'd focus. On Mimi again. Her hair was different than she remembered too. The style. A ponytail. Unusual, Kassie thought, for an executive to wear a long ponytail adorned with a red bow and a flip at the end. And the color. Where had she seen that dark silver tone, almost the shade of gunmetal, before? Her eyes narrowed as she touched the sparkly belt around her waist. Gabriella, of course. Leave it to the French to take gray, and its many silvery shades, and make it trendy for women of all ages.

"*Bonjour* again, Kassie. Sorry about that," Mimi said, remaining seated. Her ponytail swung as she swore at the computer. At least Kassie assumed Mimi swore. Whatever she said was in French, after all.

Taking her lead from Mimi, Kassie stayed seated and leaned across the desk to shake Mimi's ringless hand, which seemed warmer than she expected and a bit swollen. *Probably the July humidity.* Kassie hoped her new nail ring hadn't scratched Mimi's palm.

With that, their tête-à-tête commenced, pretty much flowing according to Kassie's checklist, which remained out of sight in the closed journal she'd rested on the desk. When Mimi asked why she happened to be in Paris, Kassie kept her response short and sweet. "Vacation. It'd been a while since I visited your beautiful city." Kassie refrained from detailing how she'd arrived there from Venice, or from saying, "I'm here with my husband's son, whom, by the way, I'm going to marry." She had no desire to be schooled on the French word for cougar . . . or stepmom.

With her right hand sitting snugly under her left palm, she thumbed the ring again. She couldn't quite figure if she was developing a nervous tic or if the ring was quickly becoming her source of strength, her totem, supplanting either the gondola or the Tower.

When it was her turn to take the lead, Kassie sucked it up, was the good corporate colleague from across the pond, and asked about Mimi's family. Not surprisingly, Mimi beamed, pointing to a photo of her daughter playing soccer. Kassie would've done the same thing if she was sitting in Mimi's seat and had family to crow about. Gratefully, this gave Kassie a segue from a painful discussion about children to a topic more to her liking: sports and France's recent World Cup victory. "Felicitations!"

"Sorry the USA was absent this year," Mimi pouted unconvincingly.

Always the competitor, Kassie squirmed, planting her feet on the floor, pushing out her chest, and rubbing her hands along the arms of the chair. "Well, we have baseball and football. American football. I predict it's going to be a championship year for the Red Sox and Patriots." *You say that every year.*

"I'm not familiar . . ." Mimi rolled her chair back, signaling a shift in the meeting's agenda. She stood with her fingers touching the desk, seeming to brace herself.

Kassie's head and shoulders reared. Her eyes grew large as Mimi's very pregnant stomach popped out of a body-hugging jumpsuit that resembled comfy jammies, adorned with a red and white polka-dotted sash below her very pregnant boobs.

"Let's move to the couch." Mimi approached Kassie, who by now was also standing out of necessity and in awe. When Mimi pointed to an adjoining sitting area and touched Kassie's elbow, she wasn't sure Mimi was being polite or if she needed to hold on to Kassie for dear life. *This woman's huge.*

"If you don't mind, I'll take the chair." Mimi laughed. "It's easier to get in and out of these days."

"I can only imagine." *That's an understatement.*

As if on cue, Patricia entered the office with a silver tray and placed it between them on the glass coffee table.

"How about tea? Croissants?"

"*Non, merci.* I had—" *How many pastries can one person eat in a day?*

"Hope you don't mind. I'm eating for three these days."

"Oh my goodness! Twins! How exciting." Kassie fake smiled. *You've got to be kidding. Not fair.* "When are you due? Oops, maybe I shouldn't have asked that."

"*Au contraire.* That is precisely the question you should be asking, Kassie. And precisely the reason Thomas and I wanted you here today."

"*Excusez-moi?*" Flummoxed beyond all comprehension by what she was seeing and hearing, Kassie blurted out one of the five or six French expressions she and almost every American knew. She hoped she hadn't given Mimi an open invitation to continue the meeting in her native language.

"With all due respect, I'm not sure I understand. Why is your having twins sometime in the not-too-distant future the precise reason I'm here today?"

Mimi ignored Kassie's declination of tea and filled a porcelain

cup for her anyway and placed a delicate matching plate with a croissant on the table in front of her as well.

"Here. This is going to take a while."

Before Kassie knew it, an hour and a half had flown by, and she
still wasn't clear as to why she was there. Mimi had spent most
of the time telling Kassie about a small firm in London they were
considering merging with—*acquiring* would be a better way to
describe it. Mimi said she and Thomas, not Tom—*if the French are
so formal, why doesn't she call me Kassandra*—decided the London
firm would open a market for the company that would complement their current portfolio and was expected to grow rapidly over
the next decade. She and Mimi discussed the pros and cons, and it
seemed the pros had it.

"Except for one small detail." Mimi stood, balancing herself with
both hands on the small of her back.

Kassie was relieved, literally, when Mimi suggested a bathroom break. Mimi directed Kassie to a ladies' room down the hall.
Naturally, Mimi had a private *salle de bain* adjoining her office. Oh,
how Kassie would love a peek in there. Everything about Mimi and
the Paris office screamed *magnifique* and *élégant*.

"I could get used to working here," Kassie mumbled as she
washed her hands in the rectangular white ceramic sink with the
soap dispenser, hot and cold water faucets, and hand dryer all conve-
niently lined up in a row. The choice of three hand lotions—lavender,
shea butter, and aloe—was a nice added touch. She considered lavender but opted for the less fragrant aloe lotion in deference to Mimi.
Didn't some scents make pregnant women gag? *I may be jealous, but
I am not spiteful.* She waved her index finger at herself in the mirror
and then combed through her hair, imagining what she'd look like
as a silvery blonde.

When she returned to Mimi's office suite, Mimi was sitting at a glass dining table overlooking the Seine.

"Thought we could continue talking over lunch. I'm starved." Mimi patted her bloated belly.

The china on the two placemats matched the teacups and plates from earlier.

"This pattern is exquisite. Unlike anything I've ever seen."

"*Merci.* I believe they're from the Philippe Deshoulieres collection."

"All the colors—red, lime green, aqua, lilac, pink—are so vibrant. The design looks like wallpaper."

"I think it's crafted in the image of Persian and Indian silk. If you like, I could find out where you can purchase place settings right here in Paris."

Kassie flashed back to the two china collections she already had, the one her mother had purchased from a door-to-door salesman back in the day, and the one she'd acquired herself one place setting at a time after she and Mike were married. Both sets were more than thirty years old and looked it. Maybe she was due something modern and chic once she and Chris were hitched. *Oh God, Chris.* She looked at her watch as inconspicuously as possible. Almost twelve thirty.

"Are you supposed to be somewhere else?"

"No, Mimi, I'm right where I should be."

"Before our break, I was talking about the merger, hmm, acquisition, and mentioned there's one small glitch . . . actually two."

25

As Luck Would Have It

On autopilot, Kassie drifted into the elevator and pressed lobby, even though someone else was a step ahead of her. She ignored the head-nod greetings of the three other occupants as she joined them for the ride down, instead fancying herself floating to the ground. If only she had an umbrella like Mary Poppins.

Acting managing director. Not full-on managing director. But she could live with that. Who knows what could happen after nine months? Nine months. She beamed as she stepped into the lobby, where the sun glared so bright she couldn't see beyond the windows to the street.

Nine months, huh. Maybe this is the baby she was meant to have all along. It just took a lifetime for her miracle to happen.

Kassie signed out with the guard with a brisk "*à bientôt*" and spun around and headed for the exit, humming "Chim Chim Cher-ee." For a brief moment, she stood on her tiptoes, still humming away, looking for Tanya. Not surprised by the coincidence as she got to the line in the song about luck, she spotted Tanya and her car to her right. Kassie waved with delight and picked up her pace. She couldn't wait to get back to the hotel to tell Chris her news, confident he'd be thrilled for her. "What a fabulous opportunity for you," she imagined he'd say. Of course, he wouldn't miss the chance to rub it in that none of this would've happened if he hadn't surprised her in Venice and whisked her away to Paris. Proving once again, he was her knight in shining armor.

It was because she stopped to retrieve her sunglasses from her purse, she didn't see Chris climb out of Tanya's car and grab clothing and shoes out of the trunk. Not until she was ten feet away did her eyes shift from the tall svelte blonde, whom Kassie had accepted as a beneficial yet annoying fixture in her life, to the handsome dude with his arms full.

"Well, hello there! To what do I owe this pleasure? What's going on?" In one fell swoop, Kassie felt conflicted, excited to see him yet confused as to why Chris was standing there holding her Skechers in one hand and her gray travel pants and a shirt in the other.

"Are we going somewhere?" She leaned up to meet Chris halfway for a kiss.

"I'll fill you in after you change. Go back inside. Here."

"Always full of surprises, aren't you?" She traded his journal for her clothes, did a pirouette, and obediently marched into the lobby.

"See," she said to the guard, "I said I'd see you soon." She held up her outfit, shrugged her shoulders, and asked if there was a ladies' room in the lobby where she could change. He handed her a card with a code and tilted his head to the left.

"*Merci!*"

After Kassie changed, she passed the guard again and shouted "*ciao*," immediately catching her mistake. "I mean, *au revoir.*" Smiling and shrugging her shoulders again, she made a mental note to have Vicki check which was better, Rosetta Stone or Babbel, for learning French PDQ. The faster the better.

This time as she approached the car and Chris and Tanya stood side by side in deep conversation, she could care less. It was her time in the sun, and nothing, no one, not even Tanya, could spoil it. Whatever adventure Chris had planned was bound to be educational, informative, and acclimate her more to Paris, her future temporary home.

Tanya held the rear door for Kassie while Chris put her dress, shoes, and so on in the trunk. She startled when he slammed it.

"How long will it take, Tanya?" Chris asked as he slid next to Kassie.

"To Charles de Gaulle, at this time of day? At least an hour."

"The airport? Where are you whisking me off to now, Sir Lancelot?" Kassie smiled and hugged Chris's arm.

"We're going home." He kissed her forehead, then whispered, "It's Mike."

26

Timing Is Everything

Still floating on a cloud an hour after she'd kissed Charlie goodbye, Karen cozied up on her rented couch and texted Mike not once but twice, giving him a heads up that she'd be at the house around six, depending on rush hour traffic. She sweetened the second message with "Dinner and . . . ?" hoping to get some kind of response from the big lug, though she had no intention of letting him anywhere near her that night, not until such time as the afterglow of Charlie faded.

He answered neither of the two messages. "What a jerk off," she said to the commercial on the television she turned on just to fill the air with a human voice to replace Charlie's. She missed the fun she'd had with him already. Charlie, she resolved, would be a good friend, with benefits, for her to keep close.

Inviting Charlie to her place wasn't as risky as it might appear, given Chris lived across the atrium and up one floor. She knew he was on the West Coast with what's her name? *Oh yeah, Lexi.* By the time he'd return from his vacation, Charlie would be long gone, *big sigh,* and she'd be back at Mike's on most nights and weekends.

Nevertheless, Karen valued her privacy and when it came to her digital assets, distrusted Silicon Valley's attempt at reassuring Americans—and the world, for that matter—that their secrets were safe with them.

Moving cross country forced her to expand her horizons in more ways than one. When Chris insisted she buy an iPhone before heading east, how could she say no? Her son actually made an overt attempt at showing he cared about her, even in the slightest way. There were no words to describe how tickled she was. Taking his lead, once she arrived in Boston, she marched herself for the first time into an Apple store—the one on Boylston Street—and took a bite out of it big time. Who wouldn't? Like a kid in a candy store, she cast aside her fear of losing privacy and wanted it all, as was her wont.

An Apple Specialist in a royal blue T-shirt with a white Apple logo greeted Karen with a great big hello and smile. Knowing she was out of her element, Karen latched herself on to the young sales lady, or was it the other way around? The gal never released her ear-to-ear grin, as Karen reckoned she must've seen neon-green dollar signs flash nonstop across her forehead.

Karen might as well have pointed and said, "I'll take one of these, and one of those," as the sales rep escorted her from station to station. White box after white box piled up on the counter, and she rubbed the palm of her hand across each as if it contained something magical and was too precious to open. She handed over a credit card, and with a single swipe of the sales rep's gizmo, Karen was the proud owner of the highest priced iPad, MacBook, Apple Watch, and their essential accessories. All compliments of one Michael Ricci, naturally.

Now sitting on her couch, Karen shrugged her shoulders and said, "What a waste," as she held her iPhone, admitting the laptop and phone were her devices of choice. She rarely used the iPad or watch, still afraid to even turn them on, though she hauled them back and forth to Mike's place, just in case he was curious about what he'd paid for. Curiouser and curiouser though to Karen was that Mike never asked her about the huge charge on his Visa card, apparently not seeming to care. The recurring itch of her scar hinted at the logical reason why.

The uptick of voices coming from the direction of the ferry dock told her the day was getting long, and she ought to get a move on. She bolted upright. She hadn't heard from Mike all day. Not a good sign. By now he'd have talked with Bill. He had to know that she'd lied about the tickets. *I bet he's pissed.* She paced twenty steps into the bedroom and back into the living room again about a dozen times, trying to come up with an excuse for her little indiscretion Saturday night.

If she was going to fulfill her pledge to get more than a fair share of what she believed was rightfully hers, she'd better suss out the situation to make sure she remained in Mike's good graces. Where to start? She collapsed on the couch and chewed her pinky nail. *Think, damn it.*

If she'd learned anything from working at Ricci and Son the last year, it was sports analogies. Before she'd moved to Boston, her friends in Elephant Butte had warned her about the insufferable Boston sports fans. They were right. Especially Monday mornings at the office when her lazy coworkers would spend at least the first hour of the day dissecting ad nauseam every play of every game and second-guessing every coach's decision. *So that's what Monday morning quarterbacking means.*

Of course, Karen hung out in the kitchen for the play-by-play even though she rarely added to the chitchat, let alone understood a thing they babbled about. To her, eavesdropping was mandatory to her cause, never knowing when something she heard might come in handy when she least expected.

Take the Monday morning after a Red Sox defeat. Karen walked smack dab into a heated debate about the meaning of "the best offense is a good defense."

"Aren't they both equally important?" she asked, resparking an argument that started with its meaning in sports and concluded with Chris expounding on the writings of George Washington during the Revolutionary War.

Now, as she sat contemplating what she'd gotten herself into with Mike, she reasoned it would be a good time to test how much that old adage held water. She'd go on the offensive, state her case before Mike had a chance to challenge her. But she had to think it through, be deliberate, not muck it up. She'd have only one chance to get it right.

Karen rifled through three kitchen drawers before she found a pen in one and paper in another. Never a problem at Mike's, where Kassie had stocked every room with ample office supplies, even the bathrooms. Mulling over that thought, she slammed the drawers shut, rattling the cabinet below as well as her cage. Whatever glow lingered from Charlie withered.

After a few meager attempts at crafting a message for Mike, she settled on the following:

"Hi M. By now the cat's out of the bag. Don't blame me. Bill was a prick 2 me Sat. Once u hear my side, I'm sure u'll c he didn't deserve tix. Tell him 2 treat me w/respect. After all, if not 4 me . . . "

Five times she reread her masterpiece. After she keyed it in, she added a smiling emoji and sent it. Then she sent one more text letting his fat fingers off the hook, telling him he needn't respond; she'd be there soon.

If she could pat herself on the back, she would. Sheer brilliance, reminding him of the role she played as his lifesaver, his guardian angel. Her act would never get old. "Look out Broadway, here I come."

Turning down Mike's street, it wasn't the lights of Broadway that welcomed Karen. Instead, an ambulance with flashing lights blocked the top of Mike's driveway behind a car she vaguely recognized, and a police cruiser with rotating blue lights was parked on the street. A police officer, directing what little traffic there was, stopped her from turning into the driveway.

"Are you related to the gentleman who lives at this address?"

"Yes, well, no. Kind of. What's going on, officer?"

"Can't let you pull in there and block the ambulance. Best you make a uey and pahk over there, across the street."

Under normal circumstances, Karen would shake her head at the officer's Boston accent and lingo, but she sensed whatever she'd driven into wasn't normal.

Neither was the scene inside the house. As she crossed the lawn and entered the wide-open front door, Karen fought her way past a collapsible wheeled stretcher and into the family room. She gasped, wrapping her right hand around her throat. Visions of her late husband, Barry, in a body bag after the ski patrol dashed him off the mountain nearly made her faint.

But then she saw that bitch, Amelia, holding Mike's hand as he reclined in his Barcalounger. *Well, at least he's alive. Thank God.*

"What the hell's going on here?" Karen directed her question seemingly to no one in particular, but clearly aimed it at Amelia.

"Give us some space here, ma'am. You'll need to go into another room until we move Mr. Ricci out." One of the two EMTs, a lady with a ponytail, chose to answer.

"Excuse me? What about her?" Karen tilted her chin toward Amelia.

"If it wasn't for Amelia, we may not have made it here in time," the other EMT piped up.

"Okay, I'm confused. Why are *you* here?" Karen pointed at Amelia, not giving her the same first-name-basis courtesy as the EMT.

"Take her away," Mike said, his weary eyes gazing at Amelia but his head tilting in Karen's direction.

"Take me away? Some nerve," Karen grumbled as she felt Amelia's hand on her elbow, leading her toward the kitchen. "Don't touch me," she said, gritting her teeth, repossessing her arm.

Once in the kitchen Karen fell back against the counter near the sink, folded her arms across her body, and glared at Amelia. "I. Want. An. Explanation."

The lady EMT interrupted. "We're ready to take Mr. Ricci to the hospital. He wants you to come with him."

"Right. I'll get my purse out of the car," Karen said.

"No, ma'am. Not you. He wants Amelia."

"Give me just a second. Let me get my mother."

Karen slapped the palms of her hands on her thighs and then up in the air. "What is this? A three-ring circus? Did I miss a party or something?" She followed Amelia into Kassie's office, where a small woman got up from the desk chair as they entered.

"No circus. We came to help Mr. Mike." The woman clasped her hands together as if she was praying.

"And you are?" Karen barely had the words out when Amelia introduced her mother, Teresa. "Oh, yes, Mike's cleaning lady. Can't imagine why we haven't met before?"

All Karen could think of was Mother Teresa, but this woman was neither dead nor a saint if she was Amelia's mother.

"How did *you* get here?" Karen barked.

Amelia rattled her car keys in the air and said she'd send an Uber to take her mother home.

"My mother will explain everything," she said as her mother hugged her and prayed to the ceiling again.

And just like that, Amelia was gone, leaving Karen staring at Teresa, who was almost on the verge of tears.

"Now, don't you cry. Tell me what's going on."

So Teresa began at the beginning. "We was, Amelia and me, up the street cleaning the Millers' house. You know the Millers? Big red house with white shutters. Two dogs. One little shedder and one big drooler. Hard to keep clean. Those dogs. Once a month Amelia comes to help. Makes it easier on me."

"I don't know the Millers or their dogs." Karen shook her head.

"Good thing, don't you think?"

"What?"

"That Amelia was with me. Or that I was with her. Haven't figured that out yet. Working on it, though."

"Whatever. Why good?"

"We was almost done for the day when Mr. Mike called Amelia to come by quick. And I have a key." Teresa dangled the key in front of Karen's face, close enough for her to read the tag: *Kassie and Mike Ricci*.

Standing there, in Kassie's office, and seeing her name made Karen's eyes blink fast. "Let's move to the family room, if you don't mind."

On a roll, Teresa followed Karen, explaining to her how she and Amelia hustled right over to the house. "Mrs. Miller was so nice. She told us not to worry about finishing cleaning. She's so nice. You should meet her someday."

"We'll see about that. Then what happened?"

"Oh my, Lord Jesus," Teresa cried out as they entered the family room. "I must clean this up right away. Will you help me, Miss Karen?"

Besides the furniture slung every which way, a pedestal end table and floor lamp angled on their sides, slick magazines lay scattered by the fireplace, an empty plastic water bottle rested atop a soaked *Boston Globe*, and a photo album lay open on the coffee table. Like the north side of a magnet, Karen was drawn to the photo album. A young Mike, the man she fell for decades ago, feeding cake to an even younger Kassie, stared back at her. She banged the book shut and in one motion flung *Our Wedding* like a Frisbee across the family room, barreling into the magazines Teresa had just picked up, knocking them out of her arms, just missing her chin.

"What are you looking at?" Karen mumbled as she picked up all the magazines and slid them into a magazine rack, then whispered, "I'm sorry."

Teresa nodded as she gathered the wet newspaper and headed to the garage.

"Wait, there's more trash." Karen moved back to the coffee table and scooped up small pieces of torn paper. The front doorbell rang. "You go." She motioned Teresa toward the garage. "I'll answer it." Holding shreds of red, white, and blue, she opened the door as the bells on the doorknob clanged.

"Where is he? I came as soon as I could. I was in a meeting downtown when he called."

"Oh, hi, Bill. He's gone."

27

Nobody Loves Me

Karen tsk-tsked at Bill, his eyes the size of dinner plates. "Mike's not dead, if that's what you're thinking. He's gone, as in on his way to the hospital, which is where I'm heading. Come in for a minute, if you must."

Bill hurried, lock-step behind Karen, into the family room that was beginning to look somewhat put back together. He pumped her with questions she couldn't answer. What happened? Is he going to be okay? Are they sure it's a heart attack? Maybe it was something he ate?

Karen felt a migraine coming on, and she didn't get migraines. Bill went on and on about how once he'd rushed Nancy to the hospital in the middle of the night thinking her heart was about to explode, when it was just a gallbladder attack from a fatty steak. What did Mike eat on the Cape?

"Lobster." Her claws stayed tucked in her pockets.

"I wish I'd taken his call. Damn it. I could've been here."

"That's great. Seems he called you first, then Amelia."

"Not you, eh?"

"I'm sure he tried. I was on my way here. I don't answer my phone when I'm driving." Still on offense, Karen didn't have to check her phone to see if Mike had called. She knew he hadn't, and she knew why.

A phone rang in another part of the house. "Yours?" Bill asked. She shook her head no. Hers was still in her purse.

Teresa walked in with a phone to her ear. "Karen's still here, and Bill too."

"You two know each other?" Karen looked at Bill.

"Of course, Teresa's our cleaning lady."

"Amelia needs to talk . . ." As Teresa said that, Karen reached toward her to take the phone. ". . . to you, Bill." Teresa handed him the phone.

WTF. No one wants to talk to me today! What am I, persona non grata? She leaned on the back of a chair, her mouth sandpaper dry, not sure she'd be able to speak even if she had to. She needed water but would be damned if she'd leave Bill alone in a conversation with Amelia. Karen grabbed his arm and led him to the kitchen. She didn't offer anything to Bill or Teresa, who was back doing whatever cleaning ladies do.

"Oh, thank God," Bill said and then started "yup-ing" and "okay-ing" and nodding as if Amelia could see him. He gestured to Karen to get him something to write with, so she pulled a purple ballpoint out of the small desk drawer. He looked at her as if to say, "Now, what am I supposed to do with this?" Taking the not-so-subtle hint, she slid a pad of paper embossed with the letter *K* on top that she'd found in another desk drawer and chuckled inwardly. Most likely Bill would think it referred to her. She knew the truth.

She peered over his shoulder, trying to read his chicken scratch. All she could make out was a *K* and two *A*s with a bunch of phone numbers.

"Who's that? Who you calling?" Karen pointed to the notepad.

"I'll try Kassie first. Then Annie if I can't reach her. She might still be in Italy." Bill ended the call.

"Who's the other *A* you wrote there?"

"Amelia. So we can keep in touch."

"Why call Kassie?"

"The hospital wants Kassie notified. She's his next of kin," Bill said as Teresa joined them in the kitchen.

"Why not me? I'm his fiancée. She's estranged—"

"Miss Kassie not strange. . . ." Teresa butted in.

"You're right about that." Bill added insult to injury as he gave Teresa back her phone and switched to his own. "Kassie would want to know what's up with Mike."

Karen exhaled loudly through her nose, as dogs do when they're settling down for a nap. She shoved her hands in her pockets and stared at the floor.

"Here, I think these belong to you. . . ." Karen pulled out what was left of the mangled Red Sox tickets, pitched them onto the kitchen counter, and took her leave.

28

There'll Always Be Paris

"Mike? This better be good. What happened? Is he dead?" Bad Kassie was AWOL. This was vintage Kassandra O'Callaghan at her finest.

"No, no. He's in the hospital. Heart attack, Annie thinks."

"Annie?"

Chris painstakingly took her through his morning. After she left, he'd showered and dressed, and thought he'd write a bit—their reunion and Paris inspired him so—but he couldn't write because she had his journal. Instead he opted for a stroll around the neighborhood and stopped at a café for coffee, where he picked up Tuesday's *Le Monde*.

Will I ever be able to read a French newspaper? Time will tell.

Kassie nudged him to keep going. She needed to know—about Mike, not about his minute-by-minute morning itinerary.

In no apparent rush, Chris said in the short hour he was at the café, he counted as many as sixteen—sixteen, mind you—people enter with their very well-behaved dogs of every shape and size and color. "Parisians do love their dogs. I love dogs. Maybe we should get a dog, Kassie. What do you think?"

"*We* already have a cat. Have you forgotten?"

"Such a gorgeous day for dog walking, *n'est-ce pas?* Before Uber, I did that as a business for a while," Tanya interjected. Kassie's sunglasses masked her eye roll. *Meow. Maybe her next act will be in the circus.* Welcome back, Bad Kassie.

"Come on, Chris . . . Annie."

"Oh, yeah. I digress." Chris held up his phone, reminding her that he'd shut it down when they were at dinner the night before at the Eiffel Tower and didn't have it with him at the café, as there was no reason to. It was off, and he'd intended to keep it that way throughout the week. So no one could reach him. He'd kept an eye on a clock at the café to be sure he returned to the hotel by noon, expecting she'd be back from her meeting by then. As he headed for the stairs back at the hotel, the concierge flagged him down and handed him an envelope. Because it was marked for the two of them, he opened it. If only her name was on it, he wouldn't have.

Kassie lifted her closed eyes toward the roof of the car and shook her head ever so slightly. *Spare me.*

"It was a message from Annie to call her right away. So I did. Good thing I didn't wait for you. If I had, we wouldn't be able to make the evening flight home."

"Goddamn it, Chris, what did she say? You are so dramatic. Just like your mother."

"Sarah? Rich, yes. Dramatic, not so much."

"No, the other one."

Chris nodded, likely in agreement, and stared out the window.

"Well . . . Annie said what?" Kassie stamped her foot.

Chris prattled on about Bill calling Annie looking for Kassie at some ungodly hour before sunrise. So early, in fact, she said Topher— see, he hadn't forgotten—was still curled up on Kassie's bed. Annie said Bill apologized for waking her; he was really trying to reach Kassie, but her phone was turned off.

"I explained to Annie that *my* phone was off because I didn't want anything to distract me from you, and that you had done the same. Essentially, we were off the grid, getting to know each other again. I think she knew what I meant because she laughed. Anyway, you were at a meeting. Of course, she didn't know anything about your meeting with Mimi, but since we were long distance, I decided that was a story you could tell her yourself."

"I appreciate that. Go on."

Chris said when Annie told Bill she wasn't home, he asked if Annie knew how he could reach her.

"Oh my God. Did she tell him about us . . . being in Paris . . . together?"

Chris kissed the back of her left hand; her wedding band hit him squarely across the nose. "No, our secret is safe for the time being. After I talked to Annie, I checked my phone. Both Bill and Karen had called. Their only message was to call them back, which of course I didn't do. Everyone in the office thinks I'm on the West Coast, three time zones and three thousand miles in the opposite direction."

"Why would they think that?"

"A red herring, my love."

"Good move. So, then what did she say?"

Chris said Annie told Bill that Kassie was still in Europe. She could reach her if there was a rational reason to do so. It would have to be something extremely important for her to interrupt her vacation. That's when Bill told her Mike had been rushed to Boston Clinic. An apparent heart attack. Mild. Resting comfortably.

"If he's resting comfortably, why do we have to go back to Boston? More than likely he'll be released before we land at Logan. You know they don't keep folks very long in hospitals these days."

"Unless they're there for observation."

Kassie gulped as a vision flashed through her mind of the fateful Easter weekend the year before when she'd learned about Mike's kidney disease and his love child, which happened to be sitting right next to her at that moment. Keeping Mike for observation that life-changing weekend spiraled into a hot mess they were still recovering from.

"There's probably nothing we can do, Chris. Anyway, he's probably got Karen doting on him," she said, not anxious to insert herself squarely in Mike's life when she'd gone through hell to escape it.

"You're kidding, right? Nothing we can do?"

"Do I sound callous? It's already Tuesday. We'll be home Saturday, just four days from now. We've only started to explore Paris. We didn't even get to the Louvre."

"Like Notre-Dame, the Louvre isn't going anywhere. We can come back."

Kassie raised her eyebrows, ready to say something about the real possibility of returning to Paris, but covered her mouth with her trusty invisible duct tape. No way was she going to tell Chris her news with Blondie sharing their air space.

"I have to go back to take care of the business."

She tilted her head away from him. "The business? Now who's callous? You're going back, interrupting our trip, because of *the business*? Not because your father had a mild heart attack?"

"Who knows how long he'll be laid up. As long as he is, I'll be running the show."

"What about Bill? He's there. He can handle everything at least until next week, if we stay."

"I'm needed there. We've got our lanes. Bill's operations. I manage the rest—business development, client engagement . . ."

As Chris rambled on about how important he was to a company he'd only joined a year ago—as a very junior partner, no less—Kassie glanced at the engagement ring. A nail. In a coffin? Whose, she wondered. She was saved from her dark thoughts as Tanya pulled alongside the airport terminal. Demonstrating this wasn't her first rodeo, Tanya deftly unloaded their suitcases, gave them each a hug and air kisses, and sent them on their way.

Always the gentleman, Chris placed his hand on the small of Kassie's back, guiding her through the sliding doors to the airline terminal.

"Hey, by the way, how was your day, honey?"

29

Culture Shock

Kassie gave up and threw her hands in the air. Standing in lines was something she decided she'd just have to get used to if becoming an international frequent flyer was in her future. Didn't matter the length of the line or where she was headed; patience was not one of her virtues. She even bristled at the lines at Fenway Park, if you could believe.

In her opinion, airports were the worst with their trifecta of potential headache triggers—check-in, security, boarding. Shifting from one foot to the other, she counted. As far as she could tell, there were at least a hundred people ahead of them and only three ticket agents available to check in that crowd and the ever-increasing throng in back of them.

Kassie pointed out the obvious and predicted to Chris, "At this rate, getting through security is going to be a nightmare." She was getting antsy . . . and itchy.

Glancing down at her luggage, it suddenly occurred to her that Chris must've packed her bags. Shocking. No one had ever done that for her. Why would they? She was the most self-sufficient person she knew. He tried to help sometimes. Like when they were getting ready to check out of a hotel, and she was busy showering, Chris would fold her clothes for her. *Sweet man that he is.* But he would never actually put her things in the suitcase, knowing how particular she was. He'd say she was fussy; she'd say fastidious.

Oh, what the hell. Give it a rest, Kassie. You're heading home. Wrinkles be damned.

Twenty-two minutes later, as she handed the ticket agent her passport, she rubbed the right side of her neck under her chin. Four bumps. She knew the root cause. Pomegranates. Haunting her still. Attacking her immune system. Damn it, she thought she had it under control. She hadn't scratched all day since she'd taken one of those French pills before she left for her meeting with Mimi. Wrong time for a flare up. She was about to be confined in a germ-infested tube with two hundred or more people on a seven-hour transatlantic flight home. With her luck and her immune system out of kilter, she was sure to contract some unpronounceable ailment that the United States had yet to approve drugs to combat. Another reason living in France for a while looked appealing.

On their way to security, Kassie grabbed Chris's hand and glared at him. "You packed my things," she said through clenched teeth, her tone more accusatory than questioning.

"You just figured that out now?"

"Did you pack the amphetamines?"

"Shh. You mean the antihistamines?" Chris laughed and reached into his pocket and dropped the small package in the palm of her hand.

"Whatever. Not funny. I need water now. Thought you forgot—"

"I think it's you who forgot something." Chris dangled the Eiffel Tower necklace in front of her face.

"Thanks, better not put it on now." She pointed at her neck and slipped the necklace in her pocket.

The line to get through security was longer than the check-in process. Since Chris had just booked their flight that day, her patience was tested again as they meandered their way through the blue-taped maze, rather than breeze through TSA Precheck. She made another note to self to be sure Vicki checked her TSA status for her future roundtrips to Paris. She'd do anything to buck the system—legally, of course.

Chris must've read her mind because as they reached the last leg of the maze, he tugged on Kassie's arm and led her to the far left side. "Lines always shorter on the left," he said as she smiled at him in relief.

My hero. Coming to save the day again.

Her relief turned into a nightmare, just as she'd foreseen. Actually, part of the process of going through security—putting her carry-on bag and purse and shoes on the black belt—went like clockwork. No problem. None of her belongings needed closer investigation than the x-ray box and the security officer's prying eyes provided. Kassie, herself, was a different matter. Obediently, and like Chris and every-one ahead of her, she entered the full-body scanner, intrigued by the newest technology. Isn't it a bit titillating, almost pornographic, to be commanded by a total stranger to stand with your hands above your head and your legs spread apart?

Her fantasy lasted only until the security officer raised his hand and signaled a woman to join them.

Oh, here we go. She'd been wanded before, a wide belt buckle usually the culprit. Though she didn't need to, she checked her waist out of habit. No belt in sight. What the hell could've tripped the body scanner sensors?

"*Venez avec moi, s'il vous plaît,*" the lady security officer said, motioning her to step aside.

Barefooted, Kassie cooperated. No way would she confront someone packing heat. She spotted Chris dutifully retrieving her bags off the belt. She caught his eye, gave him an I-have-no-clue shrug and pointed to her feet, hoping he'd get the message to not forget her Skechers.

For a second time in less than two minutes, Kassie was instructed to spread her legs. Good grief. Again she did as she was told, but this time it felt more as though she was being invaded than pleasured. The metal detector wand made a barely audible vibrating sound as the security officer moved it around her body's perimeter, first along her left side and between her legs. As the woman without a smile moved the device over Kassie's right hand, the wand went berserk. The ring.

"It's new," Kassie said, smiling and wiggling her finger.

Relieved, Kassie took four steps away from the guard, saying "*au revoir,*" pleased she'd gotten the language right that time.

"*Arrête!*"

Exasperated, Kassie stopped in her tracks. What now? Her eyes widened as her judge and jury clapped her light blue plastic-gloved hands together like a mad scientist in a James Bond movie and waved her index finger, directing Kassie to spread her loins once more. *She's going to frisk me.* How humiliating. Not seductive or pornographic. Just gross.

And pointless. Kassie took a deep breath and suppressed her embarrassment and annoyance about being made to feel like a terrorist over a ring. Her only crime that day was allowing Chris to insist they fly home when Paris still beckoned.

Just as suddenly as the security officer invaded her privacy, she tapped Kassie on the arm and said, "*Ça va. Au revoir. Bon voyage.*"

Having no clue what the guard said, she shot the woman a quizzical look and said, "*Merci,* I guess I'm good to go?"

"*Oui. La bague,*" the guard lifted Kassie's right hand, pointing to the ring.

"Told you so," she mumbled as she scanned the morass of travelers gathering the luggage off the black belts, arms flailing as they balanced to slip on their shoes, scurrying to meet up with their companions who'd left them behind. By the way, where was Chris? Ah. She spotted him standing by Starbucks, holding up a water bottle as his calling card.

"Was it fun for you?" Chris teased her as she ripped her sneakers out of his hands.

"This ring. Already making waves." Kassie showed him the ring and regretted her words as soon as they slipped off her tongue. "In a good way," she added. "All that excitement . . . and touching," she said, wanting to change the subject, "makes me have to pee."

"Come with me." Chris said he had a solution for what ailed her. He held her hand as they jockeyed around women weighed down with oversized cross-body bags, men glaring up at lighted departure boards, and unsupervised children with pictures of princesses and zombies on their backs running around as if the terminal were their own personal playground. A multitude of unfamiliar words and accents floated through the air with a sizable amount of English and French being bantered about. Clearly international travel was a cultural experience unto itself. One she vowed to embrace, rather than reject.

Above the normal airport racket, Kassie thought she heard a piano melody, live, not piped in. She squeezed Chris's hand and tilted her head in the direction her ears targeted. And they did not deceive. Smack dab in the middle of the terminal sat a red piano. How about that for a cultural experience she could get used to fast? The young lad at the keys finished his lively piece, grabbed his backpack, and went on his way to who knows where. Imagine that, a public piano. Her appreciation of the finer things of France was blossoming by the minute—the security snafu already a distant memory.

"Play something," she encouraged Chris, pushing him toward the piano.

"Seriously?"

"Seriously."

With a smile and a shrug, Chris placed his carry-on next to Kassie's feet, wrapped his arms around her, tilted her back, and kissed her deep and long, like the iconic photo of the sailor kissing the nurse at the end of World War II. She stumbled to recover when he let go, swallowing so hard her toes tingled.

He lowered himself onto the piano bench like a virtuoso and tickled the ivories the way professional pianists do, capturing her gaze and her heart. Soon a crowd gathered as Chris launched into John Legend's "All of Me," a favorite of theirs. Though he didn't sing it, Kassie knew the words and his intent. Since Friday, Chris had shown his cards—his passion, his unconditional love for her. Despite the headwinds they'd surely face back in Boston, he found her in Venice, proposed in Paris, and declared to the world—or at least to the hundred or so folks in the airport who stopped their own journey to hear him play—he couldn't live without her in his life. Without a doubt, Chris was committed to her, now and forever, just as he was more than a year ago before their relationship had gone to hell in a laundry basket. By his cumulative words and action, he showed her that for him nothing had changed.

Kassie pressed the knot forming in her stomach. *Tummy, don't fail me now.* For the first time since her meeting with Mimi, she felt anxious about how he'd react when she told him her news. Would he question whether she was as committed to him as he was to her? *Foolish girl. He's Chris. He'll understand.* He just had to.

Everyone was clapping, except for Kassie, lost in her thoughts. Someone brushed her arm, nudging her back to reality. "You're a lucky lady." She quickly put her hand on her heart, bowed her head, and blew him a kiss. Thankfully the woman hadn't referred to her as "a lucky mother."

"Let's get out of here," Chris said, laughing, seemingly embarrassed by all the attention. Kassie seconded the motion.

30

Once a Gentleman

They checked the airline departure board that was so large it was two stories tall. With two hours to kill before they needed to make their way to the gate, Chris whipped out his AMEX card and ushered Kassie into one of the airline lounges that offered a one-day entry fee.

The lounge was not a quiet place, but more peaceful than the terminal, to be sure. Travelers milled around the oak- and glass-paneled facility, passing the hours until flight time. Many were indulging entertainment apps on their electronic devices, others mesmerized by planes taxiing to and from the numerous airport terminals, some trying to read.

After Chris gave her the high sign indicating they could hang out there for a while, Kassie excused herself to make her much-needed trip to the ladies' room while Chris scoped out a place for them to hunker down and relax. She welcomed time alone to gather herself and reflect on the unexpected turn of events her day had taken; neither being offered an assignment of a lifetime in Paris, nor flying back to Boston because of Mike were on her agenda when she got up that morning. Thinking back on it, coming to grips with Chris's marriage proposal and combating a rash were more than enough to handle. "*Merci beaucoup*," she said to the woman in the lavatory's mirror.

Kassie brushed her teeth and hair, finally fresh and excited to tell Chris her happy news. She found him tucked away in a corner, dark and quiet. The smell of fresh coffee made Kassie's mouth water.

"How's this? We should be able to hear each other talk back here."

She nodded and leaned toward the area of the lounge where a buffet beckoned. First things first. The pickings were slim but sufficient—mini quiches, small ham-and-cheese sandwiches, cucumber canapés, mixed fruit cocktail, and French baguettes. They filled their plates, grabbed a bottle of water, and ventured back to their cubby. Kassie vowed to return to the buffet for dessert, which she'd learned during her short time in Paris was always far more yummy than the main course.

"Guess you're hungrier than I thought you'd be," Chris snickered. "Didn't you have lunch with Mimi? You were there long enough."

"I am, I did, and I was," Kassie answered Chris despite her mouthful of quiche. She waved her hand across her plate and picked up the cucumber canapé. She swallowed and took a swig of water. "Not quite chichitti, eh?" Her reference to when they'd first met in Venice six years ago was deliberate. By first acknowledging their love had survived events out of their control and had come full circle, she greased the skids for what was to come . . . even more separation. They'd been apart before. In fact, they were apart for most of their relationship. Nine or ten months in Paris? No big deal.

"Not quite Venice." Chris paused, shifting in his chair. "How was your lunch, your visit with Mimi? You've told me nothing."

This was her opening. Ready to start, but uncertain exactly where to begin, Kassie pushed her plate to the middle of the square table between them. Her lunch with Mimi would be as good a place as any. She described the scene—the panoramic view of the Seine, the exquisite porcelain china, the simple lunch fare typical of business offices no matter what country you worked in—a platter of cold meats, a variety of sliced and wedged cheeses, bread and rolls. In retrospect, she realized she hadn't touched much of the lunch, even passing up the pastries. No wonder her stomach was talking to her. She inched her plate closer.

Chris appeared to be listening until he excused himself and left Kassie sitting open-mouthed, midsentence, before getting to the best part of her story. Just like a man, he returned with another plate overflowing with finger food. Perhaps they should've gone to a restaurant instead, where Chris would've been able to eat a proper meal.

Nevertheless, Chris allowed her to pick up where she'd left off. "As you were saying . . ."

"You'll never guess," Kassie started. "The Paris office is expanding in more ways than one." Kassie reasoned a detailed description of how the Paris office of Calibri Marketing Group was planning to acquire a London-based firm *and* the fact that Mimi was pregnant again would serve as a logical prologue for the rest of the story. Certainly, at some point a light bulb would click inside the management side of Chris's brain, and he'd link the two events before she revealed it.

"She's pregnant again? What is it, every time you see her, she's pregnant? That didn't upset you, did it?"

"Another time, perhaps." Still determined to take Chris along her journey to a natural conclusion, Kassie proceeded to educate Chris on the most-civilized French health care system.

"Did you know in France your maternity leave starts six weeks before you're due and extends ten more weeks after the birth? They have paternity leave too."

"Sounds generous," he said, checking his phone. "Glad I won't have that to worry about."

"Guess that's one advantage to marrying me," Kassie said under her breath. If they weren't sitting as close to each other as they were, Chris would never have heard her lament.

"Give me a break, Kassie. You know there are at least two advantages to marrying you, which a gentleman, like me, would never state in public." He winked and caressed her thigh. He lifted her chin. "So, you spent four hours with Mimi today because she's having a baby."

"Two babies, Chris. Twins. And that means something really special in France." She pounded her index finger on the table, hoping to maintain his attention. "Here, if you're having twins, maternity leave from start to finish adds up to thirty-four weeks. Add the four weeks' vacation Mimi's piled up . . . she'll be out of the office for nine months, give or take."

"She told you all this? Why?"

"Didn't you hear me? Mimi will be out of the office for nine months. Just before and certainly right after the merger. Critical time for the company, don't you think?"

"Boy, she didn't time that well." Chris didn't bite.

"Depends on where you sit."

"How's that?"

"You know Tom said Mimi had an idea to discuss with me? *Acting. Managing. Director.* Of Calibri Marketing Group in Paris. What do you think?" Kassie beamed.

"Who, you?"

"You sound like an owl." Kassie put her hand on her chest, the anxiety that had built up in her lungs had escaped, and she laughed freely.

"Of course, you told her you were flattered and you'd think about it."

"Of course, I told her I was flattered and I—"

Chris's phone rang. She recognized the ringtone as the one she'd heard during dinner the night before at the Eiffel Tower. Was that only twenty hours ago? He didn't answer it.

"Come on. Time to go home." He picked up his own bags and headed out of the lounge, leaving Kassie a dozen steps behind, fending for herself. Something she wouldn't have to get used to. She already was.

31

Parlez-vous Français?

Chris turned around, and Kassie was gone. Not gone gone, but certainly not a step or two or three behind him. He spun around as if he was playing hide 'n seek with a five-year-old, and still no Kassie.

The heavy wooden door of the lounge groaned open, and there she was, not smiling.

"Thanks for waiting."

"There you are. Thought you were right behind me." He bounded toward her and put his arm around her shoulders. Was it his imagination, or did she tighten a bit when he touched her? Or was he the one stiffening, feeling guilty for shutting Kassie down when the call came in from Lexi, the second one in two days.

It'd been a month since they'd talked. He'd told Lexi he was going to try to reconcile with Kassie and was surprised when she gave him tips on how to woo her back. Sweeping her away from Venice to Paris was Lexi's idea. "If you're going to start anew, a change of scenery will do the trick. No better place than Paris," she'd said. He'd noticed she hadn't suggested Greece. *That's it,* he thought, she was probably just checking to see what progress he'd made.

"Well, I'm here now." Kassie pulled a step ahead of him.

"What did you say?"

"I'm here. Look, there's Relay's. Need something for the plane."

As they wandered separately around the store, Chris kept one eye out for her, not wanting to be accused of losing her twice in one day. If he timed it right, they'd meet at the checkout together, and he could dump some of the euros taking up space in his wallet. He didn't expect to be back in Europe in the near future. No reason to go through the hassle of reconverting once he was back in the States.

He grabbed a Lipton iced tea, a ham-and-cheese sandwich, and what looked to be the last *Sports Illustrated* World Cup issue available.

Spying Kassie, he hung back to give her space to shop to her heart's content. They still had about twenty-five minutes before boarding. He could see her thumbing through books, probably making sure they were in English.

He bided his time by amusing himself with packaging and signage around the store. As a marketer, Chris soaked in the sights and sounds of the retail world around him no matter what city or country he visited, often wondering if by doing so he could write off vacations as business trips.

Wait a minute. That's an idea.

Chris nuzzled up behind Kassie, who held two books, French cookies, and a bottle of water.

"You're going to love me for this."

"I already love you," she said.

"No, really. I think . . ." Chris paused for optimum effect. "I bet you can write off part of your vacation as a business trip. Talk to Tom. The company might, actually should, reimburse you for the airfare and hotel. Maybe some of Tanya's costs. Ooh, if I thought about it before, we could've tipped her more. And food, don't forget meals. I have receipts."

"Slow down, big guy." Kassie's smile was nearly a laugh. "I'm way ahead of you. Mimi and Tom already offered. But I like the way you think. You'll make someone a good wife."

"You talked to Tom? Today?"

"Yes. I'll tell you about it later. Shouldn't we get going?" Kassie lifted her merchandise in the air and headed toward the registers.

Chris sidled up behind her. "Here, let me get that." The salesclerk foiled his attempt at paying for both of their purchases. He must not have heard Chris or understood English as he swiped Kassie's credit card faster than fish in aquarium scarf up their food. When Kassie shook away his offer of a plastic bag, the clerk held on to one of her books.

"This is great. You'll love it." The clerk, who Chris gathered understood English but had chosen to ignore him, tilted the book for Chris to see. *The Paris Wife.*

"I'll be over there," Kassie said, reclaiming her book and stepping away.

"Can't believe you're going to eat that horrible, water-logged sandwich," Kassie said as Chris peeled open the cellophane. "Did you check the date on it? And with mustard, no less."

"Hey, it's better than cookies."

"Nothing's better. Me want cookie. Me eat cookie." Kassie did her best imitation of the Cookie Monster, good enough to get a rise out of Chris.

"Still wish we'd stayed longer." Kassie stared out the plane's window. "If I'd known we'd be cut short, I'd have shopped more. I'm bringing back no gifts."

"Me neither."

"I think I owe something to Vicki, and Annie. If it weren't for them, I wouldn't have my gifts." She held up her right hand, retrieved her necklace from her pocket, and slipped it into her purse for safe-keeping. "Who would you have shopped for?"

"Let me think . . . folks at work? Nope. No one knew I was in Europe."

"Karen? Would you have bought something for your mother while you're in Paris with me? What a hoot."

"Maybe. If only to remind her that I proposed to you there." He snickered as Lexi's call flashed through his mind. "What's that book about?" he asked, hoping to change the topic of conversation and the thoughts of another woman racing through his head.

"Hadley Richardson. Hemingway's first wife and their time in Paris . . ." Kassie paused and reminded Chris that Mike was a Hemingway buff. Perhaps she'd regift it to him when she was finished with it.

"See, you are bringing a gift back."

"To Mike of all people. Wonder if I'll ever stop catering to him?"

Chris reached for Kassie's hand as she began reading the back of the book in a low voice. His mind drifted after the first two words, "Chicago, 1920 . . ." He wondered what attracted her to that particular book. Isn't that the type of book you read when you're flying to, not away from, Paris?

"Rumor has it, of his four wives, Hemingway loved Hadley best. Be still my heart." Kassie clutched the book to her chest.

"Don't understand how you can be such a romantic. You know, deep down you're a pragmatist."

"Can't I be both?"

"Depends. What's the other book you bought?"

Kassie dragged it out of the seat pocket in front of her. *Learn French Fast.*

32

What'd She Say?

Discombobulated. That's the only word to describe Kassie as she tried to get her bearings. With the lingering effect of stagnant airplane air and waking up in the third strange bed in less than a week, she didn't know where she was or what day of the week greeted her. She failed in her attempt to open both eyes, as sleep clasped her right eye shut tight like a clam.

Her one clear eye scanned the premises, checking out what it could see. A painting of the Grand Canal in Venice at night on the off-white wall in front of her and the sun slicing the canal into uniform columns provided two clues—she was in Chris's apartment, in his bed, and it was morning. The warmth of Chris's back against hers was further confirmation, though she didn't need it. She wasn't in Paris anymore.

"Alexa, what time is it?" Kassie said in as low a voice as she could.

"The time is five thirty-seven a.m."

She calculated she'd gotten less than five hours sleep and expected her circadian rhythms would need the rest of the week to recalibrate. Too early to get up. They weren't planning to head to the hospital until late morning. She closed her eye, pulled the covers over her shoulder, took several slow and deep yoga breaths, and drifted off.

Alexa, Alexa, Lexi . . .

"Hey, Kassie, you awake? Rise and shine." The rich, toasty smell of hazelnut coffee stirred her even before Chris, all bright and cheery, all dressed in khaki cargo shorts and an aquamarine Izod shirt looking ready to go who knows where, plunked his gorgeousness at the foot of the bed.

"Ugh. Not yet. And don't say that. You sound like my mother," she said, lifting her head to get a peek at him. "And take off that shirt. Too bright and reminds me of Mike." Kassie pulled the pillow over her face, covering her now wide-open eyes.

"How about my pants?" He rested his coffee and her tea on the bureau and then unbuckled his belt.

"Welcome home," Chris said some twenty or so minutes later, give an orgasm or two. "About a year since you were here between my sheets."

Kassie pulled herself up, propping a pillow behind her back and one on her lap. She motioned for the tea, and Chris obliged.

"Thanks. We need to talk. About Paris."

Chris climbed back in bed and mirrored her pillow arrangement. "Really? I thought we resolved all that earlier."

She pounded her fists on the pillow. "You stating your opinion— that you don't want me to go—does not resolve anything. What about what I want, need?"

"Which is . . ."

"I want Paris . . . and I want you. It's not either or."

Chris put his head in his hands. "Let's talk about it later. We need to get ready to go see Mike. I called Bill. He knows we are back . . . together."

"You told him? Oh, crap, he'll tell everybody. I wanted to tell Mike. I should be the one."

"Bill won't say anything. He promised not to. I trust him. You should too."

Kassie clasped Chris's hands in hers. "You've done it again. Changed the subject. You're a master at that."

Chris didn't argue.

"We need to solve Paris before we see Mike. It's important that I tell him everything at one time. He needs to know where things stand, where I stand, where you stand, where we stand."

"Because of the divorce?"

"And the business. He's got it all tied up in a single bow. You're a central part of it now in more ways than one."

"I'll admit, when you put it that way, we are strange bedfellows." Chris instigated a fight, a pillow fight, that landed Kassie sprawled on top of him on the floor.

"Paris is an opportunity of a lifetime for me," she pleaded, pinning his arms out in a T. "We survived a five-year, long-distance secret affair. Ten months out of the closet will be a cakewalk. And we'll be planning this." She stuck the ring in front of his face.

"There is that."

"You'll just travel back and forth to Paris instead of San Francisco."

As soon as she said it, she wanted to take it back. It wasn't Bad Kassie talking. It was a mistake, plain and simple.

"Me? I'll do the traveling? Haven't I done enough of that already?" Chris lifted her off his prone body.

Kassie climbed on the bed and wrapped the sheet around her. "I didn't mean it the way it sounded. Of course, I'll come home too. Ever hear of vacations? And I could conjure up meetings every couple of months back here in Boston."

"Look around you, Kassie. I moved here for you. And then I lost you. But I stayed. And then I traveled halfway around the world to find you again. I'd be crazy to let you go."

"I won't let you let me go. You'll see we can make it all work. It has to. I already told Tom and Mimi I would do it."

Kassie stood and massaged the backs of her knees. "Where are those damn pills?"

They showered separately. They spoke sparingly. They dressed— Kassie for the first time that day, Chris for the second—without a glance, a compliment, a brush of an arm.

Kassie texted Annie to let her know they were back in town and that she'd be home, at her house, later that day. Annie asked where she'd be sleeping that night, adding an emoji with a wink. Kassie responded she didn't have a clue. It all depended. Annie sent back a half dozen question marks Kassie ignored.

How's Topher?

Purr-fect. There's a FedEx pkg here 4 u. From Mike. Divorce stuff?

Probably. Thanks. On way to hospital now. Ciao. Au revoir. Whatever.

Chris said he'd meet her in the mailroom.

"Thought you'd have had the post office hold it for you."

"Forgot. Was too excited about the prospect of you." He winked and kissed her cheek.

Kassie dumped her purse on the disheveled bed, sorting out travel essentials from everyday necessities. She left her passport,

Immodium, mini international charger, and Mimi's business card on the bed. *I'll straighten this shit up later.*

In a hurry to catch up with Chris, she took the stairs to the main floor. As she approached the mailroom, two familiar voices made her slow down. *Oh, crap. Karen. What's she doing here now? She should be at work.*

Her first instinct was to turn on her heels and make tracks to the garage. Except Chris expected her to show up in the mailroom. What the hell, she'd have to confront Karen sometime that day. The mailroom was a better option than the hospital room.

"Hey, Karen. How . . . are you?" *What's with the red hair,* she wanted to say, but opted to ignore it.

Kassie's arrival seemed to suck the air out of the mailroom. The overhead lights flickered, as did Kassie's eyelashes. *I'm good here, Mom, thanks.*

Karen stepped back from Chris and glared at him. Chris raised his eyebrows as his right shoulder crept toward his ear. Bad Kassie smirked. *Gotcha.* She'd caught him. He hadn't warned his mother that his stepmother would walk in any minute.

"Oh. Kassie. What are *you* doing here?"

Kassie stayed mum. *Take it away, Sir Lancelot. Your time to shine.*

"She's with me. We're headed to the hospital," Chris said right on cue. Almost.

Well, that was as clear as the Charles River. Kassie fastened invisible duct tape to her lips and jutted her encouraging chin toward Chris. *And . . . keep going.*

"We got in too late last night to head over there."

"Got in? From where?"

"Paris," he said.

"Really? I heard you were in San Francisco with your girlfriend, Lexi."

33

What's Age Got to Do with It?

Kassie lifted her purse's cross-body strap over her head, attempting to buy herself time to think and relieve the pain of the baseball bat she imagined crushed her shoulder blades. She had a choice. If she called out Chris about Lexi, let Karen know the truth—that he hadn't told her about Lexi—Karen would experience a sense of schadenfreude. She'd get what she wanted—a wedge between the two of them. Or she could wait to see how Chris handled this one.

Rarely Miss Patience, Kassie took the reins. "Well, Karen, you heard wrong. *We* were vacationing in Europe." She didn't want to give Karen the satisfaction of too much information but couldn't resist adding, "Together."

"What about Lexi? Chris, what about Lexi?" Karen chirped, following him out of the mailroom to the elevator. Kassie stuck close, enjoying the show.

"Lexi? She's just great. Nice of you to ask," Kassie echoed from behind. In the crevices of her mind, Kassie flipped the pages of Chris's journal to the page with green and purple words. All she could muster was "lovely, lusty, and chesty." Not what she was searching for, but it'd have to do.

"Lexi's such a lovely lady," Kassie said. "I hope to meet her chest-to-chest, I mean face-to-face . . . in person . . . sometime real soon." It was all she could do not to laugh before Karen huffed and puffed toward the lobby exit. Kassie knew her mother was watching from somewhere up above and would disapprove wholeheartedly if she continued her charade.

Looking befuddled, Chris shifted the pile of magazines and envelopes he'd retrieved from his mailbox to his left arm and grabbed hold of Kassie's sleeve.

"We're just going to drop all this off upstairs and then head out. Maybe we'll see you at the hospital." Chris pounded the up arrow elevator call button as if it was an emergency. For him, it probably was. Not so much for Kassie, whose emotions seesawed from smugness to utter despair. Her eyes twinkled and filled with water at the same time.

The nanosecond after the elevator doors clicked shut, Chris was in overdrive. "How do you know Lexi? She is lovely, but how do you know that?"

Kassie stepped out of the elevator first and sashayed her way to his door, her butt swinging in sync with her purse, a single tear streaming down her cheek.

Once inside the apartment, Chris plunked the mail on the counter and continued his twenty questions without stopping to offer an explanation. Kassie excused herself in search of a tissue—instead of turning the tables on him and asking the most important question: Who the hell was Lexi?

The time it took her to find something to wipe away her insecurity was enough for her to gather herself. An old saying of her mother's saved her. Something about when you say nothing, you're really saying more than you realize. *Okay, Mom, I'll keep my mouth shut.*

Which Kassie did until Chris collapsed on the couch in a heap, and she had to save him from himself. His face flushed red as a pomegranate rash—she should know—and his hair screamed for a good combing. It was unfair of her to let him continue his mental gymnastics when he'd never find out how she knew about Lexi without a little help.

She scanned the living room; locked suitcases rested pretty much where they were dropped twelve hours before. Their carry-ons perched open on the dining table, the jackets they'd worn on the plane draped alongside. She found his journal under his jacket and remedied the situation they were both guilty of perpetuating.

Opening to the page with the green and purple doodles, Kassie handed Chris his journal. "I met Lexi yesterday on my way over to meet with Mimi." She picked Chris's jaw up from his chest, kissed his forehead, tapped his cheek twice. "Seems like you've got some 'splaining to do."

Chris tried to open his mouth. Kassie shook her head and put two fingers over his lips. "Later. We've got all the time in the world. I'm not heading back to Paris until Labor Day."

Checkmate.

Kassie interlaced her hand with Chris's as they left the apartment for the second time that morning. This time they kept walking to the garage.

On the drive to Boston Clinic, Kassie didn't interrogate him about Lexi, though she itched to find out about the relationship he'd had after they'd split. A year ago they had no future, so he'd moved on. Could she blame him?

They passed a highway billboard that read, "You Too Can Make a Temporary Job Permanent." Of course. That's what Lexi was, a temp, a passing thing. She breathed a sigh of forgiveness. Though it hurt all

the way down to her belly button, she wouldn't let Lexi . . . or Paris
. . . destroy their reunion. Nevertheless, when the time was right,
she'd drag out of him all the skinny about the lovely, lusty, crusty, *no
chesty*, young Miss Lexi. She assumed she was young, at least younger
than she.

Kassie was relieved Chris didn't challenge her about Paris in the
fifteen minutes it took to drive to the hospital. Maybe he'd thrown in
the towel. *Careful, girl. Don't let your guard down.* This could just be
a short-lived cease fire. After all, she'd misread his initial reaction.

In the excitement of the moment yesterday, she assumed he'd be
as thrilled as she about the opportunity for her to manage the Paris
office at such a critical time as a merger. A merger! Nothing is more
complex. Leading it to a successful conclusion could be a career game
changer. Yet, once Chris explained why he didn't want her to be three
thousand miles away, she kind of understood, but gee whiz, it would
only be for nine or ten months, hardly a lifetime.

Chris took her right hand, kissed her new ring, and led the way
to the hospital lobby.

"Gosh, Chris, what the hell do you think happened around here
while we were gone?"

"What do you mean?"

"Karen's a redhead and Mike's had a heart attack. Do you think
they're connected in some perverted way?"

"Parents acting like children, perhaps. Maybe they were doin' it
when he had his attack."

"Eww, gross."

"You should talk. Your sex drive doesn't seem to be fading
with—"

"With what . . . age?" She gave him a solid poke in his arm. *Note
to self: Find out how old this Lexi person is.*

Kassie didn't have enough fingers to count the many times she
had visited the hospital in the last fifteen or so months, starting with

Easter weekend, ugh, the beginning of the big reveal and the unraveling that split Chris and her up. Then there was the kidney swap. And now, they were at the hospital again. This time hand in hand—engaged to be engaged—to check out her husband's, his father's, ticker. *You really can't make this shit up, can you?*

As they rode the elevator up to the cardiac unit, a nightmarish vision of Mike in the emergency room last year flashed through her mind. Why wouldn't it? Same hospital, just different floor. She remembered his face, pale and gray as the smoke that billowed from his cigarettes. A few days in the hospital had restored his energy and his color. Wouldn't it be the case this time? According to Bill, Mike had been there two days already. She figured there was no way he'd look as gruesome as he did back then.

They decided to walk into his room together. If gossip queen Karen had beaten them there, she would've already spilled the beans.

Kassie was wrong on all counts. A young lady, not Karen, sat beside Mike's bed. And Mike? Well, let's just say he looked as though he could use some happy news.

34

Father and Son Reunion

"Hey, you guys. Thanks for coming. How come?"

Kassie grasped the foot of the metal bed frame, seeming to almost trip over something on the floor. There was no impediment, that is, except for her chin, which had dropped at the shock of seeing Mike so frail, with circles under his eyes that appeared even darker in contrast to his pasty skin. Where was the cheery guy she'd met recently at Panera's? Even when he was in the hospital that Easter weekend a year ago, he had more zing. And could he have been crying? No, surely not the Mike she knew.

"You mean, how come we're here together?" Chris pointed to himself and Kassie as he swooped in to rescue her and the conversation.

Recovering and holding back her own tears, Kassie said it was a long story for another time. First, she wanted to know how he was.

Before he could answer, the sweet young thing who held court in a chair alongside Mike interjected, "You must be Mrs. Ricci."

Chris eased a chair under Kassie at the foot of the bed and guided her shaking body into it. His strong hands squeezed her shoulders as if he was telling her to "just hang in there." She swallowed hard and prayed Bad Kassie would stifle it and not blurt out something like "Oh my God, you look like shit." She was grateful for the distraction of someone else in the room.

"I am. And you are?" She appreciated that Chris was rubbing her arms, helping her blood circulate and travel to her brain.

Cecilia stood tall and introduced herself, shaking Kassie's hand and sporting a huge smile as she greeted Chris. If Kassie didn't know any better, Chris's description of Lexi nearly fit Cecilia. At least the lovely, chesty parts. She was way too young, maybe college age, for Kassie to brand her lusty. That would be totally inappropriate for Kassie to do, given she was old enough to be her mother. Although she wondered what words, and colors, Chris would use to paint her.

"Oh, this is Christopher Gaines. My, uh, Mr. Ricci's son."

It took Kassie a moment to recall Mike mentioning a young college student named Cecilia who was a hospital volunteer when he was there that fateful Easter weekend. She'd delivered his meals and helped direct him to the chapel and the library. He'd portrayed her as an ambitious idealist . . . and a hottie . . . who had a way with words, just like Kassie at her age.

Kassie's shoulders loosened ever so slightly. "I remember Mike telling me about you. Looks like you're still volunteering?"

"Oh, yes. Did he tell you I spend all of my time at this awesome institution of health care whenever I'm not in class or in the library with my nose in a book or sitting by the Charles writing? Did he also tell you I'm going to be a famous writer someday?"

"Yes, I remember Mike being very impressed by your dreams and aspirations. What brings you here today?"

"I was happy—well, not really happy—to see Mr. Ricci's name on the list of new patients admitted this week. I make it a habit to visit people whose acquaintance I've made, when—I mean *if*—they return to take advantage of the . . . um . . . exceptional doctoring and nursing this monumental hospital provides Bostonians."

Despite the sadness Kassie witnessed in Mike's eyes, there was also a slight glimmer as he seemed delighted by Cecilia's attention and prattle.

"Cecilia is splendid and charming company," Mike said. "She filled my morning with unceasing humor and effulgent glad tidings."

OMG, it's contagious. What the hell does effulgent even mean?

"Look it up," Mike mouthed to Kassie, able to read what was behind her furrowed brow, as a husband of thirty years naturally would.

"Mrs. Ricci, now that you're here, you might want to let the nurses know of your presence. They popped in at various intervals this morning asking if you had arrived."

Before she did that, Mike asked her to wait so he could give her and Chris an executive summary to the extent he could. He started with late Monday afternoon; he'd felt like shit so he tried to reach her, but her phone was turned off.

"Oh, Mike, I'm sorry." Her mind rewound to Monday night . . . the proposal on the bridge, the rash. Not much she could've done had he succeeded in reaching her. She was sorry, all the same.

He tried Bill; no answer either. He was with a client. So he called Amelia. Lucky for him, she and Teresa were at the Millers' house up the street, so they rushed over. They called the ambulance, and he'd been recuperating ever since.

Wait just a damn minute. Something was out of kilter. He'd called Kassie, Bill, and Amelia, but not Karen? And she wasn't at the hospital and probably hadn't been there earlier, or Mike would've known that she and Chris had reconciled. Had Chris also noticed Karen was missing in word and deed?

"You had a heart attack, they say," Chris piped in.

"Just a tremor, not a major earthquake." Mike tried to laugh but fell short, as did his three visitors.

"Nevertheless . . ." Kassie patted Mike's arm, the one without the bells and whistles attached.

Mike continued. "Amelia helped me help the hospital administrators complete all the *requisite* . . ." He winked at Cecilia. ". . . paperwork. You're listed in case of emergency, but they really wanted your signature too for some godforsaken reason."

"Probably just insurance related. We're still coinsured."

"I hope that's not why you came back from . . . where were you anyway?"

"Here, Chris, you tell Mike." As Kassie left to find the nurses' station, she heard Cecilia say her goodbyes and that she'd drop by to see him each day he was there. Kassie was touched, wondering who'd adopted whom in that odd May-December companionship.

Kassie did her duty as Mrs. Michael Ricci, maybe for the last time; their divorce would be final in two months. It hadn't occurred to her until then that both of them would have to designate new beneficiaries, new next of kin. Until a week ago, she probably would've asked Annie to fill that role for her when the time came. Under the latest circumstances, Chris would make more sense. For Mike, more than likely Karen, *eek*, would step in and fill Kassie's shoes—if Karen was still in the picture. She had a sneaking suspicion more had happened over the weekend than red hair dye and a ride in an ambulance.

Chris and Mike seemed to be having a good laugh when Kassie returned to Mike's room.

"How much did you tell him?" Kassie teased.

"Enough to know that congratulations are in order. Good for you," Mike said, nodding toward Kassie. "And good for you too, Chris. You did this all on your own. Without my help."

"Your help?" Chris said.

Mike asked if Kassie had been home yet, to Annie's. Oh, so she hadn't seen the package he'd sent. He explained he'd sent duplicate letters, one to her and the other to Chris, in one envelope.

"While you guys were canoodling in Europe, I made a minor change to my will. I know you won't mind that I carved out a small percentage for Bill. I wrote a letter, had it all notarized, and had copies sent to you, Kassie. I gave one to Bill and sent others to Stephen and my accountant. Actually, I met with Stephen on Monday. He drew up and filed a codicil so everything's square if something happens to me."

"Nothing's happening to you. You heard Cecilia. You're in the *best-est* place in town." They shared a laugh.

"Anyway, Chris, I had this bright idea, a ploy, if you will. If I sent both of the letters to Kassie, she'd be forced to get in touch with you. Then, nature would take its course. You'd find each other again, and I would be the catalyst that brought you together, making up for how I caused you to split last year."

Kassie looked at Chris. They both looked at Mike.

"That's a touching story, but you're full of shit." Kassie admitted to herself that it felt good to laugh. "A romantic you are not, not now, not ever."

Mike shrugged his shoulders; one of the monitors beep-beeped, then settled to a regular pace. "Well, you can't fault a guy for trying."

"Your heart," Chris said, placing his fist on his chest, "was in the right place. If I hadn't found her in Venice, I would've been grateful for your grand plan. I needed all the help I could get. She's not easy to pin down. Even still. I'll let her tell you all about that."

Kassie gazed at the ceiling and scratched that little obscure area behind the ear where the back of an earring rubs. She ached to tell Mike her good news, believing his reaction would be different than Chris's. With respect to Chris, though, she'd prefer knowing he was all on board before doing so. She didn't want to jinx it.

"Not sure what Chris is talking about, but if you're causing a ruckus for my son . . ."

Kassie caught Chris tilting his head with an ear-to-ear grin. Since she'd been absent from both of their lives over the past year, she wasn't sure if Mike's reference to Chris as his son was an everyday common occurrence. Given Chris's reaction, she assumed this could be a breakthrough moment.

"Nothing we can't sort out and bring to an equitable solution, Dad."

"All righty, then," Mike said, clasping his hands into a steeple. "Now, if you don't mind, Chris, I'd like to talk to my wife alone." He laughed. "May be the last time I say something like that, eh?"

35

The Forgiven

Once Chris left the room, Mike motioned Kassie to put her rear in the chair right up close to him, the one Cecilia had occupied.

"Get your ass over here, young lady. We need to talk. While I still can."

"Just because we won't be married in a couple of months doesn't mean we won't talk. There'll always be the Chris connection. Holidays may be a little weird, but we'll get used to it." She chuckled, and so did he.

Mike asked her what Chris meant when he said she was difficult to pin down. "I see a ring on your finger I don't recognize. You want to tell me about that, *Mrs. Ricci?*"

Kassie flushed, briefly covering her face with her hands. "All it means is we're engaged to be engaged. I told Chris I'm still Mrs. Ricci." She waved her left hand high enough for him to see she still wore his engagement and wedding rings, though she couldn't help noticing the tan-less imprint of his wedding band on his finger, but no ring.

"I'm just kidding with you. Let me see that ring."

She leaned in as Mike held her hand close to his face and kissed it. "A nail. Is it really a nail?"

"Exquisitely unique. Like our relationship, don't you think?"

"Shame on you, Kassie. With all your fascination with witch-craft, I'd think you'd have caught the symbolism of the ring, beyond the whole engagement thing."

"Oh my God, you're right. With all the hullabaloo over the last several days, I hadn't given it much thought."

Mike tutored her on the connection of the nail to the crucifixion and then added, "See, I did learn something during catechism class."

"The passion story, right?"

Mike nodded. "In the Bible, passion is thought to mean suffering. Over time, passion has obviously evolved to connote desire, especially of the sexual kind. Ooh la la." He inhaled deeply through his nose and exhaled out his mouth, gazing down at his hands folded on his lap, contemplating his own sexual future.

"Witches take it a step further, if I recall correctly," Kassie said, adding to the story. "Consider what a nail does. It binds one thing to another." She twirled the ring. "Protects whatever it's fastened to from being harmed. So there you have it."

"I prefer the witches' view," Mike said.

"I do too."

Kassie's phone buzzed. Unknown caller. "She'll leave a message," Kassie said, sensing it was her mother working her witchcraft from heaven above.

"You still haven't told me what Chris meant. You did say yes to his proposal?"

"Yes, but first things first. You must know I would never deliber-ately slight you by getting engaged before we were officially not Mr. and Mrs. any longer. And then there's this other itsy-bitsy complica-tion." Kassie touched her thumb and index finger together.

"Which is what?"

Kassie began the story from her vantage point, starting with the co-conspirators commonly known as Chris and Annie.

"Oh, that explains why she was at the concert." Mike shook his head.

Kassie continued with being whisked away to Paris on the craziest tourist weekend of the year, maybe of the century. The cryptic letter from Tom. The shopping spree. Tanya, the leggy queen of Uber who happened to appear whenever they needed a lift. Mike would've loved to get a gander at her. Oh, and the rash. Remember how she was allergic to pomegranates? Chris's proposal—she made him do it twice. And then the crux of the matter.

"I went to the meeting with rash and ring, but no business cards. Can you imagine me with no business cards to meet Mimi? You remember, I'd met her years before?"

"Wasn't she pregnant? I recall you freaked out about that."

"Guess what? She's pregnant again. With twins." Kassie reached her hands toward the ceiling.

Mike threw his head back. "You're kidding me. Did you think someone was playing a mean joke on you?"

"Uh, no. I'm really trying to get past all of that pulling-at-my-heart-strings kind of stuff. At my age, there's not much I can do about it. I came to realize a few years ago *mother* is not in my bio."

"I'm sorry, Kassie, truly." Mike reached for her left hand, held it as long as she'd let him. "If I could live my life over, that's the first thing I'd change. The vasectomy was cruel and selfish. Knowing I'd walked away from one child, I thought being a father, especially a good father, was not in *my* bio."

Mike frowned when Kassie tucked her chin. He lifted it and wiped a tear trickling down her cheek.

"Not as much over it as you think, me thinks. I am so sorry. Will you ever forgive me?"

"I will, if you will. When I first met Chris, I was lonely and deeply saddened by how our marriage had drifted. At the beginning, I couldn't have predicted where you and I, and he and I, would end up. I'm sure my wandering ways hurt you. . . ." Kassie traced an *A* on her forehead.

Mike bit his lower lip. "I was hurt then, and since. . . ."

"Since? Not by me, I hope. I tried to make amends when I tracked down Karen—"

Mike's eyebrows rose toward the top of his forehead. "Bingo."

"Karen? Hurt you? How? Where is she, by the way? Why isn't she here? We ran into her in Charlestown just before we headed over."

Now it was Mike's turn. Just as Kassie had, he started with Friday, omitting his romp with Amelia. No reason to give Kassie any fodder to defend Karen, as if she ever would. He told her about dinner with the Gaineses and Bill and Nancy. Karen's surprise dye job. The smoke and the game Charlie wanted to play, but that they didn't. His changing the will, the trip to the bank and FedEx. Sarah's supposed headache. Provincetown on Sunday. The proposal on the dunes.

"Oh, Guy and Dolly send their regards."

Kassie smiled and said she'd have to drag Chris out there. "Wouldn't they get a kick out of my ring?"

Mike chuckled and went on. Funny thing, though not humorous, was that even after he'd proposed to Karen, she'd declined to stay at the house that night. Again, he omitted their quickie in the back seat of his SUV. And then there was this teeny-tiny complication: Red Sox tickets.

Not surprisingly, Kassie bolted upright when he mentioned Red Sox. It was a Pavlovian response.

"She did what?"

"Shredded them. And then lied about it."

Kassie buried her head in her hands. He didn't know which

had gotten her goat more—the destruction of the tickets or Karen's prevarication.

"That was a mean thing for her to do to Bill. Wonder what that's all about? She must've had a good reason."

Mike gave her the *Reader's Digest* version of the little bit he knew about the breakfast conversation involving Sarah and Karen . . . and of course, Chris. From what he'd heard, Bill had put his two cents in. But Mike digressed.

He wrung his hands together as he proceeded to the events of Monday. He said he had this big idea of showing up at Karen's apartment unannounced to give her a chance to explain away the ticket fiasco. It was the least he could do. He owed her that much.

"So what did she say?"

"Nothing. It's not what she didn't say, but what she did." Mike felt a sudden tightness in his chest and kneaded it with his fist.

"What'd she do?" Kassie leaned in, wide-eyed.

"She was with Charlie." Mike flinched and his eyes flickered.

Kassie slumped in her chair and bombarded him with questions about what he meant by "with Charlie"—was he sure it was him? Maybe he'd gone to the apartment looking for Chris and ran into Karen instead? Maybe he was just passing time while Sarah was at her museum thingamajig?

"Maybe Sarah was in the car, picking him up on the way to the airport?"

"No maybes about it, sweet optimistic Kassie. I know what I saw. I stood there with my eyes bugging out and watched them kiss, long and deep. Tongue had to be involved. And then Charlie patted her on the ass. This was no see-you-soon-pal goodbye. More like wham-bam-thank-you-ma'am, catch you later. I know. Been there. Done that."

"Then what? Did you walk right up to her and give her the what for?"

"I should've, huh?"

"Damn right."

"I think I was in shock. Couldn't believe my eyes. I'd just proposed to her on Sunday. On Monday she shacks up with Charlie. Charlie of all people."

"Of all people? Of anyone." Kassie stood and paced the room. "And so, what happened? You went home and had a heart attack?"

"That about sums it up. In all my years, I guess I never learned how to handle confrontation well. Still don't."

"Does she know you know?"

"Yesterday, I asked her how Charlie was. I told her to leave. She did without a word. She didn't even ask how I knew. And she's not been back since."

"Do you want to see her? See if you can fix things before they release you from here? Sounds like the ball's in your court."

"Not sure. Now I'm angry. At first, I felt hurt, betrayed. Now I'm pissed. When I think back over the years I supported her, behind your back, and all that she and I have been through in the last year or so, I can't help but wonder if she was playing a game."

"What kind of a game? Everyone knew she wanted you in the worst way."

"The worst way is right. In her mind, giving me her kidney was the key to the castle. Literally. She got me, Chris, a job, my continued generosity. The signs were there. I just denied them. What is that saying? If it's—"

"If something seems too good to be true, it probably is."

"That's the one."

"Don't be so tough on yourself."

"I did push back on one thing, though. She wanted you scrubbed from my life in every which way. Last weekend she asked me to promise to get rid of everything in your office. I told her I would, but I didn't mean it. Huh. Can't imagine her reaction to you and Chris being back together."

Mike heard a light knock on the door as a nurse walked in.

"This isn't teatime here, Mr. Ricci. You need to rest. Visiting hours are over for now."

"But, but—" Mike tried to argue.

Kassie leaned toward Mike and gave him a kiss that he'd swear lingered more than a friendly peck.

"But you didn't tell me what happened in your meeting with Mimi."

"Tomorrow. I'll be back tomorrow. It'll wait until then."

Mike cocked his head to the side, pouting, as Kassie lifted her left hand and waved a slight salute with a twist goodbye.

36

Movin' On

On her way past the nurses' station, Kassie stopped and asked for the name and phone number of Mike's cardiologist. She'd call him the next day to get the lowdown on Mike's condition and prognosis. With Karen's dubious status, Kassie decided as his wife it was still her responsibility to be sure Mike was well cared for.

She texted Chris to meet in the lobby. She had no clue how she'd tell him about Karen and Charlie. His mother and his adoptive father were getting it on when his mother supposedly was engaged to his father. *Did you get that?* Would Chris?

The one common denominator in that triangle was Karen. She was the perpetrator. The only one positioned to correct the situation. She needed a comeuppance. The question was who would give it to her? *Not me. Not my job.* Would Chris step up to the plate to defend Mike . . . and Sarah?

Oh, no. Sarah. With the image of Charlie and Karen embracing on the streets of Charlestown swirling through her head, Kassie had forgotten about Sarah. She was the innocent party in this scenario.

Chris would go apeshit. No wonder Mike asked him to leave the room before telling Kassie what happened. Not sure who Chris would attack or blame.

"There you are," Chris said, wrapping his arm around her shoulder as they headed out through the automatic sliding doors, stepping aside to let a woman wheel in an elderly man who probably should've come through Emergency instead of the main lobby. Briefly, Kassie considered offering to help, but she quickly conceded there were more than enough professionals in the lobby to handle whatever the problem was.

Instead Kassie said, "Can we just go home now?" Kassie searched her purse for her sunglasses. She needed them not only to block the blinding sun but also to hide the rising panic Chris would more than likely read in her eyes. "Think the jet lag is finally getting to me."

"Home? To my place?"

"For a while. I need to see Topher . . . and Annie tonight. Okay?"

"That works. While you were with Mike, I talked with Annie. We're having dinner there tonight. There's no food in my fridge." Chris shrugged his shoulders.

"You two are good buddies these days. Seems like you guys talk more often than Annie and I do." Kassie slung her purse in the back seat of the car, contemplating all of the strange bedfellows that popped up that day—Mike and Cecilia, Karen and Charlie, Chris and Annie.

"You have a problem with that?"

"Guess not. Not anymore." She reached across the front seats and rubbed his arm.

"So, what was Mike's reaction?" Chris said as they pulled out of the parking garage.

"To what?"

"Paris. The job, silly."

"More importantly, how are you feeling about it today—after wearing the idea for twenty-four hours?"

"Still working it through my psyche. I don't relish the idea of you and me apart again. Like I told you."

"Less than a year, Chris. Come on. What's ten months after what we've been through?"

"It'll take us that long to plan . . ." Chris paused at an intersection. "If you go, first we'll need to set a date for the wedding."

"Wedding? Sounds strange. But okay, I think I can handle that. From Paris. I can have Tanya take me back to see Gabriella for the perfect dress."

Chris asked her again what Mike's reaction was. Kassie stared out the window, not ignoring him, just lost in the moment. His question forced her to replay Mike's story and feel his pain. At some point she knew she'd have to transfer that pain to Chris. Mike didn't ask her to keep it a secret. Was that his plan all along? He couldn't tell Chris, couldn't hurt him, but he was confident Kassie would break the news gently, as a woman would. Of course, that depended on which Kassie accepted the nearly impossible mission. No matter how she conveyed it, she was certain Chris would freak.

"We didn't talk about Paris. Didn't get around to it."

"What? You were up there for more than half an hour. What did you talk about?"

"Us. You and me, not him and me." She stammered but didn't lie. "The weekend. Your proposal. My rash. Oh, and my ring. He loved it."

"That's it?"

"Well, remember I wondered what happened here this past weekend? I was right. It was a whopper. Sarah and Charlie, Bill and Nancy, and Karen and Mike had dinner together Friday night. Sounds like it all went downhill from there."

"How so?" Chris asked as they arrived at the apartment.

"I'll tell you later. I need a nap."

Kassie skirted any further discussion about Mike, except for his health issues. She didn't avoid divulging the scandal because she was a coward, as Annie accused her of being when it took her years to tell Mike she wanted a divorce. Not a coward, just at a loss for words. She'd seen the toll Karen's betrayal took on Mike; she could only imagine how Chris would take a double whammy—or a triple, if you included Sarah in the mix.

Apparently, Chris wasn't as wiped out as Kassie as he left her alone in the bedroom to rest. Her pheromones must've been on hiatus too, as he didn't nuzzle up to her for an afternoon delight. For once, she was glad. She was in no mood. And age had nothing to do with it.

Nestled under the covers in her undies and a pink Red Sox T-shirt she'd pulled out of her suitcase, Kassie closed her eyes, took the deepest cleansing breath she could muster, and let her mind sort out the whole stinkin' state of affairs. When she was ready to tell Chris, should she mimic Mike's storyline—start with Friday and work her way up to his heart attack? Or just blurt it out: "Karen and Charlie are a thing." On second thought, maybe she was a coward. Maybe she'd need a little moral support from her friends—Topher, pinot grigio, and Annie.

By the time she woke up, Chris had unpacked his bags from the trip and had all but her carry-on zipped up and waiting by the door.

"Looks like you're kicking me out already."

"Thought you might want to stay at Annie's for a couple of nights before you move over here. There's Topher to consider."

"Aren't you paying for him to live here? You added him to the lease way back when, as I recall."

"Um. When we split, I stopped that charge. I'll call the office tomorrow and add him back on. Then both you and he are welcome to move in here anytime. I'll have an instant family." Chris stood with his arms folded across his body, looking like Mr. Clean with a full head of gorgeous brown hair graying a bit here and there.

Kassie looked around the apartment with a different eye than she had a year ago in April. At that time, she'd considered it temporary housing, so its smallness wasn't an issue. That was then; this was now.

"How long is your lease?"

"Up in September. Like your marriage." Chris slammed his eyelids shut. "Oops. That was low. I'm sorry."

"No, no. That's okay." Kassie's head bobbed up and down. "We can manage here until then. But we should start looking for another place. Even though I'll be in Paris part-time, we need a bigger apartment, maybe a condo like Annie's. Topher takes up a lot of space. Find something more convenient to Ricci and Son."

"And away from Karen," Chris said.

Kassie pursed her lips, not ready to go there quite yet.

"Let's go. Someone's waiting for a tummy rub."

"Me too, mommy," Chris teased as he patted her on her rear.

Good grief. Like adoptive father, like son. If he only knew.

37

Who's Who

As soon as she stepped through Annie's front door, she could tell Topher was as happy to see her as she was him. *Thump, thump* from above. A loud chorus of meows echoed down the center hall stairway; an orange tail with a white tip swung to his beat. Kassie knelt down to greet the other love of her life. "I missed you, babycakes."

"He spent most of the time curled up on your bed while you were gone. He's sure glad to see you, though I'm not." Annie greeted them, dish towel in hand.

"That's a fine how-do-ya-do." When Kassie stood to squeeze Annie, Topher rubbed up against the pant leg of his namesake.

"Guess he still remembers me." Chris leaned down and massaged Topher's chin.

"Me too. Come here, Chris, give me a hug," Annie reached out her arms to him.

"So . . . why aren't you glad to see *us*?" Kassie's eyes bounced from Annie to Chris and back again.

"Duh. Because you should still be in Paris doing whatever French

people do. Not back here dealing with all this Michael Ricci crap."
Annie waved them toward the kitchen. "His timing sucked. Do you
think it was deliberate?"

"Whoa. Now you're sounding even more cynical than I usually
am. When did that happen?"

"Probably when we were sixteen, but you were too busy surviving
your dysfunctional family to notice."

Annie handed Chris a beer as she and Kassie took their wine
glasses and the 1.5 liter of pinot grigio into the living room. Chris
and Topher followed close behind. The girls plunked down on the
sofa, while the guys—Chris and Topher—sat on an opposite chair.

"So, how's the patient? Chris said you went to see him today."

"He'll live, I think," Kassie said.

"Now who's the cynic?" Annie huffed.

"He looks like hell, though. Don't you think, Chris? Worse than
Easter weekend."

"I wouldn't know. Remember I was squirreled away in a hotel
then? But he does look like he's been through a lot."

"I'm still trying to piece together what happened. Over the weekend. And Monday." Kassie sprinkled breadcrumbs, hoping Annie
would take the bait.

"All I know is what Bill told me when he called looking for you.
Oh, and when I saw Mike at the concert."

"The concert. Saturday night? Why don't you start there?" Kassie
jumped at the chance to have Annie start the narrative, getting her
off the hook.

And she did. Annie began by saying there wasn't much to tell. It
was an oldies concert they would've—well, at least Kassie would've—
enjoyed. "Chris, you're still too young for oldies music."

"Not."

"I rest my case. Who responds *not* except people too young for
oldies concerts?"

Kassie gave Annie a quick shot in the arm. "That's my fiancé you're badgering."

"Oh, yeah. Congratulations. Tell me—"

"Oh, no, you don't. Stick to one story at a time."

"Where was I? Oh, yeah, the concert." Annie was right, there wasn't much to tell. She was there with her friend Jack, and they ran into Mike near the porta potties. "Shitty place to have a conversation."

After a communal guffaw, Annie said she'd sensed Mike was surprised to see her and was about to ask about Kassie. Not wanting to go down that path, not wanting to lie to Mike's face, she hustled Jack away. "See you later, alligator. Well, didn't say that, but should've given the concert."

"Makes sense Mike was surprised to see you. I'd told him we were planning a trip to Venice. When he saw you, he probably thought I was back."

"Well, that was that, until Bill called me Tuesday morning. Around five thirty. You know I was up, but who calls someone at that ungodly hour? Only bad news arrives then. I freaked. Thought something happened to you guys."

Kassie calculated the time difference between there and Paris. She would've been meeting with Mimi at that time, almost lunchtime. With that thought, her stomach gurgled loudly enough for Topher to raise his head off Chris's lap.

"Anyone else hungry? Should we order in?" Kassie asked, rubbing her middle.

Annie looked at her phone. "Grubhub should arrive any minute now. Let's get some plates."

Once they'd settled in at the dining table, Annie finished telling them about her call with Bill. Of course, his first priority was getting word to Kassie that Mike was in the hospital, but he blabbered on about Karen, which she thought was odd because he had to know Annie wasn't a big fan of hers and, by the way, his complaining only served to reinforce Annie's opinion. Since she wanted to be careful not to spill the beans about the two of them being in Paris, she listened to Bill with only one ear, but it was clear his anxiety about Mike extended beyond a possible heart attack.

"What did he say that made you think that?" Chris said.

"Something about Karen shredding Red Sox tickets, and Bill worried that's what caused Mike's heart attack."

"That's just the half of it," Kassie mumbled the words, regretting them as soon as they tripped out of her mouth. Whereas all eyes had been on Annie, now Kassie became the center of attention.

"What did you say?" Annie and Chris asked in unison.

Kassie clanked her fork across her plate and bowed her head. She'd gone and done it. The proverbial cat was out of the bag with no pathway to return. Didn't matter whether she was ready to show all her cards; there was no way for her to deny she knew the rest of the story.

She lifted her gaze at Chris and reached to caress his hand.

"You know when Mike asked you to leave the room today? Oh, sure, he was interested in us, in Paris, in my ring. I think he was being polite."

"Polite? Well, that'd be a first," Annie said.

Kassie shot her a just-stop-it glance. "His real intent, *I believe*, was to tell me what happened Monday, and over the weekend."

Tap-tapping her fork on her plate, Kassie continued, "It's logical Bill would've thought Karen shredding the tickets was devastating enough to cause Mike to collapse. It would've killed me dead as a doornail right on the spot."

She massaged the underside of her engaged-to-be-engaged ring and took a larger than usual swig of her wine, trying to delay the inevitable.

She returned her gaze to Chris, gulped so hard both ears popped, and plowed ahead the only way she knew how.

"It appears Karen's desire to marry Mike was not based on true love."

"How would you know that?" Annie said.

"There appears to be someone else in Karen's life."

"Who might that be?" Chris's eyebrows furrowed, seeming more curious than taken aback by the notion.

"I'm sorry to tell you this, Chris. Mike saw Karen kissing Charlie."

"You make it sound like 'I saw Mommy kissing Santa Claus.'" Chris chuckled.

Was he brushing her off? Not taking her seriously was not on the list of reactions Kassie expected from him.

"It wasn't just a kiss or a peck on the cheek, hon. It was more than that. Touching. Her ass. In public. On the street alongside your apartment, her apartment—I don't know the name of it—in Charlestown. Do you know the name of it?" Kassie directed the question to Annie.

"How the hell should I know?" Annie glared at Chris, whose mouth was closed, but his eyes narrowed, as if he were envisioning the scene.

"Whatever. Doesn't matter," Kassie said. "Mike saw Karen and Charlie leave the building arm in arm. They didn't see him." She paused, letting that sink in.

She noticed Chris's breathing getting heavier.

"When did he say this happened?" Chris asked.

"Monday afternoon. Apparently, Mike proposed to Karen—officially, by the way—on Sunday when they were in Provincetown. On the dunes."

"Poor Mike. To find out your partner is having an affair is one thing. To see it right in front of you is quite another," Chris said. "No wonder—"

"But she gave him her kidney," Annie piped in. "Why would she do that if she didn't love him?"

"Look what it got her," Chris said.

"Welcome to the Cynics Club," Annie said.

Kassie's head swiveled as Annie and Chris sorted through the pieces, trying to put the puzzle together. For Kassie, it was déjà vu; there'd been other dinners during which the two of them had their own private conversations, leaving her a bystander, or worse, an eavesdropper. Maybe it was best this way; took the pressure off her.

"A job," Kassie said, trying not to be ignored.

"More like a cushy life—a house, security, money, a future," Annie said in Chris's direction.

"Me," Chris said, flinging his napkin on the table.

"There is that. But that's only half the puzzle. What's the connection with Charlie?" Annie asked.

"They knew each other in college," Chris said.

"Wonder how well?" Neither Kassie nor Chris picked up on Annie's question, shifting instead to the innocent party.

"Does my mother—I mean, Sarah . . . does she know? Did Mike say?" Chris stood in such a huff, Kassie and Annie pushed back their chairs as if to follow his lead. "Don't get up."

Sounds of Elton John floated into the dining room until Kassie broke an unusual silence between her and Annie. "Not sure who to feel sorry for, Mike or Chris?"

The few minutes Chris was in the loo allowed them to digest the situation. In a whisper, they agreed Mike had a tough decision to make. If Karen came clean, would he forgive her and marry her? Should he confront Charlie, find out what his intentions were? How should Chris deal with Karen? Should he even? Or was it really any of his concern that his parents, at least three of them, had screwed up their lives?

Chris returned with a beer. "That bastard."

"Which one?" Annie said, still not a big Mike fan, despite his heart attack.

"Charlie. How could he do that to Sarah? They've been married forever." Chris raised his voice in a way Kassie rarely witnessed.

"Maybe that's why?" Annie glanced at Kassie. "Mike and Kassie were married forever. Look what happened to them."

"Perhaps," Chris said, shaking his head.

"All right. Let's consider this. Karen made herself available to Charlie for old times' sake. A one night—um, one-day—stand, if you will. Most men wouldn't turn down free nookie," Annie said, always the pseudo-psychologist, trying to place the blame on Karen.

They were doing it again. Excluding her. She'd fix that. She had to. Chris had taken to rubbing various body parts—his forehead, his arms, his hands.

"Wait. Before we go too far, why don't we give Karen—and Charlie, for that matter—the benefit of the doubt? Maybe it wasn't a tryst, just a friendly goodbye, a thank-you-for-the-weekend visit. Everyone deserves their day in court, don't they?" Kassie offered a scenario she didn't totally buy into herself. She just wanted to cool Chris down.

Two pairs of eyes stared at her. She turned her head, expecting to see someone hovering behind.

"What? I just think before we start waving fingers, making accusations, we should take a step back. Maybe Mike misinterpreted what he saw. He was upset when he drove to Charlestown on Monday."

Two heads were shaking.

"You're unbelievable. Where's Bad Kassie when we need her?" Annie said.

Someone's phone rang. The three amigos pulled their phones out of their pockets and placed them on the table. Chris lifted his.

He looked at Kassie. "It's Lexi. I'll call her back." He twitched his nose and started to shut down his phone.

"No, Chris. Take it." Kassie nodded toward the family room.

"Hello. What's up? Just got back . . ." Chris's voice faded.

"Who the fuck is Lexi?"

38

Home Sweet Home

And then there were two. Chris didn't stick around long after the call from Lexi. He offered no explanation for his departure, and Kassie didn't ask. Giving her a gentle kiss goodbye, he encouraged her to stay at Annie's that night. Since she had the rest of the week off, Chris reminded her she'd have more than enough time over the next few days to gather her essentials and Topher's paraphernalia and move them both to Charlestown. He gave Annie a sweet hug and pat on the head, and he was off.

Chris's headlights had barely faded when Kassie grabbed the wine bottle by its neck and made tracks to the living room.

"I'll get clean glasses and meet you there," Annie said.

Kassie changed the music. Nat King Cole was more in tune with her melancholy mood.

"You let him leave? Are you nuts? It's been five nights, and you let Chris walk out the door?"

"Just for tonight. His idea. You heard him. If you ask me, I think it's jet lag. I took a nap this afternoon, so I'm good. It's obvious he's not."

"Jet lag, my ass."

"Whatever you want to call it, I think he needs a break, we need a break. Too much happening in way too short a time." Kassie placed her hand around her throat, making both a choking gesture and gasping noise.

"Kassie, you know better. You can't play the martyr with me. I gather there's more going on besides Mike. Fill me in. Starting with Lexi."

Kassie shrugged her shoulders and poured the wine. "Cookies. I'm feeling the need for something sweet." That was true, but what she really wanted was time to recall the details about Lexi, which were few and far between. And where to begin? If she started with the journal, she'd be distracted by the Mimi meeting and the Paris offer, which she was super antsy to tell Annie about, and she'd never get around to answering her immediate question.

Annie surprised Kassie with a platter of homemade oatmeal chocolate chip cookies. "Nervous energy. I hated calling you guys about Mike, screwing up everything I worked so hard to pull off. So I baked. Some people clean. I bake."

"And I eat. As usual, you're taking good care of me."

Kassie sipped her wine, ate a cookie, and decided she'd put off the inevitable long enough. She'd honor Annie's request and start with Lexi. It was the least she could do for a friend. Her best friend. Though there wasn't much she could tell her. From what she gleaned from his journal and the brief conversation they'd had, Lexi was a gal he'd dated occasionally in San Francisco. He'd met her at work, but she'd joined another firm along the way. They'd stayed friends.

"Did he see her all those years he was seeing you? Friends with benefits?"

"Not sure, I haven't asked, but it's possible. We weren't committed. Remember I was married. I never asked him if he saw other people. I never asked him not to. I guess I hoped he didn't. I was in no position to ask him to be faithful to me."

"Are you in a different position now, Mrs. Ricci?"

"Yes, I'd say I am. But don't call me that. Chris and I are engaged to be engaged." Kassie showed Annie the ring up close. "I'll make it official once the divorce is final and switch it to the other hand. Makes sense, doesn't it? Please say so."

"Sure. Whatever you say. I'm with you one hundred percent. But where does Lexi fit in this scenario?"

"Once everything fell apart between us last year and Chris permanently joined the company, he flew back to San Francisco to pack and move here. He and Lexi got together again, I gather."

"For old times' sake, sounds like."

"You make it sound naughty."

"I call 'em like I see 'em. Did he tell her about you?"

"Kind of. He says it was her idea for us to put Venice in the rearview mirror and fly to Paris for the week."

"Seems I have competition. It was my idea for Chris to surprise you in Venice to begin with."

"I know. Don't feel bad. He told me. I love you for that." Kassie hugged Annie. "I noticed an Athens stamp in his passport. I bet they went there earlier this year. So Greece was probably out. He claims Lexi thought Paris would give us a new, fresh start."

"Why didn't I think of that?" Annie pouted.

"You did the right thing. Venice was about closure. There would've been no logical reason for me to go to Paris, to meet you in Paris."

"Except I've never been to Paris."

"Well, get ready to check it off your bucket list. You'll have a very good reason to go soon."

Annie's eyes widened as she touched the wine glass to her lips. "How so?"

Kassie held on to the couch, stood up, and wobbled around the room, bumping into end tables and chairs. Leaving nothing to Annie's imagination, she relayed the entire soup-to-nuts story, including the Uber man-eater. Bottom line, the position in Paris was the chance of a lifetime, or at least the chance of her career, even if it was temporary. Top management's clearest indicator that she'd arrived; they'd trust her to handle the merger of an international office while continuing to manage and grow the business. Kassie did a happy dance before handing Annie her glass and rushing down the hall before she wet her pants.

"How long will this opportunity of a lifetime last?" Annie asked after first asking Kassie if she'd washed her hands.

"Yes, mother. Am I supposed to ask your permission to work in Paris?"

"No, just wondering—"

"Oh my God. Topher, you're worried that I'll saddle you with him?"

"No, just wondering—"

"Don't worry, Chris will take him. Comes with the territory." She waved the ring.

"It's not Topher I'm wondering about. It's Chris-topher, you ninny."

"Why worry about Chris?" Kassie gave Annie a what-are-you-kidding-me eye roll. "I think he's good with this, or he will be when I'm finished convincing him. Anyway, he'll be super busy with his company, especially if Mike takes an extended leave—which, by the way, he should. I'll be gone less than a year. We've survived a long-distance relationship before."

Annie's eyebrows rose as high as humanly possible. "There are no guarantees. Look what happened last year. You thought you had it all figured out, and then *poof*—it was gone."

"Things are different now. And so much drama. Kidney swaps.

Ricci and *Son*. Out of the friggin' blue I became a stepmother to the fellow I was sleeping with."

"Get over it, girl. Didn't your trip to Venice teach you anything? You never were a stepmother in the truest sense of the word. You weren't then, and you're not now."

Kassie lowered her head and gripped her face with her hands. Had she replaced her motherhood obsession with a stepmother fixation? Maybe Annie was onto something.

"So why is Lexi calling him now when she thinks he's in Paris with you?"

Kassie peered straight at Annie. "I haven't the foggiest."

Annie handed Kassie a tumbler of hot tea and shooed her out the door, curtailing their plans to have Kassie stay the night. It was after eleven when she pulled into a spot under a streetlight on the road parallel to the apartment in Charlestown. She wondered whether that was the scene of the crime—the smooch heard around the city of Boston. She glanced up at the building, not knowing which apartment was Karen's, yet wondering if she saw Kassie pull in and get out of the car.

Truth be known, by the time she'd arrived in Charlestown, any notion of giving Karen a fair shake had scampered away. So it seemed, Karen was not the benevolent lady friend she'd held herself out to be when they first met in Chicago. Kassie shook her head, grasping the irony of it all. Karen's selfishness, not her selflessness, had sent Mike back to the hospital in as serious a condition as Karen supposedly rescued him from. And the latest development had the potential to hurt Chris and Sarah—the very people Karen and Charlie supposedly loved the most.

Kassie hoisted the overnight bag she'd repacked at Annie's out of the trunk and grabbed her purse and the mail that had arrived while she was away. From that moment forward, Kassie decided she didn't give a flying giraffe what Karen thought or wanted.

Kassie was home where she belonged, at least until she left for Paris.

She buzzed their apartment. He let her in . . . as did she him.

39

Breaking News

Chris held the door open, wearing the silk blue boxers Kassie had bought him the year after their first meetup in Venice and a Red Sox T-shirt. Man after her own heart. As he swallowed her in his arms, she dropped her overnight bag, her purse, her briefcase, and the mail she'd picked up at Annie's.

As usual, her knees weakened at his touch, and as she breathed his just-showered green-apple scent, their limbs tangled like octopuses in heat. On her way there, she hadn't foreseen a booty call, but what the hell.

Chris kicked the door shut, neither of them caring if they annoyed the neighbors with the racket caused when Chris shoved the coffee table and side chair out of their way. Whatever. The neighbors might as well get used to the oohs and aahs emanating from the third floor. Perhaps they'd find it inspirational instead of nerve-wracking. Needless to say, the two lovebirds didn't quite make it to the bedroom for their first go-round.

A short time later, they curled up in bed and did what Kassie intended they do when she left Annie's place.

They talked. All things Paris, Mike and Karen and Charlie, Sarah, and Lexi. Not necessarily in that order, but all relevant topics just the same. They talked. And talked. And talked. Until the wee hours of the morning. Jet lag be damned. With no place to go on Thursday, they could stay up all night if they wanted. Staying in bed all day long as if they were young lovers or newlyweds was an option they considered. Sounded good to Kassie.

Not all the problems of their world were solved that night, or was it morning? She could never figure that one out. Stymied by one of life's major flip-flops—when children are forced to parent their parents—they agreed to postpone any attempt to solve the dilemma facing Chris for another day.

To Kassie's delight, Chris unequivocally agreed and wholeheartedly supported the Paris assignment.

"Stop jumping," he said. "You'll break the bed."

"If we break it, it won't be because of me jumping." Round two commenced.

Afterward, confident in her future, Kassie raised the least discussed topic: Lexi.

"Why'd she call? If she thought we were in Paris, why'd she call you?"

Chris hemmed and hawed. Anyone with even the slightest intuition would sense he really, really didn't want to talk about Lexi. He yawned . . . a lot. And rubbed his eyes. Was she thirsty? He needed water. Hold that thought. He'd be right back.

At long last, Chris stood at the foot of the bed with his arms folded across his chest and told her what he and Lexi talked about.

"She's coming to Boston . . . soon."

"So I'll meet her."

"Looks that way."

"When?"

"She suggested Sunday."

"Sunday. Whoa. The last day of our vacation. What's the rush?"

"I don't think there's a rush." Chris wore out the carpet. "I explained how right now may not be a good time with Mike in the hospital." His fingers thinned his hair. "I'm going to be very busy at the office. I told her I'd get back to her. We'd figure out a mutually beneficial date." He slid off his boxers and into bed next to Kassie.

Kassie asked Alexa the time. "It's 2:23 a.m." She told Alexa to turn off the lights, and they spooned.

"Before I leave for Paris?"

"We'll see."

"Holy shit, whose phone is that?" Kassie bolted upright and poked Chris in the hip. Being otherwise engaged earlier, they'd left their phones where they belonged—not in the bedroom.

Always the gentleman, even when naked, Chris bounded into the living room, returning with hers.

"Local number." He handed the phone to her.

"Hello? Yes, this is Kassandra Ricci. Oh, no. Can't be." Her sleepy eyes widened as she dug her fingernails into Chris's arm.

"He's dead," she mouthed to him and pointed to her wrist.

"Alexa, what time is it?" Chris asked.

Kassie glared at him as she jumped out of bed, holding the phone in one hand and wrapping a small beige blanket around her waist with the other.

"It's 5:42 a.m.," Alexa said as Kassie passed through the doorway and into the kitchen, shaking her head. *There's a time and place for gadgets. Now is neither the time nor the place.*

Clad only in his boxers, Chris followed her into the kitchen, picking up the envelopes and flyers she'd strewn on the floor upon her late-night arrival. Despite her body shaking as it often did when she'd climb into the dentist's chair, and her hands feeling like ice, Kassie calculated what time they'd be able to get to the hospital.

"If we're there between seven thirty and eight, where should we go? Who should we see?"

Rattled, she placed the phone in the sink and slumped to the floor. Chris joined her and clutched her hands.

"Massive heart attack. Nothing they could do."

"So much for a new kidney. Wonder if the disease and the transplant were just too much for his body to handle?"

"Seems like it, though we'll never know." Kassie's voice cracked. She leaned on Chris to help her get to her feet.

"Guess we can't stay under the covers all day."

"Oh, how I'd like to." Kassie shook her hands in the air. "I'll shower and then I'll figure out what's next."

"Should I—"

"No, don't call anyone yet. Too early." She read his mind. She grabbed the FedEx envelope that was on top of the pile and retrieved her phone out of the sink. *How did that get there?*

Kassie ratcheted up the hot water as high as she could stand until Chris intervened.

"Hey, you'll set off the smoke alarm. Turn it down in there."

She gasped, almost choking on the stream of water she'd inhaled, and did as she was told. Had he heard her crying? More like weeping. Poor Mike. He'd fought a good fight with his kidneys, and then his heart shut him down.

Mirrors don't lie. With the palm of her hand, she cleared away a circle of steam. She leaned in, her nose almost touching its reflection. Her eyes, pink from tears and weary from little sleep, gave her soul away. Even though she couldn't live with him, be tied to him as his wife, she didn't want Mike to die. If that were the case, she wouldn't have gone to the ends of the earth—well, actually, just to Chicago—to locate Karen, his ultimate savior. Or so everyone thought.

Oh no, Karen. Someone's going to have to tell her.

"I'm glad you're here and not at Annie's." Chris joined her in the bathroom as she toweled off.

"How *you* doin'?" Kassie tried desperately not to sound like Joey from *Friends.*

"Sad. And disappointed." Chris's lips turned down. "We were just starting to get to know each other. To be honest, it feels more like a good friend died than a blood relative. I think I'd freak if Sarah suddenly died, or Charlie."

"Really, Charlie? Despite what Mike told me yesterday?"

"Of course. He's still my father. Sarah's still my mother. They adopted me. Mike and Karen gave me away. If I can forgive Mike and Karen for that, I should be able to forgive Charlie for being a dick with a dick."

Kassie crawled onto the bed. "Come here, sit next to me."

She massaged Chris's back and kissed his shoulder. "You're the best thing that ever came into my life."

"I could've told you that."

"Seriously. You are a sweet, caring, and gentle man. Oh, and forgiving too. Did I mention that?"

"Keep going. . . . "

"It took me forever to forgive my mother for her duplicitousness, and I'm not sure I've totally forgiven Mike yet for his, though we both tried to go down that path in the hospital yesterday."

"How so?"

Kassie related the "I'll forgive you, if you forgive me" conversation. "Mike wants us to be happy. I believe that. And now he's dead. How can I hold a grudge against someone who can't hurt me any longer?"

"Sounds like you've answered your own question. You can't."

Chris handed her the overnight envelope from Mike. "Shouldn't you open this?"

"Why? We know what's in it. He told us yesterday." She reneged, peeling the strip. "Okay, let's do this." Two envelopes fell on the bed. Kassie groaned as she moved into a yoga position. "My knees are screaming at me."

Chris rubbed them, ignoring the envelope with his name.

Kassie opened her envelope and read what appeared to be a cover letter.

Dear Kassie,

Just a quickie. LOL. If you're reading this, hopefully I've gone upstairs and joined your mother. Surely, she's in heaven with your father and not expecting me to show up and crash their party.

You'll see on the enclosed I've made some changes to my will that I'm sending on to my lawyer and accountant, oh, and to Bill. I wanted to be sure he gets a little slice of the pie for his loyalty and friendship. Needless to say, you and Chris are still well taken care of, I believe.

If I'm allowed one last confession, it is this. Years ago when we had next to nothing, I wish you had joined me in starting Ricci and Associates. I know, I know you had your own booming career. I just think we would've smashed it had it been Ricci and O'Callaghan.

When I'm gone, I know in my heart, as the new majority owner, you'll take it to the moon and back. Wave to me on your way.

Mike

Kassie was crying, again. Waterworks was not her usual modus operandi. "Clever of him, don't you think, to bring my mother into this? Always knew my hot buttons."

Chris held her and stroked her wet hair. "Do you think he had a premonition?"

"You mean after thirty years of marriage my clairvoyance rubbed off on him? What, by osmosis? Doubt it. More than likely, he wanted to do something for Bill. Make his gratitude legal."

"That may be, but the company's yours, boss. Time to get a move on."

Kassie pushed him aside, wiped her cheeks, and hopped off the bed. "Don't call me that. Just an owner, not the boss. I have my own job. It's up to you and Bill now. Speaking of which, where's my brief-case?" She rushed into the living room.

Flipping through the more than half-full notebook, she said, "I need to go to Target or Barnes & Noble today. I need a new Moleskine." Using her fingers, she mumbled, "Mike's estate. The company. Paris. Three, I need three."

"Paris, you're not . . ."

"Don't go there, Chris." Kassie pointed her index finger to the ceiling. "Not now. I'll figure this out. First things first. I think you should call Bill and decide how best to inform everyone at the office. Maybe you need to go in for a bit."

"Shouldn't you?"

"Uh, no. That would be awkward. Especially with Karen—"

"Karen. Who'll tell *her*?"

They played rock-paper-scissors.

"Not fair. She's your mother. You should tell her. Let's play again."

"No you don't. You can do this. Mike would want it to be you. Woman to woman."

Kassie lacked Chris's confidence. As she dressed, she practiced how she'd break the news to her archenemy.

40

You're Not the Boss of Me

Before heading into the lioness's den, Kassie called Annie. Six thirty could be early for some folks, but Annie would've already downed her second cup of coffee, as well as folded and put away her first load of laundry. No wonder they stayed best friends forever.

When she answered, Kassie minced no words, she just said it. Perhaps rehearsing.

"Mike's dead. Massive heart attack."

"You're shittin' me."

"Would I lie about something like that?"

"No, of course not. I'm sorry. How did you find out?"

"Hospital called *me*. Next of kin. Still his wife. Can you believe, two months to go and maybe . . ."

"What? Don't go there. They would've called Chris, if he hadn't married Karen. Except, given the events of this week, the likelihood of that ever happening was slim to none. Face it, whether today or two or three months from now, you're it, kiddo."

"People keep saying that."

"What?"

"I'm it. Chris just called me boss." Kassie gave Annie the highlights of Mike's letter. "Chris thinks I should address Mike's staff today. Not sure I'd have time even if I wanted to."

"What do you want to do?"

Kassie imagined that question floating over Annie's head like a word balloon. She let it linger, wishing she could roll back the days to a week ago. Couldn't she start her vacation all over again? Create her own *Groundhog Day*, but stop short just before Monday when Mike's heart began to fail?

"Honestly? I want to crawl back under the covers and wait for Alexa to announce it's noontime. I want this all to have been a bad dream."

"Ain't gonna happen. You making a list?"

"Started."

"Do your thing, and call me later. I'm here for you. I'll kiss your cat."

Kassie hadn't the faintest clue whether Karen would be as industrious as Annie at that hour. Yet, if she were going into the office, perhaps she would be up and getting ready. She took the stairs down to the second floor, allowing herself more time to think than the elevator ride would afford.

Kassie knocked three times on the door. No answer. *I'll knock again. No answer? I'm outta here.* Just as she raised her fist, Karen appeared four feet in front of her, wearing a three-quarter length black silk robe that looked familiar. Kassie had been searching for that among her things at Annie's, figuring she'd left it at the house when she'd moved out. Never imagining Karen would steal it.

"Nice robe," Bad Kassie said, unchecked. Kassie pursed her lips.

"You left it behind, like you did Mike, so I claimed it and

everything else you discarded. Mine now." Karen barred the threshold, her left arm clamped onto the door as though she was ready to slam it in Kassie's face given half the chance.

Kassie swallowed hard and wiped her nose with the back of her hand. With all the tears she'd already shed, how did it not occur to her to pack tissue in her pocket?

"May I come in? We need to talk." She hoped her red eyes would offer Karen a clue something was up. She wasn't a friendly neighbor needing to borrow a cup of sugar.

"At this hour? You're not serious. You are weirder than weird. I saw you pull in late last night. You two have a lovers' quarrel?" Surprisingly, despite her protestations, Karen gave more than an inch and showed Kassie into the entryway.

"Not that it's any of your business, but Chris and I are engaged." She flashed the ring, still on her right hand.

"So I've heard. A little bird . . ." Karen stood like a barricade in the small hallway between Kassie and the living room.

"What little bird?" As soon as she said it, an image of Charlie flashed like the Instamatic camera her father had given her for her ninth birthday, the year before he died. "Never mind. We're out now, so it doesn't matter."

"Shows how self-centered you are to get engaged even before the ink is dry on your divorce papers. Did you ever consider what Mike would say?"

"He knows. I mean, he knew." There. She did it again, opening her mouth a mile ahead of her brain. "Karen, I think we should sit down."

"Don't get it in your pretty little head that I'm offering you coffee."

"It's okay. Anyway, I drink tea. But then, you should know that with all the tea I left behind in the kitchen." *Down girl, you've got a job to do.*

"If you came down here just to tell me you and Chris are

engaged—" Karen rubbed her hands together and made cracking noises with her fingers as she sat on the edge of the chair opposite Kassie, who'd chosen the couch.

Something's got her spooked. Is she worried I had my own little bird whispering in my ear about Charlie? Is she gearing up for a confrontation? Don't go there. Now's not the time.

After she reassured Karen she wasn't there to discuss Chris, Kassie let it rip. There was no way to sugarcoat it. Karen could handle it. She'd seen her husband die almost in front of her eyes on a ski slope; she certainly should be able to handle this news.

"Mike had a massive heart attack a couple of hours ago." She paused, counted to let that sink in. *One Mississippi . . .*

Karen just stared at her. *Is she deaf . . . and a numbskull?*

"KAREN," Kassie said, "Mike didn't survive this one." *Don't make me shake you.*

"What do you mean?"

Oh, God, she's really gonna make me say it? "He didn't survive, Karen. I mean he died. Mike is dead."

Oops-a-daisy. Kassie read Karen all wrong. She flipped a gourd, jumping off the chair and pacing first around the living room, then the bedroom, back to the living room. For some reason, she bounded into the kitchen, opened the refrigerator door, and slammed it shut. The coat closet got the same treatment, as did the bedroom closet.

"Oh, no. Can't be true. Can't be true. This is *not* happening," Karen said over and over to no one in particular. She bent down, tossed her red hair into a frenzy, then threw her head back toward the ceiling. Did she forget Kassie was still sitting there?

Kassie was unsure how long to let her vent before intervening. She sympathized with her. Kassie'd been through the death of a loved one before with her father's sudden death and her mother's terminal illness. *She's in denial. This too shall pass.*

But there were no tears, only questions. A slew of them in rapid succession.

"How do you know? When did it happen? Were you with him? Was anyone with him? What were his last words? Why did they call *you?*"

Kassie answered the best she could, encouraging Karen to please sit down. But Karen wasn't done.

"Why couldn't they save him? I saved him. Why couldn't they?"

"Don't do this to yourself." Kassie tried to feel her pain, which had to be different than the torture Kassie was enduring, sitting there absorbing Karen's wrath. But she tried. "It was his time, apparently."

"His time? What would you know about his time? It was going to be *our time*. You're not the only one engaged, ya know."

"Yes, I know." Without thinking, Kassie swapped her rings. Maybe if she fed Karen a crumb, a fondness about Mike she could cling to in her time of hysteria, she'd snap out of it.

"Mike told me about your trip to Provincetown." Kassie stopped short of revealing the doubts Mike had shared with her and his reasons for having second thoughts. *Now's not the time.* Her mother's voice inside her head reminded her the value of saying nothing. A chill traveled up her arms and down her legs, competing with the rash that had almost healed.

Kassie rose to leave. What more was there to say? "I need to get to the hospital. Make arrangements."

"Just like that. You come in here—"

"Not sure what else I should've done. I thought you'd want to know before you got to the office. Would you really have wanted to hear this from Bill?"

Karen said nothing.

"By the way, it's perfectly all right for you to take the rest of the week off. And probably most of next week, depending on when the funeral is."

"Excuse me? You have no right. You're not my boss."

"Actually, I kind of am."

41

Initial Reactions

On the way over to Boston Clinic, Kassie and Chris caught each other up on the calls they'd made. Chris went first. He reached Bill before he left for the office. Good thing too. The letter Mike gave him on Saturday was in his bureau. If he was already at the office, he would've had to go home to get it.

"Was that his first reaction?"

"Kind of. Mike had instructed him to open it in case of his death."

"Boy, people do react strangely when people die."

"Not everyone is like you, KO. There is no prescribed checklist for how to behave when someone you care about dies. Cry for five minutes. Make arrangements. Have lunch."

The air flew out of Kassie's lungs. Is that what Chris thought of her? Had her father's suicide and her abusive childhood conditioned her to be unsympathetic?

"Survival, Chris. It's how I've survived. I didn't have an Ozzie and Harriet upbringing like—"

"Ozzie and who?"

She shook her head, the ten years between them showing.

Chris told her Bill was indeed upset and wanted to know the details, because when you're given a letter from someone on Saturday, and they die in less than a week, you kind of want to read the letter as fast as possible.

"*We* did, right?" Chris said

"And what did his letter say?"

"The same as ours. He's grateful Mike left him part of the business, but that wasn't his focus."

"What was?"

"That you're now the owner, the majority owner. So now Bill and I work for you."

"What a difference a day makes." Kassie stared out the window.

Bill told Chris he'd inform the staff that morning. Whoever wanted to go home, he'd let them. He asked Chris if he thought Kassie would be okay with that.

"Of course. I've got my hands full right now. You and Bill have got to step in."

"Understood. But . . ."

"But what?"

"We'll need a communications plan for the media and clients."

"Isn't that what you all are good at? Or do you need to hire my team at Calibri to handle this for you?"

"You're joking."

"Yes, kind of. Let's see how today goes. Let Bill know we'll meet with him tomorrow and, if that goes well, the staff right after."

"Sounds like a plan."

"Boss? Hmmph." She wondered if she'd be able to be boss on both sides of the Charles, let alone the Atlantic?

They were a block away from the hospital when Kassie gave Chris a mini version of the scene with Karen.

"Not that anything Karen says or does should surprise me, but something doesn't square." Kassie scratched her head.

"How's that?"

"No tears. Not one teardrop. A lot of door slamming, whatever that was about. And red hair flailing about."

"If she's in denial, like you said, tears will come later."

"Maybe. She said some odd things."

"Odd in general, or odd for Karen?"

"Odd is odd. She said, 'This is not happening.' In the present tense. As if something disrupted her plans. Like if you got a flat tire on the way to the airport."

Chris told her he thought she was being a bit overly judgmental and suggested Kassie cut Karen some slack.

"That's not all. She seemed baffled that the doctors didn't save him like she did. As if she was all powerful, above them. That she'd made the ultimate sacrifice, and now it was their fault he was gone."

"You got all that in fifteen minutes?"

"Ugh. Is that all it was? Felt like an eternity on steroids."

As they entered the hospital, Kassie hoped it would be the last time for a while. She'd had enough of antiseptic smells and color-coded scrubs to last a lifetime. As she held out her left hand to take his, he lifted it, winked, flashed her an ear-to-ear grin, and kissed the ring.

Standing in front of the elevator doors in the lobby, Kassie swayed from side to side.

"There's one thing she didn't ask I would've thought would've been top of mind."

"And what's that?" Chris put his arm around her as if to steady her.

"Other than saying she'd heard you and I were engaged, she didn't ask. She didn't ask about you. She didn't ask how Mike's son was doing. Odd, don't you think?"

"I wouldn't read much into it. Like I said, people behave differently."

"Oddly. They behave oddly," Kassie said as they arrived on the fifth floor. They made their way past patients' rooms to the nurses' station. Chris informed the only nurse around why they were there so early in the morning. The pretty little nurse looked up at him and smiled, of course. *I rest my case. Odd.*

They only waited five minutes in the relatives' lounge. Kassie knew the drill. She'd been there, done that two years before when her mother passed on a different floor, similar room. But this time Chris was with her, not three thousand miles away. She thanked God for this big favor.

The hospital's cardiac doctor arrived, gave his condolences, and explained in as best layman's language as he could what had happened.

"The body can only take so much wear and tear. Mr. Ricci's worked exceedingly hard over the last few years keeping him alive. I'm sorry there was nothing we could do."

Kassie and Chris sat side by side on a couch that was not made for lounging. Obviously they didn't want grieving families hanging around the hospital very long. The couch reminded her of a futon she once had where she swore the slats of the bed frame were permanently imprinted on her back. She'd have Chris check for track marks on her butt later on. He'd like that.

Focus, Kassie, focus. You owe Mike that much.

When a hospital administrator joined the doctor, Kassie knew the fun was about to begin. Well, not really fun, but the nitty-gritty of moving Mike's body out of the hospital to a funeral parlor. She scrolled through her phone. How many people have a funeral parlor listed among their contacts?

There it was. Kelly and Colombo Funeral home in Newburyport.

"Oh, yes. We're very familiar with them with all the Irish and Italian families we serve," the administrator said.

"Precisely why Mike and I chose it for ourselves. For when it was our time." Kassie noticed the woman's blank stare. "I'm Irish. O'Callaghan."

Four heads nodded.

"And we thought they sounded more like cops than funeral directors." Kassie laughed.

Three sets of eyebrows lifted.

"But they're not cops. They are very professional, caring caretakers. They'll be expecting Mike. Well, not really expecting him. But making arrangements shouldn't be too difficult." Kassie was babbling. Why, she didn't know. Things weren't going well, and her eyelids reminded her she'd had less than four hours sleep. And boy did she have to pee. She excused herself for five minutes.

The break gave her time to get her act together and analyze what was gnawing at her, what was causing her now to be the odd one. *Bingo.* They hadn't asked her the big question yet. Autopsy.

As she washed her hands—*Annie would be proud*—she looked at herself in the ladies' room mirror. At her eyes. Into her soul, as honestly as anyone could. She tried to put herself in Mike's shoes, ridiculous as it sounded, even to Bad Kassie. What would Mike want? He hated hospitals, and his body had been poked, prodded, and carved up enough over the last year and a half. She recalled from conversations they'd had on the topic that he had no desire to donate any of his body parts. If they were as damaged as his kidneys were, they'd be of no use to anyone else. Fact was, he'd had a massive heart attack. Wasn't that enough information? Why'd they need to know anything else?

Decision made, she returned to the relatives' room.

Boy, had Kassie predicted that right. A Consent and Authorization for Autopsy form sat on the small coffee table between three chairs and the couch that made her butt ache. And apparently while she was otherwise engaged, voluptuous young Cecilia joined the circle.

Kassie touched her shoulder as she passed her, returning to her rightful seat next to Chris.

"You okay?" he asked.

She inhaled deeply and nodded. She couldn't help but notice the tissues piled on Cecilia's lap along with a large plastic bag with the name of the hospital imprinted on it. *Mike's possessions.* Probably clothes, shoes, whatever he had when he showed up in the ambulance. He hadn't been there long enough to acquire much stuff. Thankfully.

The lady administrator started her spiel about the autopsy, the pros and cons, including organ donation and tissue transplantation. Everyone accepted Kassie's decision about organ donation, especially because he'd suffered a cardiac death. She didn't quite understand the nuance surrounding the cause of death but was more than relieved when they skirted that topic. On the other hand, the possibility of tissue transplantation was still on the table. Not according to Kassie. *Ain't gonna happen.*

They acquiesced and moved on. The doctor pressed for a post-mortem; the administrator seemed neutral. Especially given Mike's medical history, it could provide valuable information about not only the exact cause of death but also whether his kidneys or other organs were involved in his quick demise.

Why was he pressuring her? She hated feeling backed into a corner. She touched her chest just below her neck. The heat started there and climbed up her throat, around her ears. Her forehead dampened.

"His heart. I was married to him for thirty years. His heart killed him. I can vouch for that. Surprised it took so long." Bad Kassie blurted out, "No autopsy needed."

Four jaws dropped.

"Could you excuse us?" Chris lifted Kassie's arm, leading her out of the relatives' room.

She figured she was in for a good tongue lashing. Deservedly so.

Not only had she criticized Bill for his reaction to Mike's death, but here she was behaving her snarky best. While sad and brokenhearted, she'd be damned if she'd be forced to play the role of the distraught wife when she was two months removed from being the ex.

"You divorce for a reason," she mumbled, preparing to defend herself to Chris.

"What are you saying?"

"I'm sorry I said what I said. You know my lawyer warned me. I can't wait to call her and tell her about this change in plans." Kassie rolled her eyes. "She warned me years ago when I first made noise about divorcing Mike. 'You better do it soon. If you wait too long, he'll end up sick or impaired, and you'll be stuck in a marriage you can't get out of.' I thought I'd escaped that life sentence. But no, here I am being judged by people who didn't know Mike, don't know me, and don't know the shitshow our marriage was. And now you're going to tell me to tone it down, right?"

"Uh, no. I get you. You know I have your back."

"Then, why . . ." Kassie raised the palms of her hands in the air as if to ask, *What's this all about?*

"I think you should reconsider your position on the autopsy." Chris showed her to a bench seat in the hallway. "Here, sit."

On one hand, Kassie was relieved Chris wasn't going to chastise her; on the other, she couldn't have predicted Chris would have any skin in the game regarding the autopsy decision.

But he did. And she listened.

Ten minutes later they returned hand in hand to the relatives' room. The doctor lit up when he realized Kassie had changed her mind. She'd make the coroner happy. Not the reaction she was going for, but whatever.

She did it for Chris.

42

Words Matter

For a brief moment, Cecilia, Chris, and Kassie stared at each other as the administrator and the doctor hustled off to do whatever they needed to do to complete Mike's last visit to Boston Clinic and ship him off to Kelly and Colombo's. Kassie would give them a call once they were finished talking with—and consoling—Cecilia.

Of all people, Cecilia had shed the most tears so far that day. She'd appeared to have pulled herself together when Kassie returned from the ladies' room earlier, but it seemed the autopsy talk set her off again. Poor kid.

They played musical chairs. Chris pulled up a side chair, signaling Cecilia to move onto the couch next to Kassie.

"What a shock, Mrs. Ricci. We had such a good talk yesterday. I was so sure when I came in this morning, I'd have found he'd be released today."

Kassie placed her arm around Cecilia's shoulders, giving her a maternal squeeze.

"He was such a nice man. Kind. Helpful. Funny." Cecilia's faucet flowed steadily.

Bad Kassie opened her mouth to say something like "If you knew him like I did, you might not ascribe those adjectives to him," but she shut it before even one pejorative word slipped between her gums. No reason to burst this young lady's bubble. Kassie was struck at how a logophile, like Cecilia, was able to express her emotions concisely when it really mattered.

"Mr. Ricci inspired me to take my writing to another—" Cecilia's whimpering picked up steam, if that was even possible.

"Here." Attempting to distract, Chris spoke up. "Let's see what's in this bag, shall we? Make sure we've got everything."

His ploy worked. Cecilia emptied the bag one item at a time. It contained what you'd expect. She refolded the tan pants and dark blue shirt he'd worn on Monday neatly on the table. Kassie reached in and handled his striped boxers so Cecilia wouldn't have to. Chris did the manly chore of removing Mike's deck shoes. He handed Kassie Mike's Rolex that someone had tucked inside one of his shoes.

Nostalgically, Kassie held the watch in her hand, then glanced at Cecilia, who had started to shred the dampened tissues in her lap. "Take this, Cecilia. Mike would've wanted you to have it. You gave him joy. You know that, don't you?" She touched Cecilia's arm.

Just in time, Chris retrieved a tissue box from the far side of the room and placed it within Cecilia's reach.

"Is that all there is in the bag?" Kassie directed her question to Chris. Cecilia was of no use at the moment.

"Looks like it. Why?"

"Is this what you're looking for?"

Chris and Kassie whipped their heads up and toward the door. They'd been so consumed with comforting Cecilia, they neither saw nor heard Karen enter the room.

"What are you doing here?" Chris and Kassie stood, shocked.

Cecilia continued to sniffle, unfazed by the electric spark Karen's arrival set off.

"I asked if this is what you're looking for?" Karen approached Kassie, invading her space and dangling Mike's wedding ring in front of her eyes.

"Where'd you get that?" Kassie asked.

"Aren't you the lucky one? We were on the beach in the Cape. After he got down on one knee and begged me to marry him, he took it off. I stopped him from flinging it into the pond."

As she snatched the ring and blasted out of the room, Kassie said, "It's *on* the Cape and it's an *ocean*, you stupid slut."

43

Cecilia's Back

"Is it something I said? I just thought *she'd* want to have his ring," Karen said, standing with her hands on her hips. "I have no use for it now, except to hock it."

Cecilia gasped. "You'll have to forgive Mrs. Ricci, who is as forlorn as any lady would be who just lost her beloved husband of thirty years. The source of her utterances is a mournful, broken heart."

Praise be. Cecilia was back in rare form. She'd have made Mike as proud as a papa watching his daughter walk across the stage to accept her diploma at college graduation.

She continued, "May I ask who you are to come into this sanctified room, where this grieving family ventured into a wretched process of arranging a proper send-off for someone they'll miss from now until eternity?"

You go, girl. Chris thought calling this a sanctified room was a bit hyperbolic, but nevertheless he liked her style. If Cecilia had started in first gear, she'd shifted into third in a heartbeat. Wishing Kassie was there to witness this smackdown, he chewed the inside of his cheek, gearing up for Karen's reaction.

"Excuse me? And who are you?"

And we're off. Let the games begin.

"I asked you first."

"Um. I was Mr. Ricci's fiancée, if it's any of your business. I'm Karen—"

"Karen? The surly, ill-bred strumpet? Mr. Ricci told me all about you."

"Okay, ladies," Chris said, "I think we're finished here. Except—" He sat next to Cecilia, keyed in her phone number, and lifted her by the elbow.

"*You* wait here," he said to Karen as he escorted Cecilia to the door, where they shared a hug and solemn kisses on the cheek.

"Surly, ill-bred strumpet? Jack Benny?" Chris whispered.

"Jack who? No. William. William Shakespeare." And Cecilia was outta there.

Chris returned to find Karen situated on the couch, staring at the floor. He had no intention of an extended conversation with her at that moment. He'd make this quick. He had more important things to do.

Standing behind the side chair, his fists clutching its back, he got her attention the best way he knew how.

"*Karen.* What the hell are you doing here? This is the relatives' room. You shouldn't have come."

She lifted her head and tilted it to the right. "Do you think I can get my kidney back?"

Chris couldn't believe his ears. "Where's your dignity? Have you no sense of decency?"

"I'm just kidding, Chris. Can't you take a joke?"

He lifted the chair and bopped it against the floor. "Were you kidding when you fucked Charlie Monday?" he whispered through clenched teeth.

"Who knows about that?"

"Then it's true. Kassie thought—hoped—Mike was mistaken."

"Who knows besides Kassie and you and, oh, probably that tart, Amelia?"

"And Cecilia. You heard her."

"Oh, her. She's nothing."

"Nothing? Really? Mike didn't think she was nothing."

Karen shrugged off Chris. "Sarah. Do you think he told Sarah?" She was up and pacing the room, chewing her thumb. "Of course not. He didn't have time," she mumbled to her favorite audience—herself.

"And what if she knows?" He turned his body toward her.

Karen stopped three feet from him. He detected a familiar fragrance—Kassie's. Like everything else she'd stolen. Was there anything genuine about this woman who wanted him to renounce Sarah as his mother?

"Charlie will handle her. He always has, he always will," Karen said.

Unsure of what she meant by that remark, he filed it for later, switching gears until such time as he'd be able to give it a good think.

"Whatever. I need to ask you a favor."

"What's that, my son?"

Chris glared, his nostrils flaring. *Don't go there. Wrong time.*

"The funeral. We'll be planning it later today."

"Yeah, so?"

"Could you please keep a low profile over the next week? This is Kassie's time. Mike was her husband, not yours."

"We were going to be married. He made promises. *I* saved his life."

"Stop right there." He grabbed her arms, the first time he'd ever touched her. "It's about time you get this straight. Kassie saved him. She loved him enough to find you in order to find his son. And when it was me, she loved us both enough to give up a chance for her own happiness." He let Karen go, forcing her to fall back two steps.

"So, that's what you think? You bastard."

"You're right. That's what I would've been if it wasn't for Sarah."

44

Whose House Is It Anyway?

Kassie had a choice to make as she entered the hospital's cafeteria. Did she sit in the same exact seat she had occupied on Good Friday a year ago? It was vacant, available, waiting. Or should she break out of her comfort zone and try something new? She chuckled. If only that were the most critical decision she'd have to make that day and in the days to come.

Surprise, surprise. Kassie bought a cup of green mango tea, not her usual English breakfast, and slid into a cozy booth on the opposite side of the cafeteria than she was accustomed to. Two for two.

Baby steps. Baby? Don't go there.

The gold of Mike's wedding ring she'd slid onto the middle finger of her right hand next to her wedding band caught her eye. She wiggled the ring off her finger and twirled it, catching it before it skidded off the table. Karen's story about Mike wanting to toss it into the ocean nagged at her. Was it true? She'd never know for sure now that he was gone. Didn't matter. She'd bury the ring, and all the sorrowful and happy times they'd had together, with him. Let the past be the past; her future was now.

"Ahem."

Kassie raised her sight to Chris, greeting her with a bouquet of red roses.

"Wow. The first of many this week, I imagine."

"But these are for you, KO, not Mike."

"Aren't you afraid your allergies will flare up?"

"Nope." Chris handed her the flowers and scurried off, ostensibly to get coffee. He returned with a wide grin and a tray piled full of scrambled eggs, bacon, toast, and croissants and divided the feast between them.

"So, how did it go?" Kassie said with flakes of a croissant dangling from her mouth.

"It's done. Let's see what happens." Chris wiped his mouth, motioning for her to do the same. "You should've heard Cecilia. She gave Karen the what for. Can understand why Mike took a shine to her. There's more between the ears than she lets on."

Their phones buzzed at the same time. Word was getting out about Mike's death. They raised their eyebrows, shook their heads, and declined the calls.

Between bites, Kassie filled him in on the calls she'd made while waiting for him. Tom had no issue, of course, with her taking another week off to handle the funeral and Mike's affairs. No, she didn't discuss either her ownership of Ricci and Son or Paris with Tom. Wrong time, wrong place. She waved her fork in the air.

Annie and Vicki were lined up to organize the reception at Mike's house after the funeral, whenever that ended up being.

"You'll have to stop calling it that."

"Calling what?"

"Mike's house. It's your house now."

Kassie let that thought settle. With her primary focus on handling Mike's remains, she hadn't considered his personal assets yet, especially the assets they still shared as a married couple. The house for one. A big one.

"Should we move in there? And out of your place in Charlestown? I seem to recall yesterday—was it just yesterday?" Kassie put her head in her hands. "Weren't we talking about getting a bigger place?"

"Well, it *is* bigger. I'll give you that."

"And Topher would be comfortable there. He knows it like the back of his . . . paw." They shared a much-needed laugh as Kassie shook her paws in the air.

"Which reminds me." Kassie scrolled through her phone to find Teresa's number. She assumed Teresa still cleaned on Fridays, which meant she'd be there again tomorrow. Recalling that Teresa and Amelia had come to Mike's rescue on Monday, Kassie needed to get in touch with her asap to tell her about Mike. Wouldn't be polite to have her clean a dead man's house without knowing it.

"Maybe Teresa and her daughter would give Annie and Vicki a hand during the reception at the house. My house. Our house?"

Chris gave her a thumbs-up and continued chowing down. Kassie half expected he'd go back for seconds. But he didn't.

He sat diligently, listening to her one-sided conversation with Teresa that surely grew more interesting once Kassie got past the *I knows, I'm sorry toos*, and the "Mike and I always appreciated what you . . . and your daughter . . . did for us."

"You would do that? You think you could switch days? That would be awesome."

"She'll clean today," Kassie mouthed to Chris. He gave a second thumbs-up.

"Jimmy, the locksmith?" Kassie tapped Chris on the hand. "OMG," she mouthed.

"If you're sure about that, go ahead." Pause. "Yes, there's a concierge at the apartment." Pause. "Jimmy would do that? Thanks so much. Be sure to keep a set for yourself."

Kassie planted her phone on the table.

"What was that all about? Jimmy, the locksmith?"

"Thank goodness for Teresa. I would've never thought of it. Not yet, anyway."

She tore the second croissant in two, offering half to Chris. He declined with a slight wave indicating she could have it if she wanted it. Not as scrumptious as those she devoured in Paris, but it would do. She accepted his offer. Waistline be damned.

Kassie related Teresa's suggestion, more like a recommendation, to Chris. In all her years as a cleaning lady, Teresa apparently witnessed shady goings-on when there was a death in the family. Not only do people come out of the woodwork to get a piece of the deceased's estate, but the house becomes a target for thieves. She'd advised Kassie to be concerned about people who they'd given keys to in the past—painters, pet sitters, plumbers.

"Karen?" Chris asked.

"You win. You hit the bull's eye. A Kewpie doll for you," she replied. "It didn't occur to me, but Teresa said Karen has already moved some of her stuff over there, and I know for a fact she has some of my stuff at her place in Charlestown—"

"Excuse me? What stuff of yours?"

"I'll explain later. Anyway, what would stop her from dashing over there and helping herself to anything and everything she wanted? Or even damaging the place?"

"Hopefully that's the last thing on her mind."

"Frankly, I wouldn't put anything past her. Nor should you, Chris."

They finished what now would be considered brunch, dropped off their trays, and headed to the garage, both agreeing it was time to put Boston Clinic in the rearview mirror. Next stop, Kelly and Colombo Funeral Home in Newburyport.

On the way, Chris reminisced about the last time they'd made that drive. "Easter Sunday, wasn't it?"

That was also the day—or night, to be exact—they'd discovered his freelance job was at Mike's company. Boy, had they had their heads in the sand back then.

"Let's make a commitment to each other. Right here, right now," Kassie said.

"I'm game. What do you have in mind?"

"No secrets."

"No secrets," Chris said. "Pinky swear?"

"Pinky swear."

45

Her Just Desserts

If she couldn't get the sympathy she was entitled to from her son, Karen knew where to go to get it. Problem was the damn time difference between Boston and Chicago. It was too early to have an intimate conversation with Charlie, as Sarah would still be lurking around their house. Karen knew she flitted off to one of her pompous museum trustee meetings at lunchtime most days, so she'd wait until the coast, and the air, was clear.

Where to in the meantime? She'd planned to go into the office that day before Kassie showed up on her doorstep and dropped the Mike-is-dead bomb. She could've shown a bit more compassion given the circumstances. What could Karen really expect? Kassie had shown her true colors when she served Mike divorce papers when his kidneys were failing. If it weren't for Karen, he'd have been dead nearly a year already.

As a matter of habit, a bad habit, she headed toward the office. It was midmorning. Bill surely would've told everyone the news by then. Karen guessed she'd receive a kindhearted, sympathetic welcome in deference to Mike, if for no other reason.

What the hell? There was only one car in the Ricci and Son parking lot. Bill's. She racked her brain. It wasn't a national holiday. Where was the rest of the staff? An early lunch, perhaps?

The groan of the front door opening echoed through the vacant first floor. But with the absence of printers humming and keyboards clicking, an eerie quiet greeted Karen, rattling her nerves. She threw her purse on her desk with a thud, hoping to alert Bill she was in the building.

It worked.

"Oh, it's you." He stood in his office doorway. "I wasn't expecting to see you here today."

"Where the hell is everybody? There's a business here to run. Clients to serve." Karen thought if she showed she was calm, cool, and collected, she'd catch him off his game, and he'd forget the ticket incident.

"Chris and I agreed to let the staff decide whether they felt up to being here today."

"A free day off?" She continued on pace. "What kind of a management decision was that? You really don't think they're home crying over Mike, do you?"

"Speaking from experience, are you?"

Chris's request that she keep a low profile resounded in her mind. She stifled the go-fuck-yourself response that was about to leap from her lips.

"Do you have a minute?" Bill asked.

"Obviously, if I'm here." Karen followed him into his office and lowered herself into an armchair across from Bill, who'd parked himself behind his desk. She could tell already this was not going to be an oh-woe-are-we chitchat about the loss of the firm's fearless leader.

"I'm sorry for your loss," Bill said.

Is that the best he could do? Asshole.

"Thanks. We had our whole lives ahead of us. I'm at a loss for . . ."

Karen looked for a box of tissues. Even that was absent. She feigned a tear and used the back of her hand, pretending to wipe it away.

"A future, perhaps?" Bill paused. "We all have lost something today. Mike was a friend, our colleague, our boss."

Karen nodded. If that's all he had to say, she was ready to get the hell out of there. Since no one else was working, why should she? Though she hated to give in to Kassie's suggestion she take time off. She wrapped her hands around the chair's arms and started to rise.

"I'm not finished."

Karen let out an audible sigh, slouching her rear back down in the seat. *What else, moron?*

"You'll learn about this formally in due course, but both Kassie and Chris gave me the authority to tell the staff. And since you're part of the staff, you should know as well. Better from me than from one of your coworkers."

Spare me the drama. Karen stared at Bill, waving her palms to the ceiling as if to say, "Cut the crap."

"It's impossible to know whether Mike had any sense, any premonition, that his time was approaching. But perhaps he did. Nevertheless, among other things, Mike left a succession plan for the company, including assigning ownership rights."

Karen's back felt as though a straightening rod had been inserted. She squared her feet.

"To be fair, I'll tell you exactly what I told the rest of the team this morning."

Karen twiddled her thumbs and fixed her gaze on a crystal paperweight on Bill's desk. She imagined what the effect would be if she heaved it at him.

He continued, unharmed. "With Mike's death, Kassandra O'Callaghan—Mrs. Ricci—rises in ranks to hold majority ownership in Ricci and Son."

Big woo.

"Technically," Bill said, "that makes Kassie the boss around here."

Her thumb twiddling continued, in reverse. *That's what he thinks. I'll get my fair share, and my son will get the rest.*

As though he read her mind, he said, "Mike provided Chris a minority stake in the firm, as he did for me. To be clear, the three owners in the firm are me, Chris, and Kassie in ascending order. Which means, until Kassie directs otherwise, I will continue managing operations, and Chris will—"

"I know what Chris does around here. I know what he's entitled to. So you can stop with your MBA mumbo jumbo. Mike's succession plan isn't worth shit. I have rights too."

"With all due respect, Karen, in the eyes of the law you have no rights. No ownership rights, and frankly, no spousal rights."

She leapt to her feet. "We'll see about that."

"Before you storm out of here, you should know Mike didn't cast you aside completely. Kassie will be the one to tell you the particulars of what Mike has left for you. I have authority to tell you, though, your job here is still secure if you mind your p's and q's. In the end it'll be up to Kassie. So you might think before you say or do anything you might regret."

"Like shredding tickets?" She smirked, turned her back on him, and climbed the stairs to the solitude of Mike's office.

"Those days are over," Karen heard him say.

As she entered Mike's office, Karen waved her arms as if she were stifling an errant smoke alarm. With her physical presence recognized, the automatic recessed lights gradually took her hint.

She threw herself facedown on the couch they'd had sex on more than once and almost shed a tear for the loss of a man who was supposed to save her because she'd saved him. But all she could think of was what Bill had said.

Pulling herself upright, she wrapped her arms around a throw pillow and rocked back and forth.

"That bastard. I might not have spousal rights or ownership rights, but by golly, Chris has rights to more. A lot more." She paced the office and took the opportunity to use Mike's private bathroom. "All of this will be Chris's one day, not Kassie's, if I have anything to do with it."

She checked the time, gave Mike's leather desk chair a twirl, and keyed in her phone's password. Charlie answered on the second ring.

"I've heard. I'm sorry. I've been waiting for you to call."

"He's screwed me in more ways than one."

"Who?"

"Mike. Not only did he die before I was Mrs. Ricci, but it sounds like he left Kassie the business."

"Makes sense. Thirty years must count for something. It does with Sarah and me."

"Really? You think so? What about donating a kidney? Doesn't that count?"

"Sure, but you weren't married. And just because someone gives you an organ doesn't mean you have to provide them with diddly squat if and when you die."

Karen heard Charlie's words but wasn't listening. She went on, "And since they're still legally married, Bill of all people says she gets the house, his retirement, his money, et cetera, et cetera. I end up with shit. Shit for luck."

"Bill may be right. But still, he may have left something for you. It's too early to tell. You know, Mike was no prick."

"Speaking of pricks. They know about us."

"I know."

Charlie told her that Chris had called Sarah early that morning to tell her about Mike, and while Chris was spreading the sad news, he hinted at what little he knew about their rendezvous on Monday.

"Oh my God, what did she say?" Karen held her forehead in her hand.

"What could she say? We've been married longer than Kassie and Mike. I'm no angel. Sarah knows that. She's lived with my foibles forever."

"And she's okay with that?"

"We're adults, KC. She knows I'm not going anywhere. She's pissed because it's you. But to her, you're just one more notch on my belt."

"*One* notch?"

"Okay, more than one. So what? Life goes on, Karen. History repeats itself. Deal with it."

She wanted to argue with him. Didn't she mean anything to him? What was he going to do to help her . . . and Chris . . . get their slices of Mike's enormous money pie? Before Mike succumbed, Charlie had promised to help her legally once she and Mike were married. She needed him now. There was no later.

Charlie blew her off, telling her to slow down and take each day at a time. He and Sarah would fly out for the funeral. They could talk more then. "*Ciao*, babe," he said.

Karen spun the chair around to face the credenza decorated with photographic memories of Mike's life. Only one picture interested her. She picked it up and touched the faces. Mike's, Sarah's, her own. The glass cracked as it landed in the circular file.

She was done at Ricci and Son. At least for that day. She grabbed her keys and headed for Mike's house. Who knew what treasures she'd uncover there? She'd show the whole lot of them what a low profile looked like.

46

Under Lock and Key

Karen inserted her key into Mike's front door lock. No dice. She double-checked her key ring to be sure she'd chosen the right key. She tried again. *Shit.* She jiggled the doorknob as if doing so would magically open the door. Though she'd never entered the house through the back porch, she walked around the house to give it a shot. Maybe her key would work there. No such luck. She sighed. The only other entry point would be the garage, except she never learned the automatic door opener code, so that was out of the question.

She scratched her head and tried the front door one more time. The hum of a car's engine caused her to turn to check it out. *What's the bitch doing here?* There went her plans to rummage through the house to see what gems she might discover.

Expecting to make her heist quick, Karen had parked her car smack dab in the middle of the long driveway, forcing Kassie to pull in behind her. Maybe Karen could distract her. Tell her the lock was broken. Send her off to fetch a locksmith, giving her time to check for an unlatched first-floor window.

Conceding that climbing through a window wasn't the best plan, by the time she reached Kassie, who had one leg out of her car door, Karen changed her strategy. If she didn't have free range to scour Mike's house, she could at least retrieve her belongings before Kassie tossed her things in the trash. She wouldn't put it past her. To make this happen, though, she'd have to swallow the venom Kassie had spewed toward her earlier that day. *Slut? I'll give her that. But stupid I am not. Watch this.*

"Oh, Kassie. Thank goodness you're here. I can't get in the house." Karen waved her key ring at Kassie.

"Why are you here?"

"There's stuff in there that belongs to me." Karen stayed close behind Kassie as she headed up the driveway. "I want my things. Are you moving back?"

Kassie said nothing as she unlocked the door without a hitch.

"Why didn't my key work?" Karen chirped as she followed Kassie into the foyer. "It's worked before."

"Let's get your things." Kassie ignored Karen's questions, instead asking her if she needed a bag to carry her stuff and instructing her, as if she were a child, to wait in the hallway.

Karen grunted but did as she was told. She heard a kitchen cabinet slam, assuming it was the tall cabinet Mike shoved bags of all makes and models into—the cabinet Karen steered clear of for fear he'd suggest she organize the mess for him.

Kassie returned with a handful of brown paper shopping bags and gave her a nod to climb the stairs. Once in the bedroom, Karen emptied two bureau drawers and grabbed an armful of clothes hanging in what had been—and would be again, she surmised—Kassie's closet. *Watch her tell me to leave the hangers.* She moved to the bathroom and tossed brushes and toiletries into the bag. *Watch her accuse me of stealing her cosmetics and lotions. Just because I bought a few of her favorite things. It's a free country.*

"Hope you're happy now." Karen turned on the waterworks, tears streaking her makeup.

Her strategy appeared to break through Kassie's icy exterior. She handed Karen a tissue and rubbed her shoulder. "There's no joy in this house today, Karen. I would've preferred you and Mike shared a future together than what has occurred. If that's what you wanted . . ."

"Despite what you may think of me, I loved Mike and wanted to live the rest of my life with him." Karen sniffled for good measure. "In this house. Now I'm not even welcome here."

Kassie sat on the edge of the waterbed. Silent.

"This isn't fair." If tears wouldn't work, she'd appeal to Kassie's better angels, if she had any. The least Karen could do was walk out of the house with some idea of what provisions Mike had made for her. She stepped up her game a notch. "None of this is fair. I'm the mother of Mike's son, and Mike and I were going to marry soon, really soon."

Still no reaction.

She went for the jugular. "And then he had to go and die—"

Kassie stood. "Listen, could you give me a hand here, please?" She invited Karen to help her choose the most flattering suit in which to bury Mike.

Not what Karen was going for, but she'd bite. She sucked up her crocodile tears. Kassie pulled out a suit and shirt and laid them gently across the bed, as if Mike were stuffed in them already. At long last they agreed on something—his dark blue suit and white shirt.

"The suit will match his eyes," Karen said.

"His eyes will be closed."

Oops. The word *stupid* rattled in Karen's head.

Kassie seemed to let Karen's gaffe slide, turning their attention to choosing the right tie. Karen slid a red silk tie off the rack of fifty or more. Kassie favored a mauve one. *How ugly could she get?* Karen scrunched her nose. Kassie must've gotten the message, ceding to Karen's preference.

"Cufflinks. While I pick out cufflinks, Karen, why don't you find his wingtips?"

Shoes? *She gets to select jewelry, and I get shoes?* Again, Karen did as she was asked, keeping an eagle eye on Kassie as she removed a small brown box from Mike's top drawer and unlocked it with a key ring Karen recognized as Mike's. After touching several small items, Kassie picked something she must've found suitable.

"These are the ones. I gave these to Mike when he launched the company. From Tiffany's." Kassie held them in the palm of her hand for Karen to view.

"Gold?"

"Yes, an M and an R."

Almost on the verge of hyperventilating, Karen realized her bad timing had cost her dearly. If she'd found that box before Kassie arrived, she could've carried it right out of the house.

"You're going to bury gold with him? Don't they tell you not to do that?"

"Actually, he's my husband, and technically, my cufflinks. They'll let me do almost anything I want." Kassie returned the jewelry box to where she'd found it. She slid open the bottom drawer of the armoire, lifted out what looked like a gray metal lockbox, and placed it on the bed now crowded with clothes.

Karen edged her way next to Kassie and watched her fumble with the keys. She tried one, and then another. The box opened, and Karen's jaw and eyebrows moved in opposite directions.

"Old habits die hard," Kassie mumbled as if Karen wasn't within earshot. Without an ounce of surprise in her demeanor, Kassie counted the hundred-dollar bills. By Karen's guesstimate, there must've been eight to ten thousand dollars in there. In a flash, Kassie peeled off a bunch and handed them to Karen.

"Here, Mike would want you to have this." Kassie put the rest of the cash back in the box, locked it, and shoved it under her armpit. "Now let's go. I think you're about done here."

But Karen wasn't.

Damn it. Why hadn't she let her fingers do a little walking through his personal space before now? Karen followed Kassie's lead, scooping up an armful of clothes and heading downstairs. Kassie helped Karen out to her car.

"I stopped by the office earlier." Karen attempted to change the focus from the dead to the living. "Bill was the only one there."

"How'd that go?"

"Apparently you were right this morning. You're the boss now." Karen knew how to be a suck-up like the best of them when the situation warranted.

"Imagine that."

"Um, Kassie, thanks for the money. But that's not all, is it? Can't be all. Bill mentioned Mike may have left something for me. And that you know the details."

Kassie put her hand on Karen's unwelcoming shoulder again. "Karen, I just gave you a thousand dollars. We just picked out the clothes Mike will be buried in. Now's not the time to count chickens." She paused. "After the funeral service, Karen. I'll be here. Come see me."

47

Déjà Vu All Over Again

There was no doubt in Kassie's mind that Mike wouldn't have taken issue with her appropriating the home office when she moved back in the house on Saturday. She could've just as easily justified giving Chris her office when he moved in next month, but some things are better left unchanged. Otherwise, the saying "déjà vu all over again" would be meaningless. As such, she'd maintain her digs. Chris could have Mike's.

She sat in the desk chair she'd bought many moons ago, breathed in a lingering vanilla scent, plucked a latent cat hair off the desk lamp, and touched the photo of Topher she'd left behind. How could her life come full circle in such a short period of time? So much had changed over the last year, especially over the last week, yet here she was, back where she'd started nearly thirty years ago.

Just four days before, Kassie woke up in Paris with an itch to scratch, and her pomegranate rash wasn't the culprit.

Ambition. Ambition clawed her soul again that day. In her younger years, her passion was motherhood. An unceasing desire to have a child, be a good mother—to provide love, security, and happiness to a child in ways she'd rarely experienced. When Mike severed that hope along with their marriage, her dream lingered, remaining a secret wish tucked deep in her heart.

With almost nowhere else to turn, Kassie devoted excessive time and attention to her career. Her male colleagues labeled her ambitious, not as a compliment. Behind their backs, she gave them the finger and climbed the ladder anyway, almost but not quite to the tippy top.

Then came Christopher Gaines, and her emotions got the better of her. She spent untold hours daydreaming of waking up each morning with Chris. Once when Annie teased her about her obsession with him, she explained to her, in much too graphic detail, how if Annie spent just one night with him, she too would daydream her life away. The downside to all this lovey-doveyness was that she took her eye off the proverbial ball at work, applying most of her energy to hiding her love affair with Chris and, of course, at the same time, confronting her mother's chronic illness and ultimate death.

Last year, just as she was about to break free of Mike, he turned the tables on her. He disrupted her divorce plans—not just by getting sick but by revealing long-held secrets of his past, including the straw that broke it all, his vasectomy. At the time, she was convinced her life had hit bottom, reached a new low. Until Karen introduced her to Charlie and Sarah Gaines, and she realized she'd had a five-year affair with her husband's son.

She'd accept being called *adulteress*, even *cougar*. But stepmother to her lover? Call her inconsolable. If only Chris wasn't Mike's son. Oh, if only.

With Chris gone but never forgotten, Kassie reestablished her energy on her career. In no time at all, she was soaring again. As was Calibri's bottom line. And then came Paris. Chris's marriage proposal. Mimi. And, needless to say, Mike.

Just as he'd screwed up her plans the year before, he had done it again, but this time doubly so. Not only did he force her and Chris to cut the stepmother-son reunion short in France, but by dying and anointing her queen, Mike forced her to rethink her decision to go back to Paris, which had been difficult enough in the first place because of Chris.

She knew Tom would be at the funeral and would raise the issue. So, the day before the funeral, Kassie consulted with her mentor, Annie—the one person who could see the forest for the trees, when all Kassie saw were twinkling lights off the Seine, the glass pyramids at the Louvre, the flying buttresses of Notre-Dame Cathedral.

They made a list, assigning weight to the pros and cons. Bottom line, her decision was as plain as the nose on Cyrano de Bergerac's face.

48

Guest Wish List

The scene, that Tuesday, was reminiscent of *The Godfather*, but with a female boss wearing a black dress from Paris sitting behind a big oak desk.

It was a typical sticky, humid July day in Boston. The funeral of Michael Ricci was typical too. It had concluded an hour earlier. Since Mike and Kassie had few living relatives, close colleagues and friends filtered in to pay their respects and eat. Greeted by Teresa and Amelia, their guests would not be disappointed with the spread awaiting them.

Kassie was grateful to Chris, who suggested she take some time to be alone and gather her thoughts. They'd agreed the afternoon could be as stressful, and perhaps even more emotional, than the church service and burial in the same cemetery where her mother had been laid to rest two years before. He'd offered to bring her a glass of wine. She declined. Water would do. No wine fog for her that day.

The night before, Chris and she had discussed at length who they expected at the reception. Grabbing a yellow pad, she made a list of the people she needed to see privately, not wanting to leave to chance they'd come and go before she had an opportunity to talk with them.

Top of the list? Tom. Some might accuse Kassie of calling in her chips; she'd say it was quid pro quo. Her loyalty to Calibri was documented over decades—it was time for the company to give her some wiggle room. If they did, she'd be sure to deliver the goods.

She and Tom shared a hug and customary condolences—I'm so sorry, thank you, it's such a shame. She offered him a seat, settling in a chair facing him, their knees almost touching. Tom didn't have to ask why she singled him out to chat with first. Lately, her reputation for putting her professional career ahead of her personal needs had rebounded.

Nor was she one for beating around the mulberry bush, quickly setting the stage for the ask to come. With Mike's death, she became the majority owner of the firm. That meant she was chief executive of Ricci and Son, with full responsibility for its success or failure. Lucky for her, she had strong and capable leaders in Bill and Chris.

Tom bobbed his head, allowing her to pave the way to her proposition the only way she knew how—one rung of the ladder at a time.

Since Tom appeared to be in a positive frame of mind, Kassie's confidence grew. First, she needed him to say what he said: "We'd be lost without you. You'd be difficult to replace."

"I'm hoping you won't have to. Looks like I've been dealt a curse of riches."

Five minutes later, they had a deal Tom felt optimistic the board would approve. Kassie would accept the position in Paris, backfilling for Mimi and managing the merger. They agreed to a twelve-month window. During that time, she'd place control of Ricci and Son in Chris's and Bill's able hands. Three months before her return from Paris, they'd reassess the situation and determine the best course of action for Kassie and the two entities. And yes, in her capacity as acting managing director, she'd have to fly back to Boston for quarterly updates to the board.

Kassie chuckled when Tom raised her left hand and kissed her engagement ring.

With that agreement under her belt, she asked Chris to find Bill and Nancy. The four of them stood in her office for several minutes as Kassie shared the results of her negotiations with Tom. Chris squeezed her tight and ran off to get glasses and champagne. Moments later, they shook hands and made a toast to O'Callaghan, Mahoney, Gaines & Associates. They knew it would take the better part of a year to settle Mike's estate, and once completed, they'd rename the firm officially.

"Here's to OMG!" *Clink, clink.* At long last something to cheer about, even if for a nanosecond.

"Where's Karen?" Kassie whisked her partners through the doorway.

"I'll get her," Chris said.

"Oh, no. Permit me." Bill rubbed his palms together, as if he couldn't wait.

"I heard laughter in here. What's going on?" Karen said.

Kassie took the seat behind her desk and directed Karen to sit in the chair opposite her. She had no appetite for her one-on-one conversation with Karen to drag on any longer than absolutely necessary. Wearing two hats—employer and purveyor of Mike's estate—she'd jotted down three messages to convey to Karen.

First, because Kassie had commitments at Calibri, which she had no desire to share with Karen at that time, Bill and Chris would co-manage the firm for the next year.

Karen shook her head in agreement.

Second, it was Mike's written wish for Karen to continue as receptionist of the firm as long as she wanted—that is, as long as she performed her duties in a professional manner.

Karen squirmed in her seat, crossing and uncrossing her legs.

Kassie paused to give Karen a chance to grunt or say something pithy. Nothing doing.

"Karen? Did you get that?"

"Um. Yes. Can I have time to think about it?"

Kassie suspected her next bit of news might give Karen a swift kick in the ass one way or another.

"Remember last week when I handed you a thousand dollars?"

"How could I forget? You got more where that came from?" Karen laughed.

Kassie interlaced her fingers, placing her hands in front of her on the black desk pad.

"Yes, as a matter of fact. According to Mike's directive, in addition to long-term employment, a fund will be established that will deposit a thousand dollars tax-free into your checking account on the first of each month, for sixty months. That's five years. You'll recognize that as the same monthly stipend Mike provided after your husband's death."

"That's it? After all I did for him?"

"Check with Charlie. In retrospect and under the circumstances, I think you both might agree Mike is being more than generous."

Karen tore the edges of a small paper bag she held in her lap. Kassie recognized the Guy's and Dolly's Galleria of Jewels imprint. "Well, at least I have this goddam necklace to remember him by," Karen mumbled out of the side of her mouth, flip-flopping the bag.

Kassie's phone pinged. A text from Chris: *Just got call. Breaking news.*

Karen started to rise.

"Not so fast. We're not done yet. You can stay seated where you are."

Kassie's door opened, and it looked like a parade. First Chris, then Sarah, Charlie, and Annie, in that order. Chris motioned for her to move to one of the side chairs he'd quickly arranged so everyone could be seated in a circle close together. When she sat down, he squeezed her shoulders. She glanced up at him, trying to read his face. He gave her no clues about what he'd just learned of the lab test results conducted last Thursday.

Goosebumps shivered up her arms. With the convergence of Mike's death and the outing of Karen and Charlie, Sarah had seized the opportunity to put to rest a hunch that had nagged at her for more than forty years. Not that Kassie ever doubted Chris was Mike's son, but when Sarah suggested to Chris that they conduct a paternity test at the same time as the autopsy, Kassie took it as a sign—perhaps a message from Mike—she shouldn't ignore.

Though they didn't know each other well, Kassie admired Sarah's guts and genius. A woman after her own heart. Imagine picking up the phone one early morning to the news your adopted son's biological father was dead and his adoptive father—your husband—was having an affair with your son's biological mother. And then . . . to have the presence of mind to say three words—autopsy, paternity test.

When Chris pushed for the autopsy at the hospital, especially after Kassie adamantly rejected it, Kassie weighed the odds the results could erase the scarlet letter she'd worn for how many days now? But then, who's counting?

Fifty-fifty. Those were the odds, as simple as that. Either Mike was Chris's father, or he wasn't. If he was, nothing in their lives would change. But if he wasn't?

Chris started with the results of the autopsy. No news there. Heart attack. Massive. He spared them any of the gory details. Kassie wouldn't have understood them anyway and was too nervous to concentrate had he chosen to go down that path.

Kassie glanced at Sarah, trying to read what was going through her mind. She gave no clue as she sat straight as an arrow, clutching her petite Louis Vuitton purse. Raising her eyebrows, Kassie recalled the outrageous cost of a similar purse in Paris. Money bags, she thought. No wonder Charlie stayed put all these years. Conversely, knowing what she knew now about Charlie, someday she'd ask Sarah why she hadn't kicked him out on his arse a long time ago. Maybe forty years ago?

"As you all know," Chris began, "it's been just a year since Mike told me he was my biological father and thus Karen, my biological mother. To be honest, and I can speak from experience, it's mind-blowing at any age to meet your real parents after being raised by awesome folks you considered *real* parents, even if they technically weren't."

Oh, God, he's babbling. Since Kassie didn't know the end of his story, she couldn't save him. She reached for his hand. He let her take it. She clutched it tight.

Annie got up and stood next to Chris, probably reading Kassie's vibes.

"Okay, okay," he mumbled. "Maybe I'll just say it."

"Say what?" Karen blurted.

"At the same time the autopsy was done, they did a paternity test."

"What the fuck?" Charlie and Karen nearly shouted.

"And, dear, you have the results now, I imagine?" Sarah said.

"Yes, Mom, I do. Seems that Mike and I are not related." He stopped and breathed. "Mike is not my father."

Kassie's head fell into her hands as tears flowed like Niagara Falls. One big albatross flew off her shoulders, and she sprung into Chris's arms.

"That means I'm not your stepmother! Alleluia!"

Chris and Kassie opened their embrace and welcomed Annie into their circle. When Sarah joined their celebration, Annie stepped aside and said, "So, the ten-million-dollar question is, if not Mike, who?"

Four pairs of eyes centered on the two people who remained seated.

"Charlie? Karen?" Sarah tilted her head. "I'm waiting, Charlie. Tell me if what I suspected since our senior year is true. If not for me, for Chris."

"Yes, do tell," Chris said as he, Kassie, Annie, and Sarah all returned to their seats. Karen and Charlie didn't move. They just stared at each other.

"Could it really be?" Charlie said to Karen. "Is Chris my son? My real son? And you knew all this time?"

Karen jumped up and paced in back of the circle of chairs, causing everyone to shift in their seats.

"I didn't know. Not for sure anyway. Remember that party? The key game? And that next time we did it?"

Oh, gross, Kassie thought.

Karen didn't give Charlie time to answer. "I was seeing Mike then too. He and I were pretty darn serious. You were just a fling." She flapped her hand in the air.

"History sure has a way of repeating itself," Annie said.

Karen glared at Annie, who shrugged her shoulders. "I just call 'em as I see 'em."

"It could've been either of you." Karen put her hand over her mouth.

"I was afraid of that," Sarah said. "Did you think I didn't hear all about that party and your hookup? Sorority sisters keep secrets . . . and tell secrets . . . when necessary."

"Then why did you agree to adopt?" Karen scrunched her eyebrows.

"Simple. If there was any chance at all Charlie was the father, I wanted to be that child's mother. Not have you give him up to strangers."

"If you had an inkling, why didn't you have a paternity test done yourself? You had easy access," Kassie said.

"Good question. I thought about it, more than once. We'd signed papers. Legally Charlie was Chris's father. That was enough for me."

"Enough for me too. Good job, Mom." Chris gave her a hug and Charlie a friendly slap on the back.

"Well, it's been one helluva couple of weeks. Wouldn't you say? What do we do now?" Charlie asked.

"Why don't we all give Chris and Kassie space?" Annie ushered the parental trio out of the office. "If you three would like to talk somewhere private . . ." She turned and gave Chris and Kassie a two thumbs-up.

Chris closed the door behind them and swept Kassie into his arms.

"And you've suffered all this time. I'm so sorry. The sins of the fathers—"

"And the mother."

He pushed her gently against a wall, almost knocking down a photo of her mother and father she'd left behind when she'd moved in with Annie. Lifting her off her heels, he kissed her with renewed passion, reminding her of their first lustful kiss in front of her hotel in Venice.

"Can't wait until later," he whispered, his hands doing the talking . . . and the walking.

"Me neither."

But wait they did, because she had one more guest to see. She'd save the best until last.

49

She Is What She Is

"Come on in, Cecilia."

Chris held a chair for her as Kassie freshened herself, pinching her cheeks and running her fingers through her hair.

"I'm so glad you waited around. Funerals." Kassie grunted. You need to spend time with friends, colleagues, folks you haven't seen in years." Kassie shrugged, knowing now she was the one babbling. No harm. Right up Cecilia's alley.

"Oh, no, it's perfectly understandable, Mrs. Ricci. I'm substantially honored that you invited me into your and Mr. Ricci's warm and hospitable abode."

"Call me Kassie." She smiled, replaying in her mind the news that she hadn't been sleeping with the son of her husband, her late husband, all this time. She decided not to correct Cecilia and tell her it was just her home now that Mr. Ricci was six feet under.

Seeing how Mike cared for this young woman, almost as if she was a daughter he never had, Kassie wondered what Mike's reaction would've been to the news he didn't have a son after all. Didn't matter. She'd never know.

After a long, emotional day, Kassie relaxed and let her hair down with Chris and Cecilia. They reminisced about Mike, his quirkiness in the hospital and how he liked to give the nurses a hard time. Cecilia said he was a good talker.

"Mr. Ricci thought highly of you too, Cecilia. In fact, he's left a monetary gift for you."

Cecilia's eyes squinted as her head flipped back and forth between Chris and Kassie. "For me?"

"Let me explain. Actually, there are two components to this legacy. First is an outright gift. Mr. Ricci left instructions for you to receive twenty-five thousand dollars for you to finish your bachelor's degree. You're going into your senior year?"

"Oh my goodness. Yes."

"And there's a paid internship waiting for you at Ricci and Son."

"The timing is up to you, Cecilia," Chris said. "Depending on your course load. You can start this summer and continue through the next year, or if you prefer, you can wait until you graduate in May."

"We're very grateful for your kindness," Kassie said. "You'll always be a special part of our family, which seems to be growing by the minute."

"I'm speechless."

I thought you might be.

Not surprisingly, Cecilia gathered herself and thanked them profusely and said she couldn't wait to get home to tell her parents about their generosity and faith in her. And then like an angel, *poof,* she was gone.

The house suddenly felt eerily peaceful and quiet, except for the hum of the dishwasher in the distance. Chris stepped away, saying he'd do a fly-by around the first floor. Most everyone had gone; even all his parents had flown the coop. Vicki and Amelia scurried around collecting napkins, plates, and glassware.

Kassie heard Teresa ask Chris for a box of matches. "Candles. This house needs calming. Lavender candles will do the trick."

A few minutes later, Chris wandered back to Kassie's office, where both she and Annie had kicked off their shoes. Two best friends forever winding down, comparing manicures. Kassie showed her the remnants of her pomegranate rash. Annie one-upped her with an exaggerated tale about a rash she'd gotten after a particularly raunchy night with her boyfriend, Jack.

"Too much information!" Kassie chuckled.

"Come on in, Chris. Join us." Annie waved him in.

"Life is good, after all, eh?" Kassie reached for his hand.

"Just as it should be." Chris smiled. "Doesn't get much better than this."

Ding dong. Ding dong. Cling. Clang.

"What now?" Chris said.

"Maybe more flowers. Or somebody forgot something." Kassie shrugged.

Amelia appeared in the doorway. "Um. Chris, there's someone here to see you."

Arm in arm, barefoot and giggling, Kassie and Annie followed five steps behind Chris to the entryway.

"What are you doing here?" Kassie heard Chris say as he stood between her and the apparently uninvited guest.

"Didn't you get my message? I said I'd stop by around six."

Kassie couldn't catch his answer; he was babbling again. She let go of Annie and stepped next to Chris, coming face-to-face with a lovely, leggy, chesty woman, wearing a body-hugging jumpsuit similar to the outfit Mimi wore the week before in Paris. Her long blonde curly hair was to die for.

Chris's face drooped. "Um. Kassie, this is my friend Lexi. Lexi, this is Kassie, my fiancée. Oh, excuse me, and her friends Annie and Vicki. And you've met Amelia. Her mother, Teresa."

Kassie shook Lexi's hand, urging Bad Kassie to stifle what she was really thinking.

"Now that we've been sufficiently branded by Chris, why don't we go into the family room where there's space for everyone?" Kassie suggested. "I think things are getting back to normal . . . in there, at least."

As she turned to head that way, a door slammed upstairs. Everyone that was supposed to be in the house walked toward the family room. They looked at one another.

"Just the wind," Kassie said, suspecting her mother's spirit wouldn't let the events of that day conclude without making her presence felt.

Kassie offered Lexi wine, though she figured she'd refuse it. Chris left the room briefly, returning with a scotch. It looked like a double. Amelia got comfortable in Mike's Pleasure Chair. The rest of the crew pulled up a seat, as if they were settling in for a feature-length movie. Maybe a thriller? A mystery? A love story? All they needed was popcorn to complete the scene.

No one spoke. Most eyes were on Lexi. Kassie eyed Chris, half of her expecting him to jumpstart the conversation, the other half knowing he would leave it to her. So she started by asking what every woman asks a pregnant woman when they first meet.

"When are you due?"

"January."

Kassie calculated in her head. She knew the formula by heart. She looked at Chris, who stared into his scotch as if he wished it could swallow him up instead of the other way around.

"I know what you're all thinking. That I'm here to lay claim to Chris. Far from it." Lovely, lusty Lexi waved her hand, as if to brush away the obvious. "This . . . was an accident. I just wanted to tell Chris in person, not over the phone. I'm a traditionalist, I guess. And a big girl. I'm prepared to do this alone. No strings attached."

Annie leaned into Chris and in a stage whisper said, "Looks like you got caught with your pants down." He grimaced and bowed his head again. As he did, Kassie noticed his cheeks flushed. Embarrassment or fear? Didn't matter. She knew only she could ease what ailed him. What happened next would be up to her.

Kassie got up and walked around the family room, clinging to the gondola and Eiffel Tower charms hanging from her necklace. Adopting one of Mike's habits, she twisted the nail ring until her mother's voice in her head subsided.

She stopped in front of Chris and lifted his chin. "Have I told you today how much I love you?" She kissed him sweetly and then turned her attention to the woman who carried her fiancé's child.

Kassie pulled a yellow rose out of the bouquet on the coffee table, wrapped a tissue around the stem, and handed it to Lexi. "Welcome to the family."

Amelia clapped. A roar went up. Teresa blessed herself. Vicki and Amelia high-fived. Annie rolled her eyes as if to say, "Here we go again."

Chris swiped his forehead with the back of his hand and emitted a quiet "Phew."

Candles flickered. One blew out completely.

Kassie embraced Lexi and the future. "Just call me Stepmom."

What's Not True Playlist

On Spotify.com
https://spoti.fi/37ZKBJb

Access songs depicting the story on the *What's Not True* Playlist on Spotify.com, which is free*!

La vie en rose, *Louis Armstrong*

I Heard It Through The Grapevine, *Marvin Gaye*

Mia & Sebastian's Theme, *Justin Hurwitz*

Don't Stop Believin', *Journey*

Can't Get Enough Of Your Love, Babe, *Barry White*

50 Ways to Leave Your Lover, *Paul Simon*

West Side Story: Act 1: Something's Coming, *Leonard Bernstein*

Your Cheating Heart, *Fats Domino*

All of Me, *John Legend*

It's All In The Game, *Nat King Cole*

I Will Always Love You, *Whitney Houston*

We Can Work It Out, *The Beatles*

*Best browsers for Spotify's Web Player are Google Chrome, Firefox, Edge, and Opera.

Book Club Discussion Guide

1. When the story opens, Kassie and Chris unite after a year apart. Should Kassie have gone to Paris with Chris, or should they have stayed in Venice?

2. At that point, how honest should Chris have been with her about how he'd spent that year?

3. Has Kassie really replaced her motherhood obsession with a stepmother obsession?

4. Kassie assumed Chris would support her Paris assignment. Discuss how she handled it versus how she could have approached it.

5. Mike died thinking Chris was his son. Was that a good or bad thing?

6. Kassie waited until dinner with Annie before she divulged what she knew about Karen and Charlie. Is she a coward? Would you have handled it differently?

7. Discuss the role ambition played in the story from Kassie's and Chris's differing viewpoints.

8. Even at middle age, Kassie has a jealous streak. Does that ever go away as we age?

9. Did the "forgiveness" scene between Kassie and Mike in the hospital provide sufficient closure?

10. Do you think the stipend Mike left for Karen in his will was enough? Or maybe too much?

11. Would you ever shred Red Sox tickets?

12. What do you think the future holds for Kassie and Chris?

13. Was Kassie sincere when she welcomed Lexi into the family?

Acknowledgments

Conventional wisdom often labels authors as introverts. I, for one, can attest to that moniker. When I write, it's me and my cast of characters on a journey, having our own private conversations. However, after the writing is done, I put aside some of my introverted ways, because, after all, publishing is a team sport.

And the team starts with *readers*.

When the early readers of *What's Not Said* asked "What happens next?", I was stunned. I'd accomplished my goal of writing a story I'd carried around in my head for a decade. Could there really be more? But, of course, there was!

And thus, *What's Not True* was born. Fortunately, in the process of creating this second book in the series, I was able to rely on an exceptionally skilled team that stretches across the country.

"Best friends forever" doesn't begin to describe my gratitude to Ayse McCarthy, Lyn Englehartson, and Vicki Crumpacker. *What's Not True* would have never happened without your encouragement

319

and your willingness to invest your valuable personal time reading and critiquing my drafts.

Let it be said, there's no better *publishing team* than the professionals at *She Writes Press*.

I am deeply indebted to all of you—Brooke Warner, Shannon Green, Krissa Lagos, and Mimi Bark—who believed in me, agreeing to go through all of this all over again. As always, I depended on your expert advice, creativity, and knowledge of the industry, especially as its landscape continues to change.

Moreover, it's *community* that motivates me to rise each day, especially during the pandemic, to tackle all things I call "author-y stuff." The vast *She Writes Press* community of international authors is unparalleled as a writing resource and source of friendship and kindness.

I am beholden especially to Eileen Sanchez and Meryl Ain, who adopted me early on and brought me into the fold. You opened doors and my eyes to opportunities I, as an introvert, would've never found or ventured into on my own. Thank you for listening and for your patience and advice, even during an occasional late-night meltdown.

During 2020 as I launched *What's Not Said*, my publicity and marketing team guided me through the unprecedented challenges of launching a book during a global pandemic. I'm excited to have these professionals join me again as we roll out *What's Not True*: Jim Alkon and the entire Meryl Moss Media and BookTrib.com team, Christopher Locke and the industry experts at the Independent Book Publishers Association, digital gurus Suzy Leopold and Lauren Carr, and all the authors, bloggers, and bookstagrammers who read and boost my books.

Suffice it to say, the pandemic took a shocking and immediate toll on brick and mortar bookstores, both major chains and independent bookstores. I owe much of my sanity to Pia Ledina, owner of Turning the Page, a most charming independent bookseller in

Monroe, CT, who not only promotes my books, but also provides invaluable insight into the industry from an insider's perspective. Essential worker? You bet!

To my family—William; Lindsay, Allen, and Cecilia; and Jeanne and Ed—thank you for not asking me to explain what I mean by "I'm doing author-y stuff," and for always giving me the time to do whatever it is I do.

All in all, my team starts and ends with you, *dear readers*. No matter how you've managed to get your hands on my books, please know how grateful I am that you choose to spend your precious time with my quirky and flawed characters in the world I created for them. To be sure, I do all this author-y stuff for you.

With *What's Not Said* and *What's Not True* in the can, is a three-peat in the offing? What can I say? Yes, indeed, it's true.

About the Author

© Lifetouch, Seattle, WA

Valerie Taylor was born and raised in Stamford, Connecticut. She earned a BS in marketing and an MBA from Sacred Heart University, as well as a graduate certificate in health care administration from Simmons University (formerly Simmons College). She had a thirty-year career in the financial services industry as a marketer and writer. After her divorce, she spread her wings and relocated her career to Boston and then to Seattle. When she retired, she resettled in her home state to be near her two grown children and granddaughter. She's a member of the Westport Writers' Workshop, the Independent Book Publishers Association, and the Women's Fiction Writers Association. She's a published book reviewer with BookTrib.com. She enjoys practicing tai chi and being an expert sports spectator. *What's Not True* is the sequel to *What's Not Said*, published September 2020 (She Writes Press). The third book in the series is in the works.

WWW.VALERIETAYLORAUTHOR.COM

 valerietaylorauthor @valerieemtaylor ValerieETaylor

SELECTED TITLES FROM SHE WRITES PRESS

She Writes Press is an independent publishing company founded to serve women writers everywhere. Visit us at www.shewritespress.com.

What's Not Said by Valerie Taylor. $16.95, 978-1-63152-745-6
When a middle-aged woman's husband is diagnosed with a life-threatening illness, their secret lives collide head-on, revealing a tangled web of sex, lies, and DNA and forcing her to decide whose life to save—her husband's or her own.

The Lockhart Women by Mary Camarillo. $16.95, 978-1-64742-100-7
After Brenda Lockhart's husband announces he's leaving her for an older, less attractive woman, she—devastated and lonely—becomes addicted to the media frenzy surrounding the murder of Nicole Brown, which took place the same night her husband dropped his bombshell. In the ensuing months, her whole family falls apart—but ultimately comes together again in unexpected ways.

Play for Me by Céline Keating. $16.95, 978-1-63152-972-6
Middle-aged Lily impulsively joins a touring folk-rock band, leaving her job and marriage behind in an attempt to find a second chance at life, passion, and art.

Again and Again by Ellen Bravo. $16.95, 978-1-63152-939-9
When the man who raped her roommate in college becomes a Senate candidate, women's rights leader Deborah Borenstein must make a choice—one that could determine control of the Senate, the course of a friendship, and the fate of a marriage.

Shelter Us by Laura Diamond. $16.95, 978-1-63152-970-2
Lawyer-turned-stay-at-home-mom Sarah Shaw is still struggling to find a steady happiness after the death of her infant daughter when she meets a young homeless mother and toddler she can't get out of her mind—and becomes determined to rescue them.

Center Ring by Nicole Waggoner. $17.95, 978-1-63152-034-1
When a startling confession rattles a group of tightly knit women to its core, the friends are left analyzing their own roads not taken and the vastly different choices they've made in life and love.